THE LA
STAN

By:

L.C. VALENTINE

Copyright

Terror Tract Publishing LLC
Owned and Operated by: Becky Narron

First paperback edition 2020
Book design by: Becky Narron 2020

ISBN: 9798654337917
ISBN: (ebook)

https://terrortract.com
Twitter: @terrortract
Instagram: terrortract

Table of Contents

CHAPTER ONE

THE FINAL CHAPTER

The community hut was the centrepiece of St. Mary's Marsh Campground. It had been a little dilapidated when Ellie and her friends had begun restoring it, but when they had finished, it was ready to welcome children from all walks of life and create a summer camp experience they would never forget. They'd selected a friendly, inviting baby blue paint for the wooden exterior, and a bright white for the roof. It had been Ellie's suggestion to paint the window frames yellow, to hint at sunlight in a calm blue sky, and she'd been proud of the outcome. All of the camp counsellors had been. It was a beautiful looking building. It would be the envy of summer camps across the state. And it was. For the day or so it stood standing.

Until it was blown to bits.

The heat from the explosion seared into Ellie's back as she was thrown to the ground, the damp grass bringing little relief as flaming debris rained down around her. She felt her skin tighten from burns, and her once yellow camp counsellor shirt stuck painfully to the damaged flesh. She was glad that she couldn't see the wound. She rolled over, coughing, and threw her hand up to shield her eyes from the blazing cabin. She choked, even from there, on the thick, acrid smoke. Her eyes stung and hot tears streamed down her face as the chemical stink gagged her. It put her in mind of the time she had tried to cook for the first time and left a plastic ladle too close to the stove, causing it to melted all over the kitchen counter, only this was a thousand times that smell. She'd of course seen bonfires and camp fires before, but you could never truly understand the *stench* of a burning building until one was before you. It wasn't just the wood of the cabin, no. It was the paint, plastics and metals, all of it, making a cloying, gagging smoke as dangerous as the killer she had left trapped inside.

Painting the cabin seemed like a lifetime ago now, but it had only been that very afternoon. She remembered watching Natalie paint crude pictures on the side, Billy rushing over, arms flailing in a panic, desperate to paint over them, Sarah and Helen sneaking away to make out in the bushes, Danny offering to help her paint the high spots, Melissa sunbathing and refusing to do any work… All of them laughing and joking amongst themselves. Now all of them were dead. All killed by that creature they had mistakenly awoken. Except for her. Her and Danny. *Maybe*. Her eyes looked to Danny's body beside her, thrown clear by the blast. Was it possible? Had he survived?

Her heart rate hadn't gone back down since the first match snapped. In fact, that would have probably been her final moment, if Danny hadn't distracted the creature. He'd thrown himself in front of that deadly hand sickle long enough for Ellie to strike another match and ignite the propane.

Beside her, Danny coughed. He was still alive! He'd actually *survived*. Ellie felt every limb in her body go limp from relief, but another cough from Danny alerted her to how dire his situation was. Her heart skipped a beat and her skin pricked as she felt panic rising inside of her. Blood was everywhere, running down the front of what

6

remained of his yellow Camp Counsellor shirt. Over that, his denim jacket was badly singed. He had clearly caught the blast worse than she had. It was a blessing that he'd survived at all. He let out a groan, coughing up blood, and for a moment Ellie's entire body froze. He had survived, but for how long? He was *dying* and Ellie had no idea what to do. She was panicking, her eyes looking for help in all directions, but finding only darkness. In comparison to Danny, the cuts and scrapes she had suffered were pretty minor. She struggled to her feet, and offered him a hand. She just hoped he still had the strength to take it. Despite his injuries, his shaky fingers grasped her wrist, his free hand clutching at the huge sickle wound on his chest. Danny was much more muscular than she was, and weighed so much he nearly pulled her over as he got to his feet, but he made it. She forcibly put one of his arms over her shoulders to support him, trying not to strain too much under his weight as the pair watched the burning wreckage.

'It's over,' he said, the words coming out like a gurgled choke. His mouth was clearly still full of blood. 'It's actually over.' Fatigue came over Ellie, the entire night spent fighting for survival finally catching up with her. She found herself slumping against Danny, who seemed to move his arm from simply supporting himself in to something resembling a hug. The two kept each other propped up, each supporting the other. For a moment, all was peaceful. Even the soft roar of the blazing fire seemed gentle and comforting. And then Danny spoke again.

'Nothing could have survived that.' In the future, Ellie would learn that words had more power than anybody knew. She *knew* the rules of horror movies, of course. In fact, she probably knew them better than anyone. She was a *fan*. She'd always been fascinated by them, ever since

7

she had sneaked downstairs to watch *Halloween 4: The Return of Michael Myers* on late night cable while her parents slept. Heck, it had actually been why she'd been a little reluctant to take the camp counsellor job when Danny suggested it. Didn't he know what happened to camp counsellors in horror movies? Hadn't he ever seen any of the *Friday the 13th* films? Or *Sleepaway Camp*? But horror movies were fiction. Silly, campy things that she got a laugh out of. Slow walking killers and dumb blonde teenagers tripping over nothing as they ran away. How was she meant to know that they could really happen? That they could be *real?* That the rules she had been so proud of knowing from her favourite movies were more than just part of a speedily written film script? That there were certain phrases you should never speak? You'd never say "at least it's not raining" if you wanted to stay dry, for example. And if you ever, *ever*, survived a massacre at a camp ground by a murderous killer, the one thing you never, ever said was "nothing could have survived that". But Ellie was young and inexperienced, and she didn't yet know the power of words. So the moment that followed, when that sickle burst through Danny's chest and he was hoisted into the air, was not one that she saw coming. She screamed as she saw Danny's heart impaled on the end of the sickle, protruding from his body, letting out a desperate sob. Somehow it managed one last beat as Danny's convulsing body vomited blood. The warm liquid splattered over her, feeling wet and watery, not the thick, sticky substance she would have imagined. Another death. The horror never ended. It wasn't *fair*. They had survived! They had beaten the monster! Why did Danny have to die as well? They were going to make it out of there. They had been so close.

And there it was. The Mirror Monster, standing behind him, so completely unharmed and unconcerned. The explosion had done shockingly little damage to him. His heavy brown coat had picked up some burn marks. A little more undead flesh poked through what remained of the black shirt underneath. The shard of mirror he wore as a mask over his bald, decaying head was slightly blackened, so that when his head whipped around to stare at Ellie, her own horrified reflection was lost to a fine black mist. The old piece of rope that he used to hold the mask to his face seemed largely undamaged, although the odd frayed sections that had long ago broken away and now hung down the mask were now blackened and singed. When she had first laid eyes on them, they had oddly reminded Ellie of golden pigtails, somehow clashing with the creature's horrible, deformed appearance. Now, she couldn't look at them without picturing a hangman's noose. Somehow, that seemed far more appropriate. Despite the burn damage, however, he still moved with the same deadly vigour he had used when hunting down all of Ellie's friends. He didn't move quickly, of course, but every action was with a fierce, undeterred, unfatigued *purpose*. Ellie had never seen his face, but you could tell the strangely calm and calculated *wrath* behind his every motion, never more obvious than when he discarded Danny's lifeless corpse from his blade, and raised it to strike at Ellie.

She turned to run, as anybody would. She was aware of the heavy thumping footsteps of the zombie creature behind her, but he never approached anything resembling a run. He didn't need to. She had seen enough of him to know that the slow, lumbering killer always caught his victims in the end. The old legends of the campground had said that the Mirror Monster was once a young boy, bullied to a seeming death because of his physical deformities, who now instead reflected everything around him rather than let anybody see him for who he truly was. Ellie had remembered Danny telling that story around the campfire only last night, when life had seemed so much more innocent and safe, but she didn't remember any part of the story that explained why he seemed able to catch up with his victims when he never seemed to move at anything above a leisurely stroll. Oh, she knew the *stereotype*. She could list all of the movie slashers who seemed able to do that. She'd spent countless nights watching Michael Myers and Jason Voorhees lumber slowly after their prey, rolling her eyes at the ridiculousness of how they always seemed to catch up.

It didn't seem ridiculous now. But she didn't understand how it was *possible*. This was still the real world, wasn't it?

Again, Ellie was young, and this was the first monster she had faced. She didn't know the *rules* yet. Like the fact that you could *never* outrun the killer for long, that he always caught up to you, no matter how slowly he seemed to move, or the rule that you should never run into the woods, because escape never lay that way. Indeed, Ellie took off running directly towards the perceived safety of the tree line. Even in her naïve, youthful state, she quickly realised her mistake, for there was no light at this time of night, and the trees blocked even the glow of the moon. The warm, orange aura of the fire burning behind her soon disappeared, and she was left stumbling in the dark as branches and brambles lashed at her, and several times she stumbled over the uneven ground that was strewn with branches and twigs. She managed to stay on her feet, which was actually a considerable achievement, but began to realise that the ground was becoming increasingly boggy as she approached the marshland that had given St Mary's its full name.

Too late did she consider changing direction as her right foot disappeared into thick mud, and she stumbled. She began trying to pull it loose desperately, but her sneaker was stuck fast in the bog. Behind her, she was aware of the repeating footsteps of the Mirror Monster, thudding away as he got ever closer. Her heart raced so fast she thought she might vomit, panic overtaking her. She had to get free, and she had to get free *now*. Otherwise she knew she was going to die. She let out a slight sob, before swallowing her panic. She had to keep control. She had to find a way to get free, to keep moving. She wriggled and struggled to free her foot, desperately jerking her entire body, before squirming it enough to work it loose of her sneaker, glad that the laces hadn't been tied too tightly. She managed to free her foot, abandoning her shoe to the muck, and she ran forward, now with one foot bare, swearing that she felt the breeze of the Mirror Monster's sickle just missing her back.

The ground seemed to be firm enough to keep moving, even if she was aware that her one bare foot was now cut and bleeding as it crossed the rough terrain. She tried to swallow a whimper of pain to keep as silent as possible. Not that it mattered. There was no escape, she realised. She was the only one left, and *blowing him up* hadn't stopped that horrific beast. She was unarmed, wounded, she didn't even have both shoes. What was she going to do now? Surely this was how it ended for her...

Again, she didn't understand the *rules* yet

Oh so aware of the constant, rhythmic thumping of footsteps behind her, so slow and yet somehow always so close, she kept running, even as her exhausted, weakening legs threatened to give out from beneath her. She was beginning to lose all sense of time, of place, and worse yet, of *hope*. There was nowhere to go now. She was lost, she was alone, surely she'd die soon. And that was when she saw it. Sat in the middle of the trees. An old, dilapidated, shack. It didn't matter what was inside, or how it clearly hadn't been attended to in years, all she knew was that it had a door, and that might slow her pursuer down.

She picked up the pace, as fast as weary legs would carry her, and she threw herself through the door of the shack, immediately slamming it behind her, searching frantically for something to bar it with. She didn't take the interior of the shack in at all. She didn't notice the old, blackened wooden walls, nor what was hanging from them. She didn't notice the lack of living amenities. No table. No chairs. Just an old, rotten wooden bed frame in the corner. She didn't even notice the smell, not right away, but before she could find anything to block the entrance, it hit her. A gagging, noxious smell. It reminded her of that time she had been helping her mom empty the kitchen cupboards and found year old mouldy bread that had somehow gotten lost at the back. The stench had been unbelievable, and yet somehow milder than the one coming from the innards of the shack. It was strong enough to make her gag, to make her choke, to make her *disgusted* on some ancient, instinctive level, to speak to something in the animal part of her brain to make her wretch in horror. It was only then she understood what the smell was. The stench of death. Of rotting corpses.

Of course, she had read stories where people described smelling the stink of death, she'd seen movies and TV shows where the heroes and heroines gag at it, but she had never smelled it herself. Even after this night, where every kill had been a fresh one, she hadn't. But now, it overwhelmed her. She slowly turned to see the source, rotting corpses, mounted on the walls of the shack. Like trophies. Most were just bare skeletons, shreds of clothes hanging from them, ancient brown blood stains visible on the tatters. Some still had eyes, she noticed. Sunken, lifeless, milky orbs that made her think of rotting eggs.

She realised much too late where she had found herself. What this shack truly was. The Mirror Monster might have been a zombified beast these days, but he had started his killing spree as just a man. A man who must have lived somewhere all of those years. Who must have grown from the bullied little boy who had inexplicably survived the pranks pulled on him into the masked terror of St. Mary's Marsh. Who must have recovered somewhere. Healed somewhere. *Lived* somewhere. And who must still hide somewhere now, between his yearly killing sprees. She cursed herself. She knew the movies. The killer always had a lair.

This was the Mirror Monster's *home*. And she had stumbled right into it.

The shock had delayed her long enough for him to arrive. Or perhaps, he had just been waiting for the moment to register. Either way, the door flew open, and there he stood, seemingly breathing heavily with rage, even if Ellie knew that he didn't need oxygen to survive. Just last year, the last survivor of the massacre had chained him to the bottom of the marsh, or so the story had gone. It's why they had reopened the camp, Danny said. Ellie had told him he was just ripping off *Friday the 13th* and that he should be more original. Specifically, *Friday the 13th Part VI: Jason Lives*. The best one, in Ellie's opinion. It had that great Alice Cooper song. Although right at that moment, she could quite happily have never seen another slasher movie again as long as she lived. Which, of course, might not be very long at all.

Danny's story had seemed so *dumb*. How could she have known it was true? She'd been an idiot.

And now, she had nowhere left to run.

Something in her told her not to gawp at the killer as he made his way inside, sickle still dripping with Danny's blood. Something told her if she wanted to survive, now was the time to *think*. To find something. Anything. She ran to the edge of the shack, and spotted it in the centre of the room. A huge object, taller than she was, flat, and hidden beneath a yellowed, brittle looking sheet. Even covered, she could tell what it was. A *mirror*. She didn't pretend to fully understand the Mirror Monster's weird fascination with reflection, both his own and that of others, but she knew enough to know that the legend told around the campfire said he wanted to reflect everybody outwards to hide himself. And that meant, maybe, just maybe, his own reflection was his weakness.

She pulled the cloth from the mirror, unveiling the dusty old antique before her. She noticed that part of it had been chipped away, the exact size and shape as the shard the Mirror Monster wore as a mask. This must have been where he had first acquired it and fashioned it into a mask. If it was a real shard of mirror, she wondered how he could see through it. The thought didn't last, however, as the killer was nearly upon her. He seemed to pause for a moment, staring at the mirror, gazing at the infinite repeating loop of reflection cast off of his own soot-stained mask and the old antique itself, but if Ellie's hope had been for him to freeze, it didn't last. The reflection distracted him for only a moment, before he continued to advance, sickle raised.

She realised the reason why almost instantly. Why would a being that wore a mask be scared of his reflection while the mask was still on? But now it was too late. She had seconds left to live, and no weapon. The only thing near her was one of the rotting corpses mounted on the wall by the mirror. Basically just a skeleton in crumbling clothes. It must have been one of his first ever kills. It was her only hope.

'Sorry,' she muttered, feeling she had to say something, and she grabbed its arm. She pulled it loose easily, and wielding the skeletal arm like a club, she struck hard at the Mirror Monster's face, just as it was upon her.

Throughout that night, she had seen much more muscular people than her bravely try to strike the creature, and every time it barely flinched. Now was no different, but unlike them, she wasn't aiming to hurt him. She was aiming for the mask. She rapidly struck, over and over again, weak blows, with no real strength or co-ordination behind them, basically slapping the Mirror Monster in the face with the skeletal hand. Had she not been about to die, Ellie would have thought it must have looked hilarious. She struck, again and again, as it approached, until finally, *finally*, it worked. The old fraying rope snapped, causing the mirror mask to break free and fall to the ground, where it shattered in two.

Beneath it awaited a horrifying visage. The entire bottom half of his face was devoid of skin, purely a skeletal jaw with an unusually long tongue snaking from it, while the rest of him was made of rotting flesh, his right eyeball dangling loose from an overly large, deformed eye socket, while the left eye seemed to still be intact, but lost beneath a swell of bulbous, bubbly pus filled flesh that oozed with a vile yellowy red liquid. He let out a guttural roar, the first time she heard him make any noise, and took a furious step towards her, sickle raised above her head. This was it. Her final moment. Ellie let out a terrified scream.

And then he saw himself in the mirror. And he froze. He turned slowly to face the reflection, sickle still raised in the air. And then, with a horrific thump, he fell to his knees, the weapon clattering to the ground as he stared at himself. He let out a low moan, almost a groan of despair, and one of his rotting hands reached forward to touch the reflection. Ellie almost felt sorry for him in that moment, as if deep down, some dark sadness in the monster had been awakened. But she wouldn't let that waste her one chance.

She picked up the sickle from the ground and lifted it above her head.

'Get ready to see a lot worse! In Hell!' she screamed, and she drove the sickle down into his head. There was a sickening thud as it sunk through the skull, piercing deep inside, and he jolted his head back, letting out a terrifying scream as his skeletal jaw opened wide.

It would not be the last monster that Ellie would kill. And in the future, when she reflected on this moment, she would have one overriding thought: at least her one-liners had improved considerably since that day.

Time seemed to extend. The Mirror Monster didn't move. He was still on his knees, head back, sickle lodged in his head, and Ellie felt like she was frozen there, hands on the handle. And then, slowly, she released it. Still, the Mirror Monster stayed where it was, not moving a single decrepit muscle. Ellie's legs felt like they had turned to lead. She couldn't run even if she wanted to. Everything was still, frozen, in that one perfect moment.

And then the Mirror Monster slumped forward to the ground, body twitching for a brief second, before it was utterly still, sickle still lodged in its head. Ellie collapsed to the ground, breathing hard. Finally, every emotion hit her at once, and she found herself bursting into tears, body shaking as the adrenaline left her.

It was finally over. Nothing could have survived that, she thought.

Fortunately, she didn't say it out loud.

CHAPTER TWO

SIX MONTHS LATER

The people reminded Ellie of water cascading around a stone as they flowed through the busy mall, their groups splitting up to pass around her and reforming on the other side, never stopping, never looking, she was just another face lost in the crowd. She continued to twiddle the matchbook in her hand, a small comfort she insisted on keeping on her. She didn't even smoke. It just felt good to know that she was prepared. Her eyes darted, reading each person who passed her. So unprepared. So unready. None of these kids had ever fought for their lives. None of them had seen the horrors Ellie had seen. They were still naïve and safe. Trapped in their little bubbles. Like she had been, before St Mary's Marsh. Before she lost all of her friends. She watched each person passing, trying to imagine which ones might have the hidden strengths she had found. Which ones would survive, or which ones would have been butchered. Was she exceptional, or just lucky? Did she deserve to still be alive when everybody else was dead? Or had it been a fluke? She turned the matchbook over and over between her fingers, unpainted fingernails staring back at her. They were roughly cut and uncared for. Ellie wouldn't have said that she had been exceptionally appearance conscious before St Mary's Marsh, but she had certainly worn a little nail polish and made sure her nails were neatly presented. She had never been without make-up either, and her hair had been extremely long and at its full, natural thickness, not the practical short straightened bob cut she now wore. All those things seemed to mean so little now. Worse, they seemed foolish. Everybody had the camp had taken great care over their looks. They were a group of teenagers, after all, staying away without any real adult supervision alone in the cabins, of *course* they'd only had one thing on their minds, and somehow, Ellie couldn't shake the feeling that was exactly what had drawn the killer to them. Like he was punishing them for some perceived sin.

That's how it was in the movies, wasn't it? Jason Voorhees or Michael Myers or whoever would wait until all the teenagers were having sex and then they'd come and murder them. But those were dumb movies. Films. Films that she had used to love. It wasn't ever meant to be real life. It wasn't ever meant to happen to anybody for real.

'Eliza!' Catherine Cartwright's voice cut through her thoughts and pulled Ellie back to reality. Her mother really *was* trying, Ellie understood that. She could see it in everything her mother did. And she could see, even though her mother tried to hide it, how *difficult* she found it. She could see behind her mother's eyes her patience always wearing so thin. But to her credit, she never expressed those feelings out loud. Her mother always tried to help. She was always trying to do the right thing for her daughter.

This was something that Ellie appreciated in what she considered to be an abstract way. By which she meant she appreciated the *thought* rather than the action. It wasn't just the usual teenage rebellion that meant she wanted to spend time away from her mom. After all, it wasn't like she had any friends to run off with, but rather that she just wanted to be alone in general. Any person, even a loving mother, was difficult for Ellie to deal with now. Even six months clear of the murders.

'C'mon, Eliza, at least make a little effort...' her mom begged, and Ellie just sighed, following her out of a sense of obligation, but nothing else. There was no response to her mother's enquiry. After all, what did Ellie have to say? She had never really enjoyed clothes shopping. She had been a bit fashion conscious back in the day, sure, but no more than any of her friends. What teenager didn't want to look a *little* good, after all? But she'd never really enjoyed shopping. And at the mall? If you wanted clothes, who didn't just order them online these days? Ellie had gotten away with going to many a party in an outfit she bought online, hidden the tag on, and then returned after the event by sending it off back to the website. She always seemed to get away with it. But this was her mom for her. Online shopping was a mystery to Catherine Cartwright. She supposed this is what had been done back in her mother's day, the only thing she knew. The mall. Plus, online shopping wasn't much of a bonding activity and Ellie knew that was exactly what her mom was trying to do. How could she explain that it felt pointless? That it was just unnecessary. That she just couldn't engage with the world anymore. She didn't quite understand it herself. She couldn't quite put into words the feelings she now had. The sense of loss, yes, she understood that. Not just in the sense that her friends were dead, or that she had nearly died, but once you had lost people close to you, your entire world shattered. It no longer felt permanent. It no longer felt safe. Losing just one person made you realise that anybody could die at any time. Losing several? It left the world feeling like it was made out of a delicate paper, about to be torn down at any moment. Like everybody else you knew could be gone tomorrow just as easily as you had lost your friends. Like every life hung from a delicate thread, like everything around you, everything you saw, everyone you talked to, all of it was temporary. At any moment, everything could end.

But there was more than that. There was another feeling. Something she couldn't quite place.

She found herself looking at her cell phone, although she didn't quite remember reaching into her purse to get it. She felt dumb almost immediately after. It had been a natural movement, the type of gesture that was ingrained into pretty much everybody under the age of thirty. Things got awkward or dull and you were bored, and you escaped into the world your phone offered. But these days it didn't offer her anything. All of her friends were dead. What was she expecting? Social media was a much darker place than it had been six months ago and she found little joy in anything else. So she was a little surprised to see that she had a message waiting. Not a text message, of course (who sent those these days?), but sent over her messaging app. Apparently from a mysterious contact. She had to approve it to read it, and for a moment, she considered deleting it. It was probably just spam, after all.

But no, she decided she'd open it and give it a look. After all, whatever it was, it had to be more interesting than clothes shopping with her mom, right?

You kind of miss it, don't you? The adrenaline. The fight. The thrill.

The message was there in front of her, as clear as day. There was a name attached to it, of course. Ellie knew that privacy settings wouldn't let you send a message and hide your name. 'Nina Collins'. There was an icon too, showing the girl pretty clearly. A seemingly smiling teenager with a long blonde ponytail, a carefree girl in a pretty looking dress and big sunglasses, clearly taken during some kind of summer vacation. It was a selfie, and she was throwing up her free hand in a V peace sign. It made Ellie cringe a little, truth be told. The icon was too small to make out any real details, of course, and the message distracted her from ever thinking to search for her profile.

Her instinct was to bury her phone back in her purse immediately and pretend she had never read it, but somehow, she didn't. She kept staring.

Nothing's the same after fighting for your life. Nothing makes you feel alive.

The next message came. She paused, reading it over again. She felt her stomach knot and somersault. For a moment, she didn't quite understand what the feeling was. But it was only a moment, because then, slowly, understanding dawned on her. It was *guilt*. Remorse. Regret. Because the message was right. She felt so hollow now. So empty. Sometimes, in her darkest moments, in that small, quiet moment between sleeping and being awake, she wished she was back there. She wished she was still fighting. She missed the clarity of life or death. The real world was so complicated, so horrible, so *dull*. Back on that fateful night, fighting for her life, she had felt like everything was perfectly simple for the first time in her life. Everything was crystal clear. God, she missed that clarity...

Who are you?

She typed the message back after a pause, aware that it was perhaps the first time since that night she had actually sent a message over her phone. Oh, there had been messages of concern from various people she knew, but she had ignored them all. It felt odd to type again, so natural, and yet somehow forgotten. She realised that there was no *click* as her fingers touched the screen, no long fingernails as she used to have to make the sound. She'd never really been the type to have a manicure or false nails, but she had worn them slightly longer and neatly trimmed. Not anymore.

I'm like you. Look at the profile picture. What do you see?

Ellie frowned. What was that supposed to mean? The profile picture was nothing special. It could have been of any other white blonde teenager. Smiling, bland, enjoying the summer. What did that mean? In fact, it sort of reminded Ellie of her own, in attitude if not skin tone and hair. After all, Ellie hadn't bothered to change her profile picture since before the incident.

That was when it hit her. That was *it*. Summer had been six months ago. It had been August when the massacre occurred. Since then, Christmas had come and gone. Now it was mid-February, freezing cold, New Year's Day had passed... Who still had their profile picture from the Summer? Sure, Ellie did, but that was because changing a profile picture was the last thing on her mind after such a tragedy.

Was it the same for Nina?

What happened to you?

Ellie typed back, taking a glance up to see what her mom was doing, but she was focused on a rack of clothing, oblivious to Ellie typing away on her phone. She didn't want to have to answer awkward questions about who she was talking to.

What, did you think there was only one monster in the world? I know what keeps you up at night. If that creature that attacked you was real, if it could really exist, what else is out there? In the darkness? What else lurks in the shadows?

Ellie could only look back at her phone, that knotting sensation in her stomach moving to a dropping sensation, a roller-coaster ride taking place entirely within her insides, goose bumps bubbling up all over her skin as ice rushed through her veins. Whoever this girl was, whoever Nina Collins *was*, she knew exactly what Ellie was going through. Because she was *right*. Defeating one monster wasn't the end. Because once you accepted one monster existed, you had to accept all the others did too.

Ellie knew that her world would never be safe again.

And this Nina, whoever she was, *knew it*. Ellie didn't want to reply anymore, she didn't want to think about it, she didn't want to face it. She thrust her phone back into her purse, ignoring the message completely. Or so she told herself. But her purse felt heavier. She thought she could feel her secret fear, so perfectly given text, burning through the cheap leather of her affordable purse, searing into her soul.

'Hey, Mom. Uh, shall we grab a coffee?' she asked, only for her mother to turn and give her a startled look. She realised this was the most input she'd given on the entire day, perhaps in her entire life since the massacre.

Her mom broke into a smile at the suggestion. She was quite clearly oblivious to the haunting message on her daughter's phone, patiently waiting for a reply...

CHAPTER THREE

RECRUITMENT DRIVE

Ellie lay on her bed, staring at the old, tiny glow-in-the-dark stars on her ceiling. She had been meaning to take them down for at least the last eight years, but they were still there. Staring at them was how she spent a lot of her time now. That or being asleep. People thought sleep was a difficult thing to find after a tragedy and a loss, that dreams haunted you and kept you awake, but the truth was that sleep was about the only thing she did *well*. She spent most of the day asleep. She found herself spending almost her entire time in bed. They called it depression. She wasn't so sure. Depression, she thought, was sadness. It was pain. It was an agony that never left. All she felt was an emptiness. She felt almost *nothing at all*. No purpose. No drive. No reason to carry on. No reason to get out of bed or to open her eyes.

She didn't feel sad. She just felt *empty*.

Her therapist had tried to tell her that *was* depression. That the feeling of emptiness was normal. But she wasn't convinced. Surely if she was depressed, it would mean she *cared*, and she wasn't sure that she did anymore. Life was fleeting, life was temporary, at any moment it could be stolen away and it just didn't matter.

The only time she didn't sleep, ironically, was at night. Her mom thought it was because she spent too much time asleep in the daytime, but Ellie knew the truth. And so did Nina Collins. Whoever she was.

I know what keeps you up at night. If that creature that attacked you was real, if it could really exist, what

else is out there? In the darkness? What else lurks in the shadows?

Ellie didn't remember taking out her phone, but there she was, looking at the message. Later on, when she remembered the moment she chose to reply, she'd tell herself that had been a conflict. An indecision. That she had weighed up the pros and cons and battled to make a choice. In truth though, she had typed the response without even thinking about.

What can I do about it?

She didn't expect an immediate response. After all, just because Nina had been looking at her phone back when she sent the first messages didn't mean she would be now. It was pretty late, after all. Of course, maybe she had her messenger app on vibrate or something, but who under thirty did that *really*? But to her surprise the tell-tale three dots representing a message being typed appeared. Sure enough, moments later, there was a new message.

When the taxi arrives, get in it. Meet me. I have a plan.

Ellie blinked in surprise at the message and felt her heart skip a beat. Somehow, a taxi arriving made it feel all the more real. This wasn't just a bizarre person messaging her. This was somebody who knew who she was. Where she *lived*. Somebody who could send a vehicle to pick her up out of nowhere. She threw the phone down on the bed for a moment in shock. She could feel her heart thudding away in her chest. Her pulse had quickened. She knew that feeling. *Adrenaline*. But it wasn't the feeling of fear. She *should* have been afraid. She should have felt like a stalker was watching her. But she felt no fear.

Whoever was on the end of that phone, whoever had arranged this, she wasn't *afraid* of them. Part of her wondered if this is what everybody felt like before getting abducted, a foolish sense of trust in a person they didn't know. But the more she thought about it, the more she realised it wasn't *trust* that she felt. It wasn't that she trusted this mysterious Nina. Not at all. It was that she didn't *fear* her. Because after what she had faced, she didn't fear *anything*.

She made her decision. She'd take the taxi. It was a snap decision, almost without any doubt. Which would have been considerably more effective had the taxi actually been there to collect her. Sadly, it developed that while Nina Collins apparently had an incredible understanding of what Ellie had been through, and more importantly, what she was still going through, even *she* didn't have supernatural control over calling anybody a cab and therefore the next hour passed awkwardly.

There were challenges to be sure. The first would be to get out of the house without anybody noticing. Ellie's mom wasn't what Ellie would call controlling. In fact, she had a great deal of freedom. After how she had been acting lately however, deciding to head out late at night would seem wildly out of character. It would raise questions Ellie didn't want to answer. She wasn't sure she could explain them even if she wanted to. She considered sneaking out of her bedroom window, like she was in some kind of 1980's teenage drama, but it didn't seem practical for a few reasons. Firstly, despite what most movies made you believe, she didn't have a convenient tree outside the window to hop onto, and secondly, her window opened sideways, not upwards, making it almost impossible to actually fit through.

No, she needed another way out of the house.

That left only two options. The front door and the back door. Hardly rocket science. The back door led out into the yard with no easy way around to the front of the house, short of jumping fences, but it was pretty far from the living room and it was unlikely her mom would hear her open it, judging by the volume of the television. The front door, of course, led out on the street and was much better as far as an option went, but it'd more likely mean having to try and explain herself to her mom.

Ellie paused, letting out a sigh. This was ridiculous, wasn't it? She had fought off an unstoppable monster, now another person wanted to meet her under mysterious circumstances, and her biggest challenge was how to escape her house without her mom noticing? It was embarrassing more than anything. How did she go from feeling like the bad ass survivor who feared nothing to being somebody trying desperately to work out the best way to sneak out of her own house? Ellen Ripley never had this problem. Ultimately, she decided for the back door. After all, she was meeting up with another survivor, if her guess was right. What was the point in that if she couldn't hop a couple of fences? In a few moments, she was at the back door. She opened it gently, slipping out into the evening air.

It was cool outside, and the lawn was damp beneath her cheap canvas sneakers. She wrapped her hoodie around herself a little more, and made her way further from the house. The grass was a little long, but that was to be expected. Even before the massacre, her mom had always hated gardening and tended to avoid it in the winter months. Ever since then, she had really let the back garden go. It was nearly wild now. Ellie had always intended to offer to help out, but she hated it too. It meant that the damp grass was long enough that it soaked through the fabric of her sneakers, leaving her socks damp and her feet wet, leaving her feeling even colder.

For a moment, standing there hunched in a slightly overgrown garden in the damp cool air, Ellie felt like she was back at St Mary's Marsh. Part of her expected at any moment to turn and see that terrible creature lurching towards her. But she saw nothing. She heard nothing. The garden was silent, bar for the barking of a dog a few gardens down. That would be the incredibly unimaginatively named Fido, she thought. She didn't really know Fido's owners, but sometimes when she saw them walking past had stopped to give him a little pat or a smile. They were slightly too far away to be in that range of neighbours who knew each other, so as far as she knew, not even her mom ever spoke to them. Nobody questioned a teenage girl saying hello to a dog, however. It probably said something about your modern American family, Ellie thought, that she knew her neighbours' pet better than her neighbours themselves.

There was an old tree stump at the back of the garden, mostly covered by moss and the long grass. She climbed on to it, knowing that she could use its extra height to make jumping the fence easier. Mrs Robinson, who lived alone next door, had a side path from her garden leading out to the street. A simple jump across and her escape would be easy. She felt her feet slide a little on the slick tree stump, and regretted the Converse knock-offs yet again. If she was going to do more sneaking around, she really did need to get some more practical outfits. Her hoodie was already damp and her feet were soaking. Leather boots. That'd be good, right?

Still, at least it wasn't like she was trying to sneak around in high heels or anything like half the girls in the movies. Although she was pretty sure in horror movies the survivor girls were always the ones with practical shoes. There was probably a film theory essay in there somewhere, Ellie thought wryly, before reminding herself to focus instead on the task at hand.

She lifted herself over the fence, and dropped down onto Mrs Robinson's considerably better cared for lawn. She landed with a bit of a thump. She froze for a moment, breathing hard. She was sure she could explain herself if Mrs Robinson spotted her, but that was if she recognised her. At this distance, she just looked like a young black girl in a hoodie sneaking around somebody's garden, and Ellie knew painfully well people didn't usually assume the best when they saw that.

Still, there was no sign of light from the house, and no sign of anybody stirring. Crouching low, she moved quickly to the side path. Perhaps Mrs Robinson was out? She decided not to dwell on it. What was that old phrase? You should never look a gift horse in the mouth? She had no idea what that actually meant but she figured it meant if things went well, don't complain, and so she slipped out onto the street, feeling damp and disgusting, but at least free.

Her timing couldn't have been better either, because there pulled up the yellow cab. For a moment, she felt her heart skip a beat. If the driver went to the house, or her mom looked out to spot it, the game would be up. A tense moment passed, but it seemed the driver had been informed, because he looked around and saw Ellie, and gestured for her to get in. She followed obediently, slipping into the back seat, and relaxing with a sigh.

The driver turned his head to look back at her, a scruffy looking man with short, thinning blonde hair and thick unkempt stubble. She guessed he was in his thirties or forties. He looked tired, but somehow managed to give her an exhausted smile.

'Wasn't sure you'd show. She was a bit vague,' his voice sounded rough and ragged, as if he was a heavy smoker.

'You know her?' Ellie felt stupid saying it. He was a taxi driver. He had probably just spoken to her on the phone. Why would she assume he knew her?

'Nina? Yeah. Notice how the meter ain't running?' he tapped the meter on his dash. 'I owe her a favour or two.'

'Right.' It was all Ellie could think of to say. He looked back at her, as if expecting something. 'Uh, thank you?'

'Name's Alec, by the way. Mine was giant spiders. Pretty sure it wasn't really my story, to be honest. She said I would have just been another body to find, if she hadn't been there. I didn't even know the kids they were hunting. I was just passing through.'

'Wait, you mean… You're like me? A survivor too?' she asked, a quizzical look playing across her features. She thought it was better to ask that particular question than dwell too long on what he had just said about the nature of the threat he had faced. Ellie was just about able to cope with the idea of strange demonic mirror monsters existing out there, but had he said *giant spiders*? There was not enough screaming and running away in the world to fully convey how she felt about that particular threat. Ellie felt her recent history demonstrated what she had always suspected deep down about herself; that in a pinch she was brave, resourceful and strong, but even she would draw the line at giant spiders. Some things were just *wrong*.

'No, no,' Alec chuckled in response, turning around to face her with a dismissive wave, and taking his eyes off the road for what Ellie thought was an alarmingly long time. 'People like you, survivors, as you put it, you're the special ones. Ones who survived all on their own. Nina calls people like me, well, she calls us "damsels".'

'"Damsels?"'

'Yeah, tell me about it,' he sighed. 'Not exactly flattering, is it? So I just do the occasional job for her in payback. Y'know, free taxi fare, picking up the newbies. Like you.' Ellie realised that while he was talking she hadn't been paying attention to where they were going, but they seemed to have left the suburbs for the countryside. For a moment, she thought maybe he was taking her to perhaps an old farm or barn, or perhaps even worse. Somewhere that there were no witnesses.

How did she even know that "Alec" wasn't Nina? That this wasn't all a trap? After all, all she'd heard from Nina was over messenger online? And didn't they always say all girls on the internet were guys? That didn't seem right. After all, she'd been on the internet too, and she was pretty sure *she* was a girl. Besides that, Alec clearly knew about the monsters and demons that lurked in the darkness too. This couldn't just be some ploy.

'Here we are. Try not to be too shocked,' Alec snapped her from her thoughts, and immediately the last vestiges of concern that he was taking her somewhere sinister, somewhere removed, somewhere hidden and remote, somewhere for her body to be hidden and never found faded away. This place was many things, but 'subtle' wasn't one of them. They were in front of heavy wrought iron gates that slowly slid open, revealing a long driveway up to a distant manor house. Somehow, this was the last thing that Ellie had expected she thought as they approached, passing an ornate fountain peacefully spitting water down into fine white marble, a beautifully tendered garden, and what looked like in the distance a hedge maze.

Although, if this was Nina's home, even if she had the money to own a place like this, quite why somebody who had nearly been killed by a monster would want a hedge maze was anybody's guess. Hadn't Nina seen *The Shining*? Nothing good ever came of a hedge maze. (Although, technically, she supposed the hedge maze saved Danny in the end, but that didn't make it any less creepy).

The manor itself began to come in to view, a vast modern looking building, with eight large, ornate windows facing outwards, and its entire facade built in what Ellie had at first thought was white stone, but as she got closer, she realised it was actually baby pink.

Nina owned a *pink mansion*? Who was she? Barbie? Somehow the entire situation was becoming increasingly more surreal by the moment. It said something when Ellie thought this was the strangest situation she'd ever been in, and only six months ago she'd nearly been murdered by some kind of zombie demon monster. Alec clearly sensed her surprise, looking back at her and letting a smile break across his face.

'Not what you expected?' he laughed a little. 'Gotta admit, it still surprises me every time I see it. I mean, can you imagine the planning permission on that thing?'

'I suddenly feel underdressed.' It wasn't the funniest thing Ellie had ever said, but the quip came naturally to her, as she looked down at her still slightly muddy canvas sneakers, her jeans with the hole in the knee, and her damp grey hoodie. If she'd known she had been visiting a mansion, she might have put on a nice dress or something.

'I'm not saying anything.' Alec seemed to chuckle to himself, holding up his hands. 'Guessing I might see you again though, next time she wants you to get somewhere. Or, hey, you need a cab yourself, call me.' He handed her a business card that displayed only the name "Alec Wright" and a phone number. She cringed when she realised it was written in Comic Sans font. Alec might have been a good taxi driver (she assumed; maybe he was a bad one, who knew, but he'd got her where she was going) but he was clearly no graphics designer.

'Uh, thanks,' she said doubtfully, opening the door and getting out slowly, finding herself once again questioning what the hell she was doing there. 'Do I go and knock or do I wait for Ken to come and get me?' Alec just smirked at that, before he started the taxi engine and pulled away, leaving Ellie stood in front of the huge pink mansion in the middle of the countryside all on her own.

She paused, taking a deep breath, before walking up to the main door. It had an ornate golden knocker built in to it, framed in what she thought looked like some kind of lily. She wasn't an expert on flowers, but that was her guess. It was undoubtedly beautiful, but also more than a little gaudy, and Ellie had a sinking feeling that it might have been worth more on its own than her entire house. Still, she had come this far, and what was the point in turning back now? Even if she wanted to, Alec had left. Going onwards was her only choice. She lifted the knocker, and tapped it lightly on the door, afraid of doing any damage to anything expensive.

To her surprise, the door opened before she even managed her third knock. She couldn't even take the figure in before a high pitched, excited voice spoke.

'You knocked! You actually knocked! I thought you were gonna go home but you didn't and now you're here!' Several things struck her about the figure that stood in front of her. The most obvious one?

It was definitely not Nina Collins.

The girl stood before her, beaming a huge smile, was definitely of Japanese origin, which ruled out her being Nina from the profile picture. There was definitely a trace of an accent in her voice too, so Ellie assumed that she had probably moved to America from Japan. The second thing that she noticed, however, was that the girl was *pink*.

Not that she just wore a bit of pink. No, her hair was pink, glossy, and worn in two long pigtails coming from the side of her head, each topped off with an ornate white ribbon. Her make-up was heavy, but noticeably on her cheeks, which were, yes, pink, and topped off with shimmering pink glitter. Her eyeshadow too was pink, and her eyebrows had been dyed pink too. Her dress, although calling it a "dress" was an understatement, was a gigantic frilly *thing*, but not quite like anything Ellie had seen before. It wasn't like a prom dress or a wedding dress or anything formal, and nor was it a historical gown. No, it was a huge, flared out dress covered in laces and frills and decorated with various colourful graphics of pink unicorns on a soft pink sky laced with pink clouds and a shining, yes, pink sun. She was wearing (at this point, unsurprisingly) pink pearls around her neck and her wrists, her nails were of course a long, glossy pink, and despite standing Ellie realised several inches shorter than her own 5'4 frame, she appeared to be wearing towering pink platform stiletto heels. The only shock of colour on her that wasn't pink came from bright blue eyes, which Ellie realised must have been contact lenses.

And yet, somehow, her appearance wasn't the most overwhelming thing about her. Because as soon as the door opened, Ellie felt like she had been hit in the face by an overwhelmingly sickly sweet scent that she realised must have been perfume. It smelled like a sweet candy, and Ellie thought that it probably was quite a nice scent (not something she'd wear herself, but still, she could appreciate it) if it was about a thousand times less strong. This girl smelled like she had bathed in it. In fact, it was so overwhelming, Ellie realised she was wrong. It didn't smell like candy. It smelled *pink*. This girl *smelled pink*.

Ellie was pretty sure that was supposed to be impossible, and yet here she was, proving her wrong.

And in case the description brought to mind a child, no, this girl was at least Ellie's age. Maybe older.

'Sorry, I'm so rude, my name's Suzi. Well, it's not, it's Suzuki, but everybody calls me Suzi. C'mon in! You can probably tell, but this is my house.' She grabbed Ellie by the hand, and pulled her over the threshold into the manor. Ellie looked around with wide eyes. She realised that spotting the house's owner first had better prepared her, but she was still slightly overwhelmed by how pink everything was. Thick, pink, fluffy carpet coated the floor which left Ellie impressed that Suzi hadn't fallen flat on her face in those heels. Pink bannisters lead up a grand pink staircase. Pink wooden doors guarded the entrance of the many, many rooms she could see just from the entrance and stuffed animals were everywhere, even in the hallway, including a giant pink bear just on Ellie's right hand side. Pink-hued display cabinets were filled to the brim with Walt Disney merchandise, something that didn't surprise Ellie in the slightest. It seemed natural that this girl would be a Disney fan.

Ellie couldn't shake the feeling she'd been wrong to compare the house to Barbie before. Even Barbie would look at this house and decide that it was *too much.*

'Uh. Ellie…' Ellie introduced herself slowly, still in shock.

'Duh! I know, silly!' Suzi replied, looking at her with a big smile on glossy pink lips. 'Ah, heck with it! I'm gonna hug you!' Before Ellie could react, she had two skinny arms thrown around her, and was literally choking on that sickly sweet perfume. By the time Suzi released her, she had the sinking feeling that her clothes would smell of it for the rest of the day.

'Uh thanks. Uh…' Ellie tried to find the words to say what she wanted to say, but they just hung in the air, totally absent. She had no idea how to possibly express her confusion.

'It's okay, I know, I know, you're not here to see me. C'mon, I'll introduce you!' Again, one of Suzi's impossibly soft hands grabbed Ellie's, and began to drag her through the gaudy pink house.

She was led into what she supposed was a living room, although that description somehow seemed to understate things. It was probably the size of the ground floor of Ellie's entire house. There were multiple plush pink sofas, including at least three that seemed to be there for the exact purpose of holding an array of stuffed animals, a pink grand piano, possibly the largest television she had ever seen, an ornate metallic pink dining table, and a vast glass display cabinet which Ellie realised was displaying a range of perfume bottles. The liquids inside? All pink. There were also several mirrors around, but somehow, that didn't shock Ellie. It seemed obvious that Suzi liked looking at herself.

And then, standing out like a sore thumb, looking out of the window (the glass was pink tinted, *seriously*), was a figure all in black. A long black leather trench coat reached to nearly touch the fluffy carpet, and from behind, all Ellie could see was short, greasy looking black hair. Slowly, the figure turned to face Ellie. She looked completely different from the profile picture Ellie had seen, and yet, somehow, she still recognised her. But wow, had she changed from the day that photo was taken...

The first thing that struck her was the eyepatch. And then, her age. It was difficult to gauge, she looked a fair bit older than Ellie, but the large scar that ran down her forehead and the majority of one cheek (moving behind said eyepatch) made it difficult to tell. Her hair was just as short, ragged, and greasy from the front, with several strands dropping down over her one good eye. Ellie wasn't what she'd call a prissy girl, but she couldn't help but think it desperately needed a wash. There was something unsettling too, about how her hairline didn't quite fully form right where the scar bit in to it. The rest of her clothes matched her long leather trench coat, baggy black jeans and an oversized t-shirt bearing a generic skull, with a snake moving through the eye sockets. Ellie thought, rather unkindly, she was just a flannel shirt away from looking like she had stepped out of the nineties. Her skin was pale; she was Caucasian and definitely on the pasty side. Her profile picture had been a natural blonde, Ellie remembered, and it showed in her ghostly pale skin. The black hair, obviously dyed, somehow didn't suit her.

Heavy black eyeliner ringed her one good eye, which itself was a deep brown, and currently fixed on Ellie's own. She seemed to be enjoying playing the enigma that she was, judging by the smirk on dark red lips, and she certainly didn't seem to mind that Ellie's eyes had been taking in her appearance. She was probably used to it, Ellie thought with a sense of guilt. A big visible scar like that, the eyepatch, people probably stared at her all the time. She was being impolite.

'Sorry for the dramatic posing, looking out the window. I like to make an entrance, and it's difficult to look badass in this house.' To Ellie's surprise, she spoke with a British accent. But despite the scar, the eye patch, the strange dress, the unexpected accent, despite *all* of that, this was definitely her. And yet, Ellie felt the need to ask:

'Nina Collins?'

'In the flesh.' Nina smiled back. 'Well, what's left of it, anyway. Sorry, not quite what's advertised in my profile picture, am I? That was a long time ago. Dyed my hair since then. Those bastard things always go after blondes. This throws them off the scent,' she gestured to her hair, but it seemed obvious to Ellie that she was playing that up intentionally instead of referencing the eye patch. 'I see you've already met Suzi. She's an associate.'

'We're friends!'

'Colleagues, really.'

'Best friends!' Suzi beamed. Somehow, Ellie couldn't help but smirk. These two were such opposites. How had they ever come together?

'She's a billionaire heiress. The money's useful.' Nina seemed to guess Ellie's thoughts, but gave Suzi a look that Ellie thought made it clear she was joking.

'Anyway, I guess we'd better cut to the chase. Eliza Cartwright, it's time you started fighting back.' When Nina spoke, it was with a dramatic flair, reminding Ellie of a cheesy nineties TV show. Somehow, Ellie imagined Nina was expecting a cutaway to some upbeat opening credit sequence in that moment.

'I'm sorry, come again?' Ellie felt like she was at breaking point. Six months of trying to get her life back to normal, six months of trying to convince herself what had happened to her was a one off, and now here she was, stood in a sea of pink being told by the last goth of the nineties that she had to fight something?

It was getting to be too much.

'Sorry, big drama queen, me,' Nina replied with the air of somebody about to casually discard a cigarette. Which of course was impressive since she wasn't holding a cigarette. Something that Ellie thought was for the best since she suspected that any open flame in this house was a bad idea. There was so much cloying perfume the entire house would probably go up like a match. 'The whole "fighting back" thing is kind of a side effect. For now, it's just about saving people.'

'Alec, the taxi guy, said you saved him,' Ellie said thoughtfully as that conversation replayed in her head. 'Did you save Malibu Barbie over there too?' she asked, gesturing to the pink clad girl. She hadn't meant to be rude, but the nickname escaped her lips before she thought about it. She remembered when her friends had used to call her 'sassy'. She had hated it. She thought it was a dumb, generic word, but on occasion she could see what they meant.

'Suzi. My name's Suzi,' Suzi insisted over the pair. Nina seemed to chuckle at this.

'No, no. She's a survivor. Like me and you. Hard to believe, I know, but she killed one of those things. Alec's just a guy I helped out.'

'One of those things? You mean, a Mirror Monster? Like the thing that tried to kill me?' Ellie asked, raising an eyebrow sceptically, and giving Suzi a quizzical look for help, but Suzi just smiled and waved back at her.

'No, kid.' The "kid" seemed pretty galling, Ellie thought. There couldn't be *that* many years between them. 'Why don't you pick the seat least buried by stuffed animals, and I'll explain a thing or two to you.' Nina gestured to one of the many pink couches, and Ellie slowly made her way over, sitting down.

She sank deep down into the soft couch, and despite the fact the entire thing seemed to smell of the same *pink* smell as Suzi herself (seriously, it was everywhere), she had to admit she had never sat on a couch like it. So soft, so comfortable, it was like sinking into a nice warm bed. Not any old warm bed either, not *your* warm bed, it was the warm bed you'd always dream about rather than the harsh reality of your bed which was never quite as satisfying as you thought. She found it impossible to sit up, and ended up slouched back on the sofa, which is why she found it quite impressive when Nina sat on one opposite her and didn't seem to sink in. Maybe it wasn't so fluffy. Ellie couldn't shake the stray thought that maybe Nina was wearing the leather coat to stop all the perfume soaking into her clothes.

'Look, for you, it was the Mirror Monster. Some old urban legend from some old summer camp. But for me? Well, it started out as this escaped serial killer. Except, the bastard wouldn't die. Never did find out what he was. Only thing I know is that he was some kind of pure evil. Came back for me more than once too. They tend to do that.'

'What, like, Michael Myers?' Ellie asked after a moment.

'Right, yeah, I saw on your profile. You're a bit of a horror nerd, aren't you?' Nina smirked.

'Y-yeah. Horror films. And uh, I guess I used to like cheesy movies.' Nina just gave a small nod. It was clear she understood why Ellie had said "used to".

'Similar M.O., I guess. Had a sad clown mask instead of that creepy white thing.'

'William Shatner. It was a William Shatner mask painted white,' Ellie offered, not quite sure why she felt the need to share horror trivia.

'Huh. *Star Trek* always freaked me out. Guess now I know why,' Nina replied with a shrug. 'Anyway, you're one to talk, Miss Camp Counsellor. Your experience wasn't exactly a beacon of originality, was it?'

'It didn't really feel that way at the time.'

'Never does,' Nina agreed. 'Suzi over there? She killed a werewolf.'

'Wait, *seriously*?' Ellie asked, frowning in shock. It seemed hard to imagine that Suzi would kill anything but somebody's sense of smell, let alone a werewolf.

'Yep!' Suzi beamed proudly. 'I was the only survivor, but I got him!' For a moment, that ever cheerful facade of Suzi's seemed to crack, suggesting some kind of hidden sorrow. Ellie knew exactly what it was. That distant pain. The people she had lost, the people she had been unable to save. Ellie felt like that expression was etched on her own face at all times, but Suzi quickly replaced it with the same cheerful smile again.

'Honestly, I think it just choked to death on her perfume,' Nina mocked with a sigh. 'Point is, there's all sorts of stuff out there. Every myth, every legend you can imagine. If it's a story, it's probably got some truth to it. They show up, they kill a bunch of people, usually teenagers, of course, and then anybody else who gets in the way. Usually there's a survivor. Sometimes it's the person who managed to kill whatever monster it was. That's us. The survivors.' Nina gestured between the three of them. 'All of us I could find,' she added after a momentary pause. Ellie couldn't quite place why, but that pause bothered her. She felt like something scratching at the back of her mind, something that didn't quite add up, but she couldn't make sense of it.

She gave her head a brief shake.

'So, what? We're like, the AA for people who nearly got killed by monsters? A therapy group? Are we meant to talk about our feelings and how messed up we are? Because, I gave therapy a go and it's not for me.' In a way, she was glad she wasn't the only one out there who had faced this kind of trauma, she was glad to know there were other survivors, but if this was some kind of hug and feel support group she had no interest. And judging by Suzi's general cheerful nature and the fact that Ellie was expecting to be hugged again at any moment, that assumption seemed natural.

Except… It didn't really seem like Nina's scene. It wasn't just the all black outfit and the scar. Ellie was a modern girl, she appreciated that people could have feelings too, no matter how they looked. But nothing in Nina's attitude, or her cryptic "fighting" spiel for that matter, suggested this was just therapy. It seemed that Nina agreed because she let out a low chuckle.

'Is that how it's going to be? She's the girly one, I'm the badass one, you're the funny one?' Nina asked. Ellie paused. She was pretty sure Nina was being the "funny one" right about then, but decided not to say anything. 'No, this sure as hell isn't therapy. Unless you call stopping those bastards therapy. It certainly is *therapeutic*.' For a moment, Ellie couldn't help but be distracted by how Suzi seemed to wince at Nina's bad language. Okay, so the girl obviously defined herself by her love of childish things, that was fine, but didn't even like hearing bad language either? Wow. Ellie had to bite her lip to hide a smirk at that. Instead, she decided to focus on what Nina had been saying.

'Stop them? Haven't we already stopped them?' Ellie asked, a little cautious as she wasn't sure she wanted to know the answer.

'Okay, Rule One: If you think that the monster after you is dead, it's not. It'll come back. They always do. One way or another. Why'd you think horror movies get more sequels than any other type of movie out there?' Nina questioned.

'Honestly? I thought it was because they were cheap to make and easy to churn out quickly.'

'...Okay, yeah, that's probably it.' Nina paused thoughtfully, obviously her train of thought having been derailed. Ellie was slightly proud. Nina might have been playing the mysterious tough leader, but it was good to see she was still human underneath that gruff exterior. 'But the point remains, they always come back. So sleep with one eye open.'

'How can I sleep if I have - Ohhhh, wait, you weren't serious,' Suzi chirped in, and for the first time Ellie noticed she was listening intently. These two obviously had history and knew each other, so she knew Suzi wasn't new here. And yet, Suzi still seemed to listen anyway. It was as if she just enjoyed the company and being part of the conversation. As if she liked *people*. Ugh. Ellie wasn't sure she'd ever been that sweet, even as a kid, even before everything that happened at St Mary's Marsh, even before her world changed forever. Still, if you could nearly be eaten by a werewolf, and keep your optimism, you had to be a little admired. Even if it was from afar, Ellie decided. And possibly with sunglasses on if you had to look at her pink clad form for too long.

'Look, that's not my actual point. Yeah, we're all on borrowed time. Sorry, but that's how this gig works. Survive one encounter, and it doesn't mean you'll survive the next. Sooner or later, they're gonna get you. But, hey, way I figure it, everybody dies, right? Question you have to ask yourself is; what do you want to do first?'

Somehow, Ellie got the impression that deep down, Nina was trying to convince herself that it was okay to die, rather than Ellie or Suzi. She looked again at that angry, deep scar running down Nina's face. She could only imagine what had caused it. It looked like it cut to the bone. Surviving that must have been near impossible. Nina must have stared death in the face before. And she was pretending she accepted it. But Ellie knew better. She'd been there herself, face down in the mud of St Mary's Marsh, thinking that was the moment she was going to die, and in that moment, knowing more than anything that she wanted to *live*. 'What I'm trying to say is, yeah, we now know there are the things out there that hunted us. But we also know there are *other* things. Other monsters. Hunting people. Right as we speak, somewhere, some innocent teenager is getting shredded by some beast from her nightmares. And we're some of the only people on this entire *planet* who know about it. And that leaves us with two choices. Either we run and we hide and we pretend they don't exist, or we *do something* about it.' Ellie couldn't help but think the dramatic speech would have had a much bigger impact if she hadn't currently been sunken in to a large fluffy pink sofa with what appeared to be a giant cuddly toy of Jigglypuff by her head.

'So, what? You want us to hunt down the monsters hunting people? Go looking for them?' Ellie thought she must have sounded sceptical, but she surprised herself. She didn't feel fear. Not even a drop in that moment. No, what she felt was almost like excitement. It was a thrill inside her, the first strong emotion she could remember feeling since the massacre. Ever since then, nothing had seemed real. She had felt like she was floating through a fake world, like nothing that she said or did mattered anymore.

But *this*? This felt *real*. It felt like she could finally be doing something worth doing. She realised she hadn't even considered saying no. If that was what Nina wanted them to do, she was in. Fully.

'Why not? Suzi's loaded and can fund us. We all know what's out there. We all have experience. Bit of research, forward planning, think of the people we could save. The lives we could change.'

'We could call ourselves 'The Slasher Slayers'!' Suzi enthused.

'We're not calling ourselves that,' Ellie surprised herself because she said that at the exact same time as Nina. The two exchanged a slightly amused glance.

'Okay, you know what? I'm pretty sure you're both insane. She's *definitely* insane,' Ellie decided, pointing at Suzi.

'I'm not insane! I'm kawaii!' Suzi cheered, stopping to pose with two fingers held up in what Ellie recognised as a sideways version of the peace sign.

'What the heck is "kawaii"?' Ellie asked sceptically.

'It's Japanese for "makes you want to be sick",' Nina answered.

'No! It means, y'know, cute!' Suzi corrected, causing a slight snicker from Nina.

'*Anyway*, what I was trying to say is, I'm pretty sure you're both insane, but… I guess I must be insane too. Because… This actually sounds like a good idea.' Ellie paused again, and shook her head. 'No, scratch that. It sounds like a terrible idea that'll get us all killed, but I want to do it anyway.'

Nina broke into a smile. A youthful smile of excitement. It wasn't something Ellie thought she'd ever see on that face, and she was pretty sure she never saw it again after that day, but for just the briefest moment, despite the scar and grungy clothes and the eyepatch, she could see in Nina the same innocent teenage girl that had been her profile picture when she had sent her first message. For just the smallest split second, Ellie could see who Nina had been before the world had broken her

'I knew it!' Nina said with obvious glee and a surprisingly child-like laugh to Suzi. 'That's what I said! That you missed it! The adrenaline! The fight! After you've been in a fight for your life, nothing seems the same.'

'I already said 'yes', you don't have to keep marketing it,' Ellie replied dryly. It felt a little surreal being dry back to Nina, but she would be lying if she said she didn't enjoy the moment. 'But, uh, I don't know about you two, but I'm eighteen. I still live at home with my mom. A mom that I don't think is going to be too happy if I just disappear to fight monsters.' It was Ellie's primary concern with the plan. She was ready, she knew, to try and do something good with her life. To try and make the difference Nina believed they could.

But how would she get her mom to understand? She was so protective, so glad that she was alive after what had happened, would she ever be able to understand why her only daughter was heading back into danger? Could she even comprehend it? Ellie had told her mom many times about the horrors at St Mary's Marsh, but she was still fairly certain that she thought Ellie had imagined the supernatural elements. Her mom really believed that it had just been a masked killer that came after her.

Nina seemed to scoff at this, and rolled her one good eye.

'Screw 'em. We're talking about saving lives. Just come with us. Suzi can pay for anything you need, your mom won't ever know where you went,' she said dismissively, much to Ellie's shock. Even Suzi looked a little surprised. There was no question that Nina had had it tough, it was written all over her face, and not just because of the injury, but Ellie couldn't help but wonder what had led her to be able to so callously dismiss her mom.

'Or you could tell them you were going to live somewhere else! That's what I told my parents, that I wanted to live on my own, and move out,' Suzi explained cheerfully. Ellie sighed.

'Listen, both of you. I'm not putting my Mom through any more stress. I nearly died six months ago! She's still not over that. If I just disappear, it'll kill her. And I can't just move out, Suzi, because I'm not *rich*,' she reminded the wealthy girl. Suzi seemed awfully sweet, but she was definitely from the sheltered, spoiled end of society. She had probably had a life time of getting whatever she wanted, which was why nobody had ever told her that her current clothing and style might be a bit *excessive*. Although that was a point for another day.

'Then go home, Ellie. Because let's be real here, any choice you have is gonna stress your Mum out,' Nina said, her previously happy tone vanishing into sudden irritation. 'What, you think you can tell her the truth and everything will be okay? "Mom, I'm out hunting monsters, be back soon" and she *won't* stress? Best case scenario, she locks you up somewhere. Worse case? She'll try to follow you and get herself killed. You wanna join us, there's no easy way out of it. You've gotta break ties with your family. Your choice.' Ellie noticed Suzi looked uncomfortable, and when her eyes made contact, she looked away. Clearly she wasn't fond of confrontation, but something in her manner made Ellie think that Suzi supported Nina anyway. The worst part was as much as Ellie wanted to argue with Nina, as much as she wanted to point out all the flaws in her logic, she couldn't think of any counter arguments. Nina was absolutely correct. If Ellie wanted to do this, and she knew in heart that she really did, then she had no choice but to agree and leave her Mom behind.

'How would that work? Would we just disappear overnight? Do I leave everything behind?'

'Best way. Suzi can make sure you have plenty of clothes. Nobody's going to look for you here, and we'll be on the road most of the time anyway,' Nina answered. Suzi perked up at this idea, and Ellie gave her a reluctant look.

'I'm not wearing her outfits, am I?' Ellie asked, feeling her face drain with horror at the prospect. Somehow that was even scarier than fighting the monsters, she thought to herself.

'No, silly!' Suzi giggled a little, glad the confrontation had passed, and bad to her usual self. 'Nobody gets to wear my outfits but me! But I have some spare clothes you can use that are more your style, and we can definitely buy some more!' Ellie decided to bite her tongue, and not point out that nobody else would *want* to wear Suzi's outfits. Now didn't seem like the time. Not when she stood at the edge of making such a momentous decision about her future.

'Okay, fine,' Ellie sighed. 'But I get to leave her a message. I'm not just disappearing. She needs to know *something*.' Nina paused for a moment, her face flickering reluctance, but eventually she nodded, and Ellie headed outside, already digging her phone out of her hoodie pocket.

Ellie made her way out of the living room and down the overwhelming hallway, numb to the sheer amount of pink and expense around her, and pushed open the heavy doors to the fancy manor house. She wondered if Suzi's skinny little arms could even open the heavy, ornate door on their own, and then she recalled Suzi had opened the door for her when she arrived. Also apparently she had killed a werewolf, so she was *definitely* tougher than she looked. The cold, fresh air of the night hit her, and she gulped it down gratefully, not aware quite how overwhelming the perfume had been while she had been inside until she was free of it. If she was going to stay here for any length of time, she'd definitely be having words with Suzi about having her own room far away from the overwhelming scent.

She held the phone in her hand, staring at it, trying to figure out how to handle the gravity of what she was about to do. To say goodbye to her mom forever. Was it forever? Something about this felt very permanent, and Ellie realised that she wasn't ever intending to return. What bothered her more than the task before her, however, was the fact that she didn't really *feel* anything about it. Good or bad. She just felt numb. Inside, talking to Nina and Suzi, she had acted offended about the idea, as if it would hurt her mom, and she knew that it would, but she realised she had only been saying what common decency told her to say. The truth was that Ellie hadn't felt much of anything since that night. Even for her mom, even now, she couldn't sum up the required grief. The thought of walking away just felt natural. No, worse. It felt *freeing*.

But she had to do her duty and make sure her mom was okay. She knew it was the right thing to do, no matter how difficult it felt. She pulled out her cell phone and scrolled to her mom in her contacts list. She let it ring a few times, and it clicked to answer phone, just as it always did. She had known this was going to happen. She took a deep breath.

'Mom. It's Ellie. I'm not coming home. I know that's going to scare you. I know you're going to panic. But I'm fine. I'm okay. I just… There's something I need to do. I don't know when I'll be home or even where I'll be. But I promise you, I'm safe. I love you.' A moment passed as she waited, frozen, and then she ended the call, robotically, without emotion. It seemed woefully insufficient, but at least her mom had a message. She suspected, if she knew her mother, by tomorrow she'd have police combing through that message. She checked her phone to make sure GPS tracking was turned off. She'd seen enough movies to know they could find her that way.

Then, feeling just as numb as she had when she had stepped outside, she turned and walked back into the mansion. Her new home, she supposed.

It would definitely take some getting used to.

CHAPTER FOUR

THE OTHERS

Ellie stood in the surprisingly plain bedroom located in what Suzi had called the 'east wing' of what she was rapidly realising certainly was not a manor, nor a house, but most definitely a 'mansion'. The bedroom itself was large, much larger than any room in her tiny parent's house, including the front room, but Suzi had already apologised twice for it being 'cramped'. It was largely free of Suzi's otherwise gaudy pink decoration, and even seemed to largely have escaped the perfume scent that had soaked into the rest of the house, although with Suzi currently hovering by her side, Ellie could still smell it strongly.

Suzi threw open a wardrobe, lifting out a faded pink hoodie and some old jeans, and held them up to Ellie.

'I think these would fit!' she said cheerfully, before gesturing to the rest of the wardrobe. Inside, Ellie saw more jeans, some skirts, various crop tops and a few more hoodies, all of varying colours and styles, mostly light pastels. She supposed she shouldn't have been surprised that Suzi had reached for the pink one first. It wasn't so much the colour that concerned her; Ellie wore pink, *sometimes*. The real issue was that the outfits were clearly not *Suzi's*. Even ignoring the height difference meaning they'd be too big on her, she was pretty sure Suzi wouldn't be caught dead in any of these outfits. She could see a few shoes scattered at the bottom of the wardrobe, and while there was a pair of modest heels, the rest were flat, and definitely unflashy. She eyed Suzi's own towering pink stiletto heels. They definitely didn't belong to her.

'Whose room was this?' Ellie asked cautiously. Suzi looked panicked, her eyes darting to the side for a moment, before she looked back and giggled nervously.

'Uh, what do you mean? It's, uh, it's mine. I mean, I might wear… Uh…' She pulled out of the closet a baby blue sweater, with the picture of a VW Camper Van on it with a surfboard on top and a 'Surf's Up' caption. '....this,' she said with difficulty, as if the act of even considering wearing it physically pained her. That was ignoring the fact that it would drown her.

'Suzi.' Ellie said severely, trying to get a straight answer out of her. 'What aren't you telling me?'

'What? No. Nothing!' Suzi smiled, desperately shoving the offending sweater back into the closet. 'W-why would you think that?' Suzi fidgeted nervously, looking around desperately. Ellie suspected she was waiting for Nina to come and save her. As far as she knew, Nina was still loitering outside, having a cigarette. Maybe she had just imagined the cigarette bit, she hadn't yet seen Nina smoke, she just had the general air of somebody who did. Either way, Suzi was alone, and clearly not a talented liar. It was beginning to fit together for Ellie. That nagging thought she'd had that she couldn't place back when she'd been talking to Nina was suddenly forming into something tangible. Something that she could understand.

'When I came here, Alec, the taxi driver, acted like he'd brought people here before. Seemed like he'd seen lots of people be shocked by this place, meet you and Nina, the whole lot. I definitely wasn't the first. And yet, it's just you two. Nobody else. Nina acted like this was a new idea, but… It's not, is it? Whose room was this?'

Suzi's face flickered through a range of emotions. She looked scared, nervous, sheepish, embarrassed, and finally accepting, sighing, her shoulders slumping a little. Ellie only realised upon seeing her reaction that Suzi had been holding herself in a meticulously chosen dainty pose at all times prior. For the first time, she resembled something slightly more human than like a child's over-dressed doll.

'You're… not the first survivor we've met. Me and Nina I mean… We've… We've tried this before. And it worked! For a while it worked! But… eventually… people die. It's dangerous. People don't survive. We've… lost our entire team, at one point or another,' Suzi paused again, looking worried. No, not worried. *Scared.* Suzie was scared. '…I mean, one day it'll happen to me and Nina too. One day we'll all die doing this. But… we save people doing it. We help people. So, we accept that.'

'I know,' Ellie answered without even hesitating, although she wasn't sure at first where the words had come from. Not until she realised that it was accurate. She *did* know. She had known from the moment Nina had asked her. That simple truth. That eventually she would die doing this. And she knew that she didn't care. She wanted to do this anyway. Knowing that she wasn't the first to join only made more sense to her. Suzi and Nina's friendship, despite their differences, Nina's seemingly rehearsed speech, Alec's experience, it all made sense to Ellie that she wasn't the first. It didn't faze her. So the previous members had died. That didn't change anything. It didn't change how she felt. That same apathy towards her life, and that same enthusiasm for joining Nina hadn't been dampened. In fact, if anything, she was more confident than ever.

But while Ellie felt confidence, she couldn't help but think that Suzi was radiating the exact opposite. She seemed scared and nervous. She was obviously the source of Nina's resources, so they must have been working together, even with the others, for a while. But that didn't mean she seemed at home with the task.

'What about you? I mean, don't take this the wrong way, but you don't exactly seem like the type to fight monsters...' Ellie asked, trying to give the girl a warm smile to put her mind at rest.

'Oh. Uh, no, I guess I'm not,' Suzi replied sheepishly, her eyes fluttering down to her bulky pink attire, painfully aware of its lack of practicality. 'At first, I just helped Nina out financially. I didn't... want to face anything again. I'd nearly died once and I was happy to just hide here. But... Well, the thing is...' She looked around the room, sadness etched on her face, and Ellie realised that whoever this room had belonged to had been Suzi's friend. She doubted Suzi dealt with loss very well, and she must have been surrounded by it. '...there's no difference between me and you. Or any of the survivors that have worked with Nina. There's no excuse or reason for me to stay hiding. I know what's out there, I know people are risking their lives to stop it, so I have to help. Maybe I'm not very good at it and it's scary but if just one person is alive who wouldn't be because of me then it's all worth it. If I make a difference just once, then I have to do it. And I have. I've saved people. Not many. I mean, Nina does most of the dramatic saving. I'm just, sort of, back-up. But when I do it right, I've saved lives. There are people out there, at home, safe in their beds who would be dead if it wasn't for me. And because of that, I can't ever stop. Because if I stop today, tomorrow, the next day, whenever, somebody might die who I could have rescued. So I carry on. I do it all anyway.' Ellie was a little surprised. Scratch that, Ellie was *very* surprised. It was a deep, passionate answer from a woman that Ellie had thought would only ever feel that passionate about a particularly nice pair of shoes. And while she still struggled to imagine Suzi would have lasted five minutes if she had been at St Mary's Marsh, there had been a passion and fire blazing behind the bright blue contact lenses and false lashes she wore, clear as day in her eyes, that suggested that when there was *real* danger, Suzi would do whatever was necessary to help. And that maybe, just *maybe*, this innocent seeming girl had a real edge to her, and that she might be far more capable than met the eye.

'Lillian. Lillian McKenzie. That was her name. The girl who used to live in this room. Who's clothes they were,' Suzi spoke after the long, awkward silence between them, gesturing to the room in general. 'She was in a car when her friends accidentally knocked down some old lady. The old lady put a curse on them and they all died one by one, but she managed to survive. She destroyed the old lady's necklace which *of course* turned out to be the source of the curse. You'd have liked her. She loved horror movies, like you. She was strong and she was tough but most importantly she was *clever*. She saved a lot of people working with us, she'd always know just how to solve a mystery and stop a creature,' Suzi went on, and Ellie could tell the tiny girl was fighting back tears, which somehow seemed so odd with her carefully curated look. There was something about how Suzi spoke that made the air feel heavy, and Ellie realised that these were words Suzi had longed to say for a long time. She imagined that she didn't get to speak to Nina about emotions. Nina didn't seem the type. Again, without really knowing her, Ellie imagined she'd drink through a loss, not mourn a person. 'There was this… thing… I guess, you'd call it a demon. It was possessing people. Nina found a way to destroy it, but the person it was possessing would die too. So Lillian let it possess her, so nobody else would have to die. Nina … she had to kill them both. Lillian *and* the demon.' Suzi fell silent again. Ellie waited. She didn't know what else to say. Clearly this was a traumatic memory, but if what Suzi was saying was true, it was just one of many. Ellie was painfully aware that they had passed other rooms coming to this one in the mansion. There had been others staying here. Did they all have a story of such tragedy? Did every room hold such painful memories for Suzi?

Finally, Ellie knew she would have to break the silence.

'She sounds very brave. And like a good friend.' The words felt hollow, like they were nowhere near enough. She placed a hand on Suzi's shoulder, or at least, the large fluffy ruffles of her overly ornate dress that were where her shoulder would be. Suzi paused for a moment, and then threw her arms around Ellie, hugging her. The tender moment was only slightly ruined by Ellie letting out a small involuntary cough at the strength of the girl's perfume in this close vicinity. 'I can't… take her room. Her clothes. It'd be wrong.' She said to break away from the hug. Suzi looked up, dabbing tears from her eyes delicately with a lacy pink handkerchief. Ellie hadn't seen where she'd produced it from, but there could be a battleship hidden under that dress and she wouldn't know about it.

'She'd want you to. She wanted us to go on fighting. And she always wanted to help however she could,' Suzi paused, and suddenly, a mischievous smile flickered across her glossy pink lips. 'Unless you'd rather wear my clothes?' Ellie smiled back a little, allowing the humour to break the heavy sadness that had encroached upon the room. She knew that Suzi was bluffing, the girl had made it clear that her outfits weren't to be borrowed earlier, and they'd never fit Ellie anyway, but the act of kindness was there. A light joke to force Ellie in to accepting the gift.

'Okay, okay,' Ellie threw up her hands in mock surrender. 'I'll use these,' she said as she reached inside the wardrobe, looking at the examples. 'But I would appreciate going clothes shopping for my own outfits at some point.' Suzi's eyes lit up at this suggestion, just as Ellie thought they would. Something had told her that Suzi would be the type to love shopping, and while Ellie was actually happy wearing whatever came to hand, it was the best way she could think to return the kindness that Suzi had shown.

'That would be awesome!' Suzi smiled back. Ellie wasn't sure if Suzi knew it was a simple offer of friendship she was extending, or if the girl really thought Ellie's priorities were on clothes shopping when she had just abandoned her parents and agreed to Nina's plan, but she decided it didn't matter. Suzi was sweet, kind and obviously loyal, and she deserved Ellie's friendship, even if Ellie was pretty sure she'd never understand her… 'Nina's outside. She said to come and find her when you were ready.'

'Ready for what,'

'I don't know, she just talks like that sometimes. Usually it just means she wants to chat,' Suzi smiled and giggled a little, a goofy playful and childish giggle that suggested she had firmly moved on from their more serious conversation.

She headed out of the room, making her way through Suzi's home, taking in the displays around her. Suzi followed her, but made herself scarce pretty quickly when she saw Ellie taking in the place. She obviously knew that Ellie still had a lot of settling in to do. This wing (as Suzi had called it) of the mansion was decorated in what Ellie considered to be a slightly more typical style, she spotted an old painting of men riding horses on a hunt in an ornate gold frame, and what appeared to be a marble statue against the side of the hallway, before it reached a large door that led back out to the main hall and the staircase, where everything was pink. She assumed that Suzi had had the place decorated to her tastes, but ignored the guest wing. Either because she wanted the others in the group to have a home, or perhaps because she never went there herself outside of visiting her guests.

Once back out in to the main hall and descending the plush grand staircase and its thick pink carpet, Ellie almost found herself instantly missing the old, slightly stuffy but at least non-nauseating design of the guest wing. She soon made the large doors and stepped out into the cold air for the second time that evening.

She saw Nina not far away, stood with her back against the house, looking down at the hedge maze. Her face was lit with the orange glow of a cigarette, and one foot was behind her on the wall. She looked like the definition of try-hard cool, Ellie thought dismissively, but she regretted it afterwards. It was a harsh thought, and after all, she didn't know what Nina had been through. Not really. She imagined there was a lot of pain wrapped up in that girl's mind. Not just from the scar or the injury, but from the history. Suzi had already told her about one friend who she had killed. How many others had Nina lost?

'I knew it,' Ellie quipped, trying to make light of the situation.

'Huh?' Nina just turned, raising her one eyebrow. Ellie gestured to the cigarette. 'Oh, right, yeah. Well, it's not like we've got a long life expectancy doing this, is it? Don't exactly have to worry about staying healthy,' she explained as she dropped the cigarette on the floor and stomped it out. To Ellie's surprise, however, she followed it up by picking it up, and disposing of it in a nearby waste bin that was, yes, made out of pink metal. Nina obviously noticed the surprise on Ellie's face. 'Suzi goes mad if I litter,' she explained. 'Put the bins in just for me. Shame about the colour.' It seemed Nina was attempting to joke, but no smile appeared on her face.

A silent beat passed as the two stood there, and Nina's one eye focused on the hedge maze.

'Give you the creeps?' she asked, nodding at it.

'A bit.'

'*The Shining*, right?'

'Yeah. What kind of person who deals with the stuff you two do can keep a hedge maze and not be creeped out by it?'

'Suzi won't watch it, so I don't think the maze bothers her. She says it reminds her of *Alice in Wonderland* instead.'

'Let me guess, Suzi hates horror movies.'

'How'd you know?' Nina smirked. 'I never found *The Shining* particularly scary anyway. Sure, the hedge maze bit is creepy, but, well, in the end, the maze is the only reason Danny survives right? It *saves* the day. And Jack Torrance? I mean, what? One dude goes a bit mad and then utterly fails to kill his family? He's not exactly Jason Voorhees, is he?'

'Yeah, but he's scary while he's *trying*.'

'Only because he's Jack Nicholson and Jack Nicholson is terrifying.'

'You know, that was Stephen King's one biggest complaint about the movie? He hated Jack Nicholson in it. Apparently, he thought that Jack Torrance should be an ordinary guy, so that when he snapped, it was more shocking. He thought Jack Nicholson was too creepy from the start.' Ellie wasn't sure why the random piece of movie trivia came to her mind, but she decided to share it anyway.

'Didn't Jack Torrance beat his kid while drunk? If that's what Stephen King thinks of as "an ordinary guy", I'm kinda disturbed.' Nina raised her one visible eyebrow. Ellie shrugged.

'Hey, I'm just telling you trivia. It actually got so bad that Stephen King remade *The Shining* for TV to be more like he wanted, but they'd only let him have the rights to do so if he stopped openly criticising the Kubrick movie. In the end, he signed a literal contract that says the only element he's still allowed to publicly criticise is Jack Nicholson's casting and he has to keep quiet about the rest.'

'Wow, you really are a horror nerd, aren't you?' Nina teased. Ellie gave a slight smile and a shrug. 'Still don't see him as scary myself, though. I mean, he didn't actually successfully kill *anyone*.'

'He killed the cook!'

'Not in the novel!' Nina seemed proud to have caught Ellie out on a piece of trivia, and Ellie thought better of saying that she had actually *known* that. They were discussing the *film*, after all. 'But my point is, he totally failed at killing the people he was trying to kill.'

'I don't really think it was meant to be scary because lots of people died. It's scary because it's a look at male privilege and domestic abuse. I mean, think about it. Jack's not got any reason to be any more physically intimidating or dangerous than his wife, but when he goes mad, he *is*, and he's scary, and the only reason is because he's a *man*. He's not athletic and he doesn't take care of himself, but just through the genetic fluke of being an adult male, he's stronger, more intimidating and more dangerous than either his wife or his kid. He's not a supernatural monster. He's dangerous just because he's male. He's a man exercising his male privilege on his family to terrorise them. I find that pretty scary,' Ellie explained. Nina gave her a quizzical look, and laughed, shaking her head.

'I don't know. That sounds like some Gender Politics bull to me,' she said dismissively. 'Oh god, you're not a film student, are you?'

'I might have studied film a little in school, yeah,' Ellie said sheepishly, prompted Nina to laugh loudly. Ellie was pretty sure it was a fake laugh, but she didn't want to call her out on it. Ellie had no choice but to smile.

A moment of silence followed, and Ellie knew the entire conversation was about to take a sombre turn.

'I take it Suzi told you about the others.'

'You mean that everybody else you recruited is dead? Yeah, it came up,' Ellie tried not to sound too sarcastic, but she wasn't sure that she had succeeded.

'I'm not surprised. Suzi can't keep a secret to save her life.' Nina turned back to look at Ellie and looking at her with her one good eye. 'You still haven't left. I mean, we told you to cut out your family, and you did, we've told you everybody who's ever joined us has died, and you're still here. I don't know if I'm impressed or a tiny bit terrified of you.'

'I need this. I don't know if I can explain why, but I *know*, somehow, deep down this is exactly what I'm meant to be doing,' Ellie explained, and she meant every word. All she knew was that doing this might fill the emptiness inside. And that was something she was desperate for.

'I know what you mean,' Nina nodded, before pausing and reaching into her long trench coat. Ellie's eyes widened a little when she saw what Nina had produced; a heavy looking, dark grey automatic pistol. 'You ever fired one of these?' Nina held the weapon casually, handle extended to Ellie. Ellie found herself transfixed by the gun, eyes locked onto it; a cold metal object that she felt was drawing her in. She had never liked guns, and certainly never owned one. Neither did anybody in her family. They were dangerous objects, she believed, and she had never wanted to so much as touch one.

Nina didn't wait for an answer, because it became pretty clear that Ellie hadn't ever handled one, and sighed and shook her head.

'Seriously? You're the only American in our team and yet *you're* the one who hasn't fired a gun?' Nina sighed. 'Even Suzi has a gun!'

'Is it pink?'

'You bloody well know that it is.' Of *course* Suzi's gun would be pink. 'Look, okay, fine, I get it, you don't like guns. That's pretty fair. They kill people, and generally, we're the people who stop people getting killed. But, they're useful. Now, don't get me wrong, guns *never* work. Not on the stuff we'll be facing. You can try it. But if you think it's worked? You think, yeah, that thing is *definitely* dead this time? I promise you now, it's just waiting 'til you turn your back, then it'll calmly get back up and rip you a new one.' As Nina talked, there was passion burning in her one eye, Ellie noticed. She *lived* for this, Ellie realised. This was her life. 'Rule one; the bad guys never stay dead. Werewolf, zombie, demon, ordinary guy in a mask, it doesn't matter, you think you've killed them? Think again. Hell, it doesn't matter if you chop their heads off or burn them alive, they'll come back somehow. Bullets aren't gonna do squat against something like that. But they *do* slow them down. Especially since most of them like to play dead for the big jump scare. It means if you're smart, you can use it to buy yourself some time, and put some distance between you and them.' She gestured with the pistol, still holding it out, and Ellie realised she'd have to take it. She reached out, a hand extended, shocked by the coldness of the metal in the cool evening air. The pistol was heavier than she expected, and she had to fight the urge to just turn it straight back over to Nina. 'C'mon, let me show you how to use that thing,' Nina gestured for Ellie to follow her, disappearing into the darkness of the grounds. Ellie paused, unsure what to do with the gun in her hands, and followed Nina, holding the weapon awkwardly, not wanting to hold it as if ready to fire. She supposed she shouldn't have been surprised. How had she thought they'd stop the monsters they'd be facing? This was the only obvious solution.

She took a deep breath, and prepared herself. Well, she had always said she'd wanted to learn new skills...

CHAPTER FIVE

THE EVER BURNING FIRE

Ellie was quite pleased with herself as she re-entered the mansion. The shooting practice had gone extremely well, and Ellie had rounded off the practice by taking out a number of bottles that Nina had set up for her to shoot. (Nina had insisted it was more fun than just using the targets). She still didn't like the idea of guns, she hadn't been able to shake the feeling of tension around the cold metal object, but at the same time she was quite proud of her natural talent. She thought about making a comment to Nina that perhaps Nina herself wasn't quite as natural at it because of her lack of depth perception, but thought better of it. She doubted Nina appreciated people calling attention to her missing eye.

As soon as she entered, Ellie found it impossible to ignore Suzi, who was halfway down the grand staircase, waiting for them. It wasn't the perfume, which while ever present in the house was noticeably stronger when she was around, or even the gigantic bright pink dress and pink hair, it was more that Suzi was *radiating* some kind of excitement. Ellie had often heard people use the word 'buzzing' to describe how excited they were, she had even used it herself in plenty of social media posts, but she had never quite seen it personified as well as it was by Suzi. Ellie noticed that she was clutching a pink laptop, and gave Nina a quizzical look.

'She's got a case for us,' Nina explained quickly, immediately understanding the situation.

'A… case? I only joined you five minutes ago!'

'Well, if you wanted more time to hang out here in the Perfume Palace, why didn't you say so?'

'She thinks she's insulting my house, but I think it's a cute nickname!' Suzi piped up. Ellie had forgotten for a moment that she was obviously still listening to them. 'Anyway, people are in danger, so we've got to do something, right?'

'She's got a point,' Nina admitted with a shrug to Ellie. 'Okay, Suzi, show us what you've got.' Suzi let out a beaming grin and a slightly excited squeal, and hurried into the vast living room. Nina gave Ellie a slightly suffering smile and followed suit. Ellie trailed behind.

By the time she entered the living room, which once again surprised her with its size and, well, *pinkness*, despite the fact that she had already seen it, Suzi had already set up her laptop to sync with the gigantic pink television. Somehow the pink-themed presentation displaying itself there (hot pink background, baby pink font, and two tiny cat gifs in the top corners) pushed the entire pinkness of the room to a nauseating level. Nina seemed to be hiding a half smile to herself, as if she knew exactly what Ellie was thinking. This was long before Ellie learned that Suzi had toned these presentations down. She would later tell Ellie how Nina had felt that excessive gifs actually only harmed the seriousness of the work they did and enforced a "no more than twelve kitten gifs per presentation" compromise.

Suzi, however, was oblivious to any apprehension Ellie might be feeling. She pushed a button on her laptop, and the presentation began. Ellie raised an eyebrow.

'Wouldn't it be-' she began to say.

'Shh!' Suzi cut her off, sounding like a teacher during a school assembly. Ellie sheepishly shifted, moving down into the soft pink sofa that was to be her seat. She thought she heard a chuckle from Nina.

'So, have you ever heard of a town called Angel's Ridge?' Suzi asked, as an old black and white photograph of a nineteen fifties mining town appeared on the screen. Not that Ellie would have recognised it as such, except for the fact that the photograph had the words "Angel's Ridge - A 1950s Mining Town" written underneath it. Apart from that, it was a fairly murky photograph of a single street, old concrete buildings and the style of old store fronts that represented family run businesses. The type you only got in small towns. Ellie realised you could tell it was an old photograph by the fact there was no Starbucks there. There was silence, and Ellie realised that Suzi was expecting them to answer her question, and she dutifully shook her head. She noticed that despite Nina's laughter earlier, she did the same, apparently happy to play along with Suzi. 'It was a mining town in Texas. It was only small, with an estimated population of 1,400,' Suzi said this as she read it off the laptop screen and the same text appeared on the television. Ellie thought that Suzi might need to do a little work on her presentation skills. She sounded like a child reading out her book report. It was mildly amusing in all of its absurdity. She clicked on the laptop and another line of text appeared, which she read out. 'It was abandoned in the 1980s due to a coal mine fire.'

'Hang on, why would they abandon an entire town because a mine caught fire?' Ellie asked, giving Nina a confused look.

'If they couldn't put it out?' Nina ventured back. Suzi nodded, and Ellie wondered if she was about to give Nina a sticker for good behaviour from the enthusiastic smile she offered.

'Exactly! I thought it was crazy too at first, but if a coal vein catches fire in a mine like that, it can burn for *hundreds* of years. There's just endless fuel to burn and no way to put it all out.'

'Oh, yeah, I read a book once that said the *Titanic* sank because of a fire in its coal bunker. Because there was so much coal they couldn't put it out in time, and it weakened the hull, so when it struck the iceberg that's the reason it sank so easily.' Ellie said, remembering the novel fondly. Nina smirked and rolled her eye. 'What? I read books sometimes too! It's not all movies. Mind you, it also had an Egyptian Mummy running around on the ship, so, uh, it might not have been entirely historically accurate.' Suzi and Nina exchanged a look.

'Uh, *actually*….' Suzi began to say.

'You've gotta be kidding me.' Ellie just looked at her with disbelief. Suzi just gave an apologetic shrug.

'Well, I mean, there *is* a story…' Suzi began. Nina just sighed to cut her off. Ellie was a little disappointed. That was *definitely* a tale she'd have liked to hear.

'So, what, there's a ghost town with a big fire underneath it? Sounds spooky, but I'm not seeing how it's our thing,' Nina input casually instead, keen to move on. Ellie felt a slight tingle of excitement at the phrase 'our' thing. It felt insane that only yesterday she had been leading her normal life, and now here she was, sat discussing a supernatural case like some kind of experienced monster hunter. There was no hesitation from Nina in including her, she realised. She really was part of the team.

'It's not. I'm just *setting the scene,*' Suzi said with an exasperated sigh, as if her entire presentation had been ruined. It only lasted a second though, before that already-so-familiar smile was back. She clicked on the laptop once more, and a new slide appeared, showing a grainy, old black and white picture of an old wooden manor. It was hard to make out, it was clearly a lo-res image that Suzi had enlarged to fit her presentation template, looking even more blurry on the large television. Despite that, Ellie couldn't help but think that it looked spookily like the house from *Psycho*. 'This was Mrs Campbell's Home for Wayward Children. You see, in the late 1800s, there was an earlier disaster at the mine. A huge explosion that killed one hundred and eleven miners. It was a huge tragedy at the time, and nearly closed the mine for good. After that, there were a lot of kids without fathers, and their mothers couldn't support them. The former school mistress there, Edith Campbell, opened the home and helped raise the kids. She had a really good reputation too. Soon she was taking in kids from neighbouring towns too, and even some homeless adults. Anybody who needed help, she'd offer it to. She was a local hero, until she died in the nineteen twenties.'

'No offence Suzi, but it kind of feels like you're telling two completely different stories here. I'm so confused,' Ellie shook her head, trying to understand how this all connected.

'You're *so* the type of person who skips to the end of the book, aren't you?' Suzi said with a mock scolding tone, still playing the role of disappointed teacher. 'It's *called* dramatic tension. If I've just gotta stand here and tell you all this stuff, I'm gonna at least make it interesting!' She gestured to two additional cat gifs that had just appeared in the top corner of the presentation as if to demonstrate this. Ellie swore that she heard Nina guffaw out loud that time. 'Anyway, after she died, weird things started to happen in the house. Things moved without being touched. There were some strange accidents. Less than a year later, and everybody had moved out. The house went abandoned, but the town refused to demolish it. They said they kept it as a shrine to Edith, but really, I think they were just scared to go near it,' Suzi tried to deliver this in her spookiest voice, but truthfully, this just meant she waved her arms around in a manner that made her multiple bracelets clink together, totally undercutting any tension.

To make matters worse for any intended effect she had aimed at creating, Suzi had to then click on the laptop to move to the next part of the presentation. The next slide read 'One Year Ago' in large letters, and had a newspaper showing with the headline 'Six Teenagers Missing', which Ellie considered something of a spoiler, given the flow of Suzi's presentation..

'So, today, that old house has been abandoned for nearly one hundred years, *and* it's standing in an entire town that was abandoned shortly afterwards. So you'd think it'd be pretty safe, right?' She looked to Nina, who seemed to oblige and answer the rhetorical question with another shake of her head. Ellie had to be honest, she thought it was sweet. Nina couldn't make it any more obvious she didn't care about Suzi's dull exposition or her ridiculous PowerPoint presentation, but it was obvious it mattered to the pink obsessed girl, and therefore Nina went along with it anyway. If that wasn't true friendship, Ellie wasn't sure what was. 'Well, unfortunately, the story got out, and a bunch of teenagers decided it would be a good idea to go and try and stay the night in the creepy abandoned house in the creepy abandoned town.'

'And they were never seen again?' Nina guessed.

'Yeppers!' Suzi nodded enthusiastically, before pausing and realising that she should have probably been a bit more solemn for delivering that particular revelation.

'Anyway, that was last year. I did some browsing on social media sites though, and it looks like, hey, wouldn't you know it, a bunch of teens want to try again this year. Turns out a bunch of them disappearing only made the house seem *spookier* and more exciting to them.' Suzi gave Nina an exasperated look that was obviously put on to try and relate to Nina better, because Nina was wearing the exact same expression. Except you could tell Nina's expression came naturally, and Suzi was trying to match it. God, those two were adorable, Ellie thought to herself.

'So, what are we thinking? Ghost?' Nina asked both Ellie and Suzi, although Ellie was pretty sure she had only been included as a courtesy on that question. It wasn't like she was going to have a clue.

'Yeah, that's what I figure. I mean, Edith died, and now haunts the place. But since the town has been abandoned for so long, she's had nobody to torment. So she's probably even more frustrated and angry than ever.' Ellie gave a quizzical look between the two. She supposed she shouldn't be surprised by them discussing the concept of ghosts as a matter of fact, but it was still a little unnerving. She was just about at home with the concept of demonic zombies after the Mirror Monster, but ghosts? That was a whole new level of creepy.

'I thought you said this Edith was a lovely old lady who cared about everyone. Why would she haunt anybody?' Ellie asked, trying to look for logic in the already bizarre situation.

'Ghosts, man. Don't try to understand them. You never know what could have set them off,' Nina replied.

'The papers don't say how she died. Maybe one of the drifters she took in killed her?' Suzi suggested. 'Either way, something must have happened to make her spirit *super* angry.'

'But this is great!' The change in Nina was enough to cause Ellie to physically jolt in surprise. Before she could react, Nina was on her feet. 'A ghost! This is the perfect first job for you!' She had an uncharacteristic look on her face that was *almost*, but not quite, a smile. Ellie, meanwhile, remained seated, her eyes wide and scepticism etched into every part of her face.

'Uh, remind me how a killer ghost is a *good* thing?' Ellie asked. Even Suzi looked a little confused.

'Ghosts are *easy*.' Nina rolled her one eye as if it was obvious. 'Look, your average spirit, if it's bound to a place, and not a person or object, like this one is, is easy to get rid of. You just burn the building to the ground. The fact that it's in an abandoned town with an underground fire? That just means nobody will question it. It literally couldn't be any easier if we'd set it up.' Nina was completely without the slightest hint of concern that they were discussing a literal vengeful spirit.

'Won't the ghost try to stop us?' Ellie worried.

'Nah!' Nina practically laughed. 'Ghosts are drama queens. Very dangerous if you spend enough time around them, but they like to *build up* to an attack. Lots of jump scares, scary reflections, small objects moving, all that crap. Gets pretty intense if you're staying in the building, but if you just pop in, pour gasoline everywhere, and set the building ablaze, it's a piece of cake.' Ellie looked to Suzi for confirmation, who looked considerably more nervous than Nina, but seemed unable to come up with any reasoned argument.

'She's right. I-I-I mean, at first, I thought maybe it was a bit too dangerous. Six kids went missing, presumed dead, just last year. But, well, when you put it the way Nina did... It should be pretty easy…' Ellie gave the two a look like they were both insane, but sighed. They were the experts. She was just along for the ride. Besides, she supposed what they were saying *did* make some kind of sense. If she accepted that the ghost was real and that it had been haunting the building then the logic of simply burning the building down was pretty sound. 'I'll book us a flight on the plane. We can be there tomorrow morning.'

'The plane?' Ellie asked, noting the formality of the word 'the'. English definitely wasn't Suzi's first language, but she spoke it so perfectly and fluently she doubted it was a mistake.

'Suzi has a private plane and her own pilot. Comes in handy for when we have to get across country quickly.'

'It's not pink, is it?' Ellie asked, giving Suzi a quizzical look. Nina couldn't hide a snigger as Suzi pouted.

'No. Not even I could buy a pink plane. So unfair,' she sulked.

'Alright, rest up, you two.' Nina instructed. 'Tomorrow, we fly out, visit a town that's been on fire for decades, burn down a haunted house, and we should be home in time for tea.'

'I don't drink tea.' Ellie felt she should clear that up.

'It means dinner. Look, I'm British, and-' Nina paused, and sighed, shaking her head. 'Forget it, my point is, it's going to be easy.'

Even Nina, for all her experience, had not learned that stating something was 'going to be easy' was a dire mistake, but even if she had, not one of the girls had an inkling for just what challenges awaited them...

CHAPTER SIX

MONSTERS ON A PLANE

In retrospect, Ellie should have known something was up when Nina had insisted on taking her own car, turning down Suzi's generous offer of driving them all to the nearby airfield. After all, why take two cars for what Ellie had been assured was a short trip? And why turn down what was inevitably going to be far more luxurious than anything Nina could afford?

The answer, it turned out, was rather simple. Ellie wasn't somebody who knew an awful lot about cars, but her expectation that somebody like Suzi would have a luxurious limousine and perhaps a personal chauffeur was utterly destroyed when instead she saw what she could only describe as a hideously pink bubble shaped *thing* into which Ellie was surprised Suzi's ridiculously large dress could fit, let alone Ellie too. This was how Ellie ended up squashed into a tiny pink fur coated seat, with Suzi's huge dress threatening to crush against her, as Suzi drove with a happy smile on her face in the tiny car, its engine whining with such strain Ellie was a little afraid it was about to explode. In comparison, Nina's car, a huge black thing that looked like it was about to fall apart from rust, roared along behind them, like an eager hungry monster desperate to overtake them at any given time. Ellie couldn't afford a car of her own, and that was a fact she definitely regretted now. She'd passed Driver's Ed with flying colours, but sadly, she'd never gotten to use those skills.

Instead, she was trapped in the tiny vehicle with only Suzi and her Suzi-levels of perfume nearly choked Ellie, even with the window down, but it was mercifully a short trip. While Suzi explained that she did technically *own* the plane, in that she had bought it, her friend was the pilot and kept it on her farm nearby, which allowed Suzi and Nina their own private flights with easy access. Ellie tried to resist the headache of working out how Suzi had a friend who owned a farm; nothing about Suzi suggested she had even *seen* a farm in her life, but she decided not to question it as the car made its way down a winding country road.

It wasn't long before they made their way under an old wooden sign, seemingly with a Wild West theme, pointing out that the grounds before them was known as "Outlaw Ranch". Suzi gave Ellie a big smile as they arrived, driving down a winding path flanked by fields on both sides, each filled with horses. Suzi let out a squeal and pointed excitedly at a small white baby horse trotting along beside what Ellie assumed was its mother. Ellie focused instead on the large wooden country house not much further away.

'I'm pretty sure a ranch and a farm isn't the same thing...' Ellie pointed out after a slightly sceptical pause.

'What's the difference? They both have animals!' Suzi countered as she pulled the car up just outside the old country house. Ellie made sure to get out of the car quickly, glad of fresh, non-perfumed air while Suzi seemed to go through an almost ritualistic checking of her make-up. She looked over at Nina who seemed to have a slight smirk on her face at having left Ellie to travel with Suzi.

'A ranch isn't a farm, right?' Ellie said desperately, looking for some confirmation from Nina. Nina just shrugged.

'Honestly, there's a big strip of land to take off and land a plane and a pilot, I don't care what people call it.' Ellie looked over to Suzi, who was done with her make-up, but to Ellie's utter disbelief seemed to have decided to spray even more perfume on herself, still in the car. Even Nina seemed to sigh, before turning and heading up the small wooden porch to the door to the house.

It swung open before she could even knock and the woman standing within somehow both surprised Ellie and yet made perfect sense to her. She was tall, with long blonde hair and bright blue eyes, her bare arms tanned and showing wiry muscle, but it was her attire that made the most sense. She was wearing a leather vest and jeans, with cowgirl boots, complete with spurs, and a dark brown Stetson balanced upon her head. A smile crossed dark pink painted lips as she reached forward and embraced Nina in a big hug, something that left Nina looking considerably uncomfortable.

'Nina! Good to see you girl. Ain't seen you since the New Year's Party,' she smiled, speaking with a heavy Texan accent, Ellie noticed. Somehow, anything else coming out of her mouth would have seemed wrong.

'You can *remember* that?' Nina remarked, sounding genuinely surprised. 'You were pretty drunk.'

'Hey, I'm *Texan*, remember? I can hold my liquor,' she grinned back teasingly, before turning to make eye contact with Ellie with those bright blue eyes of hers. 'Guessing you must be Ellie.' she nodded, walking forward and thrusting out a hand for a strong handshake. 'Name's Jessamine. And no, that don't mean you can call me 'Jessie like in *Toy Story*'. I get enough Disney crap from her.' She pointed to Suzi, who was still in the car, but from here Ellie couldn't tell what she was doing. She prayed it wasn't *still* applying perfume. 'If you gotta, you can call me Jess.'

'Uh, hi. Nice to meet you,' Ellie said a little uneasily. 'I'm, well, uh, you already know.'

'Yeah, Suzi rang ahead. Told me I need to take you somewhere in my plane again.'

'*Your* plane? Suzi said it was *her* plane.'

'Oh, did she now?' the girl who liked to be called Jess shot back, smirking the entire time. 'Plane's mine.'

'Yeah, but you belong to me!' came a chirpy voice from behind, and Suzi, having finally exited the car, passed both Ellie and Nina, and moved straight into Jess's arms. Ellie watched with shocked, wide eyes as the two exchanged a kiss, and Suzi seemed to giggle, settling to turn to face the others, the taller Jess's arms around her shoulders, Suzi snuggled against her.

'Can't argue you with that,' Jess sighed in a voice that could only be described as 'loving'. Ellie realised she was staring, and quickly looked away. Any hope that she had done so without being caught passed her by quickly, however, when Nina burst out in laughter.

'You can't be *that* surprised. What about Suzi tells you she's even aware the male gender exists, let alone that she'd have any romantic interest in them?' Nina pointed out.

'Hey! I know boys exist! I just also know they're smelly and stupid.' Suzi stuck her tongue out and let out another giggle to make sure Ellie knew that she was mostly teasing.

'I'm not *that* surprised at that, but, you know, rough and tumble cowgirl on a farm and, uh, well, Suzi…' Ellie still wasn't quite sure how to describe Suzi. 'I didn't see it coming.'

'…Cowgirl?' Jess repeated after a momentary pause.

'Sorry, I mean-' Ellie tried to explain, before Jess just let out a quick laugh.

'Relax, I'm kidding. I totally see it. Rustled a few cows in my time,' she nodded. 'These days its horses though. I run this little ranch. The flying thing, that's just a hobby.'

'I bought her a plane for her birthday one year,' Suzi explained. 'So it *is* kinda mine.'

'I don't think you understand how presents work, dear,' Jess said back teasingly.

'Wow. Remind me to date somebody as rich as Suzi. My last boyfriend, I was lucky if he *remembered* my birthday,' Ellie remarked, before pausing and falling silent.

Her last boyfriend. She didn't miss him. It had been a dumb two week fling. But after that, she had grown close to Danny. She had really thought something special might happen between them. Until that fateful night at the camp. Until she lost everybody. The big personalities of Suzi, Nina and now Jess had threatened to overpower her memories of grief for a moment, but they all came flooding back in that moment. It seemed that Jess cottoned on, because she released Suzi from the embrace and moved over to touch Ellie's shoulder gently.

'Thinking about someone you lost?' she asked gently. Ellie forced a slight smile.

'Sorry, it's dumb. It's just…'

'…sometimes it catches you off guard, right? You can be talking about anything you like, just living your life, walking through the world, then it hits you like a ton of bricks. Someone close to you ain't never coming back,' Jess nodded solemnly. 'Lost my sister when I first met these two. Never did want to sign up to the life they lead myself, I was happy just staying here on the ranch, flying them when they needed it, guess it helped give me a purpose. But still, even now, sometimes I just see… A little something that reminds me of her. And I feel like my whole world freezes and comes crashing down. It ain't pleasant, but it *is* normal. And I can promise you this, there ain't nobody else in the world who understands loss better than the three of us,' she gestured to herself, Nina and Suzi. Ellie felt a lump in her throat, and swallowed hard. She knew Jess was right. That feeling of the world crashing down around her. She'd felt it, dozens of times since the camp. She had felt it again now. The sudden realisation of what she had lost. And then came the crushing guilt, the horrible knot in her stomach asking how she could have ever *forgotten* it. Guilt that the memory had ever been far from her mind. That she'd been able to smile and laugh when the people she had been so close to were gone forever.

There was an intense moment of silence between the four of them. Ellie knew each of them were experiencing the exact same thoughts that she was. She knew that Nina and Suzi had experienced real loss as well, and now Jess too. Sometimes she wondered why anybody could find the faith to carry on, when they knew so many people who had lost so much. Life felt so fleeting, so *temporary*, like at any moment the only connections you had ever made could be swept away. Maybe that was precisely why she *did* have to carry on. She had to keep forging ahead, because the past was gone forever.

It seemed Jess agreed with Ellie's distant thoughts, because her head snapped up and she carried on as if nothing had happened.

'Well, I got our ride fuelled and ready as soon as Suzi rang, so no time like the present. Just let me grab some supplies,' Jess's tone was jovial, as if no moment of sadness had passed at all. Ellie knew that was the voice of experience. Somebody who knew how to share these moments and move on. She watched in slight horror, however, as Jess reached inside and pulled from a coat stand a hanging belt, complete with a holster and six shooter and what appeared to be a lasso hanging from it. She clipped it around her waist. Ellie was conscious of the gun stuffed into the back of her jeans, the gift from Nina from the night before, but she hadn't expected to need it.

'I thought we were hunting ghosts. What are you going to do, *shoot* them?' Ellie asked sceptically, aware that she might have sounded a little rude, but being too shocked to care.

'Hey, *you're* hunting ghosts. *I'm* staying with the plane. But let's just say, after what I've seen hanging out with these two, I ain't never going anywhere unarmed again,' she explained, although her tone was casual, as if she thought nothing of carrying the weapon. Ellie still couldn't shake the feeling of the cold metal against her back, but to Jess, it was second nature. Ellie was sure there was a Texan stereotype in there, but she didn't want to comment.

'It's like I told you yesterday, it might not stop a thing, but it can sure slow it down,' Nina reminded Ellie, gesturing for her to follow as Jess took the lead, leading them around the farmhouse.

They proceeded down a path made of wooden slats laid down, a crude walkway across the field. Ellie doubted the slats were for Jess's benefit. She gave the impression of a girl who was at home knee deep in mud. She suspected that with Suzi as a girlfriend and her rather *impractical* clothing choices, Jess tried to make access around her ranch as easy as possible. They passed by a barn, in which Ellie could see a few horses, as well as notice the tell-tale smell of manure, causing her to wrinkle her nose a little. Ellie might have thought that Suzi didn't seem at home on a farm, but truthfully, neither did Ellie. She was a city kid through and through. Even being camp counsellor at St Mary's Marsh had been a novelty for Ellie and her friends, who were more at home hanging out in parking lots than the woods.

Ellie wasn't quite sure what she had been expecting, but she found herself surprised as they passed behind the barn, finding a small airstrip of flattened grass and another empty barn, with a plane sat just in front of it. She assumed that the barn was a crude form of hanger, but her eyes were drawn instead to the plane. It was smaller than she had anticipated, which made her stomach knot, with a long cone nose and two prop engines situated on either wing. The old fashioned looking engines only caused her more apprehension.

'It's got propellers. Why has it got propellers? I thought all planes were jets these days!' Ellie definitely had a trace of panic in her voice.

'Nervous flier?' Nina couldn't hide a slight smirk.

'I dunno! I've never flown before!' Ellie replied, aware that she had turned a shockingly pale shade. She could hear a chuckle coming from Jess.

'Relax, would ya? It's a Cessna 340,' Jess told Ellie calmly, before making her way towards the plane. To Ellie's shock and disgust, so did Suzi and Nina.

'What? What's that supposed to mean!? That doesn't put my mind at rest! What the heck is a Cessna.... three... whatever?'

'Damn reliable plane, that's all you need to know. Used to be used by lots of businesses for private flights,' Jess seemed to pause. 'In the eighties.' She added a little quieter.

'Eighties!? How old is this thing!?'

'Hey, relax. She might not look like much, but she's got it where it counts,' Jess assured Ellie.

'Did you just quote *Star Wars* at me!? That doesn't help!'

'Did you know you've got more chance of being killed getting crushed by a vending machine than dying in a plane crash?' Nina piped in as she began to make her way up the steps and into the plane, ducking down to get through the door.

'Is that true?' Ellie asked as she began to follow, trying to ignore the constant looping butterflies in her stomach.

'No idea, but it sounds good,' Nina shrugged. Ellie was definitely uncomfortable with the size of the plane, realising she could barely even stand up inside.

'Uh, guys, help?' Ellie was almost comfortable in her seat when Suzi's voice distracted her. It seemed Suzi's incredibly large, frilly pink dress was causing her some issues in fitting through the doorway to the plane, and Jess had to pop back out of the cockpit to pull her through.

Taking a seat and immediately putting on her seat belt, Ellie was aware that her hands were sweaty and pale as they gripped at the small table in front of her. Suzi, who had impressively somehow managed to navigate herself in to a seat despite her dress, sat opposite her.

'Relax! It's gonna be fine! Jess is the best pilot around, and this little plane has taken us all over the country!' Suzi smiled cheerfully, before resuming fussing over a potential crease in her dress from the door incident.

'Aw, you're too sweet!' Jess called back from the cockpit. 'Alright, just remember, if you're gonna spew, try and get it in a bag. I don't wanna have to clear up vomit from all over my plane.' Ellie knew the comment was definitely directed at her.

'Ewww, don't be sick! Please!' Suzi begged with a wrinkled nose.

'I'll... I'll try,' Ellie said weakly. And then, with a sudden rumble, the plane's engines sprang into life, and the propellers began to spin.

When Suzi came to tell this story later on, she would always insist Ellie shrieked at this point. Ellie, however, couldn't remember anything but blind terror.

By the time she had stopped clutching the arms of the seat with sweat drenched hands she was aware that the little aircraft was already impossibly high, and it wasn't until she looked out of the window at the landscape below that she began to feel a little calmer. Everything below was so tiny and so far away she found it difficult to comprehend that it was real. She could see the roads below with tiny cars, looking smaller than ants, and found it almost impossible to comprehend that they were in fact filled with people, each with lives as real and legitimate as her own.

Probably considerably more normal, however.

She turned back to Suzi and Nina, neither of whom seemed focused on the window. Ellie figured they must have flown a lot. Given that Suzi was Japanese and Nina was British, she had to assume they had flown over to America at some point. Suzi had said this flight should only take an hour, something Ellie was deeply glad of, despite her settling nerves. How they had withstood a flight practically half way around the world Ellie would never understand.

The first thirty minutes or so of the flight passed largely without incident. Ellie found herself adapting to the comfort of the plane, once she had convinced herself never to look at the wing out of the window again, and soon she joined in the conversation with Suzi and Nina. Suzi talked about her favourite Disney movies to watch on long flights, and how it helped to pass the time, while Nina told a story about getting excessively drunk once on a flight over from England and nearly getting arrested on landing. Ellie didn't particularly feel she could relate closely to either story, although she was hoping Nina was exaggerating. Naturally though, conversation passed to the aim of the trip, and Ellie had to admit she was slightly relieved when the topic came back around to ghosts and the mysterious forces of darkness. Pretending everything was normal was fine in theory, but in practice Ellie felt their task was hanging over them like an anvil, and she didn't want to ignore it for long.

'We've got a hire car meeting us at the airstrip, but we won't be able to drive it far into Angel's Ridge ourselves. Roads aren't safe. So once we're there, we'll be walking in,' Nina explained.

'Aw, I hate walking,' Suzi pouted. Ellie opened her mouth to say something about how Suzi might find it better in practical shoes, but closed it again, deciding it might come out as a bit mean.

'As long as we watch our step it should be fine, kids head in to the town all the time. Then, we just find the house and burn it down,' Nina said with a simple shrug.

'How are we gonna do that?' Ellie asked, mildly alarmed by how casual Nina was about the concept of arson, even if it was to an abandoned properly.

'We'll just bring a can of petrol with us, pour it around and light a match.'

'You mean gas?' Ellie asked, not quite used to the British phrasing.

'It's a liquid, it's called petrol. Why would you call a liquid 'gas'? You Yanks are weird,' Nina sighed, but a gleam in her one eye made it clear she was kidding. 'Yes, I meant a can of gas, okay?'

'Uh, is it just me, or is carrying a big tank of flammable liquid through a town that has a huge coal fire under it kinda *incredibly* dangerous?' Ellie asked.

'It'll be fine, silly!' Suzi perked up. 'The fire is underground, and besides, it's in a metal tin. It'll be perfectly safe!'

'Plus I doubt even a can of gasoline is any more flammable than all the cosmetics Suzi douses herself in, she's the one we should be afraid of,' Nina added dryly, prompting Suzi to stick her tongue out at Nina playfully. Ellie looked at the two feeling a slight twinge of irritation. She really did wish they would take these things more seriously.

'Anyway, we'll see how we get on, but once we get there, I wouldn't mind taking a peek inside before we burn it down. You know, get a chance to see this spirit face to face,' Nina said with a slightly over-eager smirk. To Ellie's surprise, Suzi nodded along, apparently equally interested.

'But what about-'

It was as far as Ellie got with her concern before the entire plane began to shake, and all thoughts of her question disappeared from her mind.

'What the hell was that!?' Ellie asked, her eyes wide.

'Oh, it's just turbulence. Don't worry.' Suzi waved a dismissive hand, trying to be comforting. Unfortunately, her point was undermined by the sudden crack of thunder, loud enough to leave Ellie's eardrums ringing.

'That's not turbulence…' Nina said with a suspicious tone, climbing out of her seat. The entire plane was shaking, and Ellie could see outside heavy rain hammering down on the windows. There was another crack of lightning and a roar of thunder, and for a moment, she thought she spotted something on the wing.

Nina, arms outstretched along the roof of the fuselage for balance, made her way to the cockpit door and threw it open.

'Did you just fly us into a storm!?' She asked Jess, surprise and concern in her voice.

'I didn't fly us in to anything!' Jess replied with her distinct Texan twang, somehow even more pronounced now with her irritation. 'It came out of nowhere!'

'How does a storm just come out of nowhere!?' Nina found herself having to shout over the roar of the rain hitting the outside of the plane.

'It doesn't. Not like this! I've been flying a long time, and I ain't never seen nothing like this!' Jess replied. Ellie wondered if the stress caused the poor grammar, or if she regularly talked like that. She didn't know her well enough yet. Suzi tried to get to her feet too, but the rumbling and shaking plane meant that, thanks to her impractical heels, she found herself falling right back in her seat in a heap of frills and bows.

'You think it's some kind of… I dunno, ghost thing?' Suzi asked from her position, trying to straighten herself out from being swallowed up by her giant dress where she had fallen.

'Never heard of a ghost who can summon a storm,' Nina yelled back to the pair, over the roar of another crack of thunder. 'And it's not exactly in the M.O. of the spirit we're investigating, even if it did somehow know we were coming.'

'Are you saying this is something else?' Suzi asked, and Ellie had to admit, she was a little impressed by the girl's calm. Everything about Suzi suggested she'd be hysterical in danger, but instead, the two were discussing the situation back and forth like seasoned pros, while Ellie was the one who sat frozen in fear.

'Must be. No idea what though,' Nina replied.

'Is something trying to kill you *again*?' Jess asked, exasperated. From where Ellie was sat, she could only make out the back of the girl's head, now sans cowgirl hat and wearing a big set of headphones instead. Even from there, Ellie could tell she was struggling to keep the plane on course.

'Apparently,' Nina sighed, taking a seat next to Jess. Ellie had no idea if Nina knew how to fly but she figured either way, having two people in the cockpit was better than one.

There was another bright flash of lightning and a worryingly close rumble of thunder. Ellie had never seen a thunder crash so close to the lightning flash before, but she didn't have time to be concerned about *that* as the flash of lightning lit up the wing perfectly, and without a shadow of a doubt, she saw something there. A small creature, with large, leathery ears and dark brown, slimy skin. It had long claw like fingernails digging into the wing to hold on, and seemed to look directly at Ellie as she saw it with deep red eyes, before hissing and climbing under the wing.

'There's something on the wing! I saw something on the wing!' Ellie suddenly found herself shouting. Suzi looked over at her with concern, and Nina glanced back from the cockpit. The look they gave Ellie surprised her; it wasn't scepticism, or amusement. Just instant belief.

These two had seen enough strange things to know not to question them.

'Did you hear that?' Nina said to Jess.

'Yeah, I heard it, and it's not that I wanna get *Twilight Zone'd* to death, but what the hell are we supposed to do about it?' she asked back, clearly still focused on keeping the plane level. More lightning crashed, and Ellie looked up as she heard the sound of scampering across the roof.

'I see it!' Suzi yelled, pointing to the far window, where the creature quickly scurried past as rain and wind continued to batter the aeroplane.

'Shouldn't we shoot it or something!?' Ellie asked, mildly surprised that her first thought was such after her discomfort around guns.

'You never seen *Goldfinger*?' Jess called back. 'Firing a gun in a plane is a bad idea!'

'It's on the engine!' Suzi shrieked, pointing out of the window in a mixture of horror and excitement.

'Dammit, if it tears that engine apart we're screwed!' Nina said, genuine panic beginning to edge in her voice.

'I know, I know…' Jess replied. 'Okay, hold on to something, I've got an idea.'

Ellie suddenly felt her stomach drop from her body as the entire plane began to climb higher, Jess pulling back on the yolk. For a horrifying moment it felt like they were flying up into the storm clouds, into further danger, and all through it the creature was still clinging to the engine. Ellie looked at it as it seemed to hang backwards with the climb, but its long claws still held fast on the metal. And then, suddenly, without warning, the entire plane lurched forward and began to dive.

The tiny creature was thrown forward and it slammed straight into the plane's propeller. It exploded in a cloud of dark green goo, torn apart by the engine propeller. Unfortunately, however, the impact didn't do the plane any favours. The entire plane lurched and rumbled and seemed to list to the side, still in its dive. Jess pulled back on the yolk, Nina helping her from the co-pilot's position, but the plane seemed to begin to scream as it crashed downwards. For a moment, Ellie thought this was how she was going to die. She had been trying to be a hero, trying to investigate a supernatural mystery, and now she was going to die in a plane crash.

Fortunately, before the imminent death could come, the plane began to level off, even if the engine out on the wing seemed to be spluttering unhealthily. It was still spinning however, and Ellie could see the claw marks on the wing clearly. It appeared that they had only left superficial damage.

It took a few moments for her to realise that she could see the claw marks easily because the storm had gone. The sky was clear and blue once more, and the only evidence there had ever been a storm was the gleaming water from the raindrops on the plane's wing, rapidly being blown away. Ellie climbed out of her seat, just wanting to be able to stand in the calmed plane, and moved towards the cockpit. Suzi followed not far behind.

'The storm's gone,' Suzi felt the need to articulate what they all already knew.

'What the hell was that!?' Ellie, however, was considerably less polite in expressing her opinion.

'Gone, whatever it was,' Nina said, breathing hard, looking over at Jess, and managing a laugh of relief. 'Nice flying.' Jess let out a slight laugh at the compliment, but Ellie noticed that her arms were shaking. Ellie didn't know much about flying planes, but she was pretty sure pulling stunts like Jess had just pulled were most certainly *not* part of a pilot's daily activities, and she recognised what adrenaline wearing off in a person after something intense looked like all too easily.

She wasn't the only one who noticed, of course, and Suzi placed a comforting hand on Jess's shoulder. Jess seized said hand with her own for a moment, before turning back to the plane's controls.

'Okay, you lot, go sit down, relax. We'll be landing shortly,' she said with a sigh, obviously trying to get her head back in the game. 'It's a pretty small private airstrip we're landing at, I better radio ahead and let them know we're coming in damaged. I'll tell 'em a bird flew in to our engine and hope nobody takes too close of a look.'

'You gonna be able to fix it?' Nina asked as she climbed from the co-pilot's seat.

'Fix it? I ain't some 1940's flying ace. I can't just patch an aeroplane back together, and I doubt a small airport like that one's gonna have any mechanics that can help to hand. Got a few contacts though, I'll get a hold of someone.'

'What, is it just like calling a car mechanic out, but for a plane?' Ellie asked, feeling naive.

'Not exactly.' Jess laughed a little. 'But, well, when your girlfriend is as rich as mine, you'd be surprised what paying people enough can do.' She turned and gave Suzi a smile. 'Now, get out of my cockpit while I make the call. And get ready for landing.' She turned to give Ellie one final mischievous look. 'Try not to scream this time.'

CHAPTER SEVEN

ANGEL'S RIDGE

Ellie's legs still felt like Jell-O, even though it was close to two hours since they had landed. She definitely didn't want to get in a plane again anytime soon, and was dreading the flight back. She had no idea how so many people were regular fliers, but she assumed that the majority of people didn't have to deal with surprise gremlins trying to tear the plane apart on their first flight. The hire car, a sleek silver Dodge Charger (according to the rental company who had dropped it off at the airport) purred along the dusty road, Nina driving with her one good eye firmly fixed on the path ahead. Behind them, Suzi was sat in the back seat, her big dress spread out all around her, making her look something like a tiny cake topping in the middle of a huge circle of frosting. She still seemed to be sulking that the hire car wasn't pink, despite the rental company representative explaining to her in detail that they didn't have any pink cars to rent out.

Ellie spotted an old, rusted sign with letters barely legible still upon it. "Angel's Ridge". They were getting closer. Sadly, the distance had long since eroded from the sign. She became aware that they had been riding in silence for quite some time. Everything seemed to happen fast upon landing. Ellie had only ever seen an airport on television, but this wasn't like she had expected. It was pretty close to the one they had left back at Jess's ranch, except this one had a few more private jets around, more tarmac, and a tiny check-in building. It seemed flights didn't come in every day, perhaps not every week, and only one member of staff was there to greet them who must have come in specially knowing that a plane was landing. After that, it was just a case of picking the car up and setting off. Suzi said some elaborate goodbyes to Jess, who was staying behind to see if she could get the plane repaired (rather gratefully, it seemed, not that she had been intending to come anyway).

Through all of it, they hadn't discussed what had happened in the air. Ellie wasn't sure if this was natural for them. After all, Suzi and Nina must have seen a lot of supernatural activity, but that didn't mean Ellie didn't have some burning questions.

'So, um, do you guys have any ideas about what happened on the plane?' she spoke up, deciding to probe for answers. Nina looked over at Ellie for a moment, before returning her eye to the road.

'No,' she said dryly, as if still deep in thought, and Ellie realised perhaps *that* had been the reason Nina had been so quiet.

'I mean, that stuff happens all the time to you two though, right? Monsters and magic and stuff?' Ellie hoped that it didn't sound *too* much like she was desperately seeking some comforting words or confirmation that what they had faced had been entirely normal.

'Oh no! I've never seen anything like that before and I've been doing this for years!' Suzi exclaimed with her usual sincerity.

'She's right. There's a pattern to how stuff happens. Things don't just strike out of nowhere and disappear again. They stalk. They hunt. They pick you off one by one. And there's always a *theme*. You don't go on a ghost hunt and get attacked by a gremlin. It just doesn't happen.'

'Uh, it looks like it kinda does,' Ellie countered. Nina shot her a bit of an annoyed look.

'It's not *supposed* to happen.'

'I'm pretty sure none of this is *supposed* to happen!' Ellie argued, before realising she had said that in a slightly heated manner. She took a breath, and decided to try another approach. 'Jess said someone might be trying to kill you? I mean, could somebody do that? Like, cast a magic spell or something?' Ellie asked. Suzi let out a snort of amusement, and even Nina rolled her eye.

'"Cast a magic spell"?' she repeated mockingly. 'This isn't…. *Harry Potter*!'

'I was more thinking of *Buffy*, actually,' Ellie said dejectedly.

'Oh! Or *Supernatural*!' Suzi seemed excited for a moment, before realising this might not be the time for pop culture reference, settling back down in her seat.

'Look, I'm not going to tell you that, I dunno, some kind of 'magic' doesn't exist.' Nina made little air quotes with one of her hands as she spoke, the other remaining on the wheel. 'We both know it does. We've both seen things. But it's not like, I dunno, you can just pick up a book and chant some Latin and magic happens. Sure, you might find the odd ritual to summon a demon or some dumb teenager reading a cursed passage they shouldn't, but you can't *control* it. Magic like that… It's evil. It's ancient. It's curses and dark wills and monsters and spirits that refuse to die. It just *exists*.'

'Okay! Okay! I get it,' Ellie sighed, despite the feeling that she very much did *not* get it. 'But if that's true, then, well, what the hell happened up there?' she asked. She was aware that Nina's one eye flickered up to the rear view mirror, to make contact with Suzi's.

'I've got no idea,' Nina confirmed. 'And if I'm being honest, that scares me to death.' Nina being scared was the most frightening thing she'd seen all day. And that included the gremlin.

The rest of the drive was spent in silence. Somehow Suzi was taking a nap, whereas Ellie was still pretty sure her adrenaline was still running from the flight. She felt like she wouldn't be able to sleep for another month. She found herself staring out of the window at the passing trees, completely unaware of time passing or where they were. Whenever she closed her eyes, all she saw were the beady glowing eyes of the creature from the plane staring back at her, and that sinking feeling that despite it being shredded, they hadn't seen the last of it. It was like Nina had said. They always came back.

She was jolted back to reality when the car stopped. She looked up to see they were still on the same road travelling through dense forest, but in front of them now was a sign stating, through heavy rust, 'Welcome to Angel's Ridge'. At least, it had once upon a time. It seemed that since then, the sign had been vandalised almost beyond recognition, graffiti paint all over even the **CONDEMNED** tape that spread across the metal like a spider's web. Aside from the numerous crude drawings of male appendages and several scrawled names (some even with 'waz 'ere' written after them, dating the vandalism far more effectively than the year written afterwards), the highlight was where some aspiring graffiti artist had thought it would be hilarious to replace the 'G' and 'E' of 'Angel' with a big 'A' and cross out the S, as well as the 'G' of 'Ridge'.

'We are clearly dealing with the mind of a criminal genius,' Ellie said dryly as she got out of the car, not even having to wait for Nina's signal. She knew this was as far as they could safely drive. Up ahead, the road was clearly cracked and damaged, although Ellie assumed that was from neglect, and not from the fires beneath the town, which she doubted extended this far to the edge.

'Wake up, princess,' Nina instructed Suzi, who awoke with a dainty yawn and began the complicated procedure of trying to extract herself in her incredibly large dress from the back of the car. As she did so, Nina made her way around to the trunk and extracted a large rucksack, which Ellie knew contained the cannister of gasoline within which they were intending to use to burn the house down. They had filled it up at a gas station on the way.

Nina and Ellie both looked up at the sign.

'Well, that tells us our missing teens weren't the first ones here, at least,' Nina observed. 'It means we're not dealing with one of those yearly death curse things. You know, bunch of kids go away to a summer camp one year and get horribly murdered, but then the *next* year a whole bunch of fresh kids go there anyway, and hey, surprise surprise, get murdered.'

'Hey! My thing was at a summer camp!' Ellie said, feeling offended as she realised that she fell right into the group of idiotic teenagers Nina was mocking.

'Yeah, and I decided to babysit on Halloween night at a house next to a mental asylum,' Nina countered with a shrug. 'We wouldn't be here if we made sensible decisions.'

'True dat,' Suzi nodded as she made her way behind them. Aware that both of them looked at her in confusion, she gave a slightly offended look. 'What? I can use hip slang too, y'know?'

'I'm pretty sure "true dat" has never been hip,' Nina corrected. 'Right, let's get going. Watch your step. Especially you, Suzi, since you still seem to think those shoes are practical.' She gestured at Suzi's ridiculous heels, not that Ellie could see them under the dress.

'You won't be laughing when I use them to stamp on a monster and escape!' Suzi insisted proudly as she began to walk along the damaged asphalt. Ellie looked over to Nina.

'Has that ever actually worked?' she asked. Nina just mouthed 'no' in response.

The trio made their way along the road, which got increasingly cracked and broken as it became more and more apparent that the town was utterly abandoned. It was only a short walk before it opened out into what had clearly once been a town square but was now nothing but utterly desolate buildings. Graffiti coated nearly everything and there wasn't an intact window in sight. The odd shop sign was still hanging, but had mostly fallen down, and near the centre of the town was a large clock tower, although the clock face had fallen out, revealing the hollow workings inside. Empty packets of chips, old disposable barbecues and rusting beer cans seemed to be everywhere, suggesting that it was a favourite haunt of teenagers to come somewhere undisturbed for the summer, despite the dangers. It was a warm day, but Ellie wondered if she was just imagining the heat rising through the tarmac.

'This is horrible.' Suzi observed, taking it all in.

'Well, I mean, it's been, what, forty years?' Nina shrugged. 'I mean, kids are kids, right? If you hear there's an abandoned town nearby, wouldn't you want to check it out?'

'Well, yeah, I guess, but I meant, how did these people ever live here? There's not even a clothes shop!' Both Nina and Ellie groaned out loud, barely able to believe Suzi had just said that. 'What?' she questioned, blinking innocently. Ellie shook her head. Nina seemed to decide it was best to ignore her.

'This is obviously the main town street. The mines are further away, and so is the old house. That means the ground should be fairly stable here, but still, watch your step,' Nina advised, reaching into her trench coat pocket and removing a large folded piece of paper. She unfurled it, until Ellie could barely see her face anymore, realising what it was.

'You brought a map?' Ellie asked, surprised.

'Preparation. It's not like we get a mobile phone signal here.'

'You mean cell phone?' Ellie shot back.

'It's a phone that you carry with you. It's *mobile*. Why would I call it a 'cell phone'? Nina paused as she examined the map. 'Here it is. The house is up this way,' Nina gestured to a side street leading away from the abandoned buildings of the centre of the town. Ellie's eyes lingered for a moment on what appeared to be an old library, wondering if any books remained inside. She doubted it. They might have evacuated quickly, but she doubted the people of this town left much behind, and anything they did would have been looted years ago by the looks of the place.

They continued down the street which grew evermore desolate. It was a more suburban district, Ellie thought, reminding her a little of her house back home, but here most of the homes were barely visible now behind tall grass and plants that had gone wild. The ground became increasingly more cracked and several times Ellie felt the fractured tarmac shift beneath her feet. There were a few wide holes in the old road, gaps that Ellie at first foolishly assumed were potholes, but she was sure she could see a heat haze rising from them. Clearly they were placed where the ground had given away to the mines below.

'Are you sure this is safe?' she asked cautiously.

'We're getting closer to the mine, which means the fire is underneath us,' Nina explained. 'So no, it's probably not safe. The house isn't far from the mine entrance.'

'Because *of course* it couldn't *not* be near the creepy death mine.' That would have been too easy, wouldn't it?

'Like I said, mate, there are rules,' Nina replied casually.

A yelp from Suzi stopped the pair, who had been a good few meters ahead. It seemed Suzi's impractical attire had been slowing her down, and now caused her to stop entirely.

'Guys! My heel's stuck!' she squealed, flailing with her arms waving in the air as she tried to dislodge where her heel had slipped into one of the cracks in the ground. Nina sighed, rolling her eyes and turning back towards Suzi, with a slight snigger.

'You really never learn, do you?' She sighed, reaching Suzi to give her a hand. Ellie watched with mild amusement as Nina took both of Suzi's arms and gave her a pull. Suzi jolted forward as she did so, freeing the stubborn heel, but as she did so there was a terrifying rumble.

The moment of mild amusement disappeared into one of pure horror as the ground gave way beneath their feet, and both Nina and Suzi disappeared as the asphalt caved in.

'Nina! Suzi!' Ellie yelled, running forward but skidding to a stop at the edge of the hole, forcing herself to take a jump back as cracked pieces of tarmac, silt and soil all flowed from beneath her feet down into the depths.

She threw up a hand, coughing at the rising dust and debris, feeling her eyes sting and water, but trying to peer down into the darkness, desperately hoping to see a hint of her friends.

'Nina!? Suzi!? Are you down there!?' She yelled into the darkness. An agonising moment of silence passed before she heard a cough and splutter.

'We're here!' came the recognisable British accent of Nina. 'I think Suzi's hoop skirts broke our fall!'

'And you said they were impractical,' coughed Suzi's voice from within the darkness.

'We're only in this mess because of your heels!' Nina countered, before coughing again.

'Are you two alright down there? I can't see you.' Ellie ignored their bickering, trying to shine the light from her cell phone down into the darkness, but it failed to illuminate the gloom. A moment later, she could see a small square of light down below, and realised one of the other girls had got out their phones. She could see the screen glow, and by the slight hint of pink around it she was judging it was Suzi's. 'Where are you?' Ellie called down.

'Looks like one of the old mine tunnels.' Nina replied with a hoarse sounding voice. 'Probably leading towards one of the shafts. I think we got lucky.'

'Because it's not on fire?' Ellie guessed.

'Well, that and the fact it's not *way* deeper.' Nina replied, her voice echoing as she shouted upwards. 'I'm guessing the coal veins run a lot deeper than this, so up here there was nothing left to burn.' Ellie hoped Nina was right, and decided not to comment on the issues of oxygen. If there was a mine fire still burning down there, even with the holes in the road granting oxygen down there, supplies would be limited.

Ellie shook her head, dismissing the thought. The immediate issue wasn't that. It was getting them out of there, by any means necessary.

'Just… sit tight! Those hardware stores back in the square that Suzi saw? I'll go check them! They must have some rope or a hose or something I can use to pull you out!' Ellie already had a plan formulating in her head. Despite the high pressure situation, Ellie had to admit, it felt good to be coming up with a practical solution.

'Forget it!' Nina called back, and Ellie deflated a little that her idea was so quickly dismissed. 'For the tunnel to be this close to the surface, we must be near the exit. We're better off trying to find our way out and meeting back up with you.' For a moment, the light from Suzi's cell phone caught her face, and Ellie realised that the poor girl was trying to illuminate Nina just for Ellie's benefit.

'I can't leave you down there!' Ellie said, the entire idea seeming utterly ridiculous.

'Those hardware stores were looted long ago. You'd be lucky to find an empty crisp packet,' Nina pointed out.

'...You mean a chip bag,' Ellie said after a slight pause, and she thought she heard a slight laugh. At least that helped keep their spirits up. 'Okay, I'll try and find the mine exit, and meet you there.'

'No, get to the house,' Nina instructed. 'Look, I had the gas tank when I fell, but I'm not carrying it with me through here.'

'In case we run into the fire!' Suzi helpfully commented, somehow her good cheer and peppy nature surviving despite the danger the pair were in.

'Exactly,' Nina agreed. 'You've got to get to that house and see if you can find another way to destroy it. We'll meet you there as soon as we can.'

'Alright, alright. Just, be careful,' Ellie sighed, hardly able to believe she was agreeing. 'I'll see you soon.'

'See you soon!' Suzi announced cheerfully. Nina stayed silent, but even from where Ellie was perched, she could hear the crunch of her boots as she began to make her way further into the darkness. Moments later, the glowing light of Suzi's phone followed, and they were gone.

CHAPTER EIGHT

THE DAMSELS

Ellie looked at her phone and sighed as the maps app failed once again to get a signal. Nina had also had the map when she had fallen, leaving Ellie to try and find the old house alone. She began to make her way down the abandoned street, much more cautious of each step than she had ever been before, afraid that if the ground was to open up beneath her as it had done for Suzi and Nina she wouldn't be as lucky as they had been.

Here she was again, she realised with a crushing feeling in her chest. The lone survivor of a horrible situation. Trapped, this time in a spooky abandoned town, all alone. The last girl standing. Just like before. Just like the horror at the camp. Was this what her life would always be? Left alone to fight against terrors most people couldn't believe existed?

But it was with an even worse sinking feeling she began to realise the truth. She *wasn't* the last girl standing. She was the one separated from the group. She was the one who was alone. She was the lone black girl exploring the haunted town away from her friends. She wasn't the *hero*. She was the girl who would be picked off and never seen again. She was just going to be another victim.

No, that was ridiculous. Sure, Nina liked to talk about patterns and how creatures behaved and act like they followed some grand narrative, but this wasn't a movie, and Ellie wouldn't let her life end like one. She was going to find that house and destroy it. She was going to survive. And so would Nina and Suzi. She had to have faith.

'Stoooooppit! It's not *funny*!' A voice snapped her out of her thoughts. A female voice, definitely. A teenager by the sounds of it. Whiny and a bit nasally. Definitely not the voice of Nina or Suzi. It had come from a side street up ahead. She was aware of laughter; the rough, loud teenage laughter of a group of friends, all of whom had clearly had a few drinks. She knew those laughs because she'd laughed those laughs, a lifetime ago.

She turned the corner, and spotted the group. A small bunch of teenagers. She quickly counted three males and three females, although she didn't form a full opinion of them yet. One, a pretty looking blonde in a very short pink skirt and light blue crop top had apparently encountered what Ellie's mind dubbed a 'Suzi' situation. Like Suzi, it seemed the cheerleader (and she was *so* obviously a cheerleader) had worn heels to this abandoned place, and gotten one wedged in a crack. One of the boys, slightly chubby with longish dark hair, was taking a photo on his cell phone as the girl pouted and struggled to free her foot. The other two boys, one a large well-built blonde in a letterman jacket, and the other with dark skin, a buzz cut and glasses, were laughing loudly. Next to them, a Latina looking girl in a leather jacket was rolling her eyes, but not able to hide a smirk. But just before Ellie could finish assessing them, another girl, a tall redhead with glasses and a neat, flowery dress, surged forward to pull the trapped girl free.

'I wouldn't do that if I were you!' Ellie suddenly called out. She'd seen this happen once already, and while the odds of it happening again were *technically* slim, she knew that they were far beyond playing by the rules of physics. And she didn't rate this lot's chances if they fell in to the mine. Nina and Suzi could take care of themselves. But these kids?

Somehow Ellie doubted it.

The group of teens turned to face Ellie, except the one with the stuck heel, who just sort of made pathetic half attempts at turning around.

'Who the hell are you?' the one in the letterman jacket snapped.

'And why wouldn't I want to help my friend?' the redhead added. Ellie paused, realising that maybe she should have approached this slightly differently.

'The ground is really unstable. Just, trust me. You need to be careful,' Ellie tried to reason.

'Seems pretty stable to me!' the one with the long dark hair commented, jumping up and down a few times to demonstrate. The redhead rolled her eyes, and reached forward, grabbing the blonde's arms.

'I mean it, don't!' Ellie rushed forward, but the redhead pulled the blonde free without much effort, and of course, nothing happened.

'Ugh, what is your problem?' the blonde asked, obviously happy that she was now free, and checking her heel for scuff marks.

'What are you lot doing here?' Ellie asked, ignoring the question.

'Pretty sure that's none of your business,' the one in the letterman jacket replied.

'Yeah, at least we're not here on our own, like some kind of *freak*,' the one with the long dark hair commented, with a too-pleased-with-himself smirk. Ellie decided he must consider himself the joker of the group.

'I'm not on my own. I just… got separated from my friends,' Ellie sighed.

'Yeah, right. Bet you've got *loads* of friends. I bet you've got a boyfriend too,' The joker laughed.

'What? No! What's that got to-' Ellie paused, shaking her head, realising she was letting him annoy her. A thought had just crossed her mind. Suzi had said that she had seen on social media that another group of teenagers were heading to the house. Could it be? Were they here already? 'Are you heading to the old Campbell place?' She asked, suddenly realising.

'Oh, yeah! You know it?' the blonde asked cheerfully, in a tone that meant more about her than just the trapped heel reminded Ellie of Suzi. The one in the leather jacket muttered something under her breath, and while Ellie couldn't hear it, she was pretty sure it involved the phrase 'none of your business'.

'Don't!' Ellie immediately warned. The redhead raised an eyebrow, and just gave Ellie a look.

'Uh, why not?' she asked.

'People who go there *die*. The last bunch of teenagers who went there, your age, *died!*' Ellie realised she was almost ranting. God, how could anybody be this stupid? Was *she* ever this bad? Surely not.

'Uh yeah, we *know,*' the one in the letterman jacket, the jock, as she'd labelled him, replied. 'Bunch of kids went up there last year, had some suicide pact. Pretty spooky but nothing we're gonna do, don't you worry.'

'Suicide pact? They were *literally never seen again*!' Ellie found herself practically yelling. 'What do you think happened? They killed themselves *then hid the bodies*!? They were clearly murdered! Doesn't that scare you!?'

'Look, it's a scary house, we're gonna spend the night and tell ghost stories, that's al,.' the girl in the leather jacket spoke up, rolling her eyes with a sigh.

'It wouldn't be any fun if it wasn't scary,' the jokester put in.

'If you go up there you are *all going to die!*' Ellie realised how loud her voice was getting.

'All right, try this on for size,' the jock stepped forward, arms folded confidently, showing his muscles beneath the jacket. He stood towering over Ellie's reasonably petite frame, and it was obvious he was moving to intimidate her. 'You're gonna leave me and my friends alone, or you're gonna have a little accident down one of these potholes. Got it?'

'Todd, don't,' the obvious cheerleader tried to reason.

'Shut it, Avril. This is my weekend with my friends, and I'm not having some crazy bitch ruin it.' He glared down at Ellie. 'So why don't you just turn around, and find those imaginary friends you got separated from.' With that, he gave her a firm push, and Ellie found herself stumbling back. A piece of debris caught her foot and she fell over onto her backside with a groan. The jock (Todd, it seemed) and jokester laughed loudly as they turned to walk away, and the silent one with the buzz cut smirked, following. The redhead and one in the leather jacket smiled slightly, but gave Ellie slightly sympathetic looks as they left. It was only Avril, the blonde, who gave her a truly sympathetic look, and mouthed 'sorry' as she turned to catch up with the group of departing teenagers.

Ellie sat for a moment, nursing both her bruised rear end and wounded pride as she watched them leave. She couldn't quite comprehend how anybody could be so incredibly *stupid*. Didn't they understand what was going to happen!? Why would people ignore such an obvious warning?

And then it hit her. Nina had spoken about the *pattern*. Ellie began to understand the *rules*. Rules that the supernatural followed. Rules that these things obeyed. She remembered St. Mary's Marsh. She remembered when she had spoken words aloud, and it seemed like they had almost summoned the monster back. Like there was a *narrative*. That was why Nina had been so freaked out by the gremlin. A gremlin on the wing of a plane didn't fit the *narrative* of an abandoned spooky house in an old town. And then she realised something else. If you believed in the narrative, if you believed there was a *story* that shaped these dark creatures, then there was one factor that was almost always present.

The crazy person delivering a dire warning before the bad thing happened.

The crazy person the teenagers always ignored. *Friday the 13th* had Crazy Ralph. *Halloween* had Dr Loomis. Even *Cabin in the Woods* had mocked that little trope.

Now that she thought about it, there had been an old man at the gas station on their way to St. Mary's Marsh who had warned them not to go. They had all laughed it off, of course. Just like those teens did now. In *this* story, Ellie was the crazy person. Ellie was the one who warned them and that they ignored. She got to her feet, feeling more agitated with herself than them. How could she not of seen how she sounded? Why didn't she just come up with a clever lie, like claiming the house had fallen down or was really unstable? Something to convince them to turn away using logic, rather than ranting about, well, whatever it was she had been saying. She couldn't even remember; the moment had been like a cloud of desperation. She was glad that Nina wasn't there at that moment, as she would have doubtlessly been amused by what a screw up of everything Ellie had made.

The teens had long since faded from sight, heading on down the winding roads, but Ellie still had a pretty clear idea of where they had gone. She could quite easily follow them, which was useful since she still had no map.

She assumed they knew where they were going. The problem now was that things had become even more complicated. Even if she could find a way to burn the old house down without the gas Nina had lost, she couldn't do it while risking the people inside. They definitely weren't going to listen to her telling them to get out of there and she couldn't wait for them to leave, because the odds were they would *never* leave. At least, not alive. She could always try and head to the mine entrance and wait for Nina and Suzi, but she realised that doing that was a risk as well. She'd be leaving the kids alone and to their horrible fate, and there was no guarantee they'd be back in time.

It was up to her. Somehow, she had to convince them she wasn't crazy. She had to get them out of that house before the ghosts could do anything. She had to save them. There was a narrative dictating how events went. Okay, fine. Ellie could accept that. But she also knew that Nina could change the narrative. She remembered Alec, the taxi driver. A man who would have been another faceless victim if the story had been followed. Nina had saved him. She had changed the story.

And now it was up to Ellie to do the same. Or come sunrise tomorrow, there would be six more dead teenagers in the town of Angel's Ridge. *Hopefully not seven*, Ellie thought to herself. She steeled herself, and went after them. She'd just have to *make* them listen.

CHAPTER NINE

DOWN BELOW

Suzi hated the entire situation. The darkness, the dust, the filth. Her beautiful dress had been ruined by the fall, and worse still, Nina was giving her the silent treatment. She suspected it was because Nina still blamed her for their current predicament. It wasn't entirely unjustified, of course, but it didn't mean it made Suzi feel any better about the situation. They did, at least, both have flashlights. Nina may have abandoned the big gas canister from her rucksack but she had kept the rest of the equipment, which included plenty of useful items. Including the flashlights. They were large, heavy metal things that Nina insisted on carrying everywhere. More confusingly, she insisted on calling them 'torches', not 'flashlights'. It must have been a British thing, Suzi decided.

The light cut through the heavy darkness and danced across the dust particles as they floated in the otherwise pitch blackness. The tunnel was quite large, but the all-encompassing darkness made it feel claustrophobic, as if it was pressing in around you from all sides. The occasional shafts of light peered through from the damaged roof, leading to the world above, but that was it. They felt like more of a taunt, a tease of a world that could no longer be reached, than helpful in any way.

'I said I was sorry!' Suzi tried to see if she could get a response from Nina, who merely sighed and pushed on. 'At least we're still alive!'

'Yeah, we are!' Nina snapped, wheeling around on Suzi. 'And now Ellie is up there all alone. And I don't need to tell you what happens to the teenage girl who gets separated from her friends in a place like this! You know the *rules*!' Suzi paused, taken aback by Nina's anger, but understanding it now. It wasn't that Suzi had caused them to fall into the mine that bothered her. It was that she was worried about what it meant for Ellie.

For all of her attempts to act like she was closed off to the world, Nina always did *care*.

'The rules… Don't always work that way. There are surprises. Twists. She might be okay!' Suzi tried to reassure her. 'There's still stuff here we don't understand! The gremlin on the plane! That didn't make sense.' Nina gave an angry look as Suzi reminded her of this, so Suzi decided to move on to something more reassuring. 'A-and, not that I'm complaining, but we should be dead!'

'The fall wasn't that far,' Nina countered.

'Yeah, but, this place was abandoned because of a coal mine fire, right? Well, even if all the coal in this tunnel had burned up, where's the toxic fumes? They say a coal seam fire is hotter than the surface of Mercury and the atmosphere is more toxic than Venus, but here we are, walking around like everything's fine,' Suzi pointed out. 'Dirty and dark, but fine!'

'"Hotter than Mercury and more toxic than Venus?" It's just a tunnel,' Nina said with a single raised eyebrow. Always a strange look on her, Suzi thought, since her other eye was covered by the patch, and you could never tell if she was quizzical or surprised.

'Exactly! But it *shouldn't* be,' Suzi explained. 'All the pictures on Wikipedia for this town, they had all these cool shots of smoke rising out of the cracks in the road and places where snow just wouldn't settle because of the heat, but we haven't seen *any* of that.' She went on. 'Heck, part of the reason the town was evacuated was the toxic fumes, it's why it's not meant to be safe here, but I can breathe fine, and we're *in* the mines,' Nina paused, turning to face Suzi, the flashlight temporarily blinding the pink clad girl. She threw a hand up to block the light and blinked at Suzi.

'What's your point?' Nina's tone definitely told Suzi that she was still feeling annoyed with her.

'*Something* is going on here. You know the rules better than even I do! But none of this, none of it, tallies up with a haunted house!' Nina opened her mouth to reply, but stopped when a distant noise cut through the air. A piercing scraping noise, like metal on stone, a noise so sharp and sudden that Suzi could almost see it visibly cutting through the darkness.

The two girls quickly shone their flashlights forward, illuminating the distant tunnel. There was silence, and then another scraping sound. The thick cloying darkness that was all around them felt like it dampened all sound, but slowly they became aware of shuffling, lumbering footsteps approaching. Something seemed to be flickering in the distant darkness, even before the light caught it, smouldering with embers, traces of smoke rising visibly from a heavy looking outdoorsman jacket. The thing made its way towards them, walking slowly, its body aglow with traces of orange fire. Just a hint, as if the body had been burned. The face was wrapped entirely in burnt looking bandages, hiding all features, and upon the head was a burned looking, wide-brimmed fedora. It let out a groan, and lifted one of its arms, revealing it not to be an arm at all, but a machete that was embedded in the severed stump. It scraped the metal along the rough stone surface once more, and let out an angry groan.

'Oh, *sod off.* I know *you* shouldn't be here!' Nina sighed. The creature was approaching slowly, and Suzi knew they had a bit of time to make a plan. These slow moving creatures, the ones Nina liked to call 'slasher monsters', never moved fast. Unless you took your eyes off them, at which point they'd be upon you before you could blink. The best way to deal with them was to keep them in your line of sight at all times.

'I'm pretty sure he definitely *is* here,' Suzi pointed out.

'I *know* that, but that's… that's your typical, zombified, slashy stabby psychopathic monster! It doesn't belong here! We're here to investigate a haunted house! None of this makes sense!' Nina raged.

'Sometimes ghosts cause hallucinations. Could it be that? A trick?' Suzi suggested calmly. In the distance, the monster groaned again, getting closer with every shuffling step.

'Hey, mate, we're trying to have a conversation here,' Nina said with irritation in the direction of the strange creature. 'Keep it down will you?' Nina turned back to Suzi. 'Nah, can't be that simple. I mean, we've not even reached the haunted house yet. Ghosts don't open with crap like this. Not until they've had a few traditional scares.'

'Could it just be two supernatural things in one place? Just a big coincidence?' Suzi suggested thoughtfully. Still, the creature got ever closer.

'No, no, it can't be that,' Nina shook her head. 'In all my years of doing this, I've never heard of two at once. Especially not totally unrelated like this.'

'Wait, wait,' Suzi suddenly realised something. 'Nina, I'm looking at you!'

'Yeah, and?'

'You're looking at me!'

'So?'

'So… who's looking at the creature?'

It was an amateur mistake to take their eyes off of it for even a moment, but a mistake that they still made, and that was why when they turned back at that exact moment it was just in time to see that strange machete arm whistling down through the air towards them both.

Suzi and Nina threw themselves apart from each other just in time, the machete only managing to tear into the edge of Suzi's large dress. While Nina was always telling her off for dressing so impractically, she did often find in these dangerous situations a large dress held out by a hoop skirt actually stopped the dangerous creatures from getting too close to her. It didn't prevent this particular creature enough, however, as it swung its machete at her throat. She ducked under it, aware of her heart thundering in her chest, feeling the blade sweep literally millimetres above her hair. Shards of the large pink bow she had been wearing on her head fluttered down on either side of her, and she realised just how close it had been.

Whoever, or whatever, the machete wielder was, it decided to try a stab next, thrusting forward towards Suzi. She jumped backwards, just out of the reach of the blade, but the creature continued to advance, swinging an arc directly at her waist. The heavy metal flashlight she was holding was her only hope, and she used it to block the incoming machete attack, causing a heavy *clang* to ring out through the darkness. The monster let out an angry roar, and brought the machete up before striking down overhead towards Suzi. She threw up the long metal torch, held in both hands, and blocked the blow, but her arms buckled under the impossible strength of her attacker, and as she stumbled back she lost balance in her heels on the rough ground, and fell painfully to the floor.

Suzi was no stranger to being in a fight with all manners of strange creatures, but she had never had Nina's talent for it. Her adrenaline and quick thinking had kept her alive so far, but now she was convinced she was doomed. She was prone on the floor, the torch gone from her hand, its light flickering and failing thanks to the damage from the machete and the creature was stood over her. This was to be her final moment, she realised. Killed in the dark underground by a creature that made no sense, even by her own considerably broad standards for illogical experiences.

It was a rather inelegant final thought, she found herself thinking, and then realising that no, *that* would now be her final thought ever. What a way to go.

Fortunately, the killing blow never came. As the machete of the creature descended, it suddenly found itself blocked with enough force to cause a flash of sparks. Nina had thrust out a machete of her own, blocking the attack. Suzi managed a slight smile. Nina's melee weapon of choice had always been the machete, since long before they met. It seemed it was a common weapon for the more stab happy monsters and she'd gotten used to using one in defence. She always carried one with her in the rucksack. At least that told Suzi where Nina had been during her own short melee; finding the weapon.

'Keep the light on it!' Nina commanded, kicking her functioning torch over to Suzi. She must have laid it down when she picked up the weapon, Suzi realised. Suzi lifted the light, illuminating the creature as Nina launched several quick, powerful attacks with the machete, wielded with a martial artist's skills. What struck Suzi as odd was how the creature blocked each attack, parrying them, almost like a sword master of its own. It was completely

114

at odds with the brutal, hacking attacks it had deployed against Suzi, and for all of her own experience, Suzi could never remember encountering a monster that also knew how to *sword fight*. Maybe a Mummy? She had never fought a Mummy, but this thing, despite the burning bandages, definitely wasn't a Mummy.

Its own skilled, rapid attacks threatened to overwhelm Nina, who while skilled herself, didn't have the creature's supernatural strength. Suzi knew that she had to act quickly. She fumbled quickly in her own dainty purse, still on her shoulder, and drew her tiny .22 pink pistol. It may have been widely mocked by the others, but right now, it could turn the tables. She still had no idea what they were fighting, but it was distracted, and at this range, she couldn't really miss.

The gunshot was deafening, echoing through the mine tunnel and causing dust to fall from the ceiling, but the shot found its mark, tearing right through the creature's head. It fell like a sack of potatoes to the ground, as if some life force had suddenly been severed. Despite Nina's council that guns never worked, everybody knew you shot a zombie in the head, so Suzi had figured it was worth a try. She hadn't expected it to work however. She was fairly certain it *wouldn't* work for long.

'Quickly! While it's down, cut off its head!' Suzi suggested, her voice rapid and ragged, still full of adrenaline.

'I know, I know, I'm not an amateur!' Both knew that despite appearances to the contrary, the odds were the creature would rise again when they least expected it. They *always* did. Nina took a step towards it, but at that exact same moment they heard a distant thunderous roar. Not a creature this time, but something more akin to an explosion, coming from behind them. They both turned, the one working flashlight flickering to illuminate something moving towards them that for a moment defied explanation. It was like a thick heavy darkness, moving in the pitch black itself, somehow darker and more oppressive than everything around it, with its own thick texture. It even swallowed the beam of light, as if it was absorbing it. But there was something else within. Embers and sparks of orange fire. Suzi realised what she was seeing almost too late. A huge cloud of toxic smoke, roaring down the tunnel right towards them. Later on, Suzi would think it was as if some floodgates had been holding it all back, and now they were open. Right now she could only think one thing. One thing that she articulated with a particularly loud scream of;

'RUN!'

It was something that Nina was already doing.

Suzi could run surprisingly fast, given her choice of attire. Even Nina herself would often make comments on how surprised she was by Suzi's physical ability in dangerous situations, but as Suzi always reminded her old friend, it wasn't like she had a choice. A lack of physical aptitude was a sure fire way to not last long living their lifestyle. She might not have quite been the fighter Nina was, or even the shot with a gun it appeared Ellie would be, but she still could run like hell with the best of them.

That didn't make the run any less terrifying though. In the darkness it was impossible to see any obstacles, and the thick toxic fumes chasing them would almost certainly engulf them with even the slightest delay. There was no room for mistakes and no time to think twice. All the pair could do was run as fast as they could and hope the passageway was clear.

'Watch out!' Nina yelled as her torch light caught something gleaming in the passageway. Suzi managed to throw herself around it, just avoiding colliding with the huge object as she ran. She thought it might have been a mine cart, but there was no time to turn and look, no time to try and work it out. There was no time to do anything but run.

Then, in the distance, finally a stroke of luck! Suzi saw beams of light peeking through something. They must have been approaching the mine exit! But her joy turned to horror as she realised the light only existed as small shafts, poking through wooden slats that had sealed the exit. They were trapped inside! The exit was sealed! With nowhere to go, the smoke would be upon them at any moment. Suzi knew they might survive it hitting them, although the heat coming from it was pretty intense, but they'd get maybe two, perhaps three breaths before they were unconscious. And down there, in that darkness, nobody would ever find them.

'One chance! Shoot!' Nina yelled. It was a pretty blunt instruction, but there was no time for anything more in depth. Despite the dead end, Nina and Suzi were still running towards it, simply because they had nowhere else to go. Nina lifted her pistol, a much heavier weapon than Suzi used, and fired several shots at the wood. Suzi, realising what she meant, did the same with her much daintier weapon. The bullets ruptured the wood, and Suzi realised what Nina meant to do. It was their only hope. Approaching the now bullet hole ridden wooden slats at full pelt, Nina and Suzi jumped, barging into them shoulder first.

Suzi remembered thinking, in that moment, either she was about to survive, or bounce off it and die in the most embarrassing way possible. Luckily, it seemed the former was the case. The gunshots, combined with the wood being exposed to the elements for so many decades, had left it fragile and splintered, and the sealed entrance burst open as both Suzi and Nina crashed through it in a shower of wood, splinters, flailing limbs and toxic smoke.

The mine exit had been at the top of a small slope, and Suzi felt several sharp jagged pains as she rolled down it, practically bouncing in her hoop skirt. Nina was nothing but a mass of flailing limbs and a very scorched looking leather trench coat and behind them the toxic smoke plumed out of the exit and high into the air, reaching up to stab the now darkening evening sky.

A few moments of silence passed as Suzi lay on her back, panting and breathing hard, and then she sat up to look at Nina. Nina was coated in what looked like soot, her face almost entirely black, her already black clothes covered in layers of the stuff, and as she wiped the ash away from her one good eye, she saw Suzi and suddenly burst out laughing. Suzi looked behind herself, confused, and then back at Nina, before looking down at herself to see what was so funny. To her horror, she saw that her entire beautifully complex and elegant pink outfit was now entirely black, the big ribbons decorating the hem of her dress either gone entirely or singed, and as she grabbed the end of her hair in reflective horror she realised her beautiful pink hair was now as black as Nina's. Her senses caught up with her and she realised her eyes were stinging, and as she reached to clear them, she realised her face was also plastered in soot.

Nina coughed a little as she finished laughing and Suzi coughed too, her lungs itching and burning, feeling as if she had just swallowed a pint of dust. The two let a moment pass between them as they wheezed and caught their breath.

'That... That was not natural,' Nina rasped. Suzi knew that she was looking for confirmation. Suzi had always been the 'smart' one of the group, or so Nina liked to say, so whenever something out of the ordinary happened Nina liked to check with Suzi that it was in fact supernatural, and not just a strange but natural occurrence.

'Uh, no. No way. It's like that creature's presence was holding the fire back, and when we killed it, it all came back,' Suzi explained the obvious, pretty sure that Nina had already figured that part out. She looked back at the smoke, still reaching up into the purple sky, blocking out the moon even as it made its early appearance. 'At least we know it's dead now. Nothing could have surviv-'

'Don't you bloody say it.'

A brief moment passed, and the two looked at each other again. Nina struggled to her feet, and offered a hand down to Suzi. Suzi's legs still felt like Jell-O and her chest was burning, but she knew better than to complain, and took Nina's hand, struggling to wobbly, shaking feet.

'C'mon. We need to find Ellie.' Nina insisted. 'That creature, this fire, that gremlin on the plane, none of it makes sense. Something else is happening here,' She articulated what Suzi was already thinking. Suzi was too polite to point out that she had already been trying to say *exactly* that.

'Well, hopefully while we've been dealing with the monster, she's been getting on okay. I mean, how much trouble could she have gotten in?'

Suzi should have learned, she realised, not to say things like that. It wasn't just the monsters that followed the rules after all. You should never tempt fate. But then again, even *she* didn't expect to find what they did as they exited the mine ground and made their way back on to the cracked street. There was Ellie, wrapped in duct tape and stuck to a lamp post, making desperate muffled gurgling noises where her mouth was taped shut and struggling against her restraints.

Helpfully, Nina burst out laughing.

CHAPTER TEN

STOP ME IF YOU'VE HEARD THIS BEFORE

Being popular, Avril often thought, was way harder than people thought. She knew even *thinking* that made her sound like your typical spoiled brat, but it was true. Popularity was fleeting. She had a reputation, of course, and some of that reputation, she thought proudly, wouldn't go anywhere. She knew she was considered the hottest girl in school, for example. A fact she was overwhelmingly proud of. While Avril would admit that some days she didn't *feel* particularly 'hot', and certainly not the best looking girl in the school, she *was* proud of her figure, of her hair, of her clothes, of everything, really. She always put maximum effort into looking good and obviously it paid off. More than that, she'd worked incredibly hard to become head cheerleader and while your average movie might make out that being pretty and popular was all you needed for that, it wasn't true at all. It was *hard work*.

But popularity was a tricky thing. You could spend years cultivating it, and then it could be destroyed in a single moment. She still remembered two years ago, when she'd barely turned fourteen, seeing Sunny Slater, everybody's favourite popular senior, have a total meltdown in the school canteen because her boyfriend wasn't wearing a designer shirt and she didn't want to be seen with him. She'd thrown such a tantrum the entire school had turned against her almost instantly, and just like that, she went from being everybody's favourite person to despised. Of course, it didn't help her boyfriend was the school's star football player. Just like Todd was. It was funny how she had gravitated to being in a relationship with him. Almost as if it was *expected* of her.

That was the reason, Avril told herself, she hadn't spoken out when Todd, Jake and Shelly had taped that girl to the lamppost. She knew it was wrong, but the girl kept bothering them and seemed kind of crazy. Maybe even dangerous. And besides, once Todd got an idea in his head, you either went along with it or you risked being his next target. Not even Avril's considerable popularity could survive Todd's wrath if it came to it. She had already fallen dangerously close when she'd gotten her heel stuck and they'd all gathered to laugh at her. She had earned no sympathy from her supposed boyfriend then.

She hadn't actually confided in anybody that she wasn't fond of this trip idea at all. The idea had originated with Shelly, always known for his jokes, making a joke about how stupid it would be to stay overnight in the 'murder house', as he called it (despite the fact the kids there apparently committed suicide). Then Todd and Jake ran with it, and Avril, not wanting to stand in the way of the boys' fun, agreed. She hadn't thought they'd take it this far, but now here they were at that awful place. She was just glad Kat and Ali had agreed to come. She'd grown up with Kat, and while they'd gone their separate ways a little in High School, they remained friends. Especially after the change, when Avril knew Kat would appreciate the support of good friends. Kat had always liked to study hard and despised sports, while Avril was terrible at schoolwork but a great cheerleader, so she was aware that in many ways they were opposites, but having her around still made Avril feel comfortable. It helped that she was *smart*. You could always rely on Kat to know what was going on. And Ali? Well, befriending Ali had surprised some people. She was tough, known as a rebel, she even smoked! But Avril felt like being popular also came with *responsibility*. She didn't want to be a Regina George, looking down on everybody who wasn't like her. So she'd befriended her and invited her along. Some might have thought she was being patronising, as if she was the noblewoman spending time talking to the peasants, but she didn't see it that way. She thought it was a friendly act and showed that she was far nicer than her 'rich, popular girl' exterior might suggest. Besides, she seemed tough and street smart, and she couldn't imagine that'd do any harm when staying overnight in a creepy town. But it had just meant to be a fun little getaway, and now they were actually there and they'd just stuck a girl to a lamp post and left her to rot. It hardly seemed right.

They arrived at the old Campbell House, and in that moment it proved to be everything the boys had hoped and everything Avril had feared. The main foyer was big, with a grand staircase in the middle leading up, before splitting off in two directions to the next floor, but the rest of it was mostly empty. There were some piles of wood covered in cobwebs that might have once been furniture, and one of the walls had rotted away leading through to another dark and dusty room that Avril couldn't quite make out. Dark mould grew up the wooden walls from the corners, and even the good, standing wall had holes in it where the wood had rotted away. There was a lighter outline of where doubtlessly a picture had once hung on the right hand wall, but the picture itself was long gone. Avril could make out half of a rusty antique frame in the dust on the floor beneath the wall. The air was heavy with an offensive, damp odour and where evening light streamed through the windows you could easily make out the dust molecules hanging in the air.

The boys were excitedly chattering among themselves about how spooky it all was and Avril realised that she was still stood frozen by the entrance, taking it all in. Kat seemed to have noticed, and headed over, a concerned look on her face.

'You okay? You look scared,' she asked with that gentle half smile of hers.

'What? Scared? No. *As if.*' Avril stepped into the room as if to demonstrate, hearing the floorboards creak. Not for the first time she regretted wearing heels on this trip. She had wanted to look good for Todd but now she was afraid the pressure would punch right through the rotting floorboards. 'I was just, uh, thinking about that girl we tied up.'

'Hey, don't get me wrong, it was an asshole thing to do,' Kat whispered so the boys wouldn't hear. 'But she'll be fine. She said she had friends. They'll find her and cut her down and just have a big laugh about it, and at least we don't need to worry about her springing out on us in our sleep or something,' she explained. Avril smiled. This was why she liked having Kat around. She spoke sensibly. She let Avril know when there was nothing to worry about.

Ali was stood in the middle of the hallway, her head craned back, looking upwards.

'Roof looks solid. At least we won't get rained on,' she commented. 'Place looks pretty undisturbed though. I doubt those missing kids ever even made it here.' Ali ran her finger along the bannister of the staircase, examining the dust that lay thickly there.

'Uh, the story is pretty clear. They all stayed here, and all committed suicide here,' Shelly said with indignation, as if he was offended his little horror story set up for them all was being ruined.

'If they all committed suicide why were there no bodies, dumbass?' Ali asked with shortening patience.

'Uh, I dunno, maybe 'cause they hid the bodies!'

'Hid the bodies? *After* they killed themselves?' Ali questioned dryly. Avril remembered that the strange girl had made the same point.

'Yeah, they could have, uh… oh. Yeah. Okay. Good point,' Shelly moped, causing Avril to actually feel sorry for him. His little horrific fantasy has been punctured. Now they were just a bunch of teenagers in an old, dusty house.

'Look, it's pretty obvious. A bunch of kids told their families they were coming here, and used it as an excuse to run away from home. Doubt anybody's even stood in this house since the town was abandoned,' Ali concluded. Avril looked to Kat for confirmation, who nodded.

'I mean, either that, or they had an accident getting here. But I agree, it doesn't look like anybody's been here for decades,' she explained. Todd, who had apparently been participating in some kind of sword fight using old pieces of wood with Jake, headed over to join them all.

'Guess we'd better baptise this place tonight, then. Show it what 21st Century people do,' he smiled as he put his arms around Avril. She might have still been angry with him about how they had treated that girl, but she didn't want to show it in front of the others. She was popular, sexy Avril Connor. She had an image to keep up.

A sudden crash from one of the upstairs rooms shattered any thought of keeping that image intact, given the shriek she gave. The entire group froze, and looked up, only to hear the sound of footsteps running along the hallway at the top of the stairs. Avril exchanged a desperate, nervous look with Kat, who seemed equally terrified for a moment. Avril was glad that Todd's arms were still around her, and she retreated a little into his grip. Even Todd seemed to be frightened for the briefest moment.

It took Ali to roll her eyes dramatically at the others and step forward, walking towards the stairs.

'Hello!? Is anybody up there!?' she called, but there was no response. The group stood in silence, and Avril could feel Todd's heart beating through his chest. She looked up at him with concern, and he seemed to take this as a sign that it was time to act as manly as possible. He let go of her, striding forward.

'Alright, you little jerks! Whoever's up there, you better come down here right now!' he yelled up the stairs, but Avril could tell he was trying to hide a quaking in his voice. 'Either you come down these stairs or I send you out the window!' he called up, but there was still nothing. The group exchanged a look. Ali sighed, and rolled her eyes again.

'It's probably just some animal.' she pointed out. 'We'd better go up there and flush it out, otherwise it might eat our food in the night.'

'You want us to go *up there*?' Avril squeaked, still painfully aware of how spooky the noise had been.

'It'll be a possum or a badger or something,' Ali countered. 'Nothing to be afraid of.'

'Actually a possum can bite pretty hard,' Kat added in, only to get a withering look from the others. Avril suspected it was just for trying to scare *her*, as none of the others looked afraid. They didn't know Kat like she did though. This was just Kat trying to be helpful. 'Uh, sorry.' she added.

'Alright, fine. The Princess can stay down here. I'm gonna go up and look for it,' Ali decided. 'Anybody else coming, or do you wanna stay with the Queen of Priss there?' She gestured over to Avril, who felt a little called out by the entire thing, but then again, she *was* scared to go up there. The demeaning nicknames had been Ali's way of rebelling since they met, always making it clear what she thought of Avril's attitude, but Avril knew deep down Ali was a true friend. Besides, as far as Avril was concerned, "prissy" was just another word for "pretty" and what was wrong with that? Plus she'd gone from a princess to a queen in two sentences, and that was clearly a promotion, so she had to be doing alright.

'I'll be right back, babe,' Todd leaned in to give Avril a quick kiss, picking up one of the big pieces of broken wood he had been fake sword fighting with earlier. Apparently he was planning to hit whatever was up there with it to chase it out.

'Don't worry, I've got his back, in case a terrifying badger tries to eat him,' Jake added with a smirk, clapping Todd on the back. Shelly looked between them, and back at the girls.

'Aw, nuts. I can't be the only guy who doesn't go,' he groaned, joining the group. Kat and Avril exchanged a look.

'Sorry Avril, I better go and check it's okay. This lot are clueless without me,' Kat gestured to the group, and hurried off to join them. Avril stayed firmly where she was standing, hands to her chest in a nervous gesture. She was fiddling with one of the rings on her well manicured hands, twirling it subconsciously. The group that were heading up the stairs paused at the bottom, clearly nervous, until Ali sighed and simply pushed past the boys to lead the way. Soon after, the others followed.

A moment of silence passed, and suddenly Avril realised she was now entirely on her own in the empty foyer. It seemed a lot darker than she had noticed before, and for the first time she began to notice the big cobwebs in the corners and hanging from the big, old, rusty chandelier that was awkwardly suspended above her head. Cobwebs meant spiders, right? She gulped and began pacing, trying not to feel too nervous. Her high heeled boots clicked and echoed on the old wooden floorboards, and that was enough to stop her moving. She paused, waiting for a moment, the quietness only broken by the creaking of floorboards above. Her friends. God, she hoped it was her friends. Why had they all gone? Why hadn't at least one stayed with her? Todd should have known not to leave her on her own! She was going to have so many words with him later.

There was a sharp creak, and she let out a startled gasp, turning. She couldn't tell where it had come from, but it didn't sound like it was from upstairs. Yet, all of the group except for her were up there, so what else could have made that noise? What if that girl they had tied up had gotten free and was after revenge? Or what if it was something worse?

It didn't take her long to make the decision and hurry to the stairs, rushing after the others. The staircase split in two directions at the midpoint, left and right, and extended up into the darkness. Avril chose to go right, thinking it was the direction the others had gone. The stairs led around to the upper walkway, which extended back over the foyer below. It was dark at the top, and Avril couldn't see much ahead of her as she stepped from the stairs onto the creaking floorboards. She hoped that they would hold. This house was old. Maybe staying on the ground floor had been a good idea.

It was too dark to easily see ahead, so Avril reached for her cellphone, lifting it up and letting the screen illuminate ahead. She didn't see anybody, and so she took a nervous step forward, trying to ignore the ominous creak as the floorboards strained, old rotten wood embracing the challenge of holding people for the first time in over half a century.

A doorway to her left lead deeper into the house, and she approached it slowly, unable to see inside. She held her phone out and as the pale white light from the screen cut into the inky blackness, she saw something. A face. Before she could react, it lunged at her, and she screamed, her phone clattering to the ground.

'BOO!' Shelly yelled at the top of his voice, jumping out in front of her and exploding with laughter. It took a moment for what he had just done to sink in, and Avril looked back at him, her fear being replaced with furious anger.

'Shelly! That's! Not! Funny!' she yelled, slapping him on the chest to punctuate each angry word.

'I dunno, it was pretty funny,' Shelly laughed. 'Oh, your face…' He stopped only to wipe a tear from his eye.

'God, you're such a child!' Avril found herself shouting, her voice echoing through the creaky old house. 'Where's Todd?'

'What?'

'Where's Todd!? Just you wait until I tell him what you did!' she threatened with as much indignation as she could muster.

'Jeez, Avril, cool down, would you?' Shelly took a defensive step back, as if somehow *he* was the one who was offended. As if it was somehow Avril's fault that she was angry with him. 'It was just a jo-' Shelly didn't get to finish his sentence, or indeed any sentence ever again, because at that moment he took a step back too far and the walkway beneath his feet gave way with a mighty crash. He managed to look Avril in the eyes, startled for a moment, before he plummeted backwards and fell down to the ground floor in a shower of splinters and rotting wood.

'SHELLY!' Avril shrieked, but she couldn't see him from where she stood.

She turned to instinctively run down the stairs when Todd, Jake and Ali ran out of the darkened passageway, having heard the crash.

'What happened?' Todd asked urgently.

'He- he- he jumped out on me, and the ground broke, and he fell!' Avril explained desperately. 'I-I think he's really hurt!'

'Shelly!?' Ali stepped forward, calling out, only to hear silence in reply. The four of them exchanged looks before bolting down the stairs together. Avril hadn't even noticed that Kat wasn't among them.

They reached the bottom of the stairway and back in to the main foyer, where they could see a pile of broken rubble. And Shelly's body. Totally stationary. Todd and Jake were in the lead, but both froze. Avril tried to approach, but Todd quickly turned around, and shielded her with his body.

'Wh-what is it? What? I want to see!' Avril tried to escape his grasp, but he held her back for a moment, silent, his eyes glazed with shock. Avril squirmed, and he released her, allowing her to pass.

Shelly's body was impaled on a huge shard of ruined, old wood, which was now coated slick with dark red blood. His lifeless eyes were still open, and his face was twisted into a grin, as if he had been laughing as he fell, before his life had so suddenly ended. Avril could do nothing but shriek, and she looked to Todd, to Jake, to Ali, all of whom looked pale and terrified. Even Ali, always so tough, always so confident, gave a look of pure fright to Avril.

'Wh-what do we do!?' Avril asked desperately, looking between the group. 'H-he's… he's dead!' She burst into tears, sobbing desperately.

'I… I don't… I don't know,' Todd stammered. 'What happened? What did you do, Avril!?' He suddenly asked, fear turning to anger as he whirled on her.

'Me!? I… I… He was just making jokes, and then, and then the walkway collapsed! I didn't do anything!' Avril defended herself desperately.

'Dammit, we should have known this place was dangerous!' Ali snapped.

'Yeah, well, I don't remember you mentioning it!' Jake yelled at her.

'Like you would have listened even if I did!' Ali countered. 'All of you! What kind of idiotic idea was it to come here, anyway!? Of *course* it was going to be dangerous!'

'Didn't stop you coming though, did it?' Jake argued back.

'Where's Kat?' Avril asked, aware that her voice was quiet. Kat would know what to do, right? She would know the answer. There had to *be* one. They just needed Kat.

'I didn't know Shelly would be dumb enough to fall through the floor!' Ali shouted.

'Oh, so now this is HIS fault? Already blaming the dead guy? Real classy, Ali!' Jake matched her volume and tone, taking a step towards her.

'Where's Kat!?' Avril asked again, this time louder, and drawing the attention of the two locked in their argument. They both span to face Avril, as if ready to answer, before they both realised at the same time neither of them knew. The argument ceased and silence descended like a blanket covering the entire hallway.

Avril looked around the house in the sudden moment of eerie silence, and largely on instinct reached for her phone.

'There's no signal!' Ali grumbled angrily. Avril remembered this, pocketing the phone again.

'Kat!? KAT!?' Todd called, striding back towards the staircase, but seeming to think better of ascending it after Shelly's fall. Only silence answered him.

'What if she's hurt too?' Avril asked in a panic.

'She was upstairs last we saw. One of us had better go up and look for her.' Jake decided, taking a deep breath and trying to calm down.

'What about Shelly!?' Avril practically shrieked.

'Well, he's not going anywhere,' Jake said, before looking away, realising that he had crossed a line. 'Uh, sorry.'

'That girl! That girl in town said she had friends!' Avril pointed out. 'Maybe they can help?'

'Yeah, or they'll think we killed him and report us for murder. We didn't exactly make a good impression on her, remember?' Ali said with a frown.

'Well, we can't just leave him!' Avril cried.

'We need to find Kat, and then we need to get out of here. Head back out of town until we get a phone signal, call the police, tell them what happened,' Todd decided, his eyes closed as he planned.

'Well, do you want to go back up there and find her!? 'cause I sure don't!' Jake argued.

'Someone's gotta, so yeah, I will,' Todd growled. 'You lot wait outside. Check your phones. Maybe one of you can get a signal out there.' he decided, turning and ascending the stairs. Avril wanted to move forward to tell him to be careful, but found her legs refusing to move. She was still frozen on the spot so she could only watch him ascend into the darkness, the stairs creaking ominously beneath his footsteps.

Ali moved towards the exit to the house, and gave the huge old wooden doors a shove. To her surprise, they didn't open.

'Huh. Door's stuck,' she said, giving it another push. This was enough to snap Avril out of her trance and get her to move towards it.

'W-what do you mean, stuck? It opened just now!' she pointed out. They had no problem getting in. 'Maybe it's locked?'

'Locked? By who?' Ali asked with a frown.

'Out of the way, you weaklings.' Jake sighed, marching past them and shoving the door himself. It still didn't budge. He gave it a look of frustration, and barged it with his shoulder, knocking it hard. Still, the door refused to yield. Ali forced down a snigger.

The amusement didn't last long however, because with a sudden repeated thud from outside the door began to jolt inwards, as if it was being battered from the outside. The trio jumped back in startled surprise, but the thumping continued, the door taking a repeated beating, straining on its hinges but somehow remaining sealed. Each thud against the door was faster than the last and always becoming increasingly aggressive, until they seemed to bypass any pace that was natural. They began to happen so quickly and so viciously that whatever it was couldn't be human, Avril began to realise. She felt her skin prickle with goose bumps and a deep gnawing fear began to knot inside her stomach. She couldn't put it into words, but she knew whatever was banging on the outside of the door was something that wasn't just *unnatural,* but something to be afraid of. It was something *evil.* Something they didn't want to get in, no matter what. A look in to Ali and Jake's eyes confirmed they felt the same way, their expressions frozen in fear, all three of them staring at the banging door.

There was a sudden crash behind them, and they all span around in shock, Avril letting loose another scream, but instead of seeing something terrifying, they saw what they expected was their salvation. A passageway had somehow blown open in the wall by the staircase. Avril was sure there hadn't been a door there before. Was it some kind of hidden passageway, perhaps? Either way, they knew it led away from the banging door, and in their fear, all three of them ran for it without even thinking twice. Beyond it in the darkness was an old wooden staircase descending into an even deeper darkness, and it was only once Avril was down that she realised they had just been perfectly shepherded into an eerie basement. She turned around, Ali almost colliding in to her, and Jake, at the rear suddenly yelping as one of the stairs split underfoot. He managed to keep moving however with a painful looking limp and blood streaming from his now injured leg, cut open by the shard of wood.

'Dammit!' he spat.

There was another crash from above, and Avril looked up to see that the passageway they had run through was now sealed. What little light that had been streaming in from the open doorway was now gone. Jake bounced up the rotting stairs the best that he could with his injury and began to pound on what now appeared to be a smooth panel of wooden wall where the entrance had been, barely lit by the light of his phone in his hand.

Avril pulled her phone out too, lighting the darkness around her, and turned, only to see a figure standing in the corner. She screamed, dropping her phone, hearing the screen crack. She backed away in utter terror, unsure of the figure she had seen, only aware of how it had *looked.* Filthy. Plastered in dust and dirt and what looked like ash, as if part of the basement itself.

Both Jake and Ali focused their own phone lights in the direction of the figure, but they didn't need to bother. There was a flash of orange light, and suddenly a soft red glow, mixed with the smell of cigarette smoke, and the figure stepped from the darkness. She was clearly a woman, in a long dark trench coat, although her entire body was plastered in the dirt and filth Avril had spotted. There was something over one of her eyes. An eyepatch, perhaps? A sudden flash of light nearly blinded Avril as she realised the woman was pointing a flashlight at them. She was flanked by one of the oddest figures she had ever seen. A Japanese woman in a frilly looking dress, only she was equally coated in filth and dirt. And beside them, she recognised the very angry looking figure of the girl they had taped to the lamppost.

'Didn't anybody ever tell you idiots? *Never* go into the creepy basement,' Nina growled. 'If I find out one of you idiots has been reciting Latin, I swear, I'm just gonna leave you to die.'

CHAPTER ELEVEN

PREVIOUSLY, ON THE LAST GIRLS STANDING...

Ellie decided that her first ever trip with Nina and Suzi hadn't really gone according to plan. She had expected some difficulty, but ending up duct taped to a lamppost certainly wasn't something she had ever considered going wrong. She couldn't decide what was more infuriating about it; that she had let them get away with it, or that she couldn't get down. When a schoolyard prank defeated you, how were you meant to stand up to ghosts and gremlins?

Fortunately, it seemed that Ellie wasn't the only one having a bad day. When Nina and Suzi appeared in her line of view, she realised that their trip through the mines hadn't exactly gone well for them either. Both were utterly coated in what appeared to be some form of dirty ash, and while Nina seemed largely unbothered, Suzi wore a thunderous expression of utter contempt at the state of herself. It didn't help that thanks to her large frilly pink dress she now looked something like a birthday cake that had been in the oven too long.

At least the sight of Ellie struggling against the duct tape must have lightened Nina's mood, because she burst out laughing hysterically the instant her one good eye met Ellie's own pair.

'Let me guess. You tried to reason with them, didn't you?' Nina said with what Ellie thought was an infuriatingly smug smile. She tried to reply, but her voice was muffled by the tape, and Suzi helpfully made her way over to tear it free, leaving Ellie wincing in pain.

'Well, what else was I supposed to do!?' she asked angrily as soon as she could speak, still squirming as Suzi set about silently freeing her from her duct tape prison. Which in itself was an amusing thing to watch, as Suzi seemed to end up sticking it to her own hand and trying to desperately shake it off without touching it with her free hand.

'Warning them never works.' Nina stepped forward to help Suzi out and get Ellie down. Once Ellie was free enough to escape, she furiously tore off the remaining duct tape, throwing it angrily to the ground. It was harder than it sounded, as it kept sticking to her, but after several frustrated tries and standing on part of it to tear it loose, she was free of the last traces of the horrible stuff. She looked at the two others covered in filth.

'Doesn't look like it went much better for you,' Ellie pointed out.

That led to Suzi beginning to retell their adventure below in the mines. Of course, she focused largely on the horrors of the fact they had gotten so dirty and that her dress was ruined, which at first Ellie considered somewhat pathetic until Nina explained a little more about their assailant. Once she'd heard that, Ellie couldn't decide if it was remarkably shallow or incredibly *badass* for Suzi to be more concerned about the state of her dress than the fact they had nearly been killed by some kind of machete handed zombie creature.

After that, things felt like they had moved fairly quickly. Despite the mysterious creatures that had plagued them so far, Nina wanted to continue onwards. Suzi was mystified, and seemed surprisingly frustrated by the fact that what they had experienced so far made no sense even by their own broad rules, but much like Nina didn't want to leave the group of teenagers to their fate, especially now that they knew the situation was so much more dangerous than a plain haunting. Ellie, despite her irritation, found herself agreeing. After all, that was why she had agreed to join them. She wanted to help people, to make a difference, to do *something* after all she'd experienced. She might have been incredibly annoyed with the teenage brats, as she thought of them, but she wasn't about to leave them to face whatever other horrors this town held.

The decision to help made, the next move was finding a way into the house. Nina explained that she didn't want to linger. Her reasoning made sense. Since it seemed that the creature they had encountered in the mines had been conclusively killed; a bullet through the head and then presumably burned up by the fire that followed it, since it was *completely impossible* for it to have survived in any way, she believed that it would most *definitely* be back.

'If it couldn't possibly have survived that, then it definitely survived that,' Nina told Ellie as if this was utterly conventional wisdom. Ellie could only nod.

They all decided that going in through the front door of the house was a bad idea, despite Ellie's suggestion that they simply burst in with their guns drawn and scare the teenagers into running away. She thought it would get rid of them, but Nina advised strongly against it. The way she explained it was that they had to be careful not to become trapped in the *story*. If they were the gun wielding psychopaths that showed up, then that made them the bad guys of the scenario. And the bad guys never survived until the end.

'These events *want* to happen. They want to occur in a certain way. That's why there's always a pattern. We can break the pattern, but if we mess up, a new pattern forms around us. We become part of the events. We become other victims,' Nina explained. Ellie wasn't sure that she entirely understood, but she nodded along. Nina was speaking with conviction, and the sad look on Suzi's face told Ellie that she had known people to become those exact victims.

So the plan, as suggested by Suzi, was to infiltrate the house by finding the secret entrance into the basement. Ellie had been surprised to hear that there was a secret entrance, and had been very impressed that Suzi knew about it. She thought perhaps Suzi had studied the house plans when she made her PowerPoint presentation. Suzi just giggled at this suggestion.

'No, silly. It's 'cause there's *always* a secret entrance to the basement of the big scary haunted house,' she explained, and Nina seemed to roll her eye at this. Ellie sighed. She had no idea how that was supposed to work; was Suzi saying the people who built this house knew that one day it would be haunted, or was it just a meaningless coincidence? Or was it just the 'story' Nina had been talking about.

Either way, Nina led them around to the back of the house and to a considerably overgrown garden. Weeds and plants grew far taller than any of the three girls, towering over them, and they smelled strongly of damp soil and wet grass. It reminded Ellie of St. Mary's Marsh. She wished things would *stop* reminding her of it, but the memories kept coming back. The three pushed their way through the plants, although Ellie wasn't too sure what they were looking for. Suzi struggled to keep up, of course, thanks to her huge dress, but at least as it was already ruined she was no longer trying desperately to preserve it from snagging thorns and leaves.

'Found it!' Nina remarked proudly. She pointed to an old gravestone, almost lost in among the weeds. The faded lettering proclaimed it the final resting place of 'Edith Campbell'. Ellie immediately recognised the name. The one time owner of this house, and their ghost suspect-in-chief.

'I thought we were looking for a way into the basement?' Ellie asked, raising an eyebrow as she eyed the old stone. Nina smirked and shook her head, as if Ellie had said something completely idiotic, and Suzi let out a high pitched giggle.

'This *is* the way in to the basement, silly.'

'Yeah, usually you're meant to come out from the other end,' Nina explained. 'Think about it, all your friends are dead, the horrible ghost is after you, you find the last minute escape route, only to burst out of the ground and find yourself right on the gravestone of the ghost itself. You're just about to win your freedom and there it is waiting for you. The big final scare.'

'And that happens a lot, does it?' Ellie asked with extreme scepticism.

'Maybe not *exactly* like that, but those kind of beats, yeah. This overgrown garden isn't a graveyard, so why is the stone here? It's gotta be the secret passage.'

'So, how do we open it?' Ellie thought it was a sensible question. Nina looked quizzical for a moment, looking around the overgrown garden, before seeming to spot something. She moved over and lifted out of the filthy weeds an old, rusty shovel, and smiled over at Ellie and Suzi.

'How'd you feel about digging?' she asked with a wry grin, heading back over and sticking it into the dirt.

'Wait, wait. Okay, I get I'm new at this whole thing, but there's some kind of story or whatever you talk about, right? Well, I mean, I'm no expert, but in a *story*, isn't digging up the grave of the person you *know* is haunting you like, a really bad idea?' Ellie was aware that her voice was edged with nerves, but even before she knew about the supernatural she wouldn't have been keen on grave digging. Now it just seemed like suicide.

'Relax, it'll be fine. She's already haunting people anyway,' Nina confirmed, before the shovel made a dull thud. 'Ah, look, a door hidden just beneath the soil. Give me a hand.' She quickly got down on her hands and knees and started scraping the filth away. Ellie sighed, not keen to join in, but doing so anyway, not wanting to seem squeamish. The soil was thick and wet and pushing it aside to reveal the rotting wooden door beneath disturbed hundreds of ants, which all seemed to squirm for shelter. The damp dirt began to get under Ellie's fingernails, and she knew she'd spend hours later on trying to get it all out.

'You gonna help?' she asked Suzi as she cleared away the dirt.

'I don't wanna get dirty!' Suzi protested, which given she was still covered head to toe in ash was somewhat silly, Ellie thought. She made that thought clear just by giving her a plain stare, and Suzi sighed, coming over to join the group, although her contribution was so minimal since she was squirming to avoid the ants and trying not to get her hands any dirtier she might as well of remained standing. All her bending down next to the group achieved was introducing Ellie to the bizarre scent that was Suzi's once overpowering perfume now apparently dampened by ash, creating the strangest battle of two scents she had ever experienced, Suzi's sweet, candy scent and the choking smell of burning battling each other at the same time.

It wasn't long until they had uncovered not only the door, but a huge metal rung built into it as well. Ellie and Suzi stood back as Nina took it and heaved. The wood strained, and for a moment Ellie thought the rusty metal rung would tear right out of the rotting wood of the door, but with a mighty creak it opened, revealing a darkened passage within, leading down old, equally rotting steps.

Nina immediately moved around to the far side of the newly opened basement entrance, and shone her torch at an angle inside.

'What's she doing?' Ellie asked Suzi as they both stood back up.

'Checking under the stairs. You don't just walk down a staircase like that in a haunted house, or something might grab your ankles,' Suzi answered as if it was common sense while largely preoccupied with futile efforts to clean wet soil from her dress, a process that Ellie was aware was utterly pointless since she was still plastered in ash.

'Looks clear,' Nina confirmed. 'Let's go.' Nina strode down with confidence, not even blinking as she practically bounced down the old wooden steps. Suzi followed, albeit more cautiously. It seemed for all her experience, Suzi still exhibited caution when heading down the old rotting staircase. Which she couldn't exactly be blamed for, Ellie thought as she followed, last and slowest, taking each step carefully, aware of the stairs painfully creaking as she moved. 'Watch the third step,' Nina said just as Ellie put her foot on it and the wood broke. She recoiled, just managing to get her footing. A second later and she'd have gone right through. She hated to think of the mess the shards of wood would have made to her leg. She readjusted her balance and took a wider step down over the shattered wood.

'I always thought it was the fourth step,' Suzi said as Ellie hurried to catch up with them.

'Nah, it's usually the third,' Nina countered.

'Uh, what?' Was all Ellie could ask, annoyed that she had nearly fallen through the staircase and they had only just warned her.

'Oh, last one down an old staircase like that, a step always breaks. Usually the third. C'mon, that's just common sense,' Nina shrugged as she led their way down the dark passageway.

Ellie sighed and rolled her eyes, shaking some wooden fragments off of her jeans. Sure, common sense. Of *course*. She followed them down the short darkened path which seemed to be leading under the garden. She looked up in the darkness, using her phone light again to illuminate the ceiling, able to see the roots of weeds and even the odd tree poking through the muddy ceiling. The odd drop of damp, muddy water dripped down with an echoing splash. She didn't have much time to focus on that, however, as the passageway was short, and at the end was an old, heavy, rotting wooden door that appeared to have come free of its hinges slightly. It was resting roughly against the stone slabs that made up the ground and was in even worse condition than the doorway they'd found under the soil. This meant that Nina had to firmly push it to open it, the wood making a loud scraping noise on the floor as it did so. She paused, for a moment apparently worried that the scraping had alerted the teens, or worse, the spirit. A silent beat passed, and Nina seemed to decide the coast was clear, gesturing for the other two to join her.

Ellie hurried out of the tunnel, glad to be away from it, unable to shake the feeling that the soil overhead would collapse on her at any moment. She went to move forward, but a sudden thumping sound from overhead stopped her in her tracks.

'Shh!' Nina gestured for her to join her and Suzi in a darkened corner, and waved to put her phone away to hide the light.

A few desperate moments passed as the trio stood sheltered in the pitch black darkness of the basement. It occurred to Ellie that hiding in total darkness was probably not the best plan, not in a haunted house anyway, and she didn't like the thought of what might be moving beyond the darkness. The thought didn't last long, however, before a crash from upstairs alerted them that the basement door had been opened, and three frightened looking teens hurried down a rotting flight of wooden stairs.

Ellie noticed that the third one seemed to splinter on the last of the teens to head down, and he cursed as he injured his leg. She tried not to give Nina the satisfaction of showing that she had noticed that. She went to move forward, but again Nina held her back, and she could just make in the shadows Nina gesturing for her to be silent. The doorway sealed behind them, and the one with the injured leg ran back up the stairs, hammering on the sealed opening uselessly. The blonde cheerleader type, as Ellie knew her, lifted her phone to look in the darkness and shone it directly into Nina's face.

The cheerleader screamed, and jumped back, dropping her phone. Nina seemed to take that as her cue, lighting a cigarette and stepping forward out of the darkness with dramatic flair.

'Didn't anybody ever tell you idiots? *Never* go into the creepy basement,' she growled. 'If I find out any of your idiots have been reciting Latin, I swear, I'm just gonna leave you to die.' Beside Ellie, she could see Suzi rolling her eyes.

'She likes to make an entrance,' Suzi explained in a whisper.

CHAPTER TWELVE

THE HAUNTED MANSION

'Who the hell are you!?' the one with the buzz cut growled towards Nina, taking an aggressive step forward, clearly ignoring the shooting pain in his bleeding leg. Nina didn't even flinch, cigarette dangling from her lips.

'I'm the one who's gonna save your life. If you shut up and do as I say,' she replied dismissively. Suzi let out an audible groan and stepped forward.

'She's just being dramatic! She's Nina. I'm Suzi. This is Ellie. We're here to help,' Suzi explained.

'Help? Help with what?' the Latina girl in the leather jacket asked with suspicion in her eyes, as if she was hiding some secret. She exchanged a glance with the one in the buzz cut, but before either could act, the blonde cheerleader pushed past them, hurrying to Suzi.

'Our friend is dead! It was an accident, I swear! None of us did anything, but he fell, and he... he...' she burst into tears, and Suzi moved quietly forward to give her a hug. Nina looked over to Ellie, a simple glance that told Ellie she was beginning to understand.

'No it wasn't,' Nina said with a shake of her head. The Latina girl, the one Ellie thought of as "the tough one", took this offensively, clearly, as she stepped forward and marched towards Nina, fire flashing in her eyes.

'How the hell do you know!? Were you there!? He fell! None of us had anything to do with it!' she yelled angrily.

'I never said *you* did,' Nina replied, still as cool as a cucumber, still drawing on that cigarette. 'But that doesn't mean it was an accident.' This seemed to defuse the angry spark in the Latina girl for a moment.

'What?' she asked sharply. The cheerleader was still crying in to Suzi's arms, and the one with the buzz cut was clearly beginning to feel the effects of his injured leg.

Nina sighed, flicking the cigarette away and bringing out her flashlight, helping to light the dim basement. All Ellie's eyes could make out were various jars on old shelving and large wooden crates, all covered in decades worth of dust, filling every corner.

'I tried to warn you!' Ellie couldn't keep it in. 'This place, it's *haunted,*' she insisted. The tough one scoffed at this, turning away with an angry laugh.

'Screw you. This is serious!' she countered.

'So am I!' Ellie argued. 'Look, you saw the door slam behind you! What did you think was going on?'

'That was just the wind!' the angry girl shouted back, and Ellie couldn't help but notice that Nina casually mimed the words "the wind" along with her as she said it, finding her answer so predictable.

'Shut up and listen to me,' Nina said simply, fixing the group with her one eye. 'It wasn't the wind. Your friend didn't die because the ground broke. This place is haunted. Let me guess, you idiots decided to split up, right?' she asked, aware that there were a lot less people than Ellie had made out.

'W-well, our friend, Kat, she went missing, and Todd, m-my boyfriend, went to look for her,' the blonde sniffled, leaving Suzi's grasp and wiping away the tears that were thick with mascara goop.

'Uh huh.' Nina nodded. 'Hate to break it to you, but they're probably dead already.'

'Don't you dare say something like that!' the blonde said through angry tears, the mascara streaking down her face now.

'Come off it, what, the blonde ditz, the fiery rebel and the jock's best friend walk into haunted house? What did you *think* was going to happen?' Nina asked angrily.

'I-I'm not a *ditz*! My name is *Avril*!' the cheerleader snapped. 'And that's Ali and Jake, and we're not some… dumb teenagers, okay!? We were just here to have a good time.'

'You came to an ancient abandoned house in the middle of nowhere, from which nobody has ever returned, for a "good time". Yeah, you're definitely *dumb teenagers,*' Nina shot back. 'But if you shut up and listen to me, you might not be *dead teenagers*, you got it?'

'You're being god damned ridiculous!' the one called Ali yelled back at Nina. 'Our friend had a horrible accident, that's all! This place isn't 'haunted'! You're all nuts! There's no such thing as ghosts!'

As soon as she finished yelling, there was a sudden flicker as the flashlight began to fade, flickering and battling to stay on. It was a battle that it appeared to be losing. Instinctively, Ellie reached for her phone light, but to her dismay, the screen was flickering on and off on there too. She noticed the same was happening to the others, all of whom were trying to produce their own light. Except for Nina, who simply seemed to let out a heavy sigh.

'You had to say it, didn't you?' she muttered, before turning to Ellie and looking her directly in the eye. 'Never, ever, say "there's no such thing as ghosts" in a haunted house. It's like saying "there's no way it could have survived that". Luckily, none of us here are dumb enough to say *that*, at least.' Ellie looked away guiltily, for the briefest moment thinking of Danny and the events of St. Mary's Marsh.

Ali looked like she was ready to offer a counter argument, but stopped when the flickering of all the available lights stopped, every device failing and plunging the group into collective darkness. A few moments of silence passed. Ellie could hear somebody, she assumed Avril, sniffling, and somebody else breathing hard, she guessed Jake, by the more masculine sounds. She also heard a very quiet countdown. Nina. Barely audible, under her breath, was very calmly counting down.

'Three... Two... One....' As soon as Nina finished, the lights flickered back on, but this time, something new was stood in the middle of the group. Its back was to Ellie, so she couldn't quite get a good look at it, and its form was hard to read, but it definitely had the shape of a person. It almost appeared to be a shadow, but one that somehow stood up within the air itself, free of any surface. She thought she could make out the remains of a tattered jacket, the shadowy texture bringing to mind tweed, and what she thought looked like some kind of workman's cap on the thing's head. She stared for what felt like several minutes, but must have been less than a second, before the thing made its move. It jerked forward, away from Ellie, but directly towards Avril, where it let out a haunting, high pitched scream in her face so deafening that Ellie found herself moving to cover her ears.

There was another flicker, and the collective lights went out, plunging the room back in to darkness, before slowly they flickered back into life, the torch slowly brightening, and everything in the room was back to normal, except for Avril, who had turned chalk white. Her eyes were wide and she was breathing hard as she looked among the group. Both Ali and Jake looked equally terrified, and Ellie couldn't help but notice that Jake had somehow taken several steps back towards the staircase, despite them being sealed inside. Nina, on the other hand, had an expression that Ellie could only describe as "bored". Suzi, perhaps, surprised her the most. She still showed no signs of being the typical, squealing girly girl who would shriek and be terrified at the sign of any danger that Ellie always expected from her. The expression she wore on her face instead was merely one of curiosity, as if she was thinking carefully about what had just happened. As if she was analysing the scenario over and over again in her head. It didn't matter how often she saw it, Ellie was always stunned by Suzi's apparent calmness in the face of the bizarre and supernatural.

'What the hell was that thing!?' Avril shrieked, apparently nowhere near as calm as either of Ellie's companions.

'I think, uh, that would be the ghost we were warning you about,' Ellie couldn't resist speaking up.

'What did it want with me!?' Avril asked, in panic, obviously desperate to work out why it had shrieked at her directly.

'Oh, come on. You're the pretty blonde one. Monsters, ghosts, demons, you name it, they all have one thing in common. They prefer blondes,' Nina explained wearily, walking forward past the group and towards the staircase. She noticed that Nina did her regular check of it, quickly glancing under it, before making her way up. Ellie watched the assembled teenagers come together in the middle of the room, close, as if forming some kind of defensive huddle without quite realising it. The three 'damsels', Ellie thought to herself. That's what Nina would have called them.

'That was a man,' Suzi spoke up, moving closer to Nina, and shooting a glance at Ellie. 'I mean, still a ghost, obvs, but a man ghost. A ghost man. Ghman?' she suggested, trying a smile, which faded when she realised nobody laughed.

'I think I flunked "spiritual gender studies", but yeah, definitely looked like a man to me.' Ellie agreed.

'Well? Blondie, you got the best look at it, was it a man?' Nina asked from the top of the staircase, where she seemed to be examining the sealed door. Avril looked up, still incredibly pale, making the thick black lines of mascara that ran down her face from her tears stand out even more.

'W-what?' Avril stammered. Ali looked over at Suzi.

'Why does it matter?' Ali asked suspiciously.

'Well, we came here to fight a *girl ghost*. Not a *boy ghost*,' Suzi explained, as if it was obvious. Ellie, who was much newer to the horrific world the two girls inhabited, felt a pang of sympathy for Avril and her friends. She knew how strange this must have all seemed.

'It was definitely a man,' Avril said a moment later, some colour returning to her cheeks, her breathing steadying as she tried to find her strength. 'God, I could smell his breath.'

'Well, we only assumed the ghost was this Edith Campbell, right? What if it's somebody else?' Ellie suggested.

'Could be. Doesn't feel right, though,' Nina said quietly. 'None of this does.' A pause passed, and suddenly she turned around, bounding down the steps to join the group. 'Right then.' she said with a sudden energy. 'Ghosts are real, you've seen one, great. Now's the part where it picks you off one by one until you're all dead. *Or*, you can go out the secret exit. The way we came in. Right there,' she pointed at the dark tunnel, where the door still hung off of its hinges. 'Most people don't get that chance. But now we're here, and things are changing. So, leave, while you can. If your friends are still alive, we'll save them. And if they're not, well, we can get revenge for you. Either way, this whole thing? It's about to end,' Nina promised, and Ellie had to admit she sounded impressive. Ellie definitely didn't want to mess with her.

Jake, Ali and Avril all exchanged glances, and Jake immediately headed towards the tunnel.

'You don't have to tell me twice. Let's get out of here!' he said eagerly. Ali seemed to pause, and turned to join him.

'Yeah, okay, I dunno what the hell is going on here, but I'm not staying here a moment longer,' she insisted. Only Avril remained, glancing between the two groups.

'You two go. I'm going with them,' she nodded towards Ellie and the others. Ellie gave her a surprised look. She hadn't expected that.

'What? Avril, are you insane!?' Ali asked. 'We don't even know these guys! For all we know, this is some set up or something! This is our chance to get out of here!'

'It's not a set up. I saw that thing's eyes...' Avril said, and Ellie recognised the expression on her face. It was the expression you wore when you'd stared into the face of unspeakable horror, when you knew that evil was *real* and facing you, and when despite all of that, you were fed up with running, and wanted to start fighting. She knew that moment only too well.

'You sure about this? It's not safe, and I can't promise I can keep you alive,' Nina said to Avril directly. Avril nodded.

'My boyfriend's up there. And if there's any chance to save him, I've gotta try,' she explained. 'Besides, you might need bait, and I'm the only blonde here.' she pointed out, fanning out her hair as if to emphasise the point. Ellie looked to Suzi and Nina in surprise at Avril's sudden courage. Suzi was smiling with delight, but Nina simply wore a tiny, small half smirk dancing on her dark lips. As if she recognised something in Avril. Ellie remembered the photograph of Nina from her social media page, pretty with blonde hair. Maybe Nina really *did* recognise something in Avril? The girl she had once been.

An uncertain moment passed, but Ali moved forward, and gave Avril a hug.

'Good luck. We'll be waiting for you,' she said bluntly. Well, so much for the others following Avril's brave example, Ellie thought.

'Yeah, yeah, see ya…' Jake didn't even approach, and was already disappearing down the tunnel. Ali quickly followed.

Avril turned back to the group and nodded.

'So, what do we do now?' She asked, hands on her hips in what was obviously an attempt to look confident.

'We find your friends, or what's left of them. Get them out if we can. Then we burn this entire place to the ground,' Nina answered simply.

'And how do we do that?' Avril asked. Ellie looked over at Nina, curious for the answer herself.

'As quickly as possible,' Nina replied with a grin, reaching into her rucksack and removing her machete. She wedged it in the sealed door and began to prise it open.

'She knows that's not what I meant, right?' Avril asked Ellie with a slightly suffering look.

'Oh yeah, she definitely knows it.' Ellie smiled back, and with a sudden crack, the sealed wooden panels came free, breaking open and revealing a way out of the basement. Nina smiled at her handiwork, and made her way through the broken opening back in to the mansion proper. Ellie followed, and then Avril.

'Help! I'm stuck!' The three girls turned to see Suzi's big dress had failed to fit through the small broken opening Nina had created, and she was trying to struggle through. Avril, who was closest, grabbed her arms and pulled her through, and the two exchanged a slight smile of familiarity.

'Wow. Ali said what I was wearing was impractical,' Avril remarked, before taking in the full extent of Suzi's ruined dress.

'I'm usually a lot prettier than this,' Suzi said, clearly upset that her clothing was still wrecked.

'Hey, it's a cute outfit. I like it,' Avril remarked. Ellie sighed.

'Okay, uh, I know Nina's in charge, but can we maybe stop discussing fashion?' Ellie asked, her gaze falling on the dead body, impaled over on wooden ruins. Avril fell silent looking over at the corpse, and her eyes filled with tears again. 'Is that your friend? The one who had the accident?' Ellie guessed. Avril nodded uneasily, trying to swallow her fear, guilt and shame, but seeing the body again was clearly bringing unpleasant memories flooding back.

'Body hasn't moved. That's probably a good sign. No zombies or anything here. Just a ghost,' Nina analysed. Ellie never thought her life would reach a point where 'no zombies' was a practical factor she had to consider, but here she was.

'Plus it means the ghost isn't gonna do that cheap, drop the body on you scare thing they sometimes do,' Suzi offered, again completely practical and serious about it, which was still unbelievably surreal to Ellie. It seemed like it was to Avril as well, who gave them both a baffled look. Ellie realised she wasn't exactly the newbie anymore. Compared to Avril, anyway.

Ellie wasn't sure if she was happy or sad about that.

'We need to find your friends,' Ellie decided it was the best course of action. She was sure that Nina had written them off as dead already and was just thinking of a way to beat whatever was haunting them, but Ellie refused to give up that easily. Maybe Nina was right, and maybe there were rules to how these things played out, but life wasn't just a *story*. It was real, it was unpredictable, and it was wild. Besides, even if you accepted that these supernatural entities followed a narrative like in horror movies, Ellie knew of plenty of horror films where the heroes rescued a victim from the killer. Hell, even Jason Voorhees was kidnapping girls instead of killing them in his new reboot.

'They went upstairs, but it's pretty big. Maybe we should split up? We could cover more ground that way,' Avril suggested. Nina and Suzi gave her immediate, identical deadpan looks.

'I *cannot believe* you just said that,' Nina sighed heavily.

'What?' Avril asked innocently.

'There are rules if you want to survive. You've seen bad horror movies, right? Never do any of the dumb stuff the kids do in those,' Ellie explained, surprising herself by offering the explanation. She noticed that Nina gave a look of approval. Was it even pride, perhaps?

'I'm not really… a horror movie fan,' Avril admitted.

'Hey, it's easy. You never, ever split up, you never ever say "there's no way it could have survived that", you never get changed in the house with the curtains open, you never ever read anything in Latin out loud, you know, stuff like that,' Suzi explained helpfully.

'Oh, I think I get it. Like, how you should never say "It's quiet... Too quiet..."?' Avril asked, complete with a deeply voiced impression of what she imagined somebody in a horror movie would sound like.

Unfortunately, the point only seemed to be proven when a door overhead slammed hard, causing all four of the girls to start, looking up in surprise. Even Nina seemed caught off-guard. The entire foyer seemed to plunge into darkness, which this time only served to mystify Ellie. Lights failing in the basement had made sense, but the foyer had huge windows. Yes, they were largely boarded up, but the old glass was still in place too, and cracks of light had been sneaking through from the setting sun outside. But now the glass just looked black, as if somebody had thrown a tarp over the entire building. Flashlights and phones flickered into life as each of the girls sought for a way to see, and Ellie, holding her own cell phone out, approached one of the old windows, curious to see what would happen if she shone her light through it, trying to work out if she could cut through the mysterious artificial darkness that had suddenly surrounded them.

She edged closer to the boarded up window and pushed her phone against a gap between two hastily assembled pieces of wood, allowing her to see the dusty glass and the blackness outside. The light from her phone's built in LED flashlight caught the darkness, and then, suddenly, there were two glowing yellow eyes looking back at her. Like the eyes of a cat catching the light, they reflected back at her, bright yellow, with slits for pupils. The eyes darted up, peering through the glass, and made contact with Ellie's own. She felt a chill run down her spine as they made contact. She jumped backwards with a slight shriek, the light from her phone disappearing from the window, and with it, the eyes were gone.

Her own shriek made Avril let out an involuntary shriek, and Suzi rushed to her side.

'What was it?' she asked, shining her own phone light at the window. But as Suzi's light made contact with it, it seemed the darkness receded, letting in eerie shafts of purple light from the evening outside. Ellie realised she was still breathing hard.

'Eyes. I saw… eyes,' she answered. Nina was heading over, even as Suzi was (with impressive bravery, Ellie thought) checking the window for clues.

'Eyes?' Nina repeated, her tone somewhere between sceptical and curious.

'Yeah. Like, cat eyes, but huge!'

'M-maybe it was just a cat, outside?' Avril stammered, heading over to join them. Ellie thought she sounded hopeful. She wanted that to be the case. Ellie didn't blame her. Nobody wanted it to be anything else.

'It definitely wasn't a cat,' Ellie answered, although she wasn't sure how she knew that. She could simply *feel* it.

'Well, the good news is that you're still alive,' Nina remarked. Ellie turned, feeling a sudden rush of anger.

'Oh, y'think? Yeah, it's definitely good news!' she found herself shouting, the adrenaline from the shock having nowhere else to go.

'I mean, it means they're still pulling that scare-tactic crap,' Nina sighed, as if the need to explain herself was somehow a massive inconvenience. 'I mean, c'mon. You wander off from the group to check something spooky out, and it *doesn't* kill you, just scares you?'

'Hey, we were all checking out that weird stuff. Why would what I do matter?'

'Oh god, don't make me say it,' Nina sighed painfully.

'What?' Ellie asked, folding her arms with irritation, having a feeling she knew exactly what was coming.

'You're... *black,*' Nina said awkwardly, her single eye refusing to make contact with Ellie's. It was as close to sheepish as Ellie had ever seen her.

'Oh. Right. Yeah. Let me guess, the black girl always dies first, right?' Ellie said sarcastically, anger in her voice.

'Well, not *first,* I mean, uh, look at him.' Suzi put in, trying to be supportive. She pointed to the corpse of Shelly, which was probably not a good idea, because it seemed to only upset Avril.

'Yeah, well, last time I checked, I was the last survivor of St Mary's Marsh, and I didn't have anybody to help me then,' Ellie pointed out, irritation burning within her. She wasn't sure who she was angrier at, Nina for bringing it up, or the ghost haunting them for possibility targeting her purely over her race.

'Yeah, uh, well, that's 'cause you're kind of a badass,' Nina said, and Ellie gave her a look that she hoped conveyed that she was perfectly aware Nina was trying to butter her up and compliment her after upsetting her. 'Plus, y'know, those aren't hard and fast rules. I mean, people surprise you! Suzi's Japanese *and* a huge girly girl. By standards of *stories*, she should be dead before we reach the second act. If she'd even be there at all!'

'Uh huh,' Ellie said dryly, and it was clear that she wasn't particularly buying this. 'I know you think this story stuff is important, but it's sounding more and more like bull to me.'

'Look, whatever. Believe me, don't believe me. Just, please be careful?' Nina sighed, and she sounded genuine. Despite how much she had irritated Ellie with her comments, she had to nod. She could tell that despite it all, some part of Nina genuinely cared. 'My point is, the ghost didn't kill any of us. It's just scaring us. That means we still have time.'

'You mean my friends might still be alive?' Avril asked.

'Yeah, if we're lucky,' Nina nodded. 'We'd better get upstairs. Start looking for them.'

Nina led the way to the staircase, with Suzi close behind. Ellie and Avril took up the rear, although Ellie had to admit, part of her was there out of stubbornness. She was pretty sure Nina would tell her that in *stories* the person at the back of the group got picked off first, and she was determined to prove to Nina that wasn't true by being there herself and being fine.

'Kat!? Todd!?' Avril called out into the silence of the upstairs hallway, her voice echoing down dusty, old corridors. 'Where are you guys!?' She seemed to break away from the group a little, searching. Ellie moved a bit faster to stick close to her, although she had no idea what she was supposed to do if the ghost did reveal itself.

'Avril!' A voice called from a door leading off in to an extended hallway, the west wing of the large house. Avril span around, a smile lightly up her features.

'Todd!' She said, practically running towards the door.

Nina leapt in, grabbing her and holding her back, blocking her passage. Avril looked up with hurt and offence in to Nina's singular eye.

'Let me go! It's Todd!' She insisted.

'Yeah, 'cause a disembodied voice in a haunted house is always your missing boyfriend,' Nina replied harshly, and Ellie felt like she was taking out frustration with herself on Avril. It wasn't really helping Ellie's opinion of her at that moment.

'It's him! I'd know that voice anywhere!' Avril insisted.

'Uh, well, there's no harm in being careful, right?' Suzi tried to mediate, and Ellie walked over to join her.

'They're... probably right, Avril,' Ellie sighed. 'I mean, after all we've seen, are you really gonna just blindly trust something you heard in this place?' Avril paused, seeming to consider this.

'Avril! Help! I'm hurt!' The voice came again, and this was enough to cause Avril to break away and run into the darkness.

'I'm coming Todd!' She yelled.

Nina, Suzi and Ellie all exchanged a look.

'Dammit,' Nina sighed.

CHAPTER THIRTEEN

ADDING AN S IS GREAT ESCALATION

Ellie couldn't help but be proud of how they all had responded. Without a word or a question, Ellie, Suzi and Nina all moved into the same darkness, chasing after the rapidly disappearing Avril. Instantly, a team. There was a slight pause when Ellie and Suzi tried to go through the doorway together, an impossibility thanks to Suzi's huge dress, but once they had detangled themselves they made it through to the other side.

Somehow, Ellie wasn't surprised that Avril was already gone.

Instead, all she could see was a darkened hallway, with multiple doors running along either wall, and a faint, flickering blue light, as if a ghostly candle was fighting valiantly back against the inky blackness. Ellie paused just behind Nina, who was obviously taking in the multiple doors.

'If I see that ghost chasing a bunch of kids and a dog from door to door, I'm out,' Ellie grumbled.

'Huh?' Suzi asked, looking confused.

'Seriously? Your house looks like you live in an actual cartoon but you missed the *Scooby Doo* reference?' Ellie laughed a little.

'Ohhhh. Yeah. Totally missed that. Ha! It does kinda look like that,' Suzi's smile disappeared as she realised things were actually serious. Nina waved a hand to hush them. The trio stood in silence, listening for a moment. There was no hint of sound from anywhere.

'Alright, let's start checking doors,' Nina decided, moving towards the closest side door. Just as her hand reached for it, however, the door burst open of its own volition, causing Nina to jump back and collide with Suzi and Ellie. Before any of them could react, something burst from the dark room and turned to face them, before screaming directly at them.

Ellie was aware that she had screamed back in shock, and a few moments passed before she realised it wasn't a ghost that stood before her, but a *girl*. Not Avril, but not just any other girl either. She recognised her. The tall redhead who had been with the gang of teenagers when they had tied her to the lamp post.

'You!' Ellie remarked.

'You!' the redhead replied. A moment passed as the two shared a moment of animosity, but also relief that they were all, apparently, human.

'You must be Kat, right?' Nina asked. The redhead, who was indeed Kat, turned and seemed a little taken aback by Nina's scarred appearance, which looked all the more intimidating in the low light. She nodded after only a brief moment of hesitation.

'Y-yeah. Who are you guys?'

'We're friends of Avril's!' Suzi said cheerfully, although Ellie wasn't sure 'friends' was the right term. They'd just met. Then again, Suzi seemed the type to befriend anybody she had more than a five minute conversation with.

'I tried to warn you. Remember? We're here to help,' Ellie said instead, deciding that explanation would make more sense, since Kat most definitely *knew* that Ellie had only just met Avril. And that they hadn't exactly been friendly when they had met. She resisted the urge to add an "I told you so".

'Help? How are you gonna do that!? Do you even know what this place is?' Kat asked desperately. Nina seemed to give a dry smile.

'Don't worry, we can handle a ghost. But our first priority is finding where Avril ran off to and then getting you both out of here.'

'Avril's missing? Where are the others?' Kat asked, before pausing, and looking back at Nina with a slightly puzzled look. 'Wait. Did you say *a ghost*?'

'Yeah. What did you think was happening here? A reality TV show?' Nina replied sarcastically.

'No, no, I mean, *a* ghost? You think there's just one?' Kat asked this in shock, looking between the three as if they were complete idiots.

Ellie exchanged a puzzled look between Suzi and Nina. Suzi had an expression of dread, and Nina a look of sudden realisation.

'Ghosts! Of course! Ghosts, plural!' she said, snapping her fingers and turning to face the others as she understood. Suddenly, she whirled on Kat. 'Wait, you've seen them?'

'Y-yeah, loads of them. But, well, they keep ignoring me. They slam doors. Make it dark. But they just sort of, flicker by, like I'm not there. I don't know why,' she explained. 'They... they were after Todd. I saw them all descend on him, and-' She paused, swallowing tears. 'They strung him up and... and... Oh my god. They hanged him. I saw... him struggling, running out of breath. I-I didn't know what to do! I ran and I hid, and... God, I don't know.' she sobbed.

'Loads? How many?' Nina asked. Ellie found herself glaring, feeling the need to interfere, putting a hand on Nina's shoulder.

'She just lost someone. Give her a moment.'

'This is *important*. How many?' Nina asked. 'You said loads of ghosts. How many did you see?'

'I-I don't know! It was like I was standing in a crowd, except they were all flickering, moving, changing. Some were shadows and some looked like people, except in really odd, old timey clothes. They moved like a tide, all around Todd. It's like there were hundreds of them!' she explained between tears.

'Hundreds?' Nina shot Suzi and Ellie a concerned look. 'That's…'

'More than there were people living here, definitely,' Suzi nodded after a moment's thought. Ellie quickly caught up with their train of thought. They were thinking the house was full of all the spirits of the people who had lived there under Edith, but that didn't match up with the amount of spirits Kat said she saw.

'Why would hundreds of ghosts be here?' Nina asked, trying to think, while Suzi at least moved to comfort the sobbing Kat.

Ellie, for her part, found herself lost in thought. She had an idea. Was it a crazy thought? She wasn't sure.

'When Edith Campbell was alive, she took in all the lost and lonely, right? That's what this place was, wasn't it? She took in anybody without a home, adult and child alike,' Ellie began, talking slowly, somewhat nervously. 'So, why would she stop doing that, just because she was a ghost?' Ellie asked. Kat looked between the trio, for a moment her curiosity breaking through her tears.

'What do you mean?' she asked, sniffing.

'The woman who used to run this place, before the mine fire, before the town got shut down, she took people in. People who had nowhere to go,' Nina began to explain. 'So you're thinking, what, she does that for ghosts now? This is like, an orphanage for *ghosts*?'

'Or a retirement home. Or, hell, I don't know, a vacation spot,' Ellie speculated.

'Ohh, like Disneyland for ghosts? A place to go and scare people for funsies?' Suzi suggested.

'I mean, I guess. It's perfect, right? Abandoned town, huge mansion, ghost lady who always took in anybody. It makes sense,' Ellie went on.

'Uh, you make them sound, well, *nice*. But they *killed my friends,*' Kat said, butting in angrily. 'A-and if we don't find Avril soon, they'll kill her too!'

'She's got a point. We can figure this out later. For now, we've got a cheerleader to rescue,' Nina nodded.

'Save the cheerleader, save the world?' Ellie grumbled under her breath, slightly sarcastically. She couldn't resist the reference.

'Ohh! *Heroes*! I know that one!' Suzi seemed thrilled she caught one of Ellie's pop culture references. Ellie was a little impressed. After all, it hadn't even been a Disney reference.

'Why does everybody assume she's a cheerleader as soon as they meet her?' Kat sighed.

'Are we wrong?' Nina asked, raising her single visible eyebrow.

'Well, no,' Kat admitted.

'Right then. Let's go. Save the cheerleader. Defeat an army of ghosts. How hard can it be?' Nina asked with a smirk, leading them further down the darkened hallway.

Nina paused after only a few steps, throwing up a hand. Ellie paused along with the others, for a split second puzzled, but feeling what had halted Nina's tracks almost immediately afterwards. She had often read that people insisted that a wave of cold air passed over you when ghosts were present. Horror movies often showed it as people's breath condensing, or give you a dramatic shot of somebody getting goose bumps on their skin. While

Ellie *did* feel her skin prickle, that wasn't what she would have used to describe the coldness she felt. Everything dropped in temperature so suddenly and so drastically it was a true shock to the system. It was the kind of cold that chilled your bones, that you couldn't escape, that you couldn't ignore, that got so deep inside of you that there was nothing you could do warm yourself back up. It made her feel dizzy. Even a little sick. It made her want to run away and hide under her bed covers, snug and warm and safe forever. It made her want to do anything but carry on moving forward.

And yet that was exactly what Nina signalled to do, gesturing to the nearest door. Ellie watched as Nina slid the sleeve of her trench coat down over her hand, as if to protect herself from the metal door handle. She realised that she must be doing so to protect herself from the cold, in case the metal was so freezing her hand would stick to it. She turned the handle, gestured for the others to follow her inside, and threw the door open.

Ellie rushed in immediately behind Nina. Suzi followed, at least this time forming a decent marching order to prevent issues with getting through the door, thanks to her attire. Kat was the last one to follow, but Ellie couldn't blame her. She hadn't signed on for this, and it took all of Ellie's will power to keep moving forward. She couldn't imagine what Kat was going through.

That was a lie. She knew exactly what Kat was going through, because she'd been there herself. She'd been the victim without a clue as to what was happening. She'd gotten through it. She had to have faith that Kat could too.

She wasn't able to reflect on this for long, however, because what she saw immediately tore her mind away from any rational thought. The memory of Nina proudly stating that ghosts liked to take things slow, build up scares and take their time flickered into her mind like an unwanted memory of a catchy song, because what she saw was the complete opposite of that.

There were ghosts. And they were definitely *ghosts*. Ellie had expected perhaps tricks of the light, things you couldn't be *certain* were real, the type of things that people could deny. But not here. What she saw were undeniably ghosts. Dozens of them. Translucent white bodies, moving like a storm, putting Ellie in mind of the thrashing of a vicious mosh pit from a concert she had attended a year ago. Some were clearly humanoid, she could make out a glimpse of a tweed jacket, a floral dress, long hair or a flat cap, all period clothing, but from a whole range of time periods. For a moment she thought she glimpsed a medieval knight. Others were somehow worse, figures that your eyes couldn't quite focus on, like moving shadows, definitely there, and solid, but only darkness in the shape of featureless humanoids. Those were the ones that chilled Ellie's bones even deeper than the cold air. There was something about the way they moved, as if they had forgotten how to walk, but with every step were trying to remember. And in the middle of them all, in a swirl of the ghostly vapours, there was Avril, being levitated into the air. Ellie looked up, and saw a long rope dangling from the rafters. They were lifting her up to hang her!

Everything seemed to happen so fast that Ellie couldn't quite keep track of it all. She wasn't sure what the others were doing, but knew she didn't have time to ask. She had to do something to help Avril. She began to take in the room, tearing her eyes away from the spirits, realising that they were in what appeared to be an old library. Bookshelves lined the walls, although they were almost entirely devoid of books now, apart from a few dusty volumes. She spotted resting against one of the bookshelves what appeared to be a rotting wooden stool. Obviously it had once been used to put books up on the higher shelves, but now she saw it as her best chance to reach Avril. She ran towards it, aware that the ghosts were passing around her, or possibly even *through* her, the coldness of their presence sinking even deeper into her bones. Her muscles tensed, nearly frozen by the cold, and yet she knew she had to push on. She made it to the stool and grabbed it, turning to rush with it towards the central mass. Right where Avril was being suspended.

Time seemed to slow down as Ellie approached and the ghosts released Avril, leaving her to fall, the rope going taught. Avril let out a strangled yelp as the rope pulled tight, and she began to kick and struggle, choking as she lost oxygen. Ellie got closer, and she knew in that moment that she was going to make it in time. She was going to save her. But then, all of a sudden, before she could reach the struggling girl, something changed. Several of the spirits snapped to face her, and she suddenly became aware of their glaring, ghostly pale eyes. In an instant, before she could even fathom what had happened, she felt her body drop to even colder temperatures, and realised that she was now flying through the air. She slammed into the old bookshelves painfully, wooden fragments splintering around her as she collapsed to the ground. Agony shot through her back. She tried to focus through blurred vision, seeing where the stool had fallen, so close but feeling so far away with the burning pain and the spirits advancing. She tried to find Nina or Suzi, but only made out a heap of trench coat flying past as Nina slammed into a wall herself. Her eyes scanned for Suzi, who seemed to be dangling upside down, trapped in some ethereal force, her long dress and apparent multiple petticoats hanging down all around her obscuring her features. Only her pink hair visible where it dangled. It would have been comical, had there not been a young girl's life on the line.

But then there was Kat. Kat was standing, looking terrified, but unaffected. She was looking desperately at Suzi, and at Nina, and then at Ellie. Ellie tried to move, but she felt like heavy lead was weighing down on every limb, pinning her to the wooden floorboards. She coughed and sputtered as she took in a mouthful of dust from the ancient floor, some unseen force pushing her face down against the old wood, choking her. Out of the corner of her eye she looked back up at Kat. Why weren't the spirits attacking her?

No, the *why* didn't matter. They had seconds to act. Kat was their only hope. With great effort, every movement feeling like moving through sludge, like gravity itself was pinning her down, she moved an arm, pointing at the stool, her finger shaking. Kat followed her point, and spotted it. She seemed to take a deep breath, and ran for the stool.

The ghosts didn't move, or react, and Kat passed harmlessly through them as she made her way to the stool. She propped it up and quickly climbed on it, grabbing Avril and allowing her to stand on it too. Avril gasped and choked for air, the rope around her neck going slack as the stool took her weight. The stool itself, old and composed entirely of the same rotting wood that made up so much of the furniture in the house, creaked with the weight of the two girls on it. Kat was trying to unknot the rope, but it was clearly tied tightly around Avril's neck and the stool was straining. Ellie realised if it broke, Avril would be hanging again, and this time they'd have no easy way to get her down in time. Furiously, Kat worked at the knot, trying to untie it, and then, in a moment, it all ended.

The stool broke, and Kat fell away, crashing to the floor painfully. But, Ellie realised, Avril came with her! She'd undone the knot in time. The two girls landed on the ground, Avril gasping and choking, her hands around her raw, reddened neck, even as Kat groaned.

There was a mighty hiss of anger, and the spirits seemed to swirl around the room, cold air blowing over all of the girls, like they were trapped in the eye of a hurricane for just the briefest moment, ghostly winds ripping around them but never quite touching. It only lasted a scant few seconds before the ghosts seemed to sink into the floorboards, disappearing. For a moment they rippled like fine mist, or the foam from a retreating wave on a beach, and then they were gone, seeping through the cracks in the wood. There was a thud as Suzi crashed to the floor too, suddenly released from whatever had held her.

There was a moment of silence, and Ellie realised the room once again belonged to the living. She groaned painfully, but pushed herself to her feet and made her way over towards Avril, who was choking and gasping on the floor. Suzi was trying to untangle herself from her own dress where she had fallen and Nina was observing the room cautiously. Kat looked on in shock for a moment.

'Are you okay?' Ellie asked, realising that it was probably a stupid question.

'There were… so many… of them…' Avril rasped, and Ellie could see that the hairs on her arms were standing on end and that she was covered in goose bumps. Despite the chill in the air having receded when the ghosts had fled, the cold had gotten deep into every part of Ellie's body and wasn't going to be shaken any time soon.

She was sure Avril felt the same way. Regardless of her own suffering, she removed her hoodie and offered it to Avril.

'Here. Put this on. Try and keep warm. Don't talk for a moment,' Ellie advised, although she hoped it wasn't obvious that she didn't actually know what she was talking about. She had no idea the best way to handle or comfort somebody who had nearly been hanged, but she hoped that this was a start. If only she'd watched more westerns instead of horror movies. She was pretty sure being saved from being hanged at the last moment was a solid western trope. She just couldn't remember what happened afterwards.

Avril struggled into the hoodie, moving painfully.

'Not exactly your style, but I think you pull it off,' Ellie smiled uneasily, rubbing her now bare arms, only having worn a simple black crop top underneath.

'Try drinking something. Your throat must be raw,' Suzi said, heading over, somehow looking even more of a mess than she had before now she had been flipped upside down, but Ellie thought better than to point it out. She could already imagine the squealing. Suzi looked over at Nina, who reluctantly produced a small metal hip flask from inside her pocket.

'Is that a good idea?' Kat asked, observing nervously.

'Relax. It's just water,' Nina said grumpily. 'I wasn't gonna admit it. Kind of ruins my image.' Ellie smirked. She had to admit, she'd been convinced it was full of whiskey.

'Poser,' Suzi teased, sticking her tongue out before bringing the flask to Avril, who took several grateful sips.

'What happens now? Where'd the ghosts go?' Kat asked, and Ellie had to admit, it was a sensible question. She wasn't sure why they had retreated, but she was pretty sure it was only a momentary respite.

'Dunno. Never seen this many in one place before,' Nina admitted. 'Usually you're only dealing with one, or maybe, if you're unlucky, a ghost family or something. But an army like that? All bets are off. They clearly have no problem attacking en masse. Dunno why they stopped.'

'We did kind of foil their plans,' Ellie pointed out.

'Yeah, but they're not like, Saturday morning cartoon villains, they're the spirits of the dead with a thirst for vengeance. Just because one plan goes wrong doesn't mean they retreat,' Nina countered.

'What if they were following orders?' Kat asked, and Nina looked at her, a perplexed expression upon her face. However, before she could say anything, Suzi planted a hand on her shoulder, eyes lighting up brightly as she got an idea.

'Ohhh, that would make sense! Think about it, that Edith lady gathered them all here. Maybe they do as she says?'

'Someone's gonna have to explain to me why a sweet old lady ghost who takes in strays now has an army trying to murder us,' Ellie grumbled.

'Told you before. Ghosts, man. Don't try to understand them,' Nina sighed. Avril struggled to her feet, and looked at the assembled group.

'What do we do now?' she rasped. 'How do we stop them?' There was a definite fire and anger in her voice despite the obvious pain talking caused her.

'We don't. We get the hell out of here,' Nina answered bluntly. 'You can't really *fight* ghosts. You might be able to stop one, *if* it happens to be tied to some kind of object you can destroy, but apart from that, your best bet is to burn down the place they haunt, and we lost our supplies to do that. Maybe we could still find the haunted object if it was just *one* ghost. But this lot? There's too many. They aren't playing games. And they could come back at any minute. We've got to get the hell out of here.'

'Isn't there anything we can do? Like, doesn't salt repel ghosts? Or something?' Ellie asked, knowing it was a pretty common tool on television at least. Come on, that summer she spent binge watching *Supernatural,* don't fail her now!

'Kind of. You can spread it around your windows and doors to stop a spirit following you home, but it's not going to stop them in their own house,' Nina answered. 'No, for now, our only hope is to get out of here.'

'What about Kat? Why did they ignore her?' Ellie asked, hoping that she didn't sound too much like she was making an accusation.

'Do you Yanks have that saying about gift horses and mouths? Because, yeah, don't look in one. Right now, just be glad, and hey, if they attack us again, Kat you might be our only hope.' Nina explained. Kat looked uneasy, giving them all a look.

'Great.' she said unsteadily, and fidgeted nervously with her hands. Ellie gave a small smile. She felt sorry for the girl. She'd gone from hanging out with her friends to being a group's last hope against an army of ghosts in the course of one evening.

That was tough.

Nina led them out of the room and back into the hallway outside, gesturing for them to follow her. Despite the urgency, none of the girls rushed, instead creeping, taking careful footsteps, hoping to avoid alerting the spirits, wherever they lurked. Even Nina, who would have happily told everybody sneaking around to avoid ghosts was foolish, was moving slowly and stealthily. It seemed even her nerves were on edge.

As they got closer to the stairs, an ominous creaking alerted them that a door next to them had opened. Ellie looked inside, shining her phone light within to try and get a look.

'Don't! Don't go in! What's wrong with you!? You don't just go in a room that creepily opened on its own!' Nina hissed, and Ellie paused, feeling a little ashamed.

'There's something in there though,' Avril said, her voice raw, pointing to something catching the light inside, looking like a dull metal.

'It's probably answers,' Suzi explained.

'Who cares about answers? I already told you, there's too many to fight! We have to get out of here!' Nina told the others, obviously irritated. Unfortunately, it seemed her words fell on deaf ears, because Kat began to move forward.

'I'm looking. They won't hurt me, remember?' Kat insisted, stepping into the darkened room. Ellie guessed she had decided that she wanted to know the reason she was being ignored, even if Nina didn't.

Ellie paused, waiting outside for a moment with the others. The *sensible* thing was to wait, of course. As Kat had pointed out, she was, for some reason, invisible to the spirits, so her heading inside made sense. But leaving somebody to go anywhere alone didn't sit right with Ellie, and after only a few moments, she turned to the others.

'Screw it,' she announced, and followed Kat inside.

The room looked like an old storeroom, with piles of objects hidden under white sheets. Ellie turned to the thing that had caught the light from outside, which Kat was currently looking closely at. Ellie realised that it wasn't a single object, but a pile of flat metal disks. She looked down to see a mouldy, old, dusty sheet on the floor, clearly having fallen off the pile. It seemed the rest of the room was filled with the same, only covered up. Kat picked one up off the top of the pile, and showed it to Ellie curiously.

'What the heck are these?' Kat asked, and Ellie immediately knew the answer. She'd never really seen one in person before, but they were pretty common objects. Especially to somebody with her interests.

'That's an old film can,' she answered. She supposed she shouldn't be surprised Kat didn't recognise them. To a film buff like her, they were obvious objects, but she guessed in times of digital downloads and Blu-rays, most *other* teenagers wouldn't recognise one. 'The type they used to record movies on and send them out to cinemas to play and stuff. The only real way to watch a film before, you know, VHS and DVDs and stuff.' Behind her, she was aware of footsteps, and whirled, but it was only Nina and the others following her inside.

'Yeah, we're not splitting up. That never ends well,' Nina sighed as an explanation for her presence, before looking at the can. 'That a film can?' Ellie wasn't sure if Nina recognised them too, or whether she'd just overheard Ellie identify them and was now pretending to know what they were.

'Yeah. There's loads of them,' Ellie gestured to the piles.

'What's the label say?' Avril asked, pointing to the faded, yellowing sticky label stuck on the underside of the can. Ellie flipped it over and took a look, trying to blow the dust off.

'I can't make it out,' Ellie said, the old pen writing long since having faded away. Kat picked up another one.

'This one is a little clearer,' she said. 'And the one underneath. I think they all say the same thing.' She began lifting each film can off, until finally she found one that was legible. 'Here we are. *Night of the Undead Vampires*. An Edward D Campbell Motion Picture,' she read out.

'Sounds thrilling,' Nina grumbled sarcastically.

'Ha, no way!' Ellie laughed, and suddenly was aware that everybody had turned to face her. 'C'mon, I'm not the only one who's heard of *Undead Vampires*, am I?' Everybody just gave her blank looks. 'It's pretty much considered the worst movie of all time! One of those old, cheesy, nineteen fifties knock-off Hammer horror movies.'

'Um…. why would we have heard of one of the worst movies of all time from the fifties?' Suzi asked, perplexed. 'I mean, why would you want to watch a terrible movie?'

'You mean you never just watched the worst thing you could find just to laugh at it?' Ellie replied, smiling a little, although the smile faded when she realised everybody else was looking at her like she was insane. 'I mean, c'mon! It's called *Undead Vampires*. All vampires are undead anyway! It's like, I dunno, naming a film '*The Killer Murderer*' or something! Or that *Doctor Who* episode called *The Deadly Assassin*. I mean, of course an assassin is deadly! Even the name is hilarious!' Ellie laughed a little to herself, before feeling foolish because nobody else joined in.

'Must be a film nerd thing,' Nina said lightly.

'Or a ghost thing. I mean, what else do they do in their free time? Maybe they watch terrible movies.' Avril suggested with a shrug. Something about it nagged at Ellie's mind. A connection she had missed. Suddenly, it hit her.

'Wait a sec! What did you say the director's name was?' she asked Kat. Kat looked back at the tin.

'Edward D. Campbell, according to this.'

'Campbell! The lady who owned this place, she was Edith *Campbell*. That can't be a coincidence!' Suzi pointed out enthusiastically, her eyes lighting up at the connection.

'You remember anything about him?' Nina asked Ellie, who suddenly felt serious pressure to be able to come up with a response.

She remembered hanging out with a few of her old friends back in the good old days. They'd watched *Undead Vampires*, but had barely paid attention to it, except to laugh at the special effects and terrible acting. She distinctly remembered a UFO she was pretty sure was a dinner plate on a piece of string. The fact that a UFO had been in a movie about vampires about summed up the quality of that particular film. She remembered laughing about it with her friends. They had thought it was so stupid.

All of those friends were dead now. God, that was a sobering thought. And yet she knew now wasn't the time. She had to think past her loss. Past the memories of the crappy movie. She had to focus on the director. What did she know about the director?

'Well, this was his one and only film. I remember that. If I remember rightly, it bankrupt him and the film company he'd set up. Nowhere would even show the film. I think he killed himself in the end.' Ellie frowned a little as she tried to remember. 'No, wait, yeah, he *hanged* himself,' she added, remembering that vivid detail and giving Avril's raw neck a significant look.

'So, what, this crappy film director, he's related to the lady who owned this house somehow?' Avril asked, before realising she received a slight look of surprise from Nina and Suzi. 'What? I pay attention!'

'A son or grandson maybe. But how do the film canisters get back to a creepy old haunted house in an abandoned town?' Nina asked.

Suddenly, the lights in their hands flickered again. Phone lights, flashlights, everything began to flicker on and off, the darkness engulfing them. The group moved closer together, instinctively on the defensive. With their backs to each other, Ellie realised they were ready to defend themselves, although quite how she hadn't thought through yet. She felt a chill down her spine. She turned, only to leap about a meter back, crashing into the piled film cans and sending them spilling out on the ground with a metallic, thunderous roar. Right behind them, in the middle of their group, stood a figure. An eerie image of a woman, in old wispy clothes, with a sunken, ancient face and long grey hair that moved in a non-existent breeze. Her entire body looked as if it was made up of a pale, swirling smoke that might blow away at any moment. One bony finger was extended, pointing at the ceiling. The crashing film canisters had gotten the attention of the others, all who turned to face her, and then slowly followed that finger pointing, up, up into the rafters.

Where an old piece of rope, mostly rotted and forgotten, still dangled.

'He hanged himself here! He came home to die!' Ellie exclaimed as she began to understand. Suzi took a step forward, towards the spirit, staring at it. She reached a hand out carefully.

'Edith?' she asked. The spirit's head snapped around to stare at Suzi, but to her credit, she didn't flinch. A tense moment passed, and Ellie found herself edging towards the spirit of Edith, in case she attacked. She had no idea what she was going to do if she did, since as far as she knew spirits were intangible, but she felt like she had to be ready. However, Edith's spirit only nodded, confirming Suzi's suspicion.

Suzi looked at Nina for a moment, with a nervous but somehow confident glance. Ellie didn't understand what it meant, but it was obvious Nina did.

'No, Suzi, don't-' Nina began, but it was too late. Suzi reached out, and touched Edith's spirit. There was a sudden howl of wind and the chill in the air increased tenfold. Ellie could have sworn she saw frost beginning to form around the edges of the room. Edith's spirit blew away into the sudden gale, looping around the room, and suddenly thundering back down, directly into Suzi. Suzi's entire body jerked and spasmed, before finally coming to a stop, deathly still. It took Ellie a few moments to realise what was so odd about that stillness, but then it hit her. She wasn't even breathing. She wasn't moving at all. She didn't even blink.

'Dammit Suzi!' Nina cursed.

'What happened!?' Avril shrieked, but Ellie was pretty sure the answer was obvious. Edith had possessed Suzi.

'The spirit is in Suzi. But while it's in there, her body doesn't need to breath, her heart doesn't need to beat, if we don't get it out of her fast, her body will be dead in minutes!' Nina snapped, moving towards Suzi quickly, moving to grab her shoulders.

'Then listen with speed,' Suzi suddenly spoke, her voice dry and hoarse, her words slightly confused, as if the speaker hadn't spoken aloud in decades. As if they were speaking with a voice that wasn't their own. Suzi's trace Japanese accent was nowhere to be found, but you could tell she was speaking with the same vocal chords, and yet an entirely different person was using them. It wasn't like an impressionist or a voice changing gimmick on a computer. Nor was it like an actor putting on an accent or faking a persona. It was simply the same voice, but a different soul driving it. It was something Ellie would never quite be able to describe. It was something, she thought, that could only be experienced.

'You're the ghost of Edith Campbell, right?' Ellie tried to talk quickly, to get things moving.

'Yes.'

'You killed my friends!' Avril suddenly snapped, tears welling in her eyes as she moved towards the Edith possessed Suzi.

'No,' Edith said bluntly, and Suzi's head moved to look directly at Avril with a jerk, the rest of her body remaining still. 'This was to be a haven. This was to be safe. Spirits had nowhere to go. Now they do. Here. I protect them. I keep your world safe from our world.'

'Doesn't look safe to me,' Ellie said, but Nina quickly waved her down.

'No time! You're in that body for a reason. No cryptic crap. Tell us what's going on and get out, now!' Nina yelled, her voice laced with more concern than Ellie had ever heard in her tone before. She realised that Nina couldn't lose Suzi. She couldn't lose another friend.

'My son. He is a director. He failed to direct in life. Now he directs in death. He always wanted to scare. He wanted to make films that filled others with terror. He could not. But here, he can. He has taken control of those who came to me for refuge. He uses them to create the horrors he never could in life.' Ellie wasn't sure, but she thought she could see Suzi's body beginning to shake as Edith spoke. As if it was beginning to convulse. Ellie and Nina exchanged a concerned look. They were running out of time.

'Why does he keep ignoring me? Why am I okay?' Kat asked, stepping forward, and Ellie saw Nina wince. It was a curious question, yes, but not one they had time for. Not now.

'He believes the world is a movie. He follows his film's plan. You cannot exist in his world.' Suzi's body was definitely shaking now. She was beginning to wobble on her legs.

'What do you-' Kat tried to ask.

'Get out of her, now! Get out or she's going to *die*!' Nina screamed, cutting her off. Edith turned Suzi's head to look at Nina, but bowed it in acceptance. Suddenly, Suzi threw open her mouth, and with another mighty gust of wind, Edith's spirit burst from Suzi's body, and swirled around the room.

Suzi collapsed, but Nina moved in faster than she could fall to catch her, lowering her gently to the ground. Suzi was suddenly gasping for air and choking as if she had just been rescued from drowning. Ellie rushed forward to be by her side too, and Avril looked on in concern, even as Kat watched the spirit of Edith disappear into the floorboards. A terrifying moment passed, and suddenly Suzi let out a horrible, spluttering cough. She looked up at the others.

'That's... one way of getting exposition,' Suzi said weakly, a faint smile on her lips.

'That was the stupidest thing you've ever done!' Nina snapped, but the concern in her voice was evident. 'And given some of your outfits, that makes it pretty *damn* stupid!' she added, but she moved and she hugged Suzi where she laid. 'Don't ever do that again!' she insisted.

'It's not exactly something I'm planning to do...' Suzi smiled faintly, before struggling to get up, Nina helping her and holding her.

'Like, what in the hell just happened!?' Avril asked, stunned.

'I let Edith possess me. If you make physical contact with a ghost, you invite it in. I realised she was on our side. That she wouldn't harm us,' Suzi explained. 'She just needed to talk to us.'

'Spirits are *never* on our side! They're all evil!' Nina insisted, concern still edging her voice.

'Hardest lesson to learn doing this, you're not always right, Nina.' Suzi said back, before sticking her tongue out.

Kat, who had been pacing a few steps away from the group, turned to them.

'What did she mean? What did she mean that I couldn't exist in his world?' Kat asked, looking at them all. A moment passed, and then Avril looked over to Ellie.

'Uh, Ellie, right? You, you know all about movies, yeah?' she asked, going off the evidence that they'd seen so far.

'A bit, yeah, but uh, I think we're beyond movies now,' Ellie answered, slightly concerned about what was coming.

'Well, um… Kat, do you mind if I tell them?' Avril looked over to Kat. Kat sighed, and nodded after a moment.

'I'll do it. Look, I wasn't… *born*… cis female. I'm trans,' Kat explained. Suzi and Nina exchanged slightly surprised glances, but it was more at the fact that Kat felt the need to reveal this information.

'Hey, you don't have to tell us. You're a girl. That's all that matters.' Nina said supportively, but Avril looked over to Ellie.

'Do you think that has something to do with it?' she asked. Ellie sighed.

'Yeah, that makes sense,' she said, her tone bitter. Ellie was angry. Not at Kat, of course not. Never at Kat. But at the situation. Because it was absurd.

'When was the last time you saw a horror movie with a trans character? Especially from the nineteen fifties?' Ellie asked. 'He can't see you, because as far as Hollywood is concerned, trans people don't exist, right? Trans erasure, as they call it. Hell, if they made a movie of this, right now, of us, they'd cast somebody cis to play you. And me and Suzi, we'd probably be white. And that's in modern day! Hollywood and equality sucks,' Ellie explained. Kat looked a little taken back.

'But I *am* a girl,' she said, rather hurt. Ellie felt a pang of guilt. She hadn't meant to make Kat feel like that.

'Yeah, you are,' Nina nodded, stepping in to support Kat, much to Ellie's relief. She turned to the others. 'And that does it. I was ready to run away, get us out of here safely. But if there's one thing I won't stand for, it's a transphobic ghost!' she said firmly. 'If this spirit wants to pull that stuff on you, then we're gonna use that to send him straight to Hell! He can't see you Kat. So we're gonna use that to send him running,' she insisted firmly.

'Uh, how?' Kat asked, looking rather nervous.

'Oh, I have a plan,' Nina gave an angry smile.

And then she began to explain.

CHAPTER FOURTEEN

THE SECOND ACT FINALE

Ellie wasn't sure how she felt about Nina's plan. It involved putting all of them in danger, but more than anybody, Kat. She felt awful about everything that was happening to Kat. Ellie was no stranger to being hated for reasons far beyond her control. She was a young black girl who had grown up in in a pretty poor area. She had spent her life hearing comments she wouldn't wish on anybody. She remembered patiently explaining to one of her white friends why she always had to make sure to get a receipt when using a self-service check out in a store, because otherwise they'd see a black girl walking out with something they had no proof they had paid for. Her friend hadn't understood. But somehow, what Kat was dealing with seemed worse. Or at least, it made Ellie feel guiltier for even bringing it up.

She couldn't quite explain why, but she felt like by even acknowledging that something made Kat different from the other girls, she was siding with the transphobes. Poor Kat didn't deserve that, Ellie knew. There was nothing different about her. She didn't deserve that treatment. And yet, now, here she was, the cornerstone of their plan, purely because of who she *was*. It didn't sit right with Ellie at all. Judging by the awkward expressions on the faces of the others, it didn't sit well with them either.

They had left the refuge of the small room they had been hiding in and headed towards the stairs and the foyer. Nina was fairly confident that any attempt to leave would prompt a ghost retaliation, and that would be their best window of opportunity. Kat was hanging back, at the rear of the group. She was quiet, and while she hadn't exactly been the most talkative of them all beforehand, it gnawed at Ellie's sense of guilt that she was clearly shaken.

'Hey, uh, you alright?' Ellie asked gently, taking a step back to check up on her.

'Yeah, uh, just, we're gonna go fight ghosts, and I might die, because I'm the only one who can stop them. Kinda nervous,' Kat answered with a slightly nervous look.

'I mean, uh, about… well, all of this,' Ellie waved a vague hand, trying to gesture at the entire situation they had found themselves in. Kat paused, and then shook her head.

'I…. don't like people knowing,' she admitted.

'That you're trans? Trust me, none of us care,' Ellie said sympathetically.

'Yeah, but I care. Being able to pass. It's what I've always wanted. Because… being seen as anything else, it *feels* like a lie. I'm not trans. Not in my head. I'm just a girl. I was always a girl. My body was wrong but that's it. I don't want to be *trans*. I don't want to be the boy who became a girl. I just want to be *a girl,*' she explained, and Ellie thought she felt her own heart break. It wasn't really something she had given enough thought to before, she realised. She was always supportive, but she hadn't thought about how it felt inside, for the people who had gone through it. She hadn't thought about how hard it must have been to feel so *certain* you were somebody else inside. And to know that people didn't see that side of you. Or worse yet, they'd always see the label, rather than the real person you were inside.

'Hey, you *are* a girl,' Ellie answered. 'Plain and simple, you're a girl. Nothing else. And if this ghost can't see that, well, that's his problem. Because it just means he won't see the girl who kicked his ass,' Ellie offered a smile, touching Kat's shoulder supportively. Kat gave an uneasy smile back.

'I wish I had your confidence in me,' Kat said unsteadily. 'I don't even know if this is gonna work.'

'It's gonna work,' Ellie nodded. 'I know, it's gonna work.' Ellie was, of course, lying. She had no idea that it was going to work, but she knew better than to say that right at that moment.

The group began to descend the stairs, back into the foyer, which was still as darkened as it had been when they left. Ellie couldn't tell if the windows were still blocking out all light unnaturally, or if that was just how dark it was outside now, night having fallen long ago. She couldn't see any stars, but that didn't surprise her. Clouds hung over Angel's Ridge at all times. Probably actually smoke and vapour from the mine fire, she realised.

'So, where are the ghosts?' Avril asked cautiously, and Ellie noticed she was rubbing her neck self-consciously where the rope had been tied. Avril more than anyone, Ellie realised, had good reason not to want to see these things again, and yet, there she was. Still standing by their side. Avril was much braver than she let on.

'The door,' Nina gestured. 'We try the door.'

Nobody moved.

'Uh, well, go on then,' Nina said, turning to Avril.

'What!? Why me!?' Avril asked, looking aghast.

'You're the screechy, easily scared one, and this guy thinks he's making a movie. You're the one he'll ambush for a jump scare when you approach the door.'

'I'm not doing it!' Avril protested.

'Well I can't. I'm too prepared. Nothing'll jump out on me. And we need Kat for the plan.'

'What about Ellie!?' Avril asked.

'Uh, yeah. No. Consider this revenge for taping me to that pole.'

'I'm not doing it!' Avril snapped.

'I'll do it!' Suzi sighed, stepping forward. 'I'm the girly one in pink! It'll totally jump out on me!'

'You gonna tell her her outfit isn't really *pink* anymore, or shall I?' Nina whispered to Ellie as Suzi moved towards the door. It wasn't a lie. Her ash and dirt stained dress barely showed a hint of pink but Ellie definitely wasn't going to point that out to Suzi.

Suzi tried the door, rattling the door handle, and the collective group tensed nervously. They exchanged looks, but nothing seemed to happen.

'It's still locked,' Suzi answered, turning around to face the others. 'And nothing appeared!'

'Give it a chance. Keep talking.' Nina smiled, holding up a hand and beginning to count down from three.

'Keep talking? Uh, what am I meant to say?'

'Uh, well, um, I guess, it's not going to jump out?' Ellie tried to input, watching as Nina gestured for them to keep on going.

'Well maybe we should-' Nina's fingers finished counting down, and at that exact moment a spirit burst out of the ground, screaming in Suzi's face. She jolted back against the door, startled, as dozens more spirits began to rise out of the floorboards, swarming around the group like a tornado.

'Classic jump scare! Won't happen when you expect it, instead, happens halfway through a casual conversation afterwards!' Nina explained, having to shout over the sound of roaring wind that seemed to accompany the swirling ghosts.

'Smug explanation later! Kicking ass now!' Ellie yelled back, over the roar. 'Kat, you ready?'

'Nope, but do I have a choice?' Kat replied with a very nervous looking shrug, standing next to Avril for comfort. Avril, for her part, didn't seem thrilled by that, taking a step away to put some distance between them. It wasn't the most sympathetic act of friendship Ellie had seen, but she understood why. Avril was clearly nervous to be standing too close to Kat since Kat was about to become the focal part of the plan.

Ellie tried to focus on the ghosts as they swirled around them, but they were moving too fast to see. She could make out the vague humanoid detail, largely lost to clouds of white mist, and the odd dark shadow seeping the room, but nothing else. It was getting harder to concentrate, the wind howling and the cold chilling her bones as the spirits surrounded them. She felt like they were caught in a vicious storm.

'How do we know which one is the director!?' she yelled to Nina over the din.

'Most spirits are pretty basic. They get stuck remembering one emotion or feeling. It's how a forceful ghost can take over and lead them. Look for the one with independent thought!' Nina instructed.

'And if that fails, the one with one of those foldy chairs and an old timey megaphone!' Suzi added with an attempted jokey smile, but it was cut off as two of the spirits suddenly veered towards her, each grabbing an arm and lifting her up into the air.

They released her, leaving her to fall, and she grabbed onto the old chandelier hanging from the ceiling. For a moment, it seemed like the entire thing would buckle, but the chains held as Suzi dangled from it, legs kicking furiously.

Nina ran to help her, but the spirits moved towards her like a wave, slamming into her legs and taking them out from under her. She fell, face first, hitting the wooden floor with force. Avril was backing away in terror, as both Ellie and Kat looked desperately for one ghost standing apart from the rest. If they could spot one, that would *have* to be Edward D. Campbell's spirit. There was a sudden sickening cracking of bone and a horrific sliding sound, and Ellie turned, distracted from her search. It was Shelly's body! The ghosts were moving him like a puppet, lifting him from where he was impaled and moving him toward her, each step taken like a lurching zombie. Avril screamed at seeing him, and Ellie couldn't blame her. He was most definitely dead, his skin cold and clammy, his eyes lifeless, and his body covered in blood from the horrific chest wound, and yet still he moved, his limbs jerking unnaturally with every forced step.

Shelly's body struck out with an arm, knocking Avril back into the hands of waiting ghosts, which began to lift her into the air. Nina still didn't seem to have moved from the floor. Unsure of what else to do, Ellie drew her pistol. She had almost forgotten that she had it. The once heavy, cold reminder she was carrying had stopped bothering her when her concerns had become the much more threatening spirits. The weapon was so pointless when fighting intangible ghosts there had been no point in remembering it anyway. But a moving body?

She levelled the pistol, and fired.

The gunshot rang out and hit Shelly's body square in the eye, his head snapping back. A moment passed, but he didn't drop, and his head levelled out again, now missing an eye, congealed blood seeping from the socket. He continued on toward her. The gunshot attracted the other spirits, all of whom seemed to turn towards Ellie. She looked around in horror at them closing in, and then she saw it. Behind all the other spirits, at the top of the stairway, a figure was pointing towards her.

'Kat! The stairs!' she yelled, but her turning around had given the ghosts puppeteering Shelly's body their chance. They grabbed her from behind, Shelly's cold dead hands grasping under her arms and pulling her back. She struggled, but it wasn't Shelly's muscle power she had to battle, but the manipulation of dozens of the spirits. She realised that they were pulling her back towards the same piece of wood Shelly had been impaled upon. They were trying to lift her up, and slam her down on it. They were trying to kill her in the same way they had killed Shelly. It figured, Ellie thought angrily to herself. Edward D. Campbell was a hack. Of course he'd use two identical death scenes. He'd already tried to use hanging twice. Why not repeat Shelly's death? Ellie was going to die, and it wasn't even in a *creative* manner.

Kat ran toward the stairs, bounding up them two at a time. She could see the spirit now, a figure separate from all others that was clearly observing. It was a misty white figure, with little detail that Kat could make out, except for the fact that a cloudy white hand was extended, directly pointing at Ellie. Kat knew that Ellie didn't have long. None of them did. Avril was in the air, pinned against a wall and struggling against ghostly hands. Nina was on the floor, possibly unconscious. Suzi dangled helplessly from the chandelier. And Ellie was about to be impaled. It was all up to her.

Her and Nina's crazy idea.

She ran towards the spirit, and reached out, grabbing the extended hand. Although her hands passed through it, she felt a freezing cold gust of air run up her arm. The contact was enough. The ghost, the spirit of Edward D. Campbell, finally saw her. His head turned to glare at her, and still Kat held out her hand, grasping where his should be.

Ellie fought against the cold grip under each arm as she tried to move, the freezing clamminess of the corpse's digits digging into her flesh. She had seen more death than anybody her age ever should have after the massacre, but she'd never taken time to stop and feel a body. She had never realised how icily cold a corpse could be until that moment, when it held her so firmly. She still gripped the pistol in her right hand, and she made a desperate decision, lifting it up over her shoulder and pointing it directly at Shelly's reanimated arm, pulling the trigger.

That close to her ear the gunshot sounded like somebody had rung church bells in her head, and her vision blurred as the sound pierced through her skull. She thought she could feel the heat of the gunshot on the back of her shoulder, burning her where the shot had been fired, but it had the intended effect. Shelly's corpse was just a puppet, and for it to be effective, it needed to have its arms connected. Firing the bullet right through his arm had caused the hand gripping her to largely become severed, and with a mighty jolt forward, she tore the hand gripping her free from the damaged wrist.

Instantly, the severed hand fell to the floor, releasing Ellie, but the other arm increased its grip, digging its fingers into her flesh with such unyielding strength she thought she heard the bones in the corpse's hand snap. The pain was immense, enough to leave her yelping in agony and causing her to drop the gun. It clattered to the ground, uselessly out of her reach. With one arm still gripping her, and the corpse powered by dozens of spirits, she was powerless to break free. She was still being pulled back toward the awaiting broken wooden shaft, and what would doubtlessly be her death. She kicked and struggled desperately.

Her eyes flickered up to Kat, hand held out, trying to take the arm of the spirit of Edward Campbell. Ellie knew she could only fight back for a few seconds longer, and then for her, it would all be over. She could only pray that Nina's plan would work. That Kat could do what they needed to do.

Even as her body was being lifted up by the one-handed corpse, even as death grew ever closer, she began to have that inkling of hope. She couldn't hear anything, her ears were still ringing, but something was happening to Kat. The spirit she had been grasping swirled in the air for a moment, and suddenly it flew in to her body, just as Edith's spirit had done with Suzi.

Kat had made contact, and allowed the spirit in. She was now being possessed!

'C'mon… C'mon… Nina, please be right,' Ellie muttered under her breath, even if she couldn't hear her own words. The moment seemed to hang, and Ellie found herself wondering if the spirits were waiting with (metaphorical) bated breath, just as she was, or if it was just her imagination that she had been given a moment's reprieve before they finished her off.

And then, all of a sudden, it was over. Kat let out a scream, and even through Ellie's ringing ears, she heard it. She threw up her arms and seemed to suddenly explode with a bright white energy, every part of her body glowing. As quickly as it began, it was over, and Kat collapsed to the floorboards, doubled over and breathing hard.

Instantly, Ellie was released, and she fell forward, away from the wooden rubble that had nearly been her doom, crashing down painfully on the old dusty floorboards. Shelly's corpse simply fell away, tumbling down to the ground in a crumpled heap. She looked up to see that the ghosts that had been attacking them all were now rounding in on Kat, able to see her, and more than that, aware that she had just done something to their leader. Their *director*. They all seemed to fly towards Kat aggressively. Ellie realised that this was something Nina definitely hadn't accounted for and began to push herself to her feet, biting back the pain and agony, knowing she had to get to Kat's side. Before she could, however, and before the swirling spirits could make contact with Kat, another ghostly figure appeared. A familiar figure. One Ellie instantly recognised.

Edith Campbell.

She appeared, perfectly stationary, on the stairs between Kat and the ghosts. The entire horde seemed to stop in their movement, hovering with what Ellie thought was an air of awe before Edith. She clearly had control of her lodgers again, Ellie thought with a wry smile. With the gesture of a ghostly wrist the spirits floated downwards, disappearing into the floorboards, much like they had in the room upstairs, only this time, instead of a crashing receding wave, it seemed peaceful. Gentle. A wave softly slinking away after gently lapping against a beach on a warm summer's day, Ellie thought. It seemed to even help calm the furious adrenaline running through every inch of Ellie's body. The ghosts were gone. Except for one. Only Edith remained.

Edith, for a moment, seemed to make eye contact with Ellie, but it was obvious that Kat was the true focal point of her attention. She turned, placing her back to the others, and seemed to deliver a small nod to Kat, before she too disappeared into the floorboards.

With a groan of pain, Ellie finished scrambling to her feet, before hearing a shriek and seeing Suzi fall from the chandelier she had been dangling from, landing with a groan, but otherwise unharmed. Nina slowly got up, wiping a trail of blood from her lip where she'd been injured in the fall, and Avril ran over to the group, sobbing, but unhurt. She grabbed Ellie in a hug, although Ellie suspected that was because she was the closest person, rather than any real affection.

One by one, the assembled group remembered exactly who they had to thank, and their eyes turned to Kat, who was still hunched and breathing heavily, but equally unharmed, looking at them all.

'You okay?' Nina called up, and Ellie shot Nina a look. She didn't really consider that enough. Ellie ran up the stairs towards Kat, refusing to acknowledge her own wobbly legs even as they threatened to buckle under her. She took her in a hug.

'Hey, you did it! You did it! Relax!' Ellie said soothingly, before Avril approached to also embrace her friend.

'I don't actually think I understand what you did, but yeah, you totally did it!' Avril cheered, equally supportively. Nina gave a slight smile as she ascended the stairs.

'Pretty simple really. You see, certain people like to pretend that there's no such thing as good and evil. They convince themselves that really, it's just different points of view. Oh, they're not a bigot, they just share a different opinion to you. Hell, how many times have you seen people arguing on the internet, sharing some hate, and then stating it's "just their opinion"?' Nina asked.

'Uh, okay, but what's that got to do with anything?' Avril asked, giving Nina a confused look.

'Well, good and evil *do* exist. There are some things in this world... that are just *evil*. And hating a person because of who they are? Because of who they are on the inside? That's evil. Just, people don't understand it. Even the people who feel that hate, they refuse to believe it's evil. They refuse to believe it's wrong. Until… they step inside that person's head.' Nina looked to Kat. 'When that ghost stepped inside your head, they saw you for who you really were. You showed him that he was wrong, that his opinions, his thoughts, his treatment of you, all of it, it was *wrong*. It was *evil*. And he couldn't stand it. He lost control.'

'What happened to him?' Ellie had to ask. She was still pretty unclear. After all, you couldn't kill a ghost, right?

'He was a spirit. All that means is that he was just left over emotions and beliefs, bound together so tightly they refuse to move on. By seeing how wrong he was, by seeing inside Kat's head, all of that resolve, all of that that strength that held his spirit together, well, it crumbled. He fell apart,' Nina answered.

'He moved on,' Suzi added.

'Moved on to where?' Avril asked.

'Not a good place,' Kat suddenly spoke up. 'I'm sure of that.' She paused, and looked at the others. 'I felt him. The hatred. The desire for success. He killed our friends, and so many people before us… I hope wherever he ended up, he suffers for that.' Her voice was suddenly cold and harsh.

Ellie felt every second in the awkward moment that passed. She hoped that Kat was right. That Edward Campbell's spirit would suffer for his crimes. The entire house now seemed eerily silent again, but this time there was something different in the silence. It wasn't *true* silence, not the haunting silence that had completely absorbed all sound before. No, now, instead, it was a natural silence. Quiet, but not without traces of sound, not without the odd creak, or the distant sound of wind pushing against the old house's frame. It was the type of change you didn't realise was missing until you heard the difference, but immediately it made the house feel more natural. Ellie began to descend the stairs, and noticed that the windows were no longer blacked out either. Soft moonlight was filtering in, albeit pale and broken up by the thick clouds that hung over Angel's Ridge.

She paused, looking at the big, heavy doors that led out of the old mansion. They suddenly opened with a creak, causing her to start slightly.

'I think that might be Edith's hint that we should leave,' Suzi said, nodding towards the open door and heading towards it.

'Wait, are we just… gonna leave the house here? I mean, isn't it still full of ghosts?' Ellie asked, looking around nervously, as if the ghosts might be eavesdropping on her.

'Yeah, but under Edith, they're *nice* ghosts again,' Suzi smiled.

'I thought Nina said there were no such thing as nice ghosts? Remember, she had this whole ominous speech about how they're evil and ancient and stuff. I mean, I remember that pretty clearly. Remember the creepy ominous speech? Anybody? Remember?' she prompted Suzi, fully aware that she was being sarcastic, although she supposed her tone must have been even mocking than she intended because she found herself on the receiving end of a glare from Nina.

'Might surprise you, but turns out I don't know everything,' Nina smirked as they stepped out into the fresh cool air. Ellie took several deep breaths, appreciating the wind on her face. Being in the presence of spirits may have kept her cold, but it hadn't exactly been refreshing. She noticed that Avril was quick to stumble out of the house and put as much distance between it and herself as possible. Kat on the other hand seemed to linger for a moment, lost in thought about what had just happened, but soon moved to join the group. 'Always said that these monsters play by the rules and follow a story, right? Well, maybe, sometimes stories end with something you didn't expect. Like a good ghost,' Nina shrugged loosely.

'Did you just try and deliver some kind of moral? You big softie!' Suzi was clearly amused. Nina just shook her head and sighed. She was about to reply, but voices cut them off.

'Kat! Avril! You're okay!' It was Ali, rushing over to them. Jake was by her side, following, obvious relief and a smile on his face. A smile that faded as he took in the assembled group, realising who was missing.

'Wait, where's Todd?' Jake asked, his face turning serious. Ali's too became deeply concerned. Avril, unable to hold it in, let out a sob and just shook her head, retreating into Ali's arms, who at least offered a comforting hug.

'He didn't make it. I'm sorry,' Nina said, although Ellie thought her tact could have used some work.

'Didn't make it? He's… dead?' Jake asked, looking a little pale and glancing at the house in shock.

'Hey, look, I know it doesn't feel like it, but all of you, walking into a situation like this, and this many of you walking back out, alive? You're lucky,' Nina tried to explain, although she sounded awkward saying it. Jake seemed to glare, and for a moment Ellie was concerned he was going to lash out and hit Nina for what she had said.

'Lucky!? You call this lucky!?' he growled. 'What? Because you were here to save us, I guess? How do we know you didn't kill him!?'

'It wasn't them, Jake,' Avril said softly.

'We didn't kill anybody,' Ellie insisted.

'We didn't save anybody either,' Nina added, nodding to Kat with a slight smile. 'That was all Kat.' Kat looked sheepish at accepting the credit, and Ellie realised it was probably something she didn't want to talk about.

'She's got a point,' Suzi admitted, gesturing to Nina. 'Without Kat, we'd have been *screwed*!'

'Kat saved you? How?' Ali asked sceptically, releasing Avril for a moment. Kat opened her mouth, about to answer, but hesitated. Ellie knew that Kat wasn't going to be comfortable talking about it, so instead Ellie just smiled.

'By being herself,' Ellie answered, placing a hand on Kat's shoulder and giving her a smile. 'That's all.'

Ellie allowed the moment to hang between them for a moment, but it didn't last long. Suzi stepped forward, with the air of a busybody with a checklist of things needing checking off. It was almost adorable, Ellie thought. Clearly Suzi knew what to do after one of these incidents.

'Okay, so, you're probably asking what now. Because, two people are dead and you're alive and you can't tell the police it was ghosts.' Even Suzi, usually sympathetic, was a bit too casual about the whole thing, Ellie thought, but her fast talking demeanour seemed to prevent any of the others raising objections. 'So, you need a story.'

'You mean, cover up the death of our friends?' Jake asked a little hotly. Kat stepped forward to join Jake, Avril and Ali, and took a deep breath.

'They're right, it's the only way,' Kat confirmed. Jake paused, looking back at the house with anger in his eyes, and then he kicked the ground hard, sending stones and pebbles flying.

'Dammit!' he cursed. 'Dammit. Fine. Right. Whatever. So what are we going to tell everybody?'

'Did anybody see you leave town together?' Suzi asked.

'What? Um, no. We drove. Avril and Todd in his car, the rest of us in mine.' Ali explained.

'Okay, well, I'm guessing *someone* saw you all leaving, so we can't just say you never met them here,' Suzi realised. 'What if you had an argument with Todd? He stormed off, Shelly went after him, you never saw them again?' Suzi suggested to Avril.

'Doesn't that kind of make everything my fault?' Avril asked, hesitating.

'No, don't be silly. This town is really dangerous. Trust me, I know!' Suzi exclaimed, gesturing to her soot plastered dress. 'They stormed off and went missing. Heck, if the police look, they'll find a big hole in the street I fell in, so they'll assume the ground collapsed under them.'

'I... really don't like this. Lying about how our friends died,' Ali said after a momentary pause.

'Neither do I, but what else can we do?' Kat asked with a sigh.

'What about their bodies?' Jake frowned. 'People are gonna look. They'll find their bodies.'

'They didn't find the bodies of the kids who vanished last year,' Nina pointed out. 'Pretty sure the ghosts will take care of that for you.' Nina seemed to pause for a moment. Ellie realised it was for show. An attempt at sympathy, but not a very convincing one. Nina had clearly had to have this conversation too many times in the past. 'Sorry, but this is how it's gotta be.'

The silence that followed was long and awkward. Ellie could feel the irritation radiating from Jake and Ali, but they didn't seem to be able to put into words. They didn't *have* a counter argument. Kat and Ellie stood by them, anguished looks on their faces, but it seemed that they all knew what had to be done. It was a horrible feeling, and one Ellie would never shake, telling people they had to lie to save themselves and to cover up how they lost friends, but there was nothing else they could do.

Finally, Ali nodded, obviously deciding to take the lead for her friends.

'Fine. Okay. We've got no choice,' she sighed. 'What about you lot? What do you do now, ride off into the sunset?' she asked.

'I think it's more of a walk, followed by a drive,' Ellie couldn't help herself, even if the sarcastic answer wasn't particularly helpful.

'We'd have all died, if it wasn't for you,' Kat observed.

'Maybe. But we'd have all died if it wasn't for *you* too,' Suzi reminded Kat. 'So, I guess, let's call it a team effort.' Another moment passed, just a beat, and Kat moved to give Suzi a hug, before embracing Ellie too. Finally, she stepped towards Nina, who despite looking very awkward, gave a hug back. Avril followed suite, hugging Suzi, Ellie and Nina, who remained looking awkward. Ali and Jake hung back, but gave curt nods. Suzi and Avril seemed to be happily swapping phone numbers, Ellie noticed.

'Don't take this the wrong way, but I hope I never see you again,' Jake said bluntly.

'Stay away from creepy old mansions and you won't,' Nina replied, lighting a cigarette, now that the goodbyes were done. Ellie was getting increasingly certain she just did that for dramatic effect, rather than because she wanted to smoke.

'I could go for saying hi every so often,' Kat admitted.

'Me too. If you ever need us… Well, just call,' Avril smiled. 'Thanks for everything.'

'See you guys around,' Nina nodded, turning away. Suzi gave a little wave and followed. Ellie hesitated for a moment, and smiled.

'Bye then, I guess,' She said. 'Take care.' And she moved to catch up with Suzi and Nina.

The trio moved through the abandoned town, making their way back along the heavily graffitied road they'd come in on. All three were still using their flashlights. It was the dead of night still, and with no functioning street lights for miles, it was a true darkness, lit only by the faint moonlight fighting through the cloud cover. Ellie cast a glance back at the group they'd left behind, barely visible, who were obviously talking before leaving themselves.

'Can we trust them not to go to the police? Not to mention us?' She asked. 'I mean, we're not exactly inconspicuous, are we?' She gestured to them all. Suzi gave herself a puzzled look, as if she couldn't figure out what about her outfits *possibly* made her conspicuous. 'If they report us, it's not gonna be hard for the cops to track us down.'

'You can trust them. You just gotta have faith,' Suzi replied with what Ellie thought was a naïve smile.

'Faith they know they'll be arrested too,' Nina added. 'Besides, even if they did go to the cops, and did tell them about us, what are they gonna do? There won't ever be any evidence we were even here.'

'It does seem so wrong though. Two people are dead, and nobody will ever know how or why. Not even their parents,' Ellie sighed.

'Hey, you told your mom what happened to you, right? Did they believe you?' Nina asked.

'No. She just thought it was some ordinary guy in a mask killing us,' Ellie admitted.

'See? People just aren't ready to understand. This way, people are protected,' Nina explained, flicking her cigarette butt away.

The group walked in silence for a bit longer, passing the hole Suzi had fallen in before, which Suzi made sure to edge around carefully. They went back past the old disused shops, which seemed much creepier in the low light. It wasn't long before they were back on the main road, and Nina's flashlight caught a glimpse of the parked rental car.

'Is that really it then?' Ellie asked. 'It's all over?'

'Oh *god*, don't say things like that!' Nina rolled her one eye dramatically. 'For god's sake, haven't you learned anything? 'It's all over'? That's just asking for something to jump out after you.' Ellie suddenly became painfully aware of the darkness surrounding them, and how at any moment something could ambush them. Moments passed, and nothing happened. 'You got lucky.' Nina confirmed, and the group continued walking.

They arrived at the car, and Nina took some time searching her dusty ash-stained trench coat pockets for the keys, luckily producing them just as Ellie was about to ask if she'd lost them. She opened the door and climbed inside.

'I think we're gonna lose our deposit,' Suzi mumbled as she climbed into the back, noticing the amount of filth and ash that was getting on the car seats from their clothes. Ellie gave a slight smile and shook her head. Somehow she figured that Suzi could afford it. Nina started the car, and soon they were back on the road, heading back towards the airport.

'Of course, it *isn't* over,' Nina said suddenly, causing Ellie to sit up slightly straighter in shock.

'What do you mean?' Ellie asked suspiciously.

'Oh, those kids are safe. The ghosts are dealt with. But that thing that attacked the plane?'

'And whatever that was in the mines!' Suzi added.

'Yeah, that too. Neither of those things were ghosts. The spirits didn't even know we were there to throw those at us,' Nina explained.

'What do you mean?' Ellie asked nervously.

'Whatever those things were, they *broke the rules* to come after us. And they did. Come after *us* specifically, I mean. This isn't over,' Nina said through tight lips.

'Well, what does that mean?' Ellie asked.

'I don't know. If this whole thing has shown me anything, it's that I really don't know everything. Something out there is playing some kind of new game with us. And I don't know what it is. Or what's going to happen next. I don't like it,' Nina said warningly.

The silence that followed was cold and chilling, almost like being the presence of the spirits again, only this time Ellie knew it was self-inflicted. She sat slumped in the car seat for a long time, but slowly her eyes began to grow heavy. Ellie didn't remember closing her eyes, but at some point, she must have drifted into sleep, because she didn't remember anything until they arrived back at the plane.

CHAPTER FIFTEEN

THE CALM BEFORE THE STORM

Ellie wasn't sure if it was the exhaustion or that after spending the night nearly being killed by evil spirits flying didn't seem like such a major thing, but the plane's take-off had been nice and smooth, and she hadn't really thought much of it. They'd left the keys in the ignition of the rental car for collection, and apart from that, their little adventure was pretty much over.

Jess was busy in the cockpit, of course. Not that Ellie minded Jess's company in the slightest, but it was definitely the one place she still wanted their pilot to be. Suzi, on the other hand, had retreated to the back of the plane and pulled a curtain across, obviously cleaning herself up and changing the best she could. That just left Nina and Ellie in the main cabin. In a moment of incredible thoughtfulness, Jess had made sure to provide coffee for both of them before take-off. Ellie was still nursing her drink as Nina was just finishing off the last of her own.

'I thought Brits just drank tea,' Ellie commented, wanting to break the silence. It was obvious even Nina was tired, but with just the two of them, Ellie figured they should at least make an effort to talk. Nina just offered a smile and shook her head.

'Nah, Britain's just like the rest of the world. Half of us wouldn't function without a morning coffee,' she replied. A moment passed, and Nina had clearly picked up on Ellie's attempts to hold a conversation. 'So, how'd you find your first mission?'

'Is that what you call them? "Missions"?' Ellie shot back, realising it was a deflection of the question but doing it anyway.

'Well, it's better than "adventure". Makes us sound like we're in a kids' TV show,' Nina countered. 'So? How was it?'

'Honestly? I don't really know. It was… different, from what I was expecting. More complicated.'

'Usually is. Things don't always get wrapped up in a neat little bow when we interfere.'

'It felt good though, helping those kids. I just wish we could have saved all of them.'

'Been doing this a long time. Don't think I've ever successfully saved everybody. Sorry, Ellie, that's just the way it is. Somebody always dies,' Nina admitted, and it was enough of a grim thought that silence followed for a few moments.

'What about you? I mean, it didn't seem like this was your regular, uh, well, "mission", as you call it,' Ellie asked.

'Every time I think I've got them figured out, something changes,' Nina replied.

'Them?'

'The spirits. The demons. I don't know, whatever you want to call them. "The forces of darkness", I guess, but that sounds a bit…'

'Kids' TV?' Ellie suggested with a slight smirk.

'Yeah. I guess,' Nina shot the smirk right back at her. 'I never thought there could be a good ghost. But… Edith proved me wrong. I've been so certain of the rules, of the way things work, and then… Something like that puts a spanner in all my ideas. It makes things pretty tense.'

'Because if you were wrong about that, what else are you wrong about?'

'Exactly,' Nina nodded. 'But if there's one thing I know I'm not wrong about, it's the other weird stuff that's been happening. The gremlin, the thing in the mine, they shouldn't have been there.'

'But you just admitted you were wrong about the ghosts. Couldn't you have been wrong about that too?' Nina just shook her head.

'No. This was different. Those things, they came after *us*. We hadn't even reached the haunted house yet, so how would any of the spirits known about us?' Nina asked. 'No. Something else is after us. And I don't think we've seen the last of it.'

'Isn't that the exact kind of ominous thing you tell me not to say?'

'Huh, I guess it is,' Nina remarked. 'See, even us pros make mistakes.' She stood up, rolling her neck slightly. 'Why don't you rest up? You look pretty shattered. I'll go check up on Jess.' she suggested, making her way down the plane towards the cockpit before Ellie could reply.

Ellie looked back around at the closed curtain, wondering how long Suzi would be. There was no sign of her emerging anytime soon. Instead, Ellie turned her eyes out of the window, to look at the distant world passing below. She'd never get used to it, she decided, trying to imagine everybody down below still living their lives while everything looked so small. So distant. She could see trees that looked like nothing more than tiny dots, smudges on the ground, and yet she knew if she were to stand in front of one, it could easily be a towering oak. She could see a road, barely a thin line across the country side, and tiny cars, still looking like ants to Ellie, making their way along it. Each car with a person inside. Each car with a story. But from here, it looked like nothing. She was sure that somewhere there was a metaphor for their current lives in there. Everybody living their ordinary, day to day lives, going to school or going to work, worrying about grocery shopping and childcare, while Ellie now lived in another world, worrying about monsters and the things that go bump in the night. A normal life now seemed as distant as the cars below. She was in another world now. A different world. And she could never touch the ground again.

It was that thought she clung to as she drifted into sleep.

Once they were back at the mansion, despite it being early afternoon, the trio dutifully trooped in through the main door and all, almost wordlessly, headed to their respective rooms. It reminded Ellie of the behaviour of a family after a long vacation returning home, every member exhausted, and all just wanting a moment of privacy. Maybe that was just her own family? She remembered it in particular being that way back when her mom and dad were still together, but perhaps that said more to the underlying tension between them that had existed even then than anything most families would show.

She didn't remember getting into bed, or even removing her clothes. Afternoon light still filtered into the room through the gap in the drawn curtains, thanks to the large window, but it wasn't enough to keep her awake. Despite all the sleeping on the trip, a very bruised and battered Ellie fell asleep almost the instant her body hit the bed.

Ellie awoke with a start, not entirely sure of how much time had passed. It was night, that much certain, and the room was dark. The only source of light came from two tiny red pin pricks over the bed. Ellie didn't give them a thought for a moment, instead groggily reaching over to check her phone. Her heart sank. No message at all from her mom. She hadn't expected that. It had been out of her mind while they had been on their little adventure, but now that it was over she found it so strange that her mother hadn't called, despite the message she sent. Did she not care? Or was this just her respecting Ellie's wish, and leaving her alone? She hesitated for a moment. Maybe she should call *her*?

She decided to get up, letting out a heavy yawn, and examining her arms, noticing the purple bruises that seemed to cover them. Her body was aching, painfully. Her legs burned, as if she had run a marathon and her arms felt shaky. She was only in a crop top and her underwear, having fallen asleep in it, her clothes bundled up on the bed. Still unfamiliar with the room, she scanned for the light switch, glad of the slight illumination from above.

It was only then that she *finally* thought to look up. Because two red pinpricks giving off a soft light? That... wasn't normal, even in a fancy mansion, right?

It was lucky she looked up when she did, because she looked straight into the glowing red eyes of the gremlin as it released itself from the ceiling, falling towards her with a screech.

CHAPTER SIXTEEN

THE ATTACK

The gremlin creature fell towards Ellie, razor sharp teeth bared, and she didn't have time to move out of the way. Instead, she did the only thing she could do and flung an arm up to protect her face. The creature landed on her arm, and immediately sank its deadly teeth into it. Ellie screamed in pain, crimson blood flowing freely as the creature clamped down. She could feel its tense jaw push down harder and harder, and she could swear the teeth were digging into the bone in her forearm.

The agony was unbearable and her arm sagged, which was enough for the creature to release it and instead launch a direct assault at her face. Ellie fell back, clutching her bleeding arm, crashing off the bed and onto the floor. This was enough that the creature's swipe at her face largely missed, instead only leaving her with a light scratch from its three long claws across her cheek. The creature, however, fell with her, landing on her neck, where it immediately went for her jugular with those vicious, deadly teeth. Without so much as a thought, Ellie struck outwards, punching forward with her bleeding, painful arm. She punched the creature directly in its slimy, leathery chest with enough force to launch it off of her. The creature sailed through the air and collided with the wardrobe, but it seemed to rotate its limbs around, digging its claws into the wooden door and immediately climbing it, rather than falling.

Ellie tried to get her bearings quickly. God, her arm hurt, and it was bleeding *heavily*. She thought she might be going into shock, if only she knew what going into shock was supposed to feel like. She tried to remember where the gun was. She must have stripped off her clothes before falling asleep, it seemed. What had she done with the gun?

She spotted her clothes piled up on a nearby chair and she made a dash for them. With any luck the gun would be in the bundle of discarded clothing. The creature was faster, however, scurrying across the ceiling and jumping down, landing on her back. She screamed again as she felt its claws dig in to her shoulders and reached behind her, grabbing it by the scruff of its neck and hurling it forward.

The creature's razor sharp claws tore into her shoulders for grip, but it wasn't able to hold on, and it flew through the air. Unfortunately, Ellie hadn't had time to think about its trajectory, causing it to collide with the chair on which her discarded clothes were sat, knocking it over. The creature landed, buried under her clothing. Exactly where she suspected the gun was.

Ellie hesitated, unsure what to do, whether to bolt for the door or try and find the weapon. Her shoulders burned with agony from where the creature had tried to grasp her. She considered her options desperately. If only she had shoes on, she could have stamped on the thing. But she didn't. And standing on something barefoot when it had that many razor sharp fangs and claws definitely didn't seem like a good idea.

Her hesitation cost her, unfortunately, as the creature burst from underneath her clothing. To Ellie's horror, it was clutching the pistol, holding it in both of its hands. Ellie silently cursed to herself. She'd forgotten to put on the safety. Nina had drilled into her that she should, but with everything that had happened at Angel's Ridge, it had slipped her mind. Ellie froze in terror for a moment, hoping that the creature was too primitive to know how to use the weapon. It let out a curious, amused squeal, and it inspected the object in its hands. It noticed the trigger, and Ellie winced as it pulled it out of curiosity. Fortunately, the gun was aiming straight up when it did, and as it rang out, the gunshot echoing loudly in Ellie's ears. The little creature was knocked flat on its back, distracted by the crumbling ceiling plaster that fell down onto it. Ellie saw her chance and she ran, bolting for the door. As soon as she was out, she slammed it behind her.

There was no way, she realised, to lock the door from the outside. She backed away into the darkened hallway, her breathing ragged. Blood was flowing easily and freely from the wound on her arm, and her shoulders felt damp with blood too from where the creature had dug its claws in. Ellie had never been particularly squeamish, but losing this much blood was making her feel woozy. Her only hope was that the gunshot had alerted Nina and Suzi, and they'd come to her aid quickly. She tried to remember where the light switch was in the hallway, but she had never looked for it before. She had no idea where it was. It was so dark now, the mansion being so overly large that the hallway was far from any windows and source of moonlight. She didn't need to worry about the lack of light for long, however. She realised that there was a sinister red glow making its way down the hallway towards her, and she turned, backing away in horror.

Dozens of red pin pricks filled the air, sets of eyes of an entire horde of the gremlin creatures, scampering over every surface towards her. Some were on the ceiling, some on the walls, some on the ground, and all of them progressing towards her slowly. Several of them emitted a low hissing, and even in the low light, just by the glow of their eyes, Ellie could make out their slimy, brown, leathery skin, their huge ears that looked almost like bat wings, and worse of all, those gleaming fangs and claws. She had already felt the sting of those. She didn't want to feel it again.

She had one stroke of luck, and that was that they were approaching from the far side of the house. They must have found their way in by a window, Ellie realised, and that meant they were effectively shepherding her towards the main staircase and the exit to the house. If she could get outside, they'd lose their advantage of scampering up the walls. She might even be able to get to a car and safety. She didn't want to abandon Nina and Suzi, but right now, she was unarmed and wounded. Escape was her only option.

She began to run, her left arm clutching her bleeding right arm, aware of the considerable flow of blood. Somehow she had always imagined that much blood would feel sticky, warm, and unnatural, but it just felt like lukewarm water in her hand, pouring with a disturbing ease from her body.

There was a horrific bang, and a flare of yellow light from down the far end of the hallway. Past the main staircase, and down the other end. Framed against it was an unmistakable figure. Nina, clad in a black t-shirt and underwear, holding what was clearly a shotgun. She pumped it forcefully and span around, facing away from Ellie, and fired again, into the darkness, where Ellie realised she could make out more pinpricks of red light. Clearly the creatures were attacking both wings of the big mansion, and Nina was busy fighting them off too.

She fired several more times, and Ellie could hear something else too. It sounded like somebody chopping vegetables in a faraway kitchen, a smooth metallic sound followed by the thud of something being cut apart. Nina fired again, and this time the shotgun light lit up the source. Suzi, armed with what appeared to be a sword, hacking at the creatures. Both of them, however, were falling back, and soon all three met at the top of the staircase.

'Okay, I am SUPER glad to see you, but I kinda don't have a weapon!' Ellie panicked right away, gesturing to the creatures behind her that were getting ever closer. Nina whirled, and fired at them, while Suzi cut at the horde that had been following her and Nina with her sword. Wearing a (predictably pink) silk kimono and wielding what Ellie now realised was definitely a Japanese katana, but one with a pink tassel and pink hand wrap, Suzi looked like the world's girliest samurai, she thought, but now wasn't the time to criticise.

'Down the stairs!' Nina yelled, gesturing for them to retreat. 'There's too many of them!' The three of them began to flee down the stairs.

'Did you just have a pump-action shotgun *in your bedroom*?' Ellie asked hysterically as they fled. Nina looked back, for a moment looking quizzical.

'Uh, yeah. Why wouldn't I?' she asked as she frantically reloaded the weapon. Ellie found it hard to argue with that right now, given that it was all that stood between them and imminent death.

'And before… you say it… I know… the whole… Japanese girl… with a katana… is stereotypical!' Suzi yelled as she cut at the approaching creatures, backing down the stairs slowly. 'But it's folded steel! … Cuts through anything!' Nina reached forward to pull her back, away from the horde that threatened to overwhelm her.

'Now! Run for the exit!' Nina commanded.

The three of them ran down the stairs as fast as they could, aware that the creatures were gathering behind them, moving faster and faster. Nina turned to fire another shot back at the creatures, putting a gigantic hole of splintered wood and frayed pink carpet in the staircase. Ellie, still clutching her arm, made it closer to the main doors, Suzi right behind her, when suddenly the big double doors slammed open, bursting inwards with enough force to remove one of them from its hinges and leave the other hanging from the doorframe. There, framed by the darkness, stood a figure. Ellie, Suzi and Nina all came to a halt, almost stumbling right into it.

Ellie quickly took in its features. It wasn't overwhelmingly tall, perhaps a few inches taller than she was, and it was wearing a heavy looking coat that smouldered with ash and smoke. Its face was wrapped in what Ellie could only assume had once been bandages, but they were smouldering and blackened too, and any facial features that she could make out even through the wrap were hidden beneath the shadow of a battered looking fedora. Something gleamed where its arm should be, and Ellie realised that it was a machete, roughly embedded in an angry looking fleshy stump where the right hand should be.

'*You!*' Suzi gasped, bringing her sword around to face it accusingly. Ellie shot her a look. 'It's the thing we saw in the mines!' Suzi explained quickly. 'It's still alive!'

'Not for long!' Nina didn't skip a beat, levelling her shotgun at it and blasting it directly in the chest. It was enough to cause the creature to jolt backwards, its body recoiling, but it only took a slight step back, as if barely bothered by it. Nina reloaded her shotgun and levelled it at the creature again, but this time the creature moved with inhuman speed, its machete arm sailing through the air and slicing into the end of the shotgun, tearing it in half.

Nina fell back from the cut, landing roughly on the floor, holding only the handle and trigger stump of her weapon. She turned quickly, aware that she had nearly fallen back in to the smaller creatures behind them, but they all seemed to have stopped, watching and waiting. In the presence of their master, Ellie realised.

Suzi looked desperately down at Nina, realising they were sandwiched between different creatures, and swung her sword at the being blocking their exit. The creature moved quickly, deflecting it with its machete, but Suzi brought it around in an upwards slice, cutting through the front of the creature's face and slicing the brim of the hat clean off.

The sliced bandages fell away and the hat flew through the air. Ellie looked at the visage that was revealed. With sunken cheeks, empty eye sockets, and hanging, rotting pieces of burned flesh that dangled from a human skull, there weren't exactly many obvious, identifiable features. The dry flesh seemed to sizzle and smoulder and the figure clearly had wisps of long scorched hair left, some of which fell down over its face, and some which draped behind it, now free from the bandages. The hair hissed and burned with a trace of soft red embers. Ellie realised there was definitely something feminine about the appearance. The big bulky coat had made it impossible to tell, but now she could see what was left of the face, the creature had clearly been a woman once. Suzi looked on in horror, letting out a sudden gasp. Nina looked stunned, the remains of the shotgun slipping from her grip where she lay on the floor. Ellie paused. The creature looked horrific, but she hadn't expected the two to react like that.

'Aw, what's the matter? Surprised to see me?' the creature suddenly spoke. Its voice was dry and high pitched, as if incredibly amused with everything it was saying. Everything about that horrible voice was unnatural, but she realised a good part of the reason was that the creature had no lips or tongue to form the words, and yet it did so anyway. It was as unnatural *looking* as it was unnatural *sounding*.

'Well, you're not exactly something you expect to see…' Ellie replied, hoping to find some courage in the quip, and break Nina and Suzi out of their shock.

'Oh, you've got no idea who I am, do you?' the creature rasped, looking at Ellie with what somehow seemed to be disappointment upon its badly damaged face. 'Rude, given you're wearing my top.'

Suddenly, it all made sense. Nina and Suzi's shock. Ellie felt her skin prickle with goosebumps. She was wearing the creature's top. But, the top she was wearing had belonged to…

'Lillian! You're…. Lillian! The girl, the girl who came before me! The one who died!' Ellie gasped, giving Nina and Suzi a horrified, understanding look. No wonder they were so shocked. So afraid. This creature… It was… *She* was… one of them. She was one of their group.

'Oh good, they told you my name. And here I thought they'd forgotten all about me,' Lillian replied with sinister glee.

'It's not Lillian!' Nina shouted, climbing to her feet. 'Lillian was possessed by a demon! She sacrificed herself to destroy it! It must still be inside her! Still controlling her, somehow!' Lillian simply laughed. It was a cold, theatrical, over-the-top "evil" laugh that would have made Freddy Krueger jealous, Ellie thought to herself.

'Oh, please. You're smarter than that. The demon died just like we planned,' Lillian replied, her jaw somehow twisting into a cold smile despite the lack of flesh on her lips. 'And you gave me the perfect origin story.' With her one remaining hand, under a thick brown leather glove, Lillian spelled out imaginary words in the air. 'Possessed by a demon, killed by her best friend, now she returns for revenge…' She lowered her arm again. 'It's perfect.'

'But why!? Why come back!? Why… as this!?' Suzi asked, barely able to comprehend what she was seeing. Nina was clearly shaken, but Suzi was *devastated*. Her eyes were tearing up. It took Ellie a moment to realise why they looked odd; they were brown, not blue. She had obviously removed the contact lenses to sleep.

'Because there *is nothing else*!' Lillian suddenly screamed, her voice raw, raspy, and yet full of hatred. It almost reverberated with strength, like a deep and powerful bass speaker. 'You die. And that's it. All of us who died fighting. All the girls Nina led to their deaths. They all just *die*. And the only thing, the *only thing* that goes on? Is *them*. The monsters. They always come back, and the humans always die.'

'So that's it, huh? Can't beat 'em, so join 'em?' Nina asked, her voice suddenly full of disdain and hatred for Lillian. There was a real anger there, pure and fierce, that Ellie had never heard from her before.

'Why not?' Lillian gave a shrug from within the heavy coat. 'Don't you get it? I *died*. And in that moment of death, all I thought was how *unfair* it was. That we all die, and yet they get to go on. Why does evil always survive while good perishes? And in that moment, in that thought, I was born again. Oh, you think you know the monsters you fight? You should see the *other side,*' she rasped passionately, her eyes smouldering with red fire as she talked.

'Other side? What do you mean?' Ellie asked, trying to keep up.

'Shut up, you. You're nothing,' Lillian waved her hand at Ellie, dismissing her. 'At best, you're here to die to motivate Nina to try and take me down, at worse, you're cannon fodder just to add to the body count. You know, get that nice hard R rating. I mean, I've got to have some generic idiots to kill before I get to the good stuff, right?' Her gaze turned back to Nina.

'That's your idea of the story? The one that'll keep you alive? You're out for revenge on me?' Nina asked.

'Oh, at first. But, y'know, after you're dead, I'll just have to reappear every summer, kill a couple of teenagers, and then I'll live forever. Nobody cares about your origin story after your first appearance,' Lillian gloated, clearly pleased with herself. 'I mean, who cares that the camp counsellors drowned Jason, am I right? By about *Part IV* you're just watching to see him kill people. You don't care why.' Ellie watched, trying to think. Just like Nina, Lillian believed in the *story*, she could see that. She believed in the rules. More than that, she was a *horror nerd*. That reference to *Friday the 13th*. She knew her horror movies. She knew the tropes. Suzi had said they had been similar. Ellie knew that was her chance. She had to play into that.

'Okay, okay, so this is the scene where I die, right?'

'No, Ellie-' Suzi tried to cut her off, but Ellie waved her quiet.

'But before that, before my horrible death, this is clearly the *exposition* scene right? The bad guy reveals themselves and tells us their backstory? I mean, there's always a scene where the survivors find out the killer's story. Usually they're way more creative than just having the killer flat out *tell* them, but hey, that's how you know you're not one of the greats.'

'Watch your tongue! Just because you're about to die doesn't mean it has to be quick!'

'She's right though,' Nina cut in, taking a step forward carefully, edging towards Ellie to guard her from attack. Ellie wasn't sure there was much point; she was feeling so woozy from the blood loss she wasn't sure how long she had left anyway. 'This is clearly the start of the third act. The big finale. You won't get another chance for your evil monologue. You've got us cornered. Might as well get it out of your system now.' Nina suggested. Lillian seemed to pause, her fiery eyes dancing between Suzi and Ellie, before finally relenting back to Nina.

'Oh, alright, fine.' If it was possible, those fiery eyes somehow rolled back in to Lillian's rotting skull for a moment, in a manner that definitely reminded Ellie of Nina. 'But let's do this properly.' She snapped her gloved fingers (which was an impressive feat in itself) and the gremlin creatures surged forward, pressing in around the three human girls. Lillian took a theatrical step forward, until she was standing right in front of the group, sneering in their faces. Suzi wrinkled her nose and looked away from the rotting flesh while Nina stared defiantly. Ellie couldn't look away from those horrible, fiery burning orbs that had once been her eyes, smouldering away within her rotting skull.

Lillian threw out her arms and let out a small cough, as if clearing her throat. Since she didn't really seem to have any skin left on her throat, Ellie was fairly sure it was for dramatic effect.

'Since you're about to die anyway, I might as well tell you everything,' she announced proudly, before pausing and one of her red flaming eyes blinked out in a wink to Nina, obviously proud of her stereotypical line. 'I've always wanted to say that,' she said with a skeletal grin.

'This is why I prefer the whole "masked silent killer" trope,' Nina grumbled, even as the gremlins seemed to close in, one hissing at her as she spoke.

'I'm going to ignore that,' Lillian muttered, although it occurred to Ellie that by saying that she most definitely *wasn't* ignoring it. 'It's just like you always thought, Nina.

The Other Side. When you die. For most people, there's nothing. Blackness. Coldness. Death. But there's one thing that can't die. One thing that lives forever. *An idea,*' Lillian explained, pausing only for dramatic effect. 'Science doesn't bring these monsters back. And it sure as hell isn't religion. It's just a simple thing. An *idea*. When I died, all I felt was hatred. Hatred towards *you,* Nina.'

'You volunteered!' Suzi shouted, desperate to defend her friend.

'Did I?' Lillian asked back with a vicious speed. 'Even if I did, doesn't make dying any easier, it turns out. But that one idea? That perfect storm, hatred, vengeance, the idea that it just wasn't fair, and all my knowledge about what lay beyond, it was the perfect catalyst to bring me back. To make me into *this*.'

'So what about the… weird things? The little gremlin monsters?' Suzi asked, gesturing to the creatures surrounding them.

'Lots of half-baked ideas on the Other Side. Creatures that don't quite have the will, don't *quite* have the full story idea to come back. They just needed a little push. They were only too happy to follow me.'

'And the fire? And the one hand?' Nina asked sceptically. 'I'm pretty sure you had two hands when you died.'

'Every good slasher needs a gimmick. Freddy had his knife glove. Leatherface has a chainsaw. Michael Myers has that weird William Shatner mask thing. The machete is a classic. So, machete hand. As for the fire, well, you *know* what that's about, don't you, Nina?' Lillian taunted gleefully.

'Sounds pretty generic to me. Forgettable,' Ellie said, trying her best to think of something to say to get under her skin. At least, metaphorically. There wasn't much skin to get under in reality. She couldn't pretend she wasn't slightly intrigued by that comment about the fire, but she wasn't going to give Lillian the satisfaction of asking about.

"Well, I can refine it. I mean, hell, Jason didn't even get his hockey mask until *Part III*. Give me a few years killing dumb brats and I'm sure I'll get more and more iconic,' Sadly, Lillian seemed unbothered by the taunt.

'Aren't you forgetting the part where the monster always dies at the end of the movie?' Nina asked.

'Oh, sure, maybe, *maybe*, after I kill everybody you know, you kill me. But even if you do, I'll be back next year. I'll kill you then. I can wait. The killer always comes back. Nobody ever gives a damn about the survivors. That's why everybody knows who Jason Voorhees is and nobody knows who Alyson Harding is.'

'It's Alice. Alice *Hardy,*' Ellie corrected. Maybe Lillian wasn't quite such a horror movie nerd after all. At least, not on Ellie's level. Ellie wasn't sure if she should be proud or embarrassed. 'Final girl in the first Friday movie. *I* know who she is.'

'Kinda proving my point there,' Lillian shrugged. 'But thanks for building up to the next part. See, not only are you new to this little group, not *only* do you have *no* personal connection to me whatsoever, but you also just revealed yourself to be the movie nerd. You know, the one in those postmodern movies there to make it clear the filmmakers know they're writing cliches, but to make it okay to write them anyway. Hanging a lampshade on it, they call it. And do you know what those film nerds have in common?' She lifted her machete blade. 'They *never see the end credits!'*

Lillian surged forward, machete blade extending to impale Ellie. She had nowhere to go, there were gremlin creatures on every side. There was no escape. Strangely enough, all Ellie felt was frustration that Lillian was wrong again. Randy Meeks survived the original *Scream*, and he was basically the original basis for the stereotype Lillian had been ranting about. Ellie closed her eyes, turning away, hearing the dull thud of the machete impacting flesh, but no pain came. Slowly, she turned back to face her attacker, and her eyes opened wide.

Nina had thrown herself in front of Ellie, and the machete had impaled her right through the chest.

'Nina!' Ellie screamed.

'No!' Suzi rushed to her side. Lillian pulled the machete back out of her body, causing Nina to collapse to the floor.

'Nina, it's going to be okay! You're… you're going to be okay.' Ellie found herself saying.

'It's … It's like I warned you before, Ellie. These events… They want to happen. Lillian was making us part of the *story*. Where I'm the final girl. And you two are victims.' She paused, coughing painfully, traces of blood oozing out of her mouth. 'But now? I die. You get revenge. We changed the story.'

'No! How dare you!? You've ruined it!' Lillian snarled, looking at the bloodied machete. 'You can't… you can't leave *them* as the hero! Neither of them are even *white*!'

'And now… she's just given you… motivation to kick her ass even more. Only one thing more satisfying than kicking the butt of a murderous villain.' Nina grinned weakly. 'Kicking the butt of a *racist* murderous villain.'

'No. No! I will not have my grand nemesis be some… some… puffy pink princess or the film nerd! I mean, you're not even the *right* stereotype, Suzi! You're the Japanese rich kid! You should be all strict and formal and worried about doing right by your family! Not like this…

pink... thing you are!' She turned to Ellie. 'And I've never even *met* you! You can't be my final nemesis!' Ellie glared back.

'Screw your story. Screw your pattern. Nina's broken it so I can kill you. And that's what I'm gonna do,' Ellie slowly got to her feet. Lillian paused.

'No, no, it's okay. I can make this work. I mean, Laurie Strode had never met Michael Myers before the first *Halloween* movie right? It was only in the sequel they revealed she was his sister. Yeah. We can fight now, and next year, next year, I can come up with some connection between us. It's gonna be fine,' Lillian said to herself, beginning to pace.

'There's no *connection* between us! I'm gonna kill you and that's it! There ain't gonna be a sequel, you're not gonna live forever, you're gonna die *here and now*!' Ellie roared, although even in her furious state she was aware that she had absolutely no plan. No way of attack. All she knew was anger. All she saw was rage.

She surged forward, but had to stop when Lillian levelled her machete arm directly at her to avoid impaling herself. She found herself looking furiously into Lillian's eyes, unable to make a move, but burning with the desire to attack.

'What? Did you think we were going to have our final showdown *here*? In Barbie's Dream House?' Lillian asked scornfully, before giving Suzi a withering look. 'I've always hated this place. But, I guess the good thing with you, Suzi, is there's so much perfume soaked into this place, I probably didn't even need the gallons of gasoline I had my little friends throw around. I bet this house is plenty flammable all on its own.'

'Flammable?' Suzi questioned, before suddenly her eyes opened wide as she understood. 'ELLIE! RUN!' Ellie understood, just in time, and ignoring the machete,

L.C. VALENTINE

ignoring the creatures, she turned, lifting Nina by ducking under one of her arms. Suzi did the same on the far side, and the trio made for the exit as quickly as they could. Nina was limp, but not yet cold. Ellie knew that she was still alive. They still had a chance to save her.

And then there was only fire, heat and pain.

CHAPTER SEVENTEEN

THE HOSPITAL

Ellie remembered it as waking with a start, suddenly sitting up in bed, hyper-aware of her surroundings. In truth, it was a much slower, much groggier return to the waking world. Her eyes fluttered open and closed again several times before consciousness managed to take hold and pull her out of the inky, dreamless darkness she had been lost in.

There was something unnaturally harsh about hospital lighting, she thought. She wondered if the bright white light was intentional, to keep you awake, or whether it was just to promote the image of a sterile environment. Either way, it *was* clearly a hospital she had awoken in, and she was aware of aches and pains all over her body, although a quick, panicked check of her skin confirmed no obvious burn marks. The deep bite mark on her arm was wrapped in tight bandage, and she was aware of similar dressings on her back underneath the thin, papery hospital gown she was wearing.

In a sudden flash she remembered the roar of fire as the mansion had exploded, and the gust of fire throwing the three of them through the heavy doors. Where was Nina? Suzi? Had they survived? Suddenly Ellie was overcome with panic. She began to try to get up, groggy, weak legs refusing to obey as she tried to swing them out of the hospital bed, only to find bars up on either side. Presumably to prevent her rolling out by accident, but they actually also served to inconvenience her attempts to escape.

'Eliza! Sweetheart, calm down.' The familiar voice cut through her panic and pulled her back to reality. Slowly her eyes began to focus, taking in the surroundings. She was on a hospital ward, with curtains pulled around her bed. In movies, patients always seemed to wake up with large cubicles all to themselves, but this wasn't a movie. This was reality. Sat next to her bed on an uncomfortable, cheap looking plastic chair was her mom, with a seriously worried expression on her face.

Ellie allowed herself to sink back down into the bed, letting out a defeated sigh. Of course her mom was there. Being rushed to hospital would have meant that her details were pulled up and her mother contacted. Of *course*. Not that Ellie regretted seeing her. In fact, after everything that had happened, a moment of normality, an inkling of her old life... it was exactly what she needed.

'Mom!' Ellie said tearfully, and her mom moved to hug her. Ellie let herself be held for several moments, before releasing her and looking at her. Her mom was tearful too, and Ellie couldn't say she blamed her. 'I'm so sorry Mom. I know... I know I was a jerk. How I just left that message and disappeared. But...'

'Shh. It's okay, sweetheart. You're safe now,' Catherine said softly, placing a gentle hand on Ellie's cheek. Ellie smiled for a moment. It was okay. Her mom was there, she wasn't mad, she had survived.

No, wait.

Ellie had survived. But what about Suzi and Nina? And Lillian was still out there! The insanity of recent events came flooding back and she sat up sharply.

'Mom! Where's Nina? Where's Suzi? My friends! Are they okay?'

'Relax, sweetie. Your friend is fine.'

'Friend?' Singular. Not plural. 'Mom, there were *three* of us.'

'Well, they only found you and that Japanese girl. Uh, Suzuki, was it?' Ellie had to resist rolling her eyes. Of *course* her mom called Suzi by her full name too.

'There was another girl, Mom. A British girl. In an eye patch.'

'They definitely only found the two of you.' Catherine gave Ellie a worried look. 'Eliza, sweetie, what *happened*? The police said they found the corpses of some wild dogs in the fire, and the doctors said you'd been bitten…' Ellie knew it was genuine concern, but she also knew that there was no way her mother would understand. She hadn't understood St. Mary's Marsh. Not properly. How would she understand an undead ex-survivor with an army of otherworldly monsters?

'I-I don't know, Mom. Animals must have gotten in the house and turned on the gas or something.' God, that was a lame excuse, but she didn't really have anything better to hand. The frown on her mom's face said that her mom felt the same way, but after a pause, she merely nodded. She probably couldn't think of a better explanation either, Ellie realised. 'Where's Suzi? I need to see her.' If Nina was missing, then that didn't mean she was *dead*, did it? Maybe Lillian had taken her. They still had time. They might still be able to save her.

'Whoa, okay, Eliza, settle down,' Catherine let out what Ellie knew too well as her 'mothering laugh'. It was the laugh her mom gave when she thought whatever Ellie's request had been was so ridiculous there was no way that she'd be allowed to do it. It was Mom for 'no chance in Hell'. 'I'm glad you're alive, I'm *so* glad you're safe, honestly. But you ran away, left me with nothing but a terrifying message, and now you've been found after a house blew up under some pretty weird circumstances.

I'm not about to let you just run off with your friends again.' Ellie knew that tone. That was her mom's tone for "there will be no argument".

It might have worked once. But Ellie wasn't a child anymore. She was nearly nineteen. But more than that, she had seen so much over the last few days. *So* much. She had come so far. And she knew that people were in danger. *She* was in danger. But not only her. So was her mom. So was Suzi. And so was Nina, wherever she was.

'Mom, listen to me,' Ellie said firmly, forcing the sides of the hospital bed down so that she could get up. 'It wasn't wild animals. It wasn't an accident. Somebody tried to kill me. *Something* tried to kill me. And it's still out there.' She swung her legs off of the hospital bed, ignoring the pain in her body as her arm throbbed where the flesh had been torn and the bruises that covered her ached. Painful reminders of the trials of the last forty eight hours, but not ones she could afford to give any attention at that moment.

'What? Ellie, then tell the police! You don't have to-'

'The Police can't help, Mom! This is St. Mary's Marsh all over again, except this time, *this time*, it's not gonna stop. It's after me and Suzi. And anybody who gets in the way. Every second I'm here puts a target on all of your backs.' It was true, Ellie realised, as soon as she said it. There was no way Lillian was done with them, and no way she'd pass up attacking a hospital. Plenty of horror clichés to exploit in a hospital.

'Well, *tell* someone!' Catherine replied, shocked but moving to stop her daughter from leaving. 'The Police can put you in, I don't know, Witness Protection or whatever they call it, if somebody is threatening you!'

'Mom, I told you before, what was after me at the Marsh wasn't human, and what's after me now isn't either. I know you've never believed me, but these things *exist*. One of them killed all my friends! Now I have a chance to save my new friends. I'm not gonna let them down,' she said fiercely. She looked around the hospital bed, spotting what little clothes she had been wearing when the house exploded piled up on the small drawer beside it. She reached over and grabbed her crop top. It was singed.

'Okay, listen, Ellie, even *if* you're right, even *if* this... thing that came after you at St Mary's, even *if* this thing now... even *if* they're some kind of, I don't know, monster... There must be people who deal with it. People who can help! There can't just be monsters and nobody knows!' Catherine's tone was growing ever more desperate, and Ellie wasn't sure if she was beginning to believe.

'There was somebody, Mom. Somebody who could help. Who would go out of her way to save the people these creatures tried to kill. Her name was Nina. Nina Collins. And right now, she's in danger. Right now, the only person who can fight back... is me.' Ellie stood a little straighter. 'You're right, there is somebody who can help. You're looking at her.' A moment passed. She wasn't sure if she had over-egged it. It *had* been a little cheesy, hadn't it?

'Okay, fine,' Catherine nodded after a moment. 'But you're not wearing that.' She gestured to the burned clothing, before she pulled a small hold-all out from under the chair she had been sat on. 'I brought you some spare clothes, for when you woke up.' Ellie gratefully took the bag, and looked through it. Jeans, a dark purple t-shirt, and she smiled to see her light leather jacket. Imitation leather, of course, and not something she often wore, but somehow, it seemed appropriate. Not quite the dramatic leather duster Nina wore, but close enough.

Better than wearing Lillian's clothes anyway. 'Your friend is in a private cubicle down the corridor. Room 3. Now go, before the nurses come around and figure out you're gone,' Catherine said. Ellie paused, looking back at her mom.

'Mom. I… I love you.' She grabbed her, and gave her a hug.

'I love you too, sweetheart. Just save your friend, and make sure you come back. I can't lose you.' It was obvious doubt edged her every word. She obviously had no idea if she was doing the right thing and truthfully, Ellie didn't know either.

'You won't,' Ellie smiled, wishing that she felt more confident, like the words weren't a lie.

'Also, your friend seems pretty wealthy. Maybe ask if she can help with the medical bills? I'm pretty sure our insurance doesn't cover it if you just walk out of the hospital,' her mom quickly added. Ellie repressed a slight laugh. That was her mom, alright. She always had her priorities right.

'I will Mom. I promise,' she replied.

And then Ellie turned and walked away. She didn't look back. She couldn't. Instead, she ducked into a nearby restroom and quickly began to change, pulling on the fresh underwear and her new clothes. She tore off the patient wristband and threw it down the toilet, before stuffing her old hospital robe back in the hold-all and leaving it on the side. She made her way back out in her new clothes, and paused for a brief moment, before hurrying down the corridor. She realised that she was slightly hunched over, as if instinctively sneaking, before pausing and forcing herself to walk a little more upright. After all, nothing looked more suspicious than sneaking around, right? As far as hospital staff knew, she was just another visitor. Besides, she could self-discharge herself if she wanted to? The hospital couldn't *make* her stay there.

She paused outside of the room marked '3', and looked in through the window. It was, fortunately, empty, bar for the patient in the bed. Had it not been for the pink hair, Ellie might have not recognised her. She realised it was the first time she had seen Suzi with absolutely no make-up. Even when she had been woken up in the middle of the night, it seemed Suzi had worn a level of make-up to bed. Her 'sleeping make-up', Ellie would later find out she called it. She was also not in pink, but in the pale blue of the hospital gown. The room was almost completely bare, and for a moment Ellie felt for her. Where were her parents? She was so wealthy, she clearly had whatever she wanted, but now she was hurt, in hospital, and there was nobody there for her? Not even a card? A further peek revealed the only decoration, on the chair next to Suzi's bed. A discarded cowboy hat. Clearly Jess was here, although it seemed she was taking a break. That thought made Ellie smile a little. At least Suzi wasn't completely alone.

Ellie pushed open the door and made her way in, and Suzi sat up sharply, giving a surprised smile. She looked bruised, but not badly hurt. She had a bandage over part of her face, Ellie spotted, and must have probably taken a nasty knock to the head, but apart from that was unharmed.

'Ellie!' Suzi said with a smile, before pausing, and taking in her clothes. 'You're... They can't have discharged you already!' She added with shock. Ellie shook her head.

'No. But I'm leaving anyway. We have to save Nina,' Ellie began. 'Her body wasn't found. If she was dead,

Lillian would have left her there. She's got to still be alive. We can still save her.' Suzi seemed to hesitate.

'Ellie, I…' She trailed off, and for a moment looked over at the empty seat, and discarded hat. It was clear that she wished Jess was there for support. 'I don't know… if I can.'

'What do you mean?' Ellie asked, slightly taken aback by Suzi's reluctance. 'Are you hurt? That explosion was pretty nasty, but-' She didn't get to finish her question.

'Ellie, my *home* is gone. Everything I ever owned, all destroyed. My best friend is probably dead. I… I can't keep doing this,' Suzi said, her voice wavering a little.

'She's not dead! We can still save her!' Ellie insisted. 'And yeah, okay, your house got destroyed. I know that's gotta suck, but, we've all lost a lot.'

'It's not *just* the house, Ellie!' Suzi snapped, and it was the first time Ellie could ever remember hearing traces of anger in her voice. 'I've lost *too much*. Over and over again people die. And now Lillian… Lillian is back, and she wants to kill us. I just… I can't take it anymore. Lillian was so good when she came to us. So pure. So brave. And look what she's turned in to. Look at what we *turned her into*.'

'You didn't do anything to Lillian,' Ellie insisted. 'And neither did Nina. Whatever twisted *thing* came back from the dead, she's not human anymore. Everything that made her human got left behind. Lillian's just a shadow now.' Ellie wasn't sure if she believed her words. They sounded good. They sounded *true*. But Ellie didn't know. She hadn't known Lillian. She didn't know if she'd always been as twisted as she seemed or if she had ended up that way after her death, but all Ellie knew was that Suzi had to be persuaded to act.

'But every time, *every time*, I think we're helping people, it comes back to hurt us! One of us doesn't make it home, or something else awful happens. How can we keep fighting? *Why*? When we always lose?'

'Because you don't lose! You win! No matter the cost, you've always won. At Angel's Ridge, we saved those guys. Without us, they'd of all ended up dead. I know I'm new at this, but are you honestly telling me you can sit there and let somebody die when you could have helped? That's not you, Suzi,' Ellie tried, and Suzi paused, looking away. She sighed.

'I honestly thought that. I always said that. That if I could save just one, just one person, if just *one* person was alive today because of me, it'd all be worthwhile. But… Lillian. We created her. Everybody she hurts, it's *because* of us,' Suzi explained.

'And everybody she saved before this, working with you and Nina, that was because of you as well. Besides, you can't blame yourself for what somebody else does. You didn't make her come back from the dead. You didn't make her come after us. You can't blame yourself. But you *can* stop her,' Ellie said fiercely. A moment passed, and Suzi sighed again, looking away, before looking back at Ellie.

'How?' She asked, but her tone had changed. It wasn't a despairing question, nor was it protest. It was practical. She wanted to know how it could be done. And that meant she was on board.

Before Ellie could answer, the door behind them swung open, and Ellie turned, startled and defensive, but relaxed as she saw Jess make her way in. She was wearing a tight denim skirt and leather vest top, and cowgirl boots, but somehow her ensemble looked a little odd without her discarded hat.

'You got through to her, then?' she commented, her thick Texan accent wrapping around each word.

'You were listening?' Ellie asked.

'Listening? Hell, I was rooting for you,' she smiled, moving to Suzi's side and giving her a kiss on the cheek. 'My girl was having a crisis of faith, but I knew it wouldn't last.'

'You knew?' Suzi asked, looking back at Jess.

'Yeah, you ain't never given up before when someone's in danger, and you ain't gonna start now,' Jess said with a small nod. 'But this time, I ain't leavin' you to go alone.'

'Huh? Wait, Jess, no-' Suzi began. Jess just shook her head.

'Nina's done a lot for me too. She's in danger. And you're down a girl. You need numbers. I'm in.'

'Welcome aboard,' Ellie smiled. She hadn't factored for Jess, but the Texan was right. They needed numbers. And Jess would be appreciated.

'Okay, okay. But you didn't answer my question, Ellie. *How*? Lillian's basically immortal now, and she has an army of those creatures.' Suzi looked between Jess and Ellie. 'How are we going to stop her?'

'I've been thinking about that,' Ellie replied. 'It's like Nina said. About the story. Lillian's writing a story for herself. The immortal slasher back for revenge. We need to change the story.'

'But how do we do that? She's after us. Anything we do, it's just playing right into her hands,' Suzi asked.

'We go *Aliens* on her,' Ellie stated, a slight smirk on her face.

'Wait, what?' Jess and Suzi said together, both looking at Ellie quizzically.

'See, she was ranting about *Halloween II*. And it got me thinking, in *Halloween II*, Michael Myers comes back, right? And he attacks a hospital, exactly like where we are, and he's more unstoppable than ever. That's what she wants. Sequel after sequel to make her more and more unkillable. She's made her debut. What she does next she thinks will only make her more powerful' Ellie explained.

'What's that got to do with a space alien?' Jess asked with a frown.

'Not an alien. *Aliens*. The James Cameron movie,' Ellie answered. 'Look, in *Alien*, right, the original one by Ridley Scott, the alien was this big, unstoppable killing machine. Just one and it wiped out the whole crew. *Alien*'s a scary, tight, claustrophobic horror movie. But for the sequel, Cameron totally changed the genre. It became an action movie. And the alien? Well, this time there were loads of them, and they just became cannon fodder. They were getting blown apart left, right and centre.'

'So... you're saying... we change the genre?' Suzi asked, her voice suddenly becoming excited as she got it. 'Lillian is counting on being the star slasher of a horror movie, but if we change the genre...'

'...We go after her. We bring the fight to *her*. No fear. No sneaking around. We go in all guns blazing...' Jess nodded as she began to understand.

'....then it's not a horror movie anymore. The slasher horror icon might always come back, but the bad guy in an action movie? They're always replaced by the sequel.' Ellie finished explaining.

'But we're not action heroes!' Suzi pointed out.

'Aren't we? We have weapons. We fight off monsters. We can do this.' Ellie said confidently. It was a faux confidence, sure, but she had to project it. She had no idea if they could do it really. But she knew they had to try. She couldn't let Nina down.

'All our weapons were at the mansion. They're gone,' Suzi said quietly, obviously troubled by the memory of her lost home.

'Sweetie, I'm your girlfriend and I'm from Texas, remember? Trust me, I've got spare guns,' Jess smiled, before giving Ellie a slightly ashamed "I'm a stereotype, so what?" shrug.

Suzi paused again, and finally nodded, moving to get out of the bed.

'Okay. Okay. Let's do it.. I think this plan is crazy, even by *our* standards. But Nina needs us. But how do we find her?'

'Lillian's clearly basing herself on classic movie slashers, right?' Ellie replied. 'Well, they've always got a lair. Freddy's got his boiler room, Jason has his shack in the woods, Michael's got his old house in Haddonfield, Leatherface has his creepy basement… She'll have a lair somewhere. Something scary, but has ties to her.'

'The crypt!' Suzi said suddenly.

'The what?' Ellie asked.

'The crypt! When we did the whole ritual thing that killed her, transferring the demon into her and all that, it was at a crypt. We needed somewhere where the connection to the demon in the spirit world was at its strongest, so we found where the first person the demon had ever possessed was buried. In this old crypt in a nearby graveyard.'

'Right. Well, "spooky crypt" sure sounds like it's up this chick's alley,' Jess agreed.

'Huh. And I was hoping for a shack in the woods,' Ellie grumbled. 'But okay. A crypt. Do you know where it is, Suzi?'

'Uh, of course. I'm not gonna forget it. A friend died there.'

'Alright, we need to gather our weapons and get ready to move out,' Ellie decided.

'A crypt's a lot of stonework. If she's got those creatures like the one that attacked my plane, guns blazing or not, it's gonna be hard work to get inside there. Ain't you never seen *Lord of the Rings?* Defending a big stone place is pretty easy, and we don't have an army of orcs to help us out,' Jess said cautiously, but she was clearly deep in thought, trying to find a solution. Ellie paused for a moment, and then slowly smiled.

'You're talking about *The Two Towers*, right? I think you've just given me an idea. Except it's a lot more *Return of the King.*' Ellie couldn't hide a grin.

'We've got friends too!' Suzi said after a moment's thought. 'I'll see if I can get some of them to help us.'

'Now there's my optimistic girlfriend.' Jess winked to Suzi.

Ellie found herself breathing a subconscious sigh of relief. Clearly Suzi was onboard. Now they just had to get moving.

'Alright, first course of action is getting out of here. I wasn't kidding about *Halloween II*. Massacre at a hospital. If we stay here, Lillian won't be able to resist that. She'll come for us here, and who knows who'll get hurt on the way.'

'Well, can you two just leave? Y'all patients here, and you were rescued from an explosion. I imagine the cops are gonna want to talk to you,' Jess asked.

'Well, we're not under arrest, and I figure they can't keep us here if we don't want to be here, right? You can medically discharge yourself from a hospital, can't you?' Ellie shrugged.

'I think so,' Suzi agreed.

'And hey, if you can't, well, they'll just have to try and stop us.'

CHAPTER EIGHTEEN

RALLYING CRY

Leaving the hospital hadn't quite been the dramatic affair Ellie had perhaps expected. Rather than risk further detention or filling out forms, she opted for the rather simplistic approach of 'just walking out'. Suzi had stopped to change out of her medical robe, although she was sulking about the plain pink dress Jess had brought her to wear. Ellie was glad however, and figured it was forward thinking on Jess's part. After all, Suzi's clothing did have a way of drawing attention to itself.

After that, they'd bundled in to Jess's pick-up truck (a vehicular choice that Ellie shouldn't have been surprised by) and made for Jess's ranch. The sun shone brightly in the sky, and it was only mid-afternoon. That was good, Ellie thought to herself. Nightfall was when things would get interesting. Lillian would wait until then before trying anything. But once the sun went down, she realised the gloves were off.

There was silence as Jess drove, and Suzi seemed to be concentrating on her pink-hued phone. Ellie realised that her own cell phone had been lost in the blast, but clearly Suzi had more than one, and Jess had brought her a replacement. The advantages of being rich, Ellie assumed.

'Okay, I've messaged Avril and Kat. They're in,' Suzi told Ellie with a nod.

'Wait, you got both of their numbers? When did *that* happen?' Ellie asked with a frown.

'What? We met them, we made friends, why wouldn't I have gotten their numbers?' Suzi replied with a look on her face that suggested *not* immediately getting all the contact details of people you met was the weird thing.

'Great. Can I borrow Kat's number? It's for an idea I have,' Ellie requested.

'You can't borrow a number, silly,' Suzi teased with a smile, and Ellie was glad to see that she was getting back to her old self. 'But I can tell you what it is!' she added.

'Actually, uh, can I just borrow your phone?' Ellie asked.

'Oh, sure! Is your phone missing? I've got spares!'

'Are they all pink?'

'One's kinda purple.'

'I guess I don't have a choice,' Ellie laughed lightly. 'For now, borrowing your phone will be okay, but yeah, I'd appreciate it.'

'If you two are calling in others, that's gonna slow us down,' Jess observed, her eyes still on the road. 'I thought you said she'd make her move tonight?'

'If we were still at the hospital, she would. Now, I'm not so sure. Maybe? I mean, she might try something. But either way, we need reinforcements,' Ellie explained.

'We can always fly and pick them up, but you gotta forgive me if I'm a bit sceptical about taking to the air again while we've got Lillian on our backs. If she sent that thing after us last time, what's she gonna do this time?' Jess pointed out.

'Crap. Didn't think of that,' Ellie admitted.

'Alright, uh, I know Nina would be mad at me for suggesting this, but we should split up,' Suzi said. Even Ellie gave her a startled 'I can't believe you said that' look. 'No, no, seriously, think about it!' Suzi added quickly. 'Lillian's after us. Me and you. If Jess goes one way, and we stay behind, if she's gonna come after anyone, it's gonna be us.'

'Sounds kinda like tempting fate to me,' Ellie said cautiously.

'You got a better idea?' Jess asked. 'I mean, we could charter a private plane for Kat and Avril, but it'll take longer. And that's if Lillian then doesn't try to target *that* plane. At least with me they've got a fighting chance.'

'I thought you were just the pilot, that you didn't do the whole monster hunting thing?' Ellie jibed playfully.

'I told you. I'm from Texas. Trust me, we Texans can take care of ourselves,' she teased back with a wink at Ellie.

'You know, I don't think I've ever heard you mention you're from Texas before...' Ellie mocked.

'Yeah, well, y'know, I keep it on the down low,' Jess replied. Ellie thought she might have even exaggerated her Texan accent while she said that.

'Jess is actually State Lariat Champion three years running,' Suzi announced proudly.

'Lariat? Like ... a lasso?' Ellie frowned.

'Hey, it's a skill, alright?' Jess countered.

'What are you gonna do, herd the gremlin things? Lasso up Lillian and put her in a barn?' Ellie teased.

'Hey, it works for Wonder Woman,' Jess said back with a smile. 'Besides, the lasso is just for showing off. I got a six shooter with Lillian's name on it too.'

'I thought you said you didn't put names on your guns anymore,' Suzi asked.

'I didn't mean *literally,* sweetie,' Jess smiled. There was a brief moment while the group regarded each other. Ellie wasn't sure if all the joking and playfulness and throwing jokey insults at each other were a result of her nerves, a sign of friendship or something else. But it helped distract from their task. She had thought it was bad enough signing up to fight monsters and ghouls, but knowing one out there was coming for you specifically? That was even worse. There was a sense of inevitability hanging over the group. The feeling that soon, *very* soon, everything would go to Hell.

In their line of work, Ellie realised, that might happen literally.

The rest of the journey occurred largely in silence after that. Eventually the trio arrived at the ranch, and Jess prepared to depart. They decided there wasn't much point in hanging around. Suzi phoned ahead to Kat and Avril to tell them Jess was on her way, and let Ellie borrow the phone for the message she had to pass on. She made sure to keep it private. It wasn't just because she wasn't actually sure if it was a good idea or not yet, but a tiny part of her wanted it to be a surprise in case it worked. It was perhaps selfish and not a great strategy, but she couldn't resist.

After Jess had left Suzi suggested they make some food, and Ellie realised how hungry she was. She couldn't remember the last time she had eaten. Suzi guided Ellie to a rather fully stocked kitchen, predictably with a fridge full of various meats and barbecue sauces. Ellie guessed Jess really did live the stereotype.

'Wow. Okay, I'm *starving*,' Ellie admitted when she saw all the food. 'I didn't realise how hungry I was until now.'

'What are we having?' Suzi asked.

'Well, it's your girlfriend's house and your idea to eat. What do you wanna cook?'

'*Cook*? Me?'

'You have no idea how to cook, do you?'

'No. I mean, back when I was growing up, we always had a family cook. Once I joined Nina's group and we used my mansion as a base, well, I guess somebody else in the group always cooked. Nina wasn't great at it but she liked to do it. She always confused me though.'

'Why?'

'Well, her favourite thing to cook was a curry. She kept saying it was a British staple.'

'Aren't curry's Indian?' Ellie raised an eyebrow.

'Yeah. Uh, that's what I thought.'

'Britain is *weird*.'

In the end the two girls settled on bacon sandwiches, mainly because they were quick, easy and definitely filled the hole that Ellie was feeling from her hunger. She thought better of asking Suzi to help with the dishes, since she figured Suzi had also probably never done washing up in her life either. She did it herself. She made sure everything was put away neatly, given that it wasn't her house, and Jess wasn't there. She didn't want Jess returning home to feel that they had left the place in a mess, after all.

It was strange, Ellie thought, that *that* was a concern when they might all be dying very shortly.

It was then that Suzi and Ellie found themselves sitting in Jess's front room, an awkward silence falling over them. The sky was darkening, and the stars were beginning to show. Suzi switched on a small lamp, bathing the room in yellow light. The sofa that they were both sat on was surprisingly comfortable, a soft deep tan fabric, and although the rest of the room had something of a rustic aesthetic (Ellie almost expected to see bull's horns mounted on the wall), she couldn't help but spot the small Suzi touches. A fluffy pillow here, a Disney ornament there. In fact, the centrepiece on her fireplace appeared to be a large statue of Mickey Mouse riding a horse, dressed as a cowboy. It was a little on the nose, Ellie thought, but clearly a gift that Jess treasured. Ellie stood up, and moved to the window, looking out over the fields outside, which stretched out as far as her eye could see, the purple evening sky making it challenging to see far.

'Why do I feel like I'm in *Zulu*? Waiting for the attack,' Ellie sighed.

'I don't think I saw that one,' Suzi replied.

'Well, it wasn't Disney,' Ellie teased.

'You say that now, but the rate they're buying things up, they'll probably own it soon,' Suzi countered. Ellie just allowed herself a smile.

'It's just… Waiting. Waiting for somebody to come. I keep expecting to see Lillian and her horde approaching over the fields,' Ellie explained. 'Hiding out on a ranch suddenly seems like a bad idea.'

'She probably won't attack us directly, don't worry,' Suzi pointed out. 'It's like you said before, remember? Lillian wants this to be a horror movie. You don't get a big army attacking in a horror movie.'

'No, I guess not. But she's gonna try *something*. I just know it,' Ellie replied as she returned to sit on the sofa.

'Well, we're ready for her, right?' Suzi said with a confidence Ellie didn't feel. Sure, they had their weapons, they knew she was coming, but how could you really be ready for a threat like Lillian? 'And tomorrow, when the others get here, *we* go after *her*.'

'Yeah,' Ellie answered uneasily.

'I've never gone to war before, but I'm guessing you don't sleep easy the night before,' Suzi said after a pause.

'No, somehow, I don't think we're gonna get a wink of rest tonight,' Ellie agreed, knowing they'd both have to stay awake and wait. It was for the best, Ellie knew. That way they'd both be on their guard. That way, nobody would get the drop on them.

It was therefore a shame but unsurprising that both girls, exhausted, aching and having faced constant physical trials, were both fast asleep within five minutes.

CHAPTER NINETEEN

NIGHTMARE ON OUTLAW RANCH

Ellie couldn't remember how she had gotten there, but she was surrounded by trees. *Familiar* trees. Beneath her feet, the mud squelched, wet and damp, and she had to watch her step to make sure her sneakers didn't disappear within. She looked down at her St. Mary's Marsh Camp Counsellor blouse, stained and torn from muck and smoke, and even blood where the blade had caught her arm.

She tried to remember. What blade? The Mirror Monster? But that had been so long ago. St. Mary's Marsh was so long ago now. How was she back there? There was a crackle of thunder and she looked up at the sky. It was a deep dark red, broken up only by dark storm clouds and flashes of crimson lightning. Rain began to fall from the sky, pouring heavily and soaking Ellie to the skin almost instantly.

Another roar of thunder and flash of lightning crashed across the landscape, the light so bright that Ellie had to shield her eyes for a moment. Spots danced across her vision, orbs swirling and pulsing, not helped by the heavy rain. Slowly, as her vision began to be restored, she became aware of a figure standing before her. Her entire body tensed, ready to run, but it wasn't the Mirror Monster she saw.

It was Lillian.

'Really? This is where your nightmare takes you?' Lillian asked, her voice deep and harsh, as if booming from the very trees themselves, and not just from her mouth. She wasn't wearing her mask or hat, but otherwise, she was dressed exactly as when Ellie had last seen her. 'Disappointing. It's just so *bland*.'

'It wasn't bland if you were there!' Ellie found herself having to shout, to make her voice heard over the roar of the weather.

'Oh, come on. Reliving a past trauma? I was hoping for something more original than that,' Lillian scoffed. 'It just goes to show… It's like I said. You're cannon fodder. You're no hero. You're no "final girl". There's nothing imaginative or special about you,' she sneered. The rain seemed to wash away some of the rotting flesh hanging from Lillian's skull, leaving gleaming, wet white bone on show beneath it.

'Oh, and you're special, are you? I mean, come *on*. Machete-for-a-hand? Real original. I mean, ignoring the whole 'killer with a deformity' stereotype, did you know they actually had Jason Voorhees do that in the spin-off comics anyway? Big crossover with Freddy and Ash from *Evil Dead*. Got his hand chainsawed off by Ash.'

'Wow, you really *are* a nerd,' Lillian scoffed.

'My point is, even your gimmick is unoriginal! And stalking some girl you feel wronged you? Wanting some deep and meaningful connection? Michael Myers called. He said welcome to nineteen seventy nine! And now this? Discount *Nightmare on Elm Street* stuff? You want to be an icon, but you haven't got an original idea in what's left of your skull,' Ellie hoped her words did the job and sounded strong and defiant, as her voice was quivering as she spoke.

'That's the beauty of it!' she boasted, throwing her arms out with a laugh, the machete cutting through the air with a whistle. 'Now I'm on the other side, there's no limits to what I can do. Whatever I can think of, I can make happen. I can enter your dreams, I can stalk you during every waking moment, I can be anywhere and everywhere, and you'll never be rid of me!'

'Only as long as the story's good enough!' Ellie replied, trying to stand her ground, even as the rain soaked through her skin. God, it was cold. How was it so *cold* during a dream? None of this was real, right? And yet she was aware of every goose pimple on her skin. 'That's how it works, isn't it? These monsters, these things, they exist to follow stories. And your story…. It *sucks.* You're a cheap knock off!'

'I'm postmodern. It's clever,' Lillian replied, but her voice was edged with something that sounded like real anger. Ellie knew that she was getting to her. She just wished she knew what that meant.

'Nobody *likes* postmodernism! Nobody even knows what it means! And if you're thinking you're being clever because you're all self-aware, *Scream* did it first, in, like, nineteen ninety six,' Ellie taunted, although she wished she had a plan beyond "make the killer mad". Maybe now wasn't a good time to be showing off her encyclopaedic film knowledge, but she couldn't resist.

'And *Halloween* wasn't the first slasher movie. But it's the one everybody remembers. You don't have to be original. You just have to be good at what you do. And I'm *very* good at this,' Lillian grinned.

'You're not *Halloween*. You're not even *Sleepaway Camp*. At best, you're *Hollywood Chainsaw Hookers*!' Ellie yelled back over the rain, determined to cut away at her pride.

For a moment, both girls were silent as the rain thundered down around them and lightning flashed

'Wait, is there really a movie called that?' Lillian suddenly asked conversationally as thunder rumbled

'Yeah. It's actually pretty great,' Ellie answered casually.

'Huh. Wow. Yeah. Sounds it,' Lillian replied sarcastically, before shaking her skeletal head. 'That's not the point! You're right. I'm not Michael Myers. I'm not Jason Voorhees. I'm not Leatherface. I'm not Freddy Krueger. I'm not Ghostface. I'm not Chucky. I'm something more. Something new. I'm all of them combined. Wanna see what I can do?' She growled. She began to advance, her machete arm slicing through the air with a threatening gleam.

Ellie turned to retreat, but became aware that the muddy ground she had been standing on, growing increasingly waterlogged by the rain, had swallowed her feet. She pulled against the mud, but it sucked back on her feet, thick and heavy. She felt like she had two massive weights strapped to her legs, and every time she tried to pull away, her strength gave out just before she could move. With each successive struggle, it seemed her feet were only pulled deeper.

'What's the matter? *Stuck*?' Lillian's skeletal face seemed to grin. Ellie began to struggle more frantically, but it only caused her to sink further and faster. This was no longer mud, she realised, but the very ground itself swallowing her up.

'God, even your taunts are unoriginal,' Ellie chided as she struggled to move, but there was no purchase. Nothing to stand on. Just impossibly heavy mud, slowly sucking her down. It was so heavy, so cloying, so *thick*. It stuck to her legs, making it impossible to move, a thick goop from which escape was impossible.

'This is *my* domain now. I control everything here,' Lillian said coldly.

'And yet the most original thing you could think of was *quicksand*?' Ellie taunted back, but she was beyond her waist now, her arms held high to hold them out of the muck, but it wouldn't last. There was no way she could move. Nothing to hold on to...

'It's a classic nightmare,' Lillian boasted proudly.

'It's a cliché!' Ellie snapped back. She was up to her armpits now, and feeling the thick, cold muck pushing down on her all around, restricting her breathing and making it so even struggling was nearly impossible. She knew all the rules from films, of course. Don't struggle. Try to float on your back. But it was useless here. She was just being pulled down no matter what she did. This wasn't real and that meant the laws of physics had no interest in being obeyed.

'Well, those were pretty lame last words. Goodbye.... You know what, I don't think I even remember your name? You'd be in the credits as "Victim Number One",' she said with a sinister skeletal grin. 'I guess lame last words suit you.'

The muck was around Ellie's neck, and she couldn't even turn her head anymore. She felt it soaking into her short bob, pulling her head back with the weight of it. Last words? Why did that echo in her mind? *Last words*. Because that was Lillian, she realised. Through and through. Last words. Lillian had to have the last word. Just like Ellie liked to taunt and argue, so did Lillian. There was no way Lillian would let Ellie die with the last word in the conversation. All she needed was the right taunt. The right thing said that Lillian couldn't let go. The one thing to make her madder than anything else. As the mud began to reach the edges of her mouth, she let out one final gurgling cry.

'Nina will stop you!'

And then there was nothing but crushing watery mud. She was drowning, but she couldn't even move. She always imagined drowning as a horrible moment in which you thrashed and writhed in desperation, but the mud was too thick, too heavy, she was suspended, unable to move a muscle. All the while furiously running out of oxygen, not even able to open her eyes in the awful darkness.

But something happened. Something changed. Suddenly, Ellie was aware that her feet were free. She was still sinking, and she was moving beyond the mud, beyond the muck, into glorious open air. There was a slurp, and like a baby spitting its foot out, the mire threw her free into darkness, and she was falling through the air, free to take desperate breaths into her burning lungs.

She landed *hard* on a stone floor. She had fallen long enough for the landing to kill her, but somehow she had survived. She wouldn't have fallen free if there wasn't a way to walk away from it, Ellie realised. Lillian had chosen this. She was surrounded by darkness and cold stone in the form of a long, narrow corridor, like some kind of small passageway carved from ancient rock. The open air that had seemed so wonderful only seconds ago now felt still and ancient, heavy with dust and an unearthly chill.

'Get up.' Lillian said coldly, and Ellie was aware that she was looming over her. Coughing up a chunk of mud, Ellie struggled to her feet, still in her camp counsellor uniform, now entirely brown from being submerged in the muck. She was breathing hard, aware that Lillian was within striking distance, but too drained from her ordeal to try and fight. She didn't know if it would do any good anyway. This was her nightmare. Could she kill Lillian here? It certainly felt like Lillian nearly killed *her*. She hadn't even questioned it. She'd seen enough movies to know exactly how the "if you die in the dream, you die in real life" rule worked.

'All of you girls are the same. Nina recruits you. The last survivor of some massacre. The last girls standing! You all think you're special. I know I did. But nobody's as special as *Nina*. She's the hero. The leader. The one you all look up to. Even now, about to die, you still think she's going to save you, don't you?' Lillian snarled. 'So did I! I thought I was different! I knew people had died before. But I thought, in that moment of death, no, this wouldn't really happen. Nina would find a way to save me! But she didn't! She let me die and she replaced me! With *you*!' The hatred in Lillian's voice came out like a snarl, and Ellie had to wipe spit from her mud plastered face.

'She didn't replace you!' Ellie yelled back. 'She cared about you! They all did! But you *died*. People don't always survive. You can't throw yourself into danger and always expect to make it out. That's the way the world works!'

'Nina always makes it out though, doesn't she? Everybody else dies, but Nina survives!' Lillian countered, before stopping, her skeletal face twisting into a sinister grin. 'Well, until now.'

'You can drop the act. There was no body, we know she's not dead,' Ellie stated firmly.

'I ran her through with my machete. She's as dead as they come, sweetheart,' Lillian mocked. Ellie faltered for a moment. There was something in how Lillian spoke that suggested she really *did* believe that, that it wasn't a ruse, but that couldn't be true, could it? There had been no body. Why take the body if Nina was dead? It had to be a bluff. Nina had to still be alive.

'Maybe she's still out there. Maybe she's abandoned us too, y'know, going it alone, like a true hero. Maybe she's coming for you *right now*?' Ellie suggested, allowing herself a smirk, knowing it was a sensitive subject. She wasn't sure what she was trying to achieve, but it seemed to be keeping Lillian off balance. Maybe she was just stalling until she woke up? That seemed like a plan. Not a *great* plan, she'd admit. After all, time worked different in a dream, right? How long had she been asleep? It could be hours yet. Hell, could it stretch to *days?* She realised it didn't matter. She just had to try to make her angry. Try to break her focus. It was her only idea.

Lillian, however, just let out a deranged cackle, and her empty eye sockets fell back to focus on Ellie.

'You still think she's such a hero, don't you?' Lillian asked. 'Didn't you wonder where we are? Let me *show* you what a "hero" she is.' Lillian spat angrily. Her one good hand lashed out, and grabbed Ellie's wrist, pulling her in a vice-like grip. Ellie had no choice but to follow. She tried to refuse, tried to pull away, but her mud soaked sneakers just slid on the stone floor, and she was pulled helplessly down through the darkness.

Ahead, she saw a crack of light and the corridor opened into a chamber. There was a huge stone casket in the middle, with a pedestal before it, and Ellie could make out a large stone staircase making its way upwards, stretching into darkness. It was some kind of tomb, she realised. A tomb that was lit by three artificial lights, on stands, stood around the casket. It put Ellie in the mind of a film set being lit, or perhaps an archaeological excavation. Lillian stopped, and thrust Ellie in front of her, so that she could see inside, but held her firmly, so that she couldn't move.

'*Watch*. Watch and see what a hero your Nina is,' she hissed.

Suddenly, there were steps and people in the chamber. They didn't enter down the stairs, but rather just appeared, as if stepping out of a smoky haze, like a memory suddenly flashing across Ellie's eyes. Except they weren't just a memory. They were physical. They were real. They were right there. God, she could even smell Suzi's perfume.

Nina stood there, hands in her pockets, her trench coat flowing behind her. She looked perhaps a year or two younger. Ellie thought her hair looked slightly fuller and better kept, and maybe a touch longer too. She wasn't sure if it was her imagination or not, but she could swear the scar beneath her eye patch looked far angrier and more raw. Suzi, in her frilly pink dress, gripped some kind of large, brown book. She looked identical to how she always did, although Ellie realised it would be impossible to see any signs of age under her heavy cosmetics. There was another girl too. She wore a familiar hoodie and jeans, and had short vibrant red hair. Ellie recognised the hoodie. She had seen it back in the closet at Suzi's house.

'That's you., Ellie realised, looking to Lillian in shock.

'Do you like the red hair?' Lillian asked dismissively. 'I'm a natural blonde, but Nina always made sure any of us blondes dyed our hair. Safer, she said. The forces of darkness like blondes,' she commented.

'Well, you look a lot better then than you do now.'

'Shut up and watch.' Lillian gripped Ellie's arm with considerable force, her bony fingers digging into Ellie's muscle and causing her to bite back a yelp of pain.

Out in the chamber, the figures of Nina, Suzi and the human Lillian were moving around the casket.

'Get ready,' Nina ordered, and Ellie could see gleaming in her hands a shotgun. She wondered if it was the same one she had used in defence of the house, but she couldn't tell. Not from this distance. A long moment seemed to pass. Suzi stood behind Nina, clutching the book. From where she was hidden Ellie could see was wrapped in a crinkled, brown leather, with what looked like a screaming, wide eyed face embossed onto the cover, as if the leather it was made from was human skin, and the face had been stitched directly to it. It was very *Evil Dead*, Ellie thought.

'Uh, nothing's happening,' the human Lillian pointed out. Nina paused, and then grabbed the top of the crypt.

'Give me a hand,' she ordered, and between them, Lillian and Nina pushed the lid of the crypt free. It crashed to the ground loudly, and they peered inside. A few moments later, Suzi, still clutching the book, joined them.

'Uh, wasn't the demon meant to arise when we read that passage?' Lillian asked. 'It looks pretty dead to me still.'

'The passage is supposed to make the demon *mortal*. So we can kill it,' Suzi reminded Lillian. 'Yeah, great, so where is it?' Lillian questioned.

'It's a possessor, right?' Nina said after a moment's thought. 'I mean, we've never seen it in its real form before. Maybe it doesn't have one,' she suggested.

'Yeah, right, so this is the body of the first person it ever possessed. It should return here,' Lillian waved a hand at the casket, and Ellie could only imagine the rotting corpse that was inside. From her point hidden in the shadows, she couldn't make it out. She wasn't sure why she was hiding. This was Lillian's memory, wasn't it? That meant she couldn't interfere. And yet, somehow, it just felt right. To observe from the shadows and not interfere.

'I told you that you couldn't trust that thing.' Lillian said, turning to point at the book in Suzi's hand. 'I mean, god, don't any of you watch movies? Never read the creepy ancient language out of something called "The Book of the Dead". It never ends well!'

'Ha. Don't worry about it. If I had a dollar for every time I encountered some creepy ancient tome that called itself "The Book of the Dead" I'd be richer than Suzi,' Nina said dismissively. 'Demonic libraries must get really confusing. Same title everywhere,' she remarked. Suzi smiled a little at the joke, but Lillian seemed to remain concerned.

'Sure, fine, but we've just read a demonic resurrection passage, and it's nowhere to be seen. Doesn't that concern anybody!?' Lillian asked desperately.

'Well, we might have made it mortal, which means we can kill it, but it still needs a host, right? I thought, well, I thought it'd come back into the corpse, but I guess it needs a *live* host,' Suzi pointed out after a momentary pause of thought.

'So, it gets into a live host, and then we kill it from there?' Nina asked. Suzi nodded.

'How do we do that without killing the host?' Lillian questioned.

'We don't,' Nina answered, without missing a beat. 'To kill that thing, the host has to die as well,' she said, but her voice quaked with a sudden anger. It was a sudden realisation of what they had to do, Ellie realised.

'Dammit! I knew this was too easy! I knew that damned book would find a way to screw us! I told you not to trust it!' Lillian snapped angrily.

'It doesn't matter. That demon's killed hundreds of people over the years. If somebody has to die to stop it, it's one life for hundreds,' Nina pointed out with a surprising calm, having taken a deep breath to swallow her anger. Ellie was a little shocked to hear it. She had always known Nina could be practical, but to be so *cold* about it, so calm... It stunned her.

'Easy for you to say! Who are we gonna kill? Some poor random bystander on the street?' Lillian asked furiously.

'Maybe we can, uh, direct it into, like, a prisoner on death row or something?' Suzi suggested hopefully.

'And how do we do that? That thing's not stupid. Everybody it's possessed so far, it's tempted into accepting its power. It's smart. It picks its hosts well. It's not gonna jump into the body of somebody who's gonna die,' Lillian argued.

'Then it could go anywhere!' Suzi pointed out, her voice edged with panic. 'W-we have to find the next host, and stop it!'

'No,' Nina said firmly, turning to look at the other two. 'It has to be one of us.'

'*What*?' Suzi shrieked.

'You're asking one of us to *die*!' Lillian echoed Suzi's disbelief.

'Or we let some random innocent civilian die!' Nina shot back, a mixture of anger and despair in her voice. 'I don't like it any more than you do, but how can we just let somebody die, when we know we can stop it?'

'Oh, and are you volunteering?' Lillian asked hotly.

'How will it even work?' Suzi questioned.

'The demon wants a willing host, right? We just have to be willing,' Nina explained. 'We just have to accept it in.'

'There's got to be another way!' Suzi said loudly.

'We don't have *time*. If we don't do it soon, it'll find another host out there. It's already been hostless for too long. We've got a few minutes, if that! And then *that* person will have to *die*. And anybody it kills before we get to it will die too! No, it has to be one of us!' Nina's voice was desperate.

'You mean it has to be *me*, right?' Lillian asked, her voice laced with anger. 'You're the leader, you can't die, and Suzi finances us. In other words, I'm the expendable one. You want it to be me!' Nina looked taken aback, and Ellie glanced at the undead Lillian, still gripping her. The monstrous Lillian merely hissed at her, and forcefully turned her head to force her to still watch.

'Lillian, *no,*' Nina actually looked hurt. 'I can't… I can't ask any of you to do this,' she said. 'That's why… we should all do it.'

'What?' Lillian and Suzi asked together.

'Russian Roulette. All of us welcome the demon. And then, whoever it picks, they're the one we kill,' Nina suggested.

'You want us to play a game with our lives!?' Lillian asked, disbelievingly.

'I want us to *save* lives. If one of us has to die to do it, it's how it has to be,' Nina said firmly. The girls seemed to hang in an awkward silence, but there was an unshakeable sense of urgency to it. Each fidgeted for a moment, before finally Suzi spoke up.

'Okay, okay. I say yes. We've gotta do it,' Suzi nodded. 'We always knew we weren't gonna live forever. We've gotta do this!' she declared, her voice nervous, but edged with a surprising confidence. Lillian, the *human* Lillian, took a step away, and let out a frustrated groan, before turning back to the others.

'Fine. Fine! If this is what it means, we do it,' Lillian said grimly. 'How's this work?'

The figures faded back into the darkness, becoming wisps of smoke as they disappeared. Ellie was painfully aware of the only figure still present; the undead form of Lillian beside her, still holding her in that painful grip.

'We can skip this bit,' Lillian said dismissively. 'It's all reading the book and finding the right words. Boring stuff. I want to show you the *good* bit,' she hissed. Ellie watched, but she was at a loss for words. It was all happening so fast. Three young girls deciding one of them had to die. Suzi had told her that Lillian had volunteered, but not like this. She had pictured some kind of noble sacrifice. Not this horror. Not this horrible moment of facing mortality together. Not three friends having to gamble with their lives for the greater good. Ellie had to ask herself what she would have done if she was there. Would she have stopped it? Would she have volunteered? There was no better idea, was there?

The figures reappeared from a smoky haze, now all stood around the casket in a triangle. Ellie almost expected them to be holding hands, but it was impractical. They were too far away. Still, they formed a basic triangle, and could easily look into each other's' eyes.

'Alright, here goes nothing,' Nina grumbled. 'Let's say it together.' All three of them closed their eyes, and then they spoke.

'To the demon Furcas, soldier of the darkness, I accept you as a willing host.' All three spoke at the same time, and then there was silence. One by one, their eyes reopened.

'Uh, did it work?' Lillian asked.

'I don't think so,' Suzi said thoughtfully. Nina looked like she was about to say something, but before she could, the entire chamber began to rumble. A dark red storm cloud seemed to be forming over their heads, swirling and looping, small bolts of crimson lightning crackling all over it. It expanded into a thick mist, blocking Ellie's vision completely. It was like being stood in a heavy fog, only it was dark red, and somehow far more terrifying.

Then, as quickly as it had appeared, it was gone. The three girls were still exactly where they had been stood, waiting. They looked at each other for a moment.

'Was that-' Suzi began to speak, but before she could say anything else, Nina drew a gun, and shot Lillian directly in the head. Lillian's body fell to the floor instantly, head snapping back, blood spraying everywhere. Suzi screamed, and even Ellie, watching from afar, jumped out of her skin.

'Got it,' Nina said grimly.

'Wait, what?' Suzi questioned desperately. 'Y-you shot Lillian!'

'The demon was in her,' Nina explained, her voice cold and detached.

'How did you know!?' Suzi asked, rushing to Lillian's side, but it was too late. She was long gone.

'Demons are attracted to people with darkness in their souls. It wouldn't go near you. You couldn't be more cotton candy themed if you tried. So it was between me and Lillian. And as soon as I realised that thing wasn't in me, I knew it had to be in her,' Nina explained, holstering her pistol back under her jacket.

'But you didn't even give her a *chance*! What if it wasn't in her at all!?' Suzi was near tears, distraught at what had just happened.

'If I'd given it a chance it would have killed all of us,' Nina said firmly. 'We knew what we were doing. We knew the price we'd have to pay. We all agreed,' she went on, although the sheer determination in her voice made Ellie think that maybe Nina was trying to convince herself more than Suzi.

'Do you see?' The undead Lillian whispered in Ellie's ear. 'She manipulated me. She knew all along one of us would have to die, and she knew it wouldn't be Suzi. I bet she knew it wouldn't be her. It was all a game to her. She told you I *volunteered,* I bet? Did it sound like I volunteered?' Ellie just looked on, trying to understand what she had seen, trying to square it with her opinion of Nina. *Had* Nina done wrong? From their discussion, it had been the only way to stop what was coming, right? She had put her life on the line too. Or was Lillian right? Had it all been a trick?

'We should get the body out of here. W-we need to get her back to her parents. Make sure she gets a proper funeral,' Suzi said through tears that were ruining her once flawless mascara.

'No,' Nina said, already lifting the body up. 'We need to burn it. We made the demon mortal, but that doesn't mean we know a head shot will do the job,' she went on. pushing Lillian's dead body into the open casket in front of her.

'You're just gonna burn her and leave her here?' Suzi asked, aghast.

'Hiding a body in a grave seems like a pretty good idea to me. It's exactly where you'd expect to find a dead person,' She said matter-of-factly as she emptied something from a small hip flask into the casket. 'Okay, stand back.' She lit a match, and threw it in. The body immediately went up in flames as Suzi turned away, sobbing.

The smoke from the fire plumed up into the chamber, swirling around the figures until they were gone, just a memory fading away. The smoke quickly faded afterwards. Only Lillian and Ellie remained. Lillian threw Ellie forward to the floor, and she turned to look at her skeletal face. The eyeless sockets bore down on her, fire burning deep within, and she couldn't help but take in her skeletal form. *Really* take it in. Burn marks and bone covered her, but so little skin. There had been nothing left of Lillian after she had burned. Ellie involuntarily turned to look at where Lillian's human body had just been burned in the casket, not daring to look inside.

'*That's* your precious Nina. *That's* your hero,' Lillian spat. 'She manipulated me and then she *killed me* without even a second thought. Didn't you ever wonder how she always survived when everybody around her died? We're all expendable to Nina. And yet she *always* survives.'

'You agreed. You could have said no, but you agreed to the whole thing,' Ellie tried to reason, but she wasn't sure she believed her words. Yes, Lillian had agreed to go along with it. But she had clearly been reluctant. Nina had forced her hand. There was no denying that.

'Agreed? *Agreed?* Like she gave me a choice! She pushed me into it! She didn't even give me time to think it through!' Lillian growled.

'Th-there wasn't time…' Ellie stammered.

'According to who? *Her?* You might be a nerd, but you're no salesperson. Classic technique. Limit the buyer's time. Make them rush the decision. She *manipulated* me!' Lillian raged. 'And what about that "attracted to darkness" crap? You *heard* that. She never mentioned that before! She hid the truth so that it would be me who died!' Ellie paused, hesitating. What was she supposed to say to that? She had just seen the scene. She knew that Lillian had a reason to feel wronged. But that didn't justify what she had done now, did it? It didn't justify her coming after them.

'Okay, so Nina wronged you. But you killed her. So why keep hurting us?' Ellie asked. Lillian simply allowed her skeletal features to contort into something resembling a smile.

'It's like I told you. I'm immortal now. There's nothing like dying to give you a taste for *never doing it again,*' Lillian snapped. 'Killing. Being this monster I've become. It's the only way to come back. To *stay* back.'

'Oh, don't try it. Don't try playing that "misunderstood villain" crap now,' Ellie found herself saying. She wondered if she was braver in her dreamscape than in reality, because it seemed gutsier than she could ever imagine her saying to an armed undead monster.

'Well, why *shouldn't* I!?' Lillian argued. 'I died. And do you know what? There was no God waiting for me. No Heaven. It was eternal death or it was this. Why do only the bad get to live forever? Why do only the evil get to return? *I wanted to live!*'

'No,' Ellie said firmly.

'What?' Lillian asked, for a moment so shocked her voice sounded almost normal.

'No,' Ellie repeated. 'You wanted *power*. You're enjoying this. Every moment. Nina said there was darkness in your heart. Admit it. This power is what you've always wanted,' she dared.

'Well, I admit, I am having fun,' Lillian grinned. 'I hope you're right, you know? I hope Nina *is* still alive. Because killing her once wasn't enough. I can't wait to kill her again.' She lifted the machete hand. 'But for now, you'll have to do.'

'I don't think so,' Ellie replied defiantly.

'You can't stop me here. I control everything,' Lillian taunted.

'Then what's that sound?' Ellie asked, and suddenly Lillian paused, listening.

'It sounds like…' Lillian said thoughtfully, trying to place it.

'...an aeroplane landing outside. I'd say that's my alarm clock,' Ellie smiled. 'See you soon.'

'NO!' Lillian thrust the machete out at Ellie.

Ellie started awake on the couch, aware of the morning light filtering in through the windows and the noise of Jess's plane touching down on the runway outside.

That had been too close.

CHAPTER TWENTY

THE REUNION

Ellie saw Suzi stir beside her, waking up where she had fallen asleep on the couch. She was much sleepier than Ellie had been, and much more gentle in her waking, which gave Ellie hope that Suzi hadn't shared the encounter that Ellie had done.

'Suzi, are you okay!?' Ellie thought she'd better check anyway.

'Huh? Wha-?' she said through bleary eyes, letting out a yawn and a stretch, before suddenly sitting upright. 'Aw, no! We fell asleep!' she muttered. 'We're *really lucky* Lillian didn't decide to attack!'

'I think she did…' Ellie muttered, lifting up her arms and looking at fresh bruises from her "fall" within the dream.

'Are those from the attack on the mansion?' Suzi asked.

'No. They came from last night. Lillian came after me in my dreams,' Ellie answered with a slight wince of pain.

'In your dreams? What? Like *Nightmare Before Elm Street*?' Suzi questioned.

'It's *Nightmare ON Elm Street*. I think you're thinking of *Nightmare Before Christmas*. Very different movies,' Ellie replied, a slight smile. Of course Suzi would get it confused with a movie owned by Disney. 'But yeah. Guess Lillian doesn't have an original thought in her head,' she added in a grumble.

'Are you sure you didn't just… dream it?' Suzi asked in what Ellie thought was an intentionally delicate manner.

'Pretty sure,' Ellie confirmed. She stood up and stretched out, rolling her neck. It ached. Apparently sleeping on the couch all night hadn't done her any good. 'Aren't you going to go and welcome your girlfriend back?' Ellie asked.

'Oh! Yeah! Uh, hang on! I've gotta go sort myself out!' Suzi said in a panic, and Ellie just shook her head as Suzi rushed off to the restroom. Presumably to fix her make-up and hair. There was no way Suzi would let anybody see her after just having woken up, least of all her girlfriend, Ellie figured. She was surprised she hadn't attempted to blindfold Ellie the instant she had woken up.

Ellie cared a lot less about such things, especially after nearly being murdered in her sleep, and so made her way to the entrance, opening it just as she saw Jess, Kat and Avril approach.

'Hey guys,' she gave a sleepy smile. It was good to see them, but they had obviously just learned of Nina's situation, and possible death, and it wasn't a time for too much enthusiasm.

'Hey Ellie,' Avril moved in and gave Ellie a hug. Ellie noticed that at least this time Avril was wearing white sneakers. Probably a part of her cheerleader uniform, Ellie thought to herself. But still, better practical wear than she'd been wearing at Angel's Ridge. Now if only that would rub off on Suzi.

'Hey,' Kat smiled, moving in and also hugging Ellie. 'Wow, you look, uh, kinda… Are you okay?' Kat tried to ask.

'She means you look like crap,' Jess smirked, who somehow looked as lively and flawless as ever, even though she must have flown through the night, cowboy hat still upon her head, hips cocked to the side where she stood, the spurs on her cowgirl boots catching the early morning sun.

'Yeah, rough night,' Ellie admitted. 'Thanks for coming, you two.'

'No problem,' Kat replied. 'We said we'd help you out if you ever needed us.'

'Gotta admit, we thought it'd be longer than a day,' Avril added.

'But, well, if you need us, we're here,' Kat nodded. 'Sorry Jake and Ali didn't come.'

'Hey, it's okay, I figured they wouldn't. But trust me, we need you. We didn't fly you out here for a sleepover,' Ellie replied. 'But it *is* good to see you,' she added quickly, as she didn't want to seem ungrateful. 'Did you manage to-'

'Yeah, it's all sorted. I just hope your idea works,' Kat replied. Jess raised an eyebrow.

'At some point you're gonna have to let me in on this plan,' she commented.

'Yeah, I'll fill you in, don't worry,' Ellie replied.

'What *is* the plan?' Avril asked. 'I-I mean, like, I'm totally here to help out, but uh, what are we gonna do?'

'Let's go inside, and I'll explain.' Ellie gestured to the house, and they moved inside.

Once inside, they took seats while Jess went to make them all coffee. Even Ellie was grateful for that. She was still drowsy but definitely had no intention of falling back to sleep. An excited squeal from the kitchen told her that Suzi and Jess were reunited, and soon the entire group were gathered around, ready to hear what Ellie had to say. She felt like she should have had an attack strategy drawn up on a board and a stick to point at it with, like a military general briefing her troops.

'I take it Jess has told you about Lillian?' Ellie began, unsure if she should lead their little impromptu meeting or Suzi. Suzi had more experience *and* knew Lillian, but she seemed happy to let Ellie lead and she had to admit, it came naturally to her. She was no Nina, that was for sure, but she knew somebody had to take charge, and it seemed that somebody was her.

'Crazy psycho who used to be one of you. Has a machete for a hand and an army of gremlin thingies. Anything else?' Avril replied, her tone verging from "casual" to "unable to believe she was saying that" all in one sentence.

'Apparently she can attack us in our sleep now too,' Ellie added.

'Oh, like in *Friday the 13th*?' Avril asked.

'*Nightmare on Elm Street,*' Both Ellie and Kat said together, before exchanging a look and a slightly amused smile.

'Definitely not *Nightmare Before Christmas!*' Suzi chimed in.

'*Friday the 13th* is the one with Jason and the hockey mask,' Kat expanded.

'Oh yeah. Put me off going to summer camp for life!' Avril said.

'Wish I'd learned that lesson,' Ellie grumbled. 'Basically, we don't *really* know what she's capable of. Seems like she can do anything she wants now. She can come after us in our dreams, she's immortal, she's armed *and* she has an army.'

'And I did Ju Jitsu for about two years and Avril is quite good at gym…' It was one of the first times Ellie had heard Kat be sarcastic. 'So how are we meant to stop her?'

'Her power comes from stories. The reason she's so powerful is because she knows all the scary stories,' Suzi explained.

'So we fight back by changing the story,' Ellie added. 'We all go together to stop her. Attack her where she's hiding.'

'The crypt, right?' Jess asked, making sure that she was on the same page.

'Yeah. The crypt,' Ellie nodded.

'How do we get in without getting killed?' Kat asked.

'Yeah, um, I wanna help you, but like, I don't wanna die,' Avril added.

'About that...' Ellie said thoughtfully. 'I think Lillian gave me the answer.'

'What? She... what?' Suzi was stunned. 'But she hates us!'

'Yeah, but she's not as smart as she thinks,' Ellie smirked. 'When she showed up in my dream, she showed me what happened. How she died.'

'Oh god. Ellie. I'm so sorry. It must have looked so bad...' Suzi's heart clearly broke. She had never wanted her friend to see what had happened back then. It was obvious that Suzi blamed herself, even though Ellie knew there had been nothing Suzi could have done. She wanted to comfort her. Tell her that she understood. But now wasn't the time. She didn't want to bring it up in front of Avril and Kat. Not in the detail that was needed, anyway. It wasn't a discussion to be had lightly.

'I don't know, I kind of got the cliff's notes version, and even then, I don't know enough about what was going on. Maybe Nina was right to do what she did. This isn't about that,' Ellie explained with a shake of her head. She wasn't sure that the words she had just said were true. She still had no idea how she felt about Nina after what she had seen. But none of that mattered at that moment in time. She noticed Avril and Kat exchange curious looks. She felt bad for moving on, but she knew they couldn't dwell on that topic. Not while Lillian was still out there. 'It's about *where* we watched from.'

'What do you mean?' Jess asked with a frown.

'She just wanted me to be watching from a distance, right? But she placed me in this little hallway. Like a tiny side passage. Away from the main steps,' Ellie explained.

'I don't remember a side passage. We came in to the crypt through a big staircase,' Suzi interjected.

'Exactly. Which means she accidentally showed me another way in. A hidden passageway!' Ellie went on, smiling. 'Lillian showed me a way into her hideout and she didn't even realise it.'

'So, we take the secret passage in?' Kat asked. 'Then what?'

'Lillian can't defeat us all. Think about it. These slashers, these maniac killers in movies that she's so desperate to model herself on… They always kill individuals. One at a time. Against all of us, she's vulnerable,' Ellie answered.

'And if she's not?' Jess asked with concern.

'Then I have a back-up plan too. But, god, I hope it won't come to that,' Ellie replied with a sigh. 'For now, let's just focus on Plan A.'

'Okay. So we're gonna attack a creepy crypt and fight an army of monsters and a possibly immortal evil girl?' Avril asked with what Ellie thought was incredibly justified scepticism. 'Do we at least have, like, weapons?' She added. Jess smiled.

'Now weapons I can do. Follow me.' She led the girls out of the living room and outside.

They crossed over the field as Jess led them out past where the plane stood and to a small wooden shack, not far from the old barn that Ellie assumed she used to store the plane when it wasn't in use. She pulled a key off her belt and undid a heavy padlock, before swinging open the door.

'Welcome to the workshed!' she said proudly, flicking on a light.

'*Evil Dead* reference. Nice,' Ellie smiled. Her smile changed to slight awe as the light flickered and she saw what was inside.

The wooden walls were lined with weapons. Shotguns, rifles, machetes, swords, axes, even whips and lassos. Ellie even thought she spotted a chainsaw, but that might have been her imagination.

'Holy crap!' Ellie remarked.

'Well, they needed a back-up in case anything happened to the mansion. And nobody questions the Texas farm girl owning a few guns,' Jess beamed proudly.

'Uh, you have a strange definition of 'a few',' Kat interjected.

'Oh, this one's mine!' Suzi said proudly, reaching for a katana on the wall with a noticeable pink wrap around the handle.

'Isn't that a bit of a stereotype?' Kat asked.

'We've covered that one already,' Ellie answered with a slight smile. 'Okay, so, we've got weapons.' She looked on the wall, reaching for a pistol. 'I've never fired one of those big ones, so I'll stick to the handguns,' she decided, not that she felt comfortable about that either. In fact, she had a strong feeling that several of these weapons must have been illegal. While she didn't actually follow what gun laws were that closely, she had been a bit of an advocate for gun control before all of this. Not enough to study the laws closely, but enough to know that she didn't like them. Now, she wasn't so sure. She was all for restricting access to firearms, but she felt there should be a caveat in the law; "unless you're using them to kill undead zombie creatures or killer gremlin monsters". Regardless, now wasn't the time for a moral debate on gun control. They had to stop Lillian. She stuffed the pistol into the back of her jeans, and began to wonder if she should invest in a holster.

'Better take this too,' Jess suggested, passing Ellie a machete.

'I'm not really much of a fighter,' Ellie said nervously.

'That ain't what I've heard,' Jess smiled a little, nodding to Suzi as her source of information. 'Besides, you can't just rely on a gun. Trust me, you run out of ammo, you're gonna want that,' she explained, passing the machete to her. Luckily it was in a protective leather sheath. Ellie took it, and looped it through her belt. She supposed it couldn't hurt.

'I took an axe throwing class once,' Kat volunteered, reaching for one of the big axes on the wall.

'Wait. You took a *what*?' Ellie asked.

'Axe throwing. It's a sport. You throw axes,' Kat explained.

'I, uh, I figured *that* part out,' Ellie answered with a stutter. 'It just, uh, seems kinda out of character for you.'

'It was at a comic convention if it makes you feel any better. There were these Viking re-enactment guys,' Kat explained.

'You learned from LARPers?' Ellie asked sceptically.

'Hey, don't knock them. I mean, if anybody is going to know how to use old fashioned weapons, it's going to be the guys who beat each other up with foam versions every weekend, right?' Kat pointed out.

'Well, since I've never been to a comic convention, but I have like, two brothers who love paintball, I'm gonna take a rifle,' Avril commented, reaching for a gun.

'Wait, you've done paintballing?' Ellie asked.

'And airsoft,' Avril replied, checking the rifle. 'Plus my dad's into shooting.'

'You see? This is why we're gonna win,' Suzi chirped in. 'Lillian thinks in stereotypes. But people, they *aren't* stereotypes. Avril can be the preppy blonde cheerleader *and* know how to shoot. Kat can be the quiet bookish girl *and* know how to throw axes. People are three dimensional!'

'Yeah, thanks, we'll put that moral in after the credits if we live through this,' Ellie sighed. She knew Suzi was right, however. They weren't just their stereotypes. And they were going to prove it.

Jess pulled a large rifle off of the wall and slung it over her back, before taking a leather belt with two hip holsters, and adding two six shooters. She grabbed one of the whips and added it to her belt, alongside a lasso, and took a knife and slipped it into the top of one one of her cowgirl boots. She realised the others were looking at her.

'What? I might need to stay mobile. I didn't wanna take *too* many weapons,' she commented.

'....I take back what I said about stereotypes,' Suzi said playfully.

'Love you too,' Jess winked, giving Suzi a quick kiss.

'Okay, so we're like, armed, and we've got a plan. How do we rescue Nina though?' Avril asked, after waiting for their little moment to end.

'Honestly? In my nightmare, Lillian claimed not to know Nina was still alive. But that could just be part of the trap. Basically, shoot anything that's not us and has more than one eye,' It wasn't a fool proof plan, but it was the best Ellie had.

'Unless it's a big cyclops monster! Shoot that too!' Suzi said with a helpful smile. Ellie just shook her head with a smirk.

'Okay, let's get moving,' Ellie didn't mean for it to sound like an order, but they took it that way, filing out of the work shed. Ellie followed.

They were all waiting for her, and turned to look at her, waiting for her to lead. She stepped forward, and then she realised she was missing an important detail.

'So, uh, where's this crypt?' She asked Suzi with a slightly embarrassed smile.

CHAPTER TWENTY-ONE

THIS TIME, IT'S WAR

Luckily, it turned out Suzi knew exactly where the crypt was. The journey there was surprisingly short. It was only a few hours from the farm. That actually put it not too far from St. Mary's Marsh. Ellie wasn't sure if that was the type of situation you'd describe as 'ironic', but it felt that way. It had all started for her in that campground, and now, here she was at the end only a stone's throw away.

She was surprised by that thought. 'The end'. Why was this the end? She realised there was definitely an air of finality hanging over the group. She wondered if this was how it felt to prepare to go into battle. If this is what a soldier felt before facing the enemy's guns. After all, that was what they were doing, wasn't it? Going into battle?

She tried to shake the thoughts from her mind.

They had stopped to prepare a little better. Jess had provided bullet proof vests for the group to wear, and Ellie felt the awkward, heavy Kevlar pushing down upon her chest. Jess had assured them that they were largely stab resistant as well as bullet proof. The best armour she could get for them. Suzi had also changed into the closest thing Ellie had ever seen to her being in a practical outfit. She wore a long pink skirt and a kimono style top. Almost like a samurai of old, Ellie thought. If they did a Barbie version of a samurai, that was. But still, at least the frills were left to a minimum and either she was getting used to it or Suzi was wearing less perfume than before. That had to be a sign that she was serious. She also had her own, customised pink bullet proof vest over the top. Of *course* Jess had a pink bullet proof vest in reserve for her.

They had returned to Suzi's house, still behind police tape after the fire, but sneaking in was simple. It was no longer observed. It was just to keep people out of an unsafe structure. Nobody suspected foul play in the fire, especially since Suzi hadn't reported any. It was simply to pick up a second vehicle, since they didn't want to all be bundled into Jess's pick-up truck. They soon tracked down Suzi's tiny pink car, but quickly noticed something was missing.

'Where's Nina's car?' Ellie asked. 'Wasn't it parked here with yours?'

'Yeah,' Suzi confirmed, before pausing. A hopeful, nervous pause. 'You don't think…'

'…Nina took it. That she's still alive?' Ellie guessed Suzi's thoughts. The two exchanged a look, but it was a hope they didn't want to dwell on any longer. It was just as likely the car had been damaged in the fire and removed as it was unsafe.

Unfortunately that only left Suzi's car to travel in, alongside Jess's pick-up truck. The pick-up truck was battered, covered in mud from working on the farm, and had a rough and ready look to it. Ellie didn't mind riding that into war. Suzi's car, however? It slightly killed the mood. And *of course* Ellie was the one who ended up riding with Suzi, while the others shared with Jess. She felt ridiculous, bundled in the tiny pink thing while armed to the teeth and heading off for the grimmest of tasks she had ever faced.

It didn't help that Suzi insisted on putting a Disney mix on while they drove.

The drive took a few hours, and Ellie was relieved when she finally saw the old graveyard looming. It was getting dark, and storm clouds seemed to be gathering. Of *course* storm clouds were gathering. In her head, Ellie heard Nina telling her that you couldn't raid a spooky graveyard and have the night's sky be clear. She guessed even nature had a dramatic flare.

It was a foreboding vision, or would have been, had the latter half of *Hakuna Matata* not been blasting out of Suzi's car at that point. They drove through the main entrance, and down the main path of the cemetery.

'The crypt is pretty old. It's near the back,' Suzi explained as she pulled her car onto the grass and began to navigate further towards it. 'I'll get us as close as I can.' she added.

'Lucky the groundskeeper isn't here tonight...' Ellie observed as it began to rain. Suzi stopped the car, and the two listened to the rain thunder down on the roof for a moment. She turned off the car's lights.

'I'm no master strategist,' Suzi admitted. 'But I think if we go any further, we'll give the game away.'

'Yeah, this car isn't exactly inconspicuous,' Ellie teased. They both got out, to see Jess's pick-up stopping behind them. Suzi reached into the dash and pulled out a big, plasticky pink rain hat to protect her hair. Ellie decided to just let herself get wet.

'On foot from here, I guess?' she asked, climbing out alongside Kat and Avril, who both looked uncomfortable in the heavy Kevlar vests.

'Seems like our best best,' Ellie confirmed. 'Now to see if we can find that secret passage.' Jess nodded, and Suzi reached into the trunk of the car, pulling out some flashlights to hand out among the group.

'See, I'm prepared!' she said proudly. 'Oh, just in case, sometimes, some supernatural stuff can mess with electronics so, here's a flare each,' she handed out the tubes, and Ellie took one, looking at it curiously.

'Is it safe to carry one of these? Don't they like, catch fire?' she asked nervously.

'So do matches, and you don't moan about carrying those,' Jess pointed out. 'Just, if you need it, twist the end off and strike it, like you would a match.' She instructed, and Ellie found herself putting it in her waistband of her jeans. She never thought there'd be a day she carried a pistol and a flare with her. Then again, she never thought there'd be a day she headed off into an ancient crypt to battle an undead killer. It was strange how life worked out.

That was, perhaps, a bit of an understatement.

Their flashlights flickered through the otherwise deserted graveyard, and soon Ellie fell in behind Suzi, who seemed to know where she was going.

'The crypt belonged to the first ever guy possessed by the demon that got into Lillian. The one that we killed inside of her. When we first summoned it, we thought it'd return to its original body, but it turned out it needed a living person,' Suzi explained as they walked.

'I caught the backstory in my dream, thanks,' Ellie confirmed. 'God, that's a sentence I never thought I'd have to say.'

'Well, I guess when it possessed this guy, the demon helped him accumulate wealth and all that stuff, because, well, look,' Suzi pointed her flashlight at a grand looking crypt, sat near the back of the graveyard. It was large enough that her flashlight failed to fully light the front, and was lined with what appeared to be marble columns that brought to Ellie's mind images of a Greek temple. She half expected thunder to crash and lightning to strike behind it as they took it in, but nothing quite that dramatic happened. The rain was pretty constant though, making it hard to look. Ellie turned. Both Kat and Avril were sensible enough to have hoods up, and rain dripped off the brim of Jess's hat, but otherwise kept her dry. Ellie, on the other hand, was getting soaked.

'So, that's the crypt. We're not going through those doors, right?' Avril pointed to the huge wooden doors at the entrance, held firmly shut with what looked like old rusted bolts.

'No. We need to find the passage,' Ellie instructed. 'Its got to be here somewhere. A weird looking tree or something…'

'It could be anything!' Jess protested. 'This is gonna take forever!'

'Yeah, and my feet are getting wet! These sneakers aren't waterproof!' Avril complained.

'Wet feet is probably the least of our worries,' Ellie replied. Although it was pretty uncomfortable. Her feet were getting wet too. 'Stop complaining and start looking. It could take us a while, it could be anything, but if we all look, hopefully we'll find it in the next few hours and-'

'Found it!' Kat announced suddenly.

'Wait, what? You *have*?' Ellie was startled. That was much quicker than she had expected.

'Pretty sure. Look at that headstone over there,' Kat pointed to one. Ellie moved closer, flanked by the others who all lit it up with its torch light.

The stonework was old and weather worn and the name was difficult to read, but Ellie made an attempt anyway, shining the torchlight closely upon it.

HAROLD REMINGTON
BORN 1812
DIED 1867
RIP

It was a remarkably plain looking grave. There was no loving message, nothing written in Latin that could be interpreted as a code, and the name meant nothing to Ellie.

'What makes you think this is the secret passage?' Ellie asked Kat curiously. She found it harder to imagine a more generic gravestone if she tried.

'Don't look at the headstone. Look at the plot,' Kat shone her flashlight down on the grass in front of the stone. It was noticeably completely flattened, as if something had crushed it. Ellie looked around, realising that the rest of the grass was standing tall and overgrown. Apparently nobody visited this part of the graveyard very much.

'I get it!' Suzi beamed in. 'You think the gravestone moves?'

'Yeah. Like the graves in the graveyard in *Ocarina of Time,*' Kat explained. Ellie gave a blank look to Kat. 'It's a video game. I can do pop culture references too, y'know?'

'Okay, well, let's try it,' Ellie agreed, and the group moved around to the back of the graveyard. Except for Jess, who seemed to pause, having spotted something out near the trees.

'Uh, hey, y'all... Is that what I think it is?' She asked, shining her flashlight on a metallic object in the distance. The others turned to look, and saw it there, plain as day.

Nina's rusty black muscle car.

'Nina! She's here!' Suzi beamed with excitement.

'Or at least her car is,' Kat pointed out.

'Yeah, how do we know it's not a trap?' Avril asked.

'We don't,' Ellie replied. 'But it doesn't change the plan. Either way, we have to go in there, and we have to stop Lillian. All this means is that there's definitely a chance Nina is still alive. We knew that anyway. Don't let it distract us. We have to stick to the plan,' Ellie wished she believed her own words, but she was already hoping beyond hope that Nina would emerge from the shadows at any moment and take charge. To tell her if her plan was right or wrong. To tell her if this was the right thing to do. She just needed guidance. She felt so lost.

But nobody appeared. Ellie was aware that all eyes were on her. She turned to the others, and gave a short nod.

'Okay, let's move this thing,' She got behind the gravestone, and began to push it. The rain had made the grass slippery, and her sneakers slipped on the wet soil, but soon the other girls came to help, and with all of them pushing they felt the grave begin to slide forward. It was heavy and difficult to move, but clearly on some kind of ancient rails, and sure enough there was a dark passageway lurking beneath it.

'There's always a secret entrance,' Ellie repeated Nina's lesson. She shone her flashlight down, spotting the old wooden steps. 'Skip the third one,' she instructed as she began to make her way down. It seemed to be an invaluable lesson as the group made it to the stoney floor without the giveaway crack of a breaking step. Even Avril, who was last down, arrived safely.

Ellie shone the flashlight down the tunnel. It was long, narrow and the walls were stone shelves. On each shelf there were the unmistakable shapes of human skulls. It was, after all, a crypt, Ellie realised, but it wasn't exactly the type of decor she had expected. This was just the tomb of one person, wasn't it? This looked like a set-up from a bad horror movie. She realised that was probably the point. Of *course* it did. This was Lillian they were talking about. She could even see the odd skeletal arm and hand poking out, making it a nightmare gauntlet to move down.

Worse still, they'd need to kill the lights. She clicked off the flashlight, and heard the sound of a deep breath as they all paused nervously, waiting in the dark.

'The flashlights will tell her we're coming,' Ellie was whispering now. 'Grab the back of the shirt of the girl in front of you, and follow me,' she instructed, feeling Suzi tug on the back of her top and knowing that way they'd stay together. Slowly, she began to make her way forward, the small part of moonlight from the open passageway quickly disappearing and leaving the girls plunged into total darkness.

Ellie felt her way along the wall, pausing only to wince when she felt her fingers make their way into what she could only assume was a dusty eye socket of an old skull. They were all moving so quietly, and the only obvious noise was the dripping of water from the open passageway behind them, but still Ellie thought every sound, every shuffle, every footstep was magnified tenfold, and she felt certain that at any moment Lillian would hear them coming. Soon enough though, light began to filter through from the end of the tunnel as it widened, and slowly Ellie came to recognise where they were. It was the same opening she had stood in with Lillian back during her nightmare. Except here it was real, and the crypt beyond it loomed, bathing the entrance of the chamber in a strange orange light. It felt odd to be stood in a place she had only seen in a dream, knowing it was so perfectly real. Every piece of stone work, every old inscription, it was exactly as she had seen it in her nightmare.

She paused, gesturing behind her with a flailing hand for the other girls to stop too. Her eyes adjusted, beginning to take in more of the shape of the crypt. It was very similar to before, but she began to notice differences.

This time the casket that she had seen Nina, Suzi and Lillian gathered around in the past was closed. On top of the heavy stone lid of the casket there was an ancient corpse pinned, surrounded by burning candles. Ellie was pretty sure she could make out a pentagram painted on in what she hoped was red paint, but she suspected was blood, beneath the corpse.

Ellie was aware of Suzi and Jess's heads appearing over her shoulder, and Avril and Kat flanking them also. They were all peering into the chamber. Suzi and Ellie exchanged a silent look, which was one of joint confusion. What was going on? Where was Lillian?

As if to answer their question, there was a sudden movement. The scurrying of small shadows. Lillian's gremlin creatures, no doubt. And then Lillian herself, her face bandaged once again, her hat in place, as she stood before the crypt and the body.

'I wish I'd brought a chair. They'll be here soon. I could have been looming on a big, ancient stone throne,' she said out loud to her minions. There seemed to be a hiss of chatter back. 'You're right, that's more cocky supervillain than scary slasher. Better off scaring them.' She made her way back out of sight, and everything fell silent for a moment.

Ellie reached for her gun, and gestured for the others to do the same. She gave a nod. This was it. Time to fight. She tried to keep her hand from shaking, but it was difficult. As soon as Lillian reappeared, she'd open fire, and they'd storm in. All guns blazing. No horror tricks, no jump scares. It was time to rewrite the narrative, just like they planned.

It was time to go to war.

Ellie edged closer to the entrance from the passageway, gun in her hand, looking for any sign of

Lillian. There was nothing. Only darkness. She couldn't even see the gremlins anymore.

And then with a horrific screech, Lillian's face appeared directly in Ellie's.

Ellie leapt out of her skin instinctively. Lillian was snarling, bandages gone again, her burned, skull-like face on show for all to see, screaming directly at Ellie. Before Ellie could react, her one gloved hand grabbed her and hurled her cross the room. She flew through the air effortlessly, crashing into the casket, colliding with it painfully before dropping to the ground and knocking several of the candles over. She realised she had been an idiot. The *skulls*. The creepy decor! It had all been a sign that Lillian knew they were coming! She'd known the exact path they'd follow!

It had all been a set-up.

She heard gunshots from the secret passageway and saw the flashes of light, causing Lillian to stumble back, along with screams. There was a distant crash, and Ellie didn't have to be there to know it was the secret passageway's escape route closing behind them, cutting off their escape. She struggled back to her feet, ignoring the pounding pain in her skull and the trickle of blood from where she had bashed her head. Her mouth felt dry and the ground swayed beneath her feet, but now wasn't the time to focus on that.

There was a clang, and a shower of sparks, and Ellie could make out Suzi, pushing the offensive, her katana in hand, clashing against Lillian's own machete. Ellie began to run towards Suzi to help, but something tripped her, and one of the gremlins was on her, teeth gnashing directly at her. Behind her, she heard a sickening cracking, something that she could only describe as dry bone moving against dry bone, and she had a horrible idea she knew what was happening.

Avril, Jess and Kat were being forced out of the secret passageway by something that had filled them with terror. Avril was screaming, and even Jess, who seemed pretty unshakable, was firing blindly back into the tunnel. Just as Ellie had feared, they were being followed. Forced out of the tunnel by something. Skeletons. The bones they had passed had animated, coming to life, now forcing them back.

The gremlin made its move to bite at Ellie's neck, but Ellie was ready for it this time. She pulled the machete from her belt, and drove it directly into the gremlin's body, causing it to squeal and fall from her, even as she was bathed in its disgusting blood. She struggled to her feet to watch the chaos.

Avril, Jess and Kat were surrounded. They had been pushed out of the passageway by the skeletons and directly into a waiting horde of gremlins. They had nowhere to go, even as Jess fired wildly into the group. Kat swung her axe and took the skull directly off one of the skeletons, but its body just kept moving. Meanwhile, Suzi and Lillian fought, katana against machete, and the clang of metal on metal ringing out and echoing throughout the crypt.

'To think, you always played the little pink princess. The girly girl. But look at you. You're a *fighter*,' Lillian snarled at Suzi. 'Maybe you're my final girl. Maybe once I kill this lot, you'll be the last one standing,' she taunted. Ellie knew that Suzi was in trouble though. It was true, Suzi was doing incredibly well, but Lillian had the kind of strength on her side only the undead could possess. There was no way Suzi could last much longer.

There didn't seem to be anybody else threatening Ellie directly, so she took the bloody machete in her hand,

and began to run towards Lillian, ready to help Suzi. But before she could get there, Lillian twirled her blade, causing Suzi to lose grip on her sword. The katana flew through the air, whistling past Ellie's face, delivering a fine thin cut to her cheek. Now unarmed, Lillian grabbed Suzi, and held her machete to her throat.

'Guess not,' Lillian hissed. 'Okay, stop!' She raised her free her hand in the air, and the gremlins and skeletons stopped advancing for a moment. Not that it helped. The others were boxed in, surrounded, even with their weapons in their hands. Ellie could move, but she was right by the flaming candles, in plain sight. There was no way she could get to Lillian in time.

'Do you like what I've done with the place? The corpse doesn't mean anything, by the way,' she gestured to the body laid out on top of the casket. 'Just, you can't go wrong with Satanic imagery, y'know? Inject a little supernatural mystery into the situation,' she boasted. 'This was *your* plan, was it?' she asked, looking directly at Ellie. 'Storm the place? Let me guess, you were thinking 'action movie sequel' right?' Her eyeless sockets scanned the group, and then focused back onto Ellie. 'That was your big idea, huh?'

'Worked for *Aliens*,' Ellie replied. She was trying to buy time.

'Really? I think you might have forgotten the hive scene in *Aliens*. It didn't work out so well for the marines,' she taunted back. Ellie had to resist a curse. She was right, of course. Sure, the aliens were cannon fodder in that movie, but very few people made it out alive. Especially in the scene where they first stormed the hive. Ellie had thought this was the finale, but Lillian had turned it right back on them. This was going to be a *slaughter* scene. Less common, but they did happen in horror movies. A scene where a great big chunk of the cast were killed off. And Lillian knew it.

There had to be a chance. She had stopped the attack for a reason. Ellie tried to think. Lillian wanted to be a slasher villain *so badly*. An unstoppable horror killer. But she *talked*. That was it. She couldn't just kill them. She needed her moment of glory. Ellie just had to keep her talking.

'You knew, didn't you? You knew we'd use the passage,' Ellie knew it was a desperate gambit, but she had to appeal to that ego. Get her talking.

'Of course. I showed it to you, after all,' Lillian replied with a casual shrug. 'Besides, Nina taught me the same as she taught you. There's always a secret passage.'

'And where is Nina?' Ellie asked. 'We saw her car!' Nina was that one topic that always made her mad. Maybe that could get them somewhere.

'Oh, were you hoping she'd show up at the last minute to rescue you?' Lillian asked with mocking sympathy. 'Sorry to disappoint you, but I stole her car after I destroyed Suzi's mansion. I figured, what's the one thing movie killers never have? Their own iconic vehicle! Nina's is pretty cool, with a few modifications, I could be the first!' she said proudly.

'*Duel* did it first,' Ellie replied, allowing herself a smile. Steven Spielberg. A duel between vehicles.

'Nobody remembers that film!' Lillian snapped.

'What about *Death Proof*? That's Tarantino. Nobody forgets a Tarantino.' Ellie shot back.

'*Death Proof* is his worst movie! It doesn't count!' Lillian was furious, and held the machete closer to Suzi's neck.

'*Jeepers Creepers* has the truck,' Ellie continued, aware that this was definitely infuriating her. It was a risk, but she had to have faith she wouldn't kill Suzi. Not until she got the last word anyway.

'It doesn't matter! I don't need your approval! I've *won*! I've got you all right where I want you! You all die, right now, and I become a legend!'

'Not yet you don't,' Ellie taunted back. 'You've got us, sure. But if you kill us all, you just murdered a bunch of people at once in a crypt. That doesn't make for a good slasher story. You have to hunt us down, one by one. You kill us all now, you know what happens next?'

'I'll find some dumb bimbo high schoolers and slash them up too. You can just be the backstory,' Lillian replied.

'No. What happens next… is Nina comes for you,' Ellie replied.

'Nina is dead!' Lillian screamed. 'I killed her!'

'There was no *body*!' Ellie countered. God, she wished she believed it, but instead she was just buying time. Nina was still the perfect button to push to make Lillian lose focus.

'So what!? Happens all the time in horror movies. Somebody dies off screen! It just shows they weren't important! Nina is gone and she's not coming to save you! You all die, right here, right now!' she yelled furiously.

Ellie suddenly became aware of a sudden temperature drop, feeling her skin goosepimple. She was aware the others did too, because they began to look around. Not Lillian though. She'd sacrificed her skin and her senses a long time ago. Kat looked over to Ellie, and smiled, giving a nod.

'And what if we stop you?' Ellie asked.

'How are you going to do that?' Lillian replied furiously.

'We'll keep fighting,' Ellie answered plainly.

'You're outnumbered! And I have an army of the damned! You'll last two seconds!' Lillian spat.

'I dunno, I reckon we can take them,' Ellie smirked.

'Yeah, you and what army!?' Lillian taunted. Ellie's smirk broke into a smile.

'*Thank you,*' she replied proudly. 'I wasn't sure I was going to get you to say it, but you never let me down for a stereotype.'

'What do you-?' Lillian began to say.

'*This one!*' Ellie yelled, throwing her arms open.

With a sudden ghostly howl, the chamber was filled with distinct, wispy shapes. Familiar shapes. Shapes all the living girls in that room had seen before. The shapes from Angel's Ridge. The ghosts. At their lead, the familiar figure of the ghostly Edith Campbell, her pale eyes flashing red for a moment as she focused on Lillian.

'NO! What have you done!?' Lillian screamed, moving to slash Suzi's throat, but before she could she was picked up and thrown across the chamber by the ghosts. Suzi ran back towards the others as several of the gremlins were tossed away from the group, and the skeletons began to be smashed to dust. The girls regrouped, breathing hard, covered in small wounds, but watching in awe as the army of ghosts took on the army of monsters.

'I told you. *Return of the King,*' Ellie said proudly. 'Aragorn brings an army of ghosts to help him out.'

'And I thought you just knew horror movies,' Suzi smiled in delight, grabbing Ellie in a hug.

'Is it too much to hope you read the book?' Kat asked sarcastically, joining them in the hug. Avril frantically grabbed Ellie's arm, however, pulling her away.

'Look! I think Lillian's fighting back!' She pointed, and Lillian was slashing with her machete. Somehow, it seemed that the supernatural powers bestowed upon Lillian allowed her to cut at the ghosts and keep them back.

'This was your crazy plan all along, huh?' Jess asked in surprise. 'You definitely got guts. Nina would be proud,' she smiled.

'Nina would never have thought of it. That's how I knew it'd work on Lillian,' Ellie explained. 'Nina told us that all spirits, all supernatural entities were bad. But we saw first-hand that Edith Campbell wasn't. Lillian learned all of her lessons from Nina, so the only way to surprise her was to use a lesson we'd learned on our own.'

'Uh, nice recap, but she's not stopping!' Avril pointed to the advancing Lillian, who was slicing her way through the spirits, her empty eye sockets now burning with an orange fire of rage.

'This isn't over! You're going to die, right here!' Lillian screamed, and Ellie realised that all of Lillian's ire was now focused on her.

'You keep saying that, but I keep *not dying*! Are you sure you're any good at this?' Ellie yelled back. It probably didn't help matters, but it definitely made her feel better.

'So, uh, what now?' Suzi asked as the group began to back towards the main entrance to the crypt, and the huge staircase.

'Well the plan was rescue Nina. But she's not here. So, uh….' Ellie paused, uncertain, as Lillian advanced.

'I got a plan! *RUN!*' Jess answered, grabbing Suzi's hand and bolting for the stone steps that led to the main entrance. Ellie quickly followed, Avril and Kat by her side. They reached the top, and the heavy doors that were the formal entrance to the crypt. They began to bang on them.

'They're locked!' Suzi pointed out the obvious.

'She's right behind us.' Jess announced, seeing the advancing Lillian, her eyes smouldering with fiery rage. She fired off several gunshots directly at the approaching villain, but Lillian took them in her stride, not even missing a step.

'We've got nowhere to go!' Avril panicked.

'Just keep pushing! We can break the door!' Jess said quickly, ramming against the door with her shoulder as hard as she could. Ellie joined in, as did the others, but Lillian was getting closer.

'Hold on!' Kat turned, and in one smooth movement hurled the axe out of her hand. It lodged perfectly into Lillian's skull, snapping her head back and leaving her body crashing down the stone steps. 'Told ya! Axe throwing!' Kat said proudly.

'That won't stop her!' Suzi warned, and sure enough, the group could see Lillian getting back to her feet, axe now lodged in her head above her eye.

'Keep pushing! It's moving!' Jess cried, and slowly they felt the door begin to move. The heavy wood refused to budge, but the old rusty hinges began to strain, and with a sudden crash, the entire thing fell forward, the wood splintering around the bolts as the old hinges gave way. Nice design work, Ellie thought. The hinges gave out before the bolts ever did.

Ellie fell forward with the door, landing flat on her face, and scrambled to her feet just as the axe came down exactly where she had been moments before. Lillian was right behind her now, axe in one hand, machete for the other, a huge gash over her eye and into her skull, although there was no blood left to flow from the wound. Ellie scrambled to her feet, slipping slightly on the slick wood and then wet grass, and she fell down again, landing face first in the soil.

She cursed. She wasn't going to die this way! The hapless girl who tripped running from the killer! She rolled over just in time to see Lillian lifting the axe, and suddenly something lashed around the undead villain, pulling her back.

It was a lasso! Jess was stood there, rope extended, wrapped around Lillian, pinning her arms to her side. Avril, Kat and Suzi grabbed the rope, to pull Lillian back from Ellie, giving her chance to scramble to her feet. With a roar of anger, Lillian flexed her arms, tearing the rope apart, her chest rising and falling with rage. It was a gesture of anger, not a requirement to breathe, Ellie was sure.

'Axe wound over the eye? Jason Voorhees did *that* first too. *Friday the 13th Part III*. Even when you're losing, you can't do it originally,' Ellie taunted, although part of her wished she'd shut up, as she was out of ideas.

'Worse creatures to be like,' Lillian snarled back. She was obviously a Jason fan.

'Jason's the lamest killer anyway! I mean, he's the one with the hockey mask, right?' It seemed Avril at least knew *that* when it came to horror movies. It was obvious she was joining in the taunting. Taking digs at Lillian's icon.

'That mask just gives him big puppy dog eyes? It's not exactly scary!' Kat seemed to pick up on the idea, and joined in.

'How did he ever beat Freddy anyway?' Jess asked. Ellie smiled at that. *Freddy vs. Jason*. The one big crossover slasher movie to end them all.

And that was it. That was the idea. *That* was how Ellie was going to beat Lillian!

'Suzi! Keys! Now!' Ellie snapped quickly.

'What?' Suzi blinked.

'Car keys!' Ellie explained. Suzi quickly fished around and pulled out her keys, throwing them to Ellie, who snatched them out of the air. It was definitely a lucky catch, but Ellie wasn't complaining.

'It won't work! Cars never start when you're being chased!' Suzi pointed out.

'Unless the killer wants a car chase. C'mon, Lillian! You wanted your big iconic vehicle showdown! Let's see what you're made of!' Ellie taunted, and ran as fast as she could towards Suzi's car.

CHAPTER TWENTY-TWO

TERROR AT 130MPH!

Ellie didn't have time to look back, but she was already certain Lillian was angry enough to pursue her no matter what. She reached Suzi's car, skidding to a halt on the wet grass and quickly throwing the door open. God, she wished she'd asked Jess for the keys in retrospect, she thought as she climbed inside. Suzi's little pink bubble car was much less likely to make it all the way she needed it to, she knew.

She turned the keys. The engine strained.

'C'mon, c'mon, let me be right about this,' she turned the keys again, and again the engine struggled to turn over. With perfect timing, she was suddenly bathed in light from headlights behind her. Lillian in Nina's car, ready to pursue. She turned the keys yet again, and this time the engine spluttered into life, just as Nina's car was beginning to accelerate towards her.

She slammed her foot down on the accelerator only to hear the wheels hiss. Suzi's car had tiny, soft wheels and they were spinning helplessly on the slick grass. The car was stuck!

'Nonono, c'mon!' Ellie said desperately. Nina's car was approaching ever closer. Unable to go forward, Ellie slammed the car into reverse. The wheels span, but the car began to back up, just in time as Nina's car raced past where Ellie had been just seconds earlier and smashed directly into a gravestone.

The damage to Nina's car didn't look too bad, and Ellie could hear the engine struggling to restart as Lillian tried to get it going again. Ellie took the opportunity to try and get Suzi's car back to the road, the wheels spinning on the wet, slick grass as she tried. They hissed and she kept coming to a stop, having to back up and retry. She felt like she was getting further with every attempt, but every time she was near the solid road, again the wheels would spin and the car would become stuck. With a roar Nina's car came back to life, and backed away from the grave, one of its lights flickering where it had been damaged, and began to turn to ram Suzi's car. Ellie put her foot down as hard as she could. She had no more time to back up again, and still the wheels span and span, the car inching towards the safety of the tarmac...

...until it finally made it, just as Nina's car shot past behind Ellie again. Suzi's car lurched forward as Nina's car span out of control on the wet grass, but it quickly readjusted its path to follow. Ellie was picking up speed now, back on the road out of the graveyard, but Nina's car was fast. Much faster than Suzi's and gaining ground. The car screeched as she took a corner too hard out of the graveyard and onto the main road, which luckily was deserted at this time of night. She sped along it as fast as Suzi's car could carry her. Behind her, the ominous flickering headlights of Nina's car grew ever closer.

'Dammit Suzi. Why couldn't you have bought a jeep? Or a sports car?' Ellie muttered under her breath, bracing herself as Nina's car rammed into the back of Suzi's. The entire car buckled forward, and swerved, but Ellie managed to keep it on the rain slick road, despite the squealing, protesting tires. That wouldn't last for long, however. Ellie realised she couldn't take another hit quite like that without crashing off of the road, and she still had a fair distance to go.

Fortunately, she knew the way.

Nina's car was getting ever closer again, and Ellie could see Lillian's fiery eyes glaring behind the wheel. At the last moment, before it collided again, Ellie turned the steering wheel as hard as she could. Suzi's car went spinning wildly, throwing up white smoke on the road as it turned, skidding out of control, but it meant that Lillian in Nina's car sailed past ineffectually, and had to skid to a stop itself. Ellie managed to recover, glad that there had been no other traffic to collide with her while the car had spun out of control, and quickly began to accelerate again, shooting past Lillian in Nina's stopped car. She felt sick and dizzy from the spin, her head wound not helping, but she couldn't stop now. Lillian didn't stay stationary for long, and immediately began to pick up speed. This time, Lillian pulled up alongside Ellie, and she saw Lillian's red eyes glaring at her. God, even in Suzi's tiny car, with its engine whining like a lawnmower, they were flying along the road, faster than Ellie had ever driven before. The speedometer said they were at 130 mph. Not quite the spectacular car chase speeds some might expect, but not bad for such a tiny vehicle. Lillian moved her car out, and back in, and rammed the side of Ellie, causing the entire car to skid to the side. Ellie fought to keep control, barely keeping it on the road, several extended branches snapping against the side of the car as she nearly crashed into a nearby bush. She felt the glass of the driver's side window as it shattered from the impact cut into her arm. She noticed that Lillian actually seemed worse off, her car swerving all over the road to recover.

She didn't have two hands, Ellie realised! Always keep two hands on the wheel! A nice simple instruction, and clearly Lillian hadn't exactly had much time to learn to drive in her new form. Having a machete for an arm made quite the difference, Ellie imagined. Driver's Ed didn't tend to cover that part.

Still, she had the faster, and sturdier, vehicle, and soon she was alongside Ellie once again, ready to try ramming her once more. This time, however, when the car swung out to hit her, Ellie slammed the breaks. Suzi's car skidded to a halt and Nina's vehicle missed her completely, crashing off the road into the nearby trees. Quickly, Ellie put her foot down again and the car began to accelerate once more. She looked in her rear view mirror, which itself was now cocked sideways. There was no sign of pursuit.

Ellie knew, however, that it wouldn't end there. You couldn't defeat the killer that way. She'd be back any moment. Ellie watched, her eyes torn between the road in front and her rear view mirror, looking for any sign of movement. She was nearly there. She just had to hold out a bit longer.

Her eyes flickered back to the road, and then were drawn back to the rear view mirror, a creeping realisation sinking in. She looked into the reflection, then she screamed. Staring back at her were two fiery eyes. Lillian was on the backseat, blade arm whistling through the air. Ellie ducked and it slammed into the side of the car door, wedging for a moment.

'It's a cheap scare tactic, but when all else fails, nothing beats a teleporting killer, appearing where they shouldn't!' Lillian said with satisfaction. 'I already told you!' She pulled her blade free of the car door. 'You can't beat me! I know all the tricks! All the *rules*!' She stabbed forward, directly through the back of Ellie's seat.

Ellie had no choice. She reacted just in time, unbuckling herself from the seat belt and throwing herself into the passenger seat. With nobody left driving, the car veered off the road towards the trees.

Ellie could only throw her arms up for the inevitable collision. There was a huge crash, metal screeching and crunching, wood snapping and breaking as the entire car seemed to flip and Ellie lost all sense of what was happening. Then there was only noise, pain, movement and finally darkness.

Ellie coughed painfully. It wasn't unconsciousness. She was *alive*! More than that, she was awake! The darkness was the thick, inky blackness of night, the moon hidden by the tree canopies. A cold gust of wind brushed against her. She was outside. In the darkness. Surrounded by trees. Familiar tree. She had made it.

She struggled to her feet with a groan. Blood was flowing freely down her face, and her body was covered in cuts. It seemed she'd been thrown through the windscreen, but somehow landed in a nearby pile of leaves, still alive.

She groaned, climbing out of the wet leaves, holding her throbbing arm, which seemed to be bleeding heavily. She could see Suzi's car, now on its side, wheels still spinning, a soft hissing sound emanating from its engine. It looked like a definite write-off. She hoped Suzi wouldn't be too mad. One of its lights was still on, flickering, providing slight illumination in the damp forest.

Suddenly, the door on the side of the car now facing upwards flew off into the air and landed with a thud between Ellie and the wreck. Lillian climbed out, standing on top of the vehicle, framed by what little moonlight was filtering through the trees. She jumped, landing in front of the car, and began to stride towards Ellie.

'I suppose you think you're a real hero, don't you? Luring me away from the others?' she growled. Her voice was furious and full of rage. There was no control there now. No reasoning. She was ready to slash Ellie to pieces. 'Well, I've got news for you, *sister*! You're not Laurie Strode! You're not Nancy Thompson! Or Sidney Prescott or Alice Hardy or Sally whatever-the-heck-her-name-was in *Texas Chainsaw Massacre*! You're not the final girl! You're not the last girl standing! You're just another dead idiot! You're a nobody! Killed at the halfway point! Poor little black girl who nobody remembers! Did you really think you could beat *me*?' she snarled. She was upon Ellie so quickly that Ellie didn't have time to move in her wounded state. Lillian hoisted her into the air, and slammed her back against a large wooden sign.

'Look… where… we… are…' Ellie gasped for breath. Lillian looked behind Ellie to read the huge sign she had pushed Ellie against.

ST MARY'S MARSH CAMPGROUND
WHERE THE FUN NEVER STOPS
EST. 1928

Lillian dropped Ellie with a laugh.

'That's it? That's your big final move? You brought me, what, to the place where you killed your first killer?' she asked in disbelief. 'What, did you think you could off me here too? It doesn't work that way, *princess*. I've got no ties to this place! There's nothing here you can use against me!' she snarled. Ellie pushed herself to her feet, rubbing her neck carefully.

'Not that *I* can use, no,' she admitted. 'But… you said it yourself. Last time I was here, I killed a killer,' she stated. 'The legendary Mirror Monster. Hunter of camp counsellors for *years*. And I defeated it.'

'Yeah, so what?' Lillian asked. 'What's that got to do with anything?'

'And now, me, the lone survivor, has come back. Come back to where I killed the Mirror Monster. Where I made sure it'd never hurt anybody again,' Ellie went on, circling Lillian, who looked on in confusion.

'So wh-' Suddenly, Lillian paused. 'Oh no, don't say it.'

'Yeah, that's right! I killed the Mirror Monster! I drove a sickle right through its skull! It's gone for good! I know it is!'

'Don't you *dare* say it!'

'Because…..'

'DON'T!'

'….nothing could have survived that!'

With a mighty roar, the ground between the two burst apart, and the huge, hulking form of the Mirror Monster tore itself from the very pits of Hell, sickle in its hand, ready to kill once more.

And behind the shard of mirror that was its mask, its eyes locked on its prey.

Lillian.

St. Mary's Marsh wasn't big enough for two killers.

CHAPTER TWENTY-THREE

WHOEVER WINS, WE LOSE

Ellie threw herself aside, without a care for where she landed. She crashed into a bush, feeling the twigs and branches scrape her face. She ignored the pain, and scrambled to fight her way through it and to the other side. She knew she had to keep her distance.

Pitching the Mirror Monster against Lillian was a play she was proud of, but she was also painfully aware that it might have been a very stupid one. After all, now instead of being stranded in the woods with one psychotic immortal killer, she was stranded with *two*.

Safely behind the bush, she began to make her way around to a vantage point that would allow her to see. She was aware of her hand landing in something wet as she crawled, and she lifted it to her nose and sniffed. Gasoline. Leaking from wreckage Suzi's car. Well, *that* couldn't be good. She didn't really have time to worry about that now, however. Not with two immortal killers fighting to their undeaths only a few feet away.

'You think you can stop ME!? You!? Some lame, summer camp killing Jason Voorhees knock-off!?' Lillian yelled, swiping viciously with her machete arm. The Mirror Monster didn't reply. Ellie had never seen it speak, and she was pretty sure that it couldn't. Instead, it merely took a calm, lumbering step back, so that the machete whistled past its mirror mask, and then with surprising speed, stomped forward, bringing its sickle down. It clanged against Lillian's machete, and the Mirror Monster took that as an opportunity to further its attack, grabbing Lillian by the scruff of her heavy coat, and flinging her with so much force she slammed into a tree and caused it to splinter in two. The tree seemed to remain standing for a moment, and then with a horrible, slow, creaking groan it began to fall, branches snapping on the other trees as it passed them, shards of wood flying everywhere.

Ellie's hiding spot was unfortunately directly in the path of the falling tree, and she had to scramble to her feet and throw herself aside to avoid being crushed. Face down in the dirt once more, she grumbled to herself about bright ideas, and pushed herself back to her feet, observing the battle over the fallen tree that now provided her cover.

Apparently, being thrown through a tree did little to quell Lillian's rage, who came storming forward, again swinging her machete over and over. The Mirror Monster blocked with a lumbering, repetitive motion, but Lillian was faster, and pressing her advantage.

'You… you stupid, slow, boring idiots! You never deserved to be legends! You're all the same! Some slow moving imbecile in a creepy mask! *I'm* the future! I'm faster than you, I'm better than you, I'm self-aware and evolving! I'm the smarts of the survivor with the powers of the killer! I'm the *ultimate slasher!*' Lillian drove her machete arm directly into the chest of the Mirror Monster, and for a moment Ellie felt her heart catch in her throat. Had it all been for nothing? Could Lillian defeat the Mirror Monster so easily?

It seemed not. The Mirror Monster barely responded to the blade lodged in its chest. It looked down at it as if it was a mild inconvenience before bringing its powerful arm down onto it in a dramatic sweep. There the scream of metal tearing as it broke, and Lillian let out a cry, stumbling back, her machete arm now gone, still lodged in the chest of the Mirror Monster.

It was now the Mirror Monster's turn to push the offensive, and it did so viciously, swiping again and again with its sickle, slicing at Lillian who barely stayed one jump ahead of it with every retreating footstep. Finally it swept, catching her on the chest, and she fell back into the bushes with a cry of rage.

The Mirror Monster stomped and ripped open the bush, but Ellie already knew what it'd see. Lillian was gone. She appeared behind the Mirror Monster, lunging out of the shadows, a vicious looking hunting knife in her hand.

'You think that's my only weapon!?' she screamed, plunging it into the Mirror Monster's neck, and stabbing over and over again, thick, black congealed blood splattering everywhere out of the Mirror Monster's zombified skin. It stumbled back, reaching for its neck, and then with a wet thud on the damp ground, fell back, arms splayed out.

Lillian stood over the fallen Mirror Monster for a moment, and Ellie could see that she was breathing hard. There was an angry rising and falling of her chest. A subconscious effort, no doubt. Like the Mirror Monster, Lillian didn't need to breathe, but it seemed she had forgotten that. An apparent of the effort and how close the battle had been.

'You see, Ellie, I *am* the ultimate killer!' Lillian cried out into the darkness. 'You'll never defeat me! You can't escape me! And you definitely can't *kill* me! So show yourself, and get this over with,' she called.

Ellie knew she had no choice. Slowly, she stepped out from behind the tree, her hands raised in surrender.

'Okay, okay, you win,' Ellie admitted.

'Really? No more tricks?' Lillian scoffed. 'You called in your friends. They failed. You called in an army of ghosts. *They* failed. Then you pitched me against this stupid creature. That failed too. You finally ready to admit defeat?'

'Uh, yeah, if this last thing doesn't work out,' Ellie said, allowing herself to flash a smile.

'What last thing?' Lillian's voice was annoyed, but no longer angry. As if this was one more minor inconvenience before her inevitable victory now.

'C'mon, now, I thought you knew the *rules,*' Ellie replied. 'You knock the killer down, it doesn't matter how dead it seems… it always gets back up.'

Lillian turned, but not in time. The Mirror Monster was on its feet, marching towards Lillian, and in one quick gesture it pulled the machete out of its chest and drove it directly through Lillian's stomach, lifting her up into the air. Its march broke into an angry, stomping run, and it thrust the machete and Lillian into the underside of the wreckage of Suzi's car, pinning her to it. She gasped, struggling, and made to free herself, attempting to pull the machete out with her one arm. However, as her arm made contact with it, the Mirror Monster's sickle whistled through the air, and in one clean sweep, it cut off her remaining arm. The severed limb flew through the air, landing at Ellie's feet, where it twitched and spasmed, before its fingers curled up like the legs of dying spider. She jolted back, but tried to ignore it. Lillian hissed angrily, and the Mirror Monster simply cocked its head to one side, as if bored by her. It struck with one fierce backhand, and with a sickening crunch, Lillian's neck broke, leaving her head dangling to the side.

It was so very nearly over.

The Mirror Monster turned to face Ellie. It paused, seeming to recognise her. Ellie took a deep breath.

'C'mon. You've won. I brought you back. I know how these crossovers end. Mutual respect. We worked together. You go your way, I go mine,' Ellie said, more to herself than the Monster, with desperate hope. A few moments passed, a few seconds dragging into what felt like forever, but then the Mirror Monster simply inclined its head in a small nod, and it turned away, stomping off into the darkness.

Now there was only one thing left to do.

Ellie stepped out, once she was sure it was gone, and approached Lillian's body, still pinned to the car.

'You should have known. The only thing that can kill an immortal slasher, and I mean *properly* kill it, is a crossover with a more popular slasher. The Mirror Monster's been doing this for years. You were the newbie. You didn't stand a chance,' she explained, approaching her. 'Still, we both know what happens next. C'mon. Give it to me.'

Lillian's corpse just hung there, limp, her neck at an impossible right angle.

'C'mon...' Ellie said. Wham! Lillian's head snapped back to life, and she jerked forward, her bony jaw snapping in an attempt to rip out Ellie's jugular with her teeth. Ellie jumped back in time. She had been ready for it. 'The final jump scare. I knew you couldn't resist.' She allowed herself a smirk.

'This isn't over! I'll be back! You'll never be rid of me!' Lillian growled furiously, wriggling on the machete where she impaled, but unable to escape due to her missing arms.

'That's where you're wrong.' Ellie's voice was perfectly calm. 'See, all the time, you thought you were, what? Michael Myers? Jason Voorhees? Leatherface? Freddy Krueger? Hell, I'd bet you'd settle for Chucky.'

'I'm more than them! I'm better than them! I'm all of them and more!' Lillian hissed.

'No, you're not. See, this isn't your origin story. It's *mine*. And you? You're just another dumb zombie bitch for me to kill,' Ellie answered fiercely. 'You were right about one thing. I'm not Laurie Strode. I'm not Nancy Thompson. Or Sidney Prescott or Alice Hardy or Sally *Hardesty*.' She made it clear she knew that last name, just to rub into Lillian that *she* was the horror expert there. 'You wanna know who I am?'

She grinned.

'I'm the one who hunts monsters. The one who fights back. I'm not the victim. I'm not the final girl. Let me put this in horror terms for you, so that you understand. I'm Buffy Summers. I'm Sam and Dean Winchester. No, you know what? I'm Ash Williams. And this?' She pulled out from her waistband the only weapon she had left. The flare. 'This is my *boomstick*!' Ellie smiled, lighting it.

'NO!' Lillian screamed, but it was too late. Ellie threw the flare down onto the leaking gasoline and turned to run, not looking back.

Suzi's car went up in a gigantic explosion, throwing Ellie to the ground once again, the heat and fire and the smell of burning metal filling the air. Once again she ended face down in the dirt, like she had so many times before, but this time she knew that there would be no final jump scare. Lillian wouldn't emerge from the flames. She had won. Because this had never been *Lillian's* story. This had been *Ellie's*.

Slowly, she rose to her feet, and took in the burning wreckage. There was only one thing she could think to say to herself.

'Groovy.'

She heard an engine and spotted headlights on the road, and turned to make her way towards it. It was Jess's pick-up truck, and she broke into a huge smile as Suzi, Avril and Kat jumped out, before Jess joined them. They all ran over, grabbing her in a big hug.

'Did you do it!? Is it over!?' Avril asked excitedly.

'Don't be stupid. It's not over. That's how Lillian planned to always come back. The story ends, and the sequel opens the door for her. Which is why this isn't the end. It's just the beginning,' Ellie smiled back. 'One monster down. A lot more to go.' Suzi smiled at this.

'I think you're finally getting it,' she said happily. 'It's not *their* story. It's ours.,

'What was it Lillian called us? In my nightmare? She said we were the last girls standing.' Ellie asked. 'Had a nice ring to it. The Last Girls Standing. That's us.'

'So, what, you're saying… we hunt monsters now?' Kat asked.

'You can go back to your old life if you want. But there'll always be more people in danger. More horny dumb teens getting stalked in the shadows. And they'll always be us to stop them.'

'Alright,' Kat nodded. 'I'm in.'

'Me too,' Avril said. 'The Last Girls Standing. Sounds fun.'

'Guess I've sat watching on the side-lines for long enough. I'm in too,' Jess agreed.

'I'm glad Nina wasn't around to see you blow up her car,' Suzi added in her chirpy voice, looking towards the burning fire.

Ellie paused.

'Uh, Suzi, that wasn't *Nina's* car,' she explained a little sheepishly. Suzi gave Ellie a curious look for a moment, and then caught sight of a piece of burning pink metal and realised. She threw her hands up in the air.

'Aw, *c'mon!*' she complained. 'Okay, next time, somebody *else's* stuff gets blown up!'

EPILOGUE

Reconstruction on Suzi's mansion had begun, but it would be a long time before they could all move back in there. For the time being, the Last Girls Standing, as they now officially called themselves, operated out of Outlaw Ranch. The advantage of Jess's farmland was that it had plenty of room, even if Ellie suspected it wasn't quite as luxurious as Suzi was used to.

Avril and Kat had taken a little longer adjusting to life there. They had gone through similar difficulties to those Ellie had in what to tell their parents, but ultimately Ellie convinced them to try honesty. It had worked for her mom after all. Kat seemed to fit in pretty naturally, but it seemed Avril's life as the popular high school cheerleader had left her slightly less well adapted to the chores of living together, especially on a farm. She doubted Avril had ever done her own laundry in her life. But even Ellie had to admit, the memory of watching Jess teach Avril how to muck out the horse stables was one she would treasure forever.

When they weren't doing chores, they were researching to find their next case. While Suzi was the pro at it, Ellie thought they should all be involved, and it was her turn to do so when Suzi walked in and found her on the laptop Suzi had gifted to her. It was, amazingly, not a shade of pink. Personal laptops for the entire team had been a gift from Suzi, and of course, hers was the only pink one.

She looked over Ellie's shoulder, curiously peering at the search bar.

'Eye patch. Trench coat. British?' Suzi repeated the keywords. 'You're looking for Nina. Still?'

'I know what Lillian said. Dying "off screen" doesn't mean anything in a horror movie. But... Well, Nina wasn't your average horror movie protagonist, was she?' Ellie replied.

'No. I used to say she was more like some kind of weird mysterious British superhero,' Suzi shrugged.

'Exactly. Trench coat. Eyepatch. Bringing us all together. She's not some horror movie victim. She's Nick Fury,' Ellie explained.

'The *Avengers* guy?' Suzi asked.

'Yep. Bona fide comic book character. And you know the thing about comic book characters?' she smiled.

'If there's no body, then they're never truly dead!' Suzi beamed a smile as she understood.

'You got it!' Ellie smiled back. 'Plus, y'know, Nick Fury is *really* hard to kill. I swear he comes back to life like every second movie,' she added with a shrug.

'You know.... She wasn't always a good person. Lillian was right about that. What we did to Lillian... I still don't know... If it was right or wrong,' Suzi admitted.

'Neither do I,' Ellie agreed. 'But there are a lot of people out there who are only alive because of Nina. We owe it to her to keep looking.'

'You really think Nina's still out there?' Suzi asked.

'I know it,' Ellie replied, closing the laptop. 'And we're gonna find her. Because we're not horror victims. None of us are. We're goddamn superheroes. And superheroes never stay dead.'

Printed in Great Britain
by Amazon